Kate's lips parted eagerly...

...at the first thrust of his tongue. She'd told herself she imagined it, that her memories of kissing Tommy Ibarra had been exaggerated, overblown. Her brain, soaked in the throes of first lust, followed by the worst trauma she'd ever known, had infused the memories of that summer with a kind of intensity that couldn't have existed.

She couldn't have been more wrong, and the realization shook her to the core. Her memories of Tommy's kiss, his touch, didn't come close to what she was feeling now. It was like being thrust into a vortex full of heat and light, where nothing mattered but the taste of him, the soft rasp of his tongue against hers as he tasted every corner of her mouth.

This—this was the reason she'd broken the rules, been willing to give Tommy anything and everything he wanted, even if he was too much of a gentleman to ask for it.

He wasn't a gentleman now...

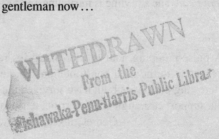

Praise for
Jami Alden's Novels

Run from Fear

"Alden's each and every well-placed word demonstrates to readers what a superior storyteller of suspense she is. Her latest has a solid plot, a strong battle-tested heroine, and tension to the extreme. This is one story that will have readers turning pages well into the night."

—*RT Book Reviews*

"A tense suspense and a captivating romance make *Run from Fear* an exciting read."

—RomRevToday.com

"Alden has written another gripping romantic suspense in *Run from Fear*. The storyline is intriguing and fast-paced."

—BookLoons.com

"A pulse-pumping, taut thriller that grips readers from the first threat to the final confrontation. The lead couple is an interesting pairing as both have survived the baptism of fire. The support cast augments a terrific, tense tale."

—GenreGoRoundReviews.blogspot.com

Hide from Evil

"4½ stars! Anyone who says that romantic suspense is no longer a hot commodity hasn't read Jami Alden. She's quickly making a name for herself as one of the top writers in the genre. Her latest novel continues her streak of excellent, gripping stories and brings captivating recurring characters along for the ride."

—*RT Book Reviews*

"Sexual chemistry engulfs these two and spills from the pages with the force of a tsunami...The best way I can describe this story is an emotional adrenaline rush...Alden's portrayal of Sean is brilliant, and pairing him with the hard-nosed, determined prosecutor was risky but proved to be perfect. I've been looking forward to reading this novel for months, and Jami Alden didn't disappoint."

—*USA Today*'s Happy Ever After blog

"The sexual tension and chemistry between them was absolutely delicious, especially when compounded by their previous bad history together. Overall, I adored this one."

—Romanceaholic.com

"Brilliant, simply and utterly brilliant!...This book moves Ms. Alden into the big leagues and most definitely onto my 'Must Read' author's list...*Hide from Evil* is a flat-out scorcher...The dramatic finish to this book leaves me absolutely rabid for Talia and Jack's book. If it's better than this one, it'll have to be written in gold."

—YouGottaRead.com

GUILTY
as SIN

GUILTY
as SIN

Jami Alden

FOREVER

NEW YORK   BOSTON

Copyright © 2013 by Jami Alden
Excerpt from *Run from Fear* Copyright © 2012 by Jami Alden

Forever
Hachette Book Group
237 Park Avenue
New York, NY 10017
www.HachetteBookGroup.com

Printed in the United States of America

First Edition: July 2013
10 9 8 7 6 5 4 3 2 1

OPM

Forever is an imprint of Grand Central Publishing.
The Forever name and logo are trademarks of Hachette Book Group, Inc.

The Hachette Speakers Bureau provides a wide range of authors for speaking events. To find out more, go to www.hachettespeakersbureau.com or call (866) 376-6591.

The publisher is not responsible for websites (or their content) that are not owned by the publisher.

To Gajus, who is always there to remind me I can do it, especially when I'm convinced I can't

Acknowledgments

As always, I have to thank the amazing Monica McCarty. I don't know what I'd do without you, on so many levels. Thank you also to Kim Whalen, agent extraordinaire, equal parts sweetheart and badass and pure pleasure to work with. And most of all, I have to thank you, my readers. Your emails, tweets, and posts keep me inspired to find ways to tell the stories of the people wandering around in my head.

Acknowledgments

GUILTY *as* SIN

Prologue

Y ou understand what a big responsibility this is, don't you, Kate?" her father said. "You understand that this is your chance to prove we can still trust you?"

Up until three weeks ago, there had been no reason for Senator Beckett and his wife not to. Sixteen-year-old Kate had always been the good twin, the sensible twin. The twin who kept her head on straight and never, ever threatened the senator's image as an upstanding citizen who fully embraced so-called family values.

But that was before he'd caught her making out in the sunroom with Tommy Ibarra. While her parents had never fully embraced Kate's unlikely friendship with the local rancher's son three years her senior, they'd tolerated it. Mostly because Kate's mother thought it was good for her kids to be exposed to people who existed outside their exclusive circle of Washington, D.C.'s elite. And because as far as they knew, Kate and Tommy's relationship hadn't seemed to go beyond a big brother/little sister dynamic.

Not until this summer, at least.

And to say her father wasn't okay with it was the understatement of the century. Kate was afraid he was going to have an aneurysm when he caught them.

Yet not even his wrath could compel her to keep her promise to stay away from Tommy Ibarra for the rest of their annual vacation on the shores of Lake Pend Oreille.

"Of course," Kate replied with a smile.

Her father gave her a smile and bent to kiss her on the cheek. "That's my good girl," he said, patting her shoulder as he straightened up. "Even after what happened, I know we can still count on you."

"Of course you can," Kate replied. As she looked into her father's eyes, full of warmth and love, she felt a flash of guilt for what she had planned.

"I know you think I'm too strict sometimes, but I just want what's best for you and our family. And I know you can do a lot better than Tommy Ibarra."

Her guilt dissolved in a flash of anger, and she fought to keep her hands from curling into fists. Her father had no idea who Tommy really was, had no idea that there was no such thing as doing better than Tommy Ibarra. All he saw was an older local boy trying to take advantage of his teenage daughter.

And while she knew her father loved her and was genuinely concerned for her welfare, he was equally concerned about the scandal that might erupt if the press got wind of her summer romance. As a U.S. Senator whose platform centered on conservative family values, he couldn't have his daughter's steamy make-out sessions with inappropriate suitors become public knowledge.

She pulled her mouth into a guileless smile. "Everything will be fine."

Her father nodded and gave her another quick squeeze. "All right then, we'll be home tomorrow around lunchtime."

"Here's the number where we can be reached." Kate's mother pressed the slip of paper into her hand as she was walking to the door.

"I know, you already taped it on the refrigerator," Kate said impatiently.

Her mom leaned down to kiss her cheek, enveloping Kate in a cloud of perfume and hairspray.

"And your father has his cell phone, not that the darn thing ever seems to work when we need it."

Kate closed the door behind them and practically danced a little jig. The situation couldn't have fallen into her lap more perfectly. Her parents would be gone for the night attending a fundraiser in Boise. Her fraternal twin sister, Lauren, was spending the night at the Burkharts' house with her friend Hailey. Kate knew that was code for she was going to stay out all night partying because everyone except for Kate's parents knew the Burkharts let them do whatever they wanted as long as it didn't end in an arrest.

Which left Kate to stay home with Michael, who had come down with a nasty summer flu and wasn't going anywhere except the living room couch.

Normally Kate would have resented having to be on little-brother detail when there was so much going on, but not tonight. Tonight all she had to do was throw him a cup of soup and send him to bed, and the house would be all hers.

Hers and Tommy's.

She went into the great room where Michael was sprawled in front of the TV, his attention focused on the Game Boy that seemed permanently grafted to his hand. An empty glass of melting ice and a box of Kleenex sat on the coffee table in front of him. He was surrounded by a dozen or so crumpled-up tissues.

"Can I get you anything?" Kate asked, wrinkling her nose as she picked up a tissue between her thumb and forefinger and threw it in the trash.

Michael's eyes, blue to match hers, slanted in her direction. "Maybe a pizza?"

"You threw up all morning. I'm not getting you a pizza. How about some toast?"

He shrugged, which Kate took as yes. The phone rang just as she was putting some bread in the toaster.

Kate rushed to answer. She'd told Tommy her parents were leaving at five and to call any time after. "Hey," she said breathlessly.

But it wasn't Tommy's voice on the other line. "Hey, Kate, it's John."

"Oh, hi," she said, her brow wrinkling as she wondered why he might be calling her. She'd known John Burkhart almost her entire life—her father and his had been close since college, and they'd been vacationing here in Sandpoint together for the past six years.

"Is something wrong with Lauren?" She looked at her watch. It was only five thirty, presumably too early for her and his younger sister, Hailey, to have gotten themselves into trouble, but you never knew.

"Uh, no," he said, clearing his throat uncomfortably. "Nothing's wrong. I was just wondering, uh, I mean I know you're home alone with Michael..."

"Yes," she prompted as his voice trailed off. But the uneasiness in her belly made her unsure if she really wanted him to go on.

"I was thinking I could maybe come over with a pizza and a movie or something and keep you guys company."

"Aren't your next-door neighbors hosting their big bonfire tonight? You never miss it."

"Yeah, well, I've been enough times, one summer isn't going to matter. And I think this would be a good chance for us to hang out."

"Since when do you want to hang out with me?" Kate asked with genuine confusion. John was twenty, a junior at the University of Colorado, and had always acted like he was way too old and way too cool to hang out with Kate and her sister.

He blew out a harsh breath. "Please, Kate, the fact that I'm interested in you can't be a total surprise. Why do you think I'm always giving you and your sister rides and going to parties with you?"

Kate practically dropped the phone in shock. John Burkhart was interested in her? Since when? "Uh, I thought it was because you were giving Hailey a ride anyway and we were tagging along."

He gave a forced-sounding laugh. "Okay, fine, you want me to lay it out there? I like you, Kate. I've been interested for a while, but I was waiting till you got a little older to make my move. So what do you say? Can we stop with the pretense that I'm nothing more than a family friend? Let me come over."

Kate spared a moment to wonder what kind of phero-mone she was putting out that suddenly made guys take interest. Kate was the quiet sister who stood around the edges of the crowd while the boys chased Lauren. In any case, though she truly did view John as little more than an acquaintance she never would have known had their parents not been friends, she wanted to let him down easy. "You know my father would go ballistic if he knew I was home alone and had someone over."

"Kate, it's *me*. Your father's known me all my life. He trusts me."

"And, more important, he trusts *me*," she said, feeling a little pinch of guilt at the knowledge that he no longer had good reason too, "and I can't risk violating that, even for you."

"We don't have to tell him."

"Even if I don't, Michael might, and even so, I'm not lying to my father." *Not for you, anyway.*

"Tomorrow then. Let me take you to Mary's for dinner," he persisted.

"I don't think that's a good idea," Kate said warily.

"Kate, do you have any idea how many girls in this town would kill to go out with me?" John snapped.

His arrogance brought an edge to her own voice. "Then ask one of them."

"What's the matter, Kate, am I not man enough for you? Do you only get turned on by guys who get dirty and work with their hands, like that gardener of yours? You ever wonder what he does when he's on his ranch, all alone out there with his sheep—"

Kate's grip around the phone tightened. Apparently news of her hookup had made it to the Burkhart house. "Good night, John," she said, and hung up. She buttered Michael's toast, put it on a plate, and poured herself a Diet Coke over ice. But the sweet fizziness wasn't enough to chase away the bad taste the conversation had left in her mouth.

The awkwardness was going to be unavoidable—they'd be thrown together constantly for the rest of the summer. She could only hope John would let it go and they could just pretend the whole thing had never happened.

The phone rang again fifteen minutes later and Kate picked it up with no small trepidation, worried it was John going in for another round. But this time it was Tommy. Keeping her voice low, she said, "I think Michael's going to zone out pretty soon, so I'll call you after he goes to bed."

Kate made herself a sandwich and settled on the couch to watch *Dumb and Dumber* with Michael, who, much to her consternation, didn't seem in any hurry to head up to bed.

When the movie ended and he asked her to put *Jurassic Park* into the VCR, she replied, "Aren't you ready for bed?" unable to conceal the exasperation in her voice.

"What's the difference to you? It's not like you have anywhere to go."

Kate gave a little huff of impatience and checked her watch. It was after nine. How long would Tommy wait by the phone before he gave up and came over on his own, revealing everything to her nosy little brother?

Or, worse, decided she wasn't worth the wait and went out for the night?

"Or maybe," Michael said idly, his gaze still glued to the television, "you're waiting for someone to come over here."

"What makes you think that?" she said, too quickly.

Michael, ever perceptive, slanted a look at her. "It's Tommy, right?"

"Of course not," she snapped. "I promised Dad I wouldn't see him anymore."

"Oh, come on, Kate, you think I don't hear you and Lauren gossiping all night? I can totally hear you two from my room."

"Only if you sit with your head glued to the air vent," she snapped, and snatched up a throw pillow to clobber him over the head.

"Hey, what else am I supposed to do?" Michael threw down the Game Boy and flung his arms up to protect his face. "You guys are the ones with the TV and the VCR player in your room. I don't have jack crap."

"Promise you won't say anything to Dad."

Michael narrowed his eyes. "What's it worth to you?"

Kate glared right back. "My allowance for the next month?"

He shook his head. "Not good enough. I want a ride to and from school every morning. The bus blows."

"I can promise rides in the morning but not afternoons. Lauren and I will start SAT prep soon and you've got soccer—"

"Fine," Michael conceded. "Rides in the morning and two months of allowance."

"Fine," she bit out, and called him a jerk under her breath.

They were silent a few more minutes watching the movie, then Michael said, "Just so you know, I've known for about a week and probably wouldn't have said anything. Tommy seems like a cool guy. I don't know why Dad gets all up in his head about it."

Even her father's disapproval of Tommy couldn't erase sixteen years of being a daddy's girl. Kate automatically jumped to his defense. "Because of who he is, he has to worry about how everything will look, and he has very specific ideas about the kind of people Lauren and I date."

Michael snorted. "He'd have a stroke if he knew what Lauren's been up to."

"How do you know what Lauren's up to?"

"I know a lot more than you think."

More silence, then Kate asked. "So if you weren't going to tell, do I still have to give you my allowance?"

"Hell yeah," he replied. "Between your two months and the six I already have from Lauren, I'll finally be able to buy that Jet Ski Mom refuses to let me have."

"You can buy it, but that doesn't mean you can keep it."

"Dad will have me covered."

Kate rolled her eyes and didn't argue. It was no secret that while their dad adored and was proud of all of them, he had a particular soft spot for Michael and always let him get away with more. Whether it was because he was the only boy or the youngest or a combination of both, Kate had learned a long time ago not to let the favoritism get to her.

Satisfied Michael wouldn't narc on her any time soon, she dialed Tommy. Her heart squeezed as the phone got to its fourth ring.

It's too late, she thought. He got tired of waiting...

"Hello?" he answered, a little breathless as though he'd been running.

"So, um, you can still come over if you want to," she said.

"Of course I still want to!" he said, the unrestrained eagerness in his voice making her smile.

For the next twenty minutes or so Kate watched the front windows, starting at the sight of each pair of headlights going by.

"He lives outside of town," Michael reminded her after the third time. "It'll take him at least fifteen minutes to get here."

"Aren't you getting really tired and needing to go upstairs to bed?" she shot back.

He gave an exaggerated stretch. "I've been sleeping like, all day, so now I'm not even tired. I could probably stay up all night at this point," he said with an innocent smile she didn't buy for a second.

Just then there was a firm knock at the door. She rushed to answer, shooting Michael a glare over her shoulder.

"Hi," she said, unable to hold back her grin at the sight of Tommy, the harsh planes of his face illuminated by the overhead light. "You got here quicker than I expected." She moved aside to let him in.

"I might have sped a little," he said with a sheepish smile. He reached out and placed his hands on her hips as he bent his head to kiss her hello.

"Hey, Tommy." His head snapped up at the sound of Michael's call, and there was a flash of panic in his eyes.

"It's okay," Kate said, taking Tommy by the hand and leading him into the great room. "We worked out a deal."

Tommy raised a hand in greeting. "Hey. Kate said you've been sick."

"I'm better today," Michael said, and turned his attention back to his Game Boy.

"But you really should get your rest," Kate said. "Sleep is really the best thing for your body."

"I'm getting plenty of rest right here on the couch," Michael replied.

"Let's go out on the deck," Tommy said. Kate shot another glare at her brother as Tommy led her outside. He settled them onto a wicker love seat facing the lake.

He slipped his arm around her shoulders, and she snuggled eagerly into his side.

"You sure we're okay?" Tommy said.

Kate found it hard to focus with his fingers tracing up and down the sensitive skin of her inner arm. "Yeah," she finally managed. "He named a price for his silence and I caved."

Tommy gave a soft chuckle. "I hope it wasn't too bad."

"Just some money and having to put up with a smelly thirteen-year-old in my car every morning on the way to school."

Tommy gave a soft laugh. "Remind me to keep him away from my sister Emilia. She's only nine but she's already figured out the blackmail thing."

"I'm glad you could come over tonight," Kate said, anticipation buzzing in her veins as she thought about what was going to happen.

"Me too," Tommy whispered, and bent his head to kiss her. He smelled delicious, soapy and the fresh citrus smell of shaving cream. As always, the second his lips touched hers she went spinning out of control, her mouth hungry against his, her hands clutching at him as though she couldn't get close enough.

And tonight they would be as close as two people could be—

The sharp sound of shattering glass startled them apart. Kate surged to her feet and started for the kitchen where Michael stood, bathed in light from the overhead fixture. He wore a guilty look on his face, and there was a puddle of lemonade and shards of glass surrounding his bare feet.

"You're such a klutz," Kate fumed as she marched into the kitchen.

"I'm sorry, I was just thirsty."

"More like nosy," Kate muttered. "You know damn well the mini fridge under the bar is totally stocked. Don't move!" she ordered when Michael would have stepped forward.

Tension knotted in her shoulders as she and Tommy mopped up the sticky liquid and swept up the glass. Way to set the romantic scene, she thought, spending an evening trying to dodge her thirteen-year-old brother.

"I'm sorry, Kate," Michael said as she threw away the last of the mess.

"Can you just go to bed?" She sighed tiredly. "Tommy and I really want to be alone."

Her gave her an exaggerated leer. "What are you going to do?"

She punched him in the arm hard enough to make him wince. "None of your business. Go upstairs."

His mouth set in a petulant line. "I'm not tired. You can be alone in your bedroom. You go upstairs."

Kate's cheeks flooded with heat at the memory of Tommy in her bedroom three days ago, his rangy body stretched out on the twin bed across from Lauren's. But there was no way she was taking him up there now—not with Michael still awake and tracking their every move.

It was one thing to flirt with her inner bad girl and sneak

a guy in her bedroom when the house was empty, but she wasn't brazen enough yet to do it under her nosy brother's ever-watchful eye. Knowing Michael, he'd either be at the door with a glass to his ear or hunkered next to that damn air vent.

"Fine. You can hang out in our room," Kate said, grateful Lauren wasn't there to punch her in the face. "You can watch movies as late as you want. Just don't come back down."

"Awesome." He tucked the Game Boy under his arm and rushed to the great room to retrieve a stack of cassettes. A few seconds later he was pounding up the stairs.

"And stay out of our stuff!" Kate called after him, knowing full well their room would be ransacked inside of ten minutes.

But it would be worth it, she thought, turning with a little shiver of anticipation back to Tommy, who was watching her from the doorway that led from the kitchen to the great room.

His thick dark hair shone under the lights, picking up the faint gold streaks from all the time he spent in the sun. His deep-set eyes watched her carefully, and as he looked in her face she wondered if he sensed her plans for tonight.

She was suddenly nervous, not sure how to proceed. She couldn't exactly blurt out that she planned to let him take her virginity that night. Deciding that the best course of action was to let things unfold naturally, she let him lead her to the big leather couch and watched as he made a show of picking out a movie they had no intention of watching.

He had her stretched out under him before the opening credits had rolled, and soon after his shirt was on the floor and hers was tugged from the waistband of her skirt.

Tommy's hand was making slow, careful progress up her stomach when they heard a large crash and roar. It took her a few seconds to register that the noise came from the TV upstairs, turned up obnoxiously loud, no doubt for their benefit.

But that did nothing to calm the adrenaline spiking in her system and the realization that there was no way she could do this with her little brother in the house.

As though he read her thoughts, Tommy said, "It's weird having Michael here. I'm afraid he'll bust in any second."

"I'm sorry." She sighed, frustrated. "I totally thought he'd be asleep and wouldn't even know..."

"I know someplace we can go," Tommy said, tugging her up from the couch. She followed, hesitating as he reached for the handle of the front door.

"I can't leave." She shook her head. "I know he's a pain in the ass, but I can't leave him alone."

"We won't go far, I promise. Close enough for us to hear if he calls for you, but nowhere he can bust in on us. Come on."

Kate's eyes flicked involuntarily up the stairs. She could hear the roar of the television, hoped Michael would stay occupied or fall asleep soon.

"Okay." She followed Tommy, first to his truck, where he retrieved a sleeping bag and a pillow he'd stashed in the back. Then he led her down the beach, past the last house where the lake was still bordered by forest. Kate smiled in delight as he stopped at a bare patch of sand sheltered on either side by bushes. He spread the sleeping bag out and knelt down and reached out his hand for her to join him.

Though this was not exactly what she'd imagined for her first time, she didn't hesitate to follow him down when he stretched out on his back.

Kate couldn't stifle a moan as strong hands slid under the hem of her shirt and slid up the bare skin of her back. Her own hands swept hungrily over the muscular swells of his chest and shoulders.

She loved the way his breath sped up to match hers, the way his skin heated under her touch until she could smell the arousal coming off him in waves. His hand slid farther up her back until it met with the clasp of her bra. His fingers traced it for a second before sliding away.

Not tonight, she thought with a pulse of anticipation that was nearly as arousing as his touch. She pushed up so she was sitting next to him. She could hear the surprised hitch in his breath as she unbuttoned her shirt and let it slide off her shoulders. Then, before she could psych herself out, she reached behind her and unhooked her bra.

"Kate..."

Tommy's hushed whisper, almost reverent, rushed through her and gave her that last bit of courage she needed to let her bra follow her shirt onto the ground.

Grateful that the nearly full moon was muted by the tree branches, she sank back down until they were chest to chest and felt his own gasp echo hers at the first touch of skin on skin. It shouldn't be such a huge deal; he'd touched her under her clothes dozens of times. But the feeling of being naked—from the waist up anyway—the sensation of being completely bare against him—sent a wicked thrill that went straight to her core.

Taking her mouth hungrily with his, Tommy rolled her to her back, one big hand immediately swallowing up the curve of one breast. She pushed aside the fleeting moment of embarrassment that she was so small and gave herself up to the sensation of his strong fingers kneading her, the feel of his thumb and forefinger closing over her nipple in a gentle squeeze that startled a cry from her throat.

His mouth licked and sucked its way down her neck, across

her bare chest. And before she could give in to the flutter of panic, his lips closed gently over one hard tip.

"Tommy!" she cried, her hands fisting in his hair.

He immediately lifted his head. "Do you want me to stop?"

"No." Her whisper dissolved into a sigh as his mouth closed over her again. Her body shifted restlessly under his, intense sensation wracking her.

Her legs came up to cradle his hips and her skirt shifted up her thighs. Tommy instinctively moved lower so she wouldn't have direct contact with the rock-hard pillar she knew was straining against the fly of his shorts.

Kate slid her arms around his body and moved her hands down until they were resting on his hips. She tugged at him and rocked her hips until his body was perfectly aligned with hers. Pleasure hit her with the force of an electric shock, every fiber in her body pulling tight.

"Kate." Tommy groaned, his hips rocking as though he couldn't stop himself from moving against her. "We don't have to—"

"I want to," she said quickly before she lost her nerve. "I want to feel you against me. And in a little while, I want us both to get naked and feel you for real."

Tommy groaned and kissed her again, hard, like he wanted to consume her.

"I want you to be my first," she whispered against his lips.

He swore softly against her mouth. "We don't have to rush it, Kate. There's so much other stuff we can do to make each other feel good."

Kate slid her hands down the back of Tommy's shorts and dug her fingers into the firm muscles of his butt. "I don't want to do other stuff," she said, and gave his earlobe a little nip. "I want to have sex."

"Kate." The single word betrayed an agony of frustration.

Kate muffled his protests by covering his mouth with hers and reached one hand in between their bodies, feeling a hot thrill race through her as her hand closed over him through the fabric of his shorts. Two weeks ago, she would have thought herself incapable of such boldness.

But tonight, in the moonlight, her whole body quivered with anticipation as she explored every inch of him, so hard, so hot he seemed to burn her palm even through the heavy fabric of his shorts.

Tommy went stock still, every muscle locked and trembling as his breath heaved in his chest.

"Tommy, I know you're worried I'm not experienced, but I'm sure about this. I'm sure I want you—"

Her words caught in her throat as his hand closed over her wrist in a grip that bordered on painful. "We can't," he ground out.

Kate sat up and jerked her hand from his grip as dread closed its fist in the pit of her stomach. "Don't you want to? I thought—"

"Of course I want to!" Tommy said in a harsh whisper. "I've wanted to since the first time I touched you."

"Then why can't we?"

Tommy sat up, shoving away from her until he'd put a couple feet of distance in between them. "Your dad, for one thing," he said.

"Why does what my dad think matters?"

"Age of consent is eighteen in Idaho, Kate. You think your dad would hesitate for a second to bring me up on statutory rape charges if he found out?"

"He'd be just as likely to want to sweep the whole thing under the rug so the press doesn't find out his perfect princess of a daughter isn't as pure as he'd like everyone to think," she shot back.

Tommy shook his head. "I can't risk it. My scholarship has a morals clause, and anything like this..."

Kate's eyes stung with frustrated tears. One escaped to roll down her cheek. Tommy reached out to brush it away with his thumb. The light brush of his callused finger on her skin sent a jolt of awareness through her body, making her all too aware of the unfulfilled desire humming through every nerve. "So what are you saying? Hit you up again when I turn eighteen? That's over a year from now." On edge and embarrassed at the idea that on some level he still saw her as a kid, more trouble than she was worth, Kate scrambled in the dark for her bra and shirt and quickly slipped them on.

She stiffened as Tommy's arms wrapped around her from behind but let him pull her against him, her back to his chest. His breath was warm in her hair and she could feel his heart still beating double time against her back. "For now I think that's our only option," he replied.

Kate made a scoffing sound. "What, like you'll really wait for me? Like you won't hook up with anyone else for the entire school year?"

He was silent for several seconds, each one of them agony as she waited for his reply. "We never really talked about that," he said carefully.

Kate wished that the ground would open up and swallow her as humiliation threatened to overwhelm her. "Forget it," she said quickly. "I didn't mean to back you into a corner. I didn't really expect this to go anywhere, and I know you're not serious—"

"Shut up," Tommy said softly. He caught her chin between his fingers and turned her around to face him. His mouth settled over hers in a kiss that went beyond hunger. Corny as it seemed, to Kate it almost felt like a promise.

"You don't know how I feel, or what my plans are, because we haven't talked about it."

"What are your plans?" she asked softly.

Even in the dark, there was no missing the flash of white teeth as he grinned. "Hell, Kate, I wasn't even sure you wouldn't slap me the first time I tried to kiss you. And after everything with your dad, I've pretty much been winging it and not getting my hopes up too much."

"You have hopes? What kind of hopes?"

He tucked her back against his chest and rested his chin on the top of her head. "That maybe this doesn't have to end when I go back to school and you go back to D.C."

He didn't say anything else, and though her brain was screaming with questions about what exactly that meant, Kate didn't push him to elaborate. Instead she wanted to focus on this unexpected gift, on the amazing guy cradling her in his arms and telling her—her! quiet, Goody Two-Shoes boring Kate—that he didn't want what they had to end when the summer did.

They sat there for several minutes. Once again Kate became aware of the warmth of him against her back, the scent of him teasing her nostrils. The way the hard muscles of his arms brushed against the sides of her breasts. "So," she said, trying her best to sound nonchalant, "what are some of the other ways?"

"What other ways?"

She turned to face him, rising to her knees so she could settle in his lap, face to face. "You said there were other ways," she said, bending to deliver a soft nip to his bottom lip, "that we could make each other feel good."

Tommy kissed her hard, his low groan rumbling through her until once again she was primed, every cell tight with awareness, ready to explode at the slightest touch.

His hand slid up the outside of her thigh, up under the hem of her short skirt until it rested just below the juncture of where her leg met her hip. His fingers spread, his thumb brushed the inside of her thigh, making her jump with nervousness and anticipation. His hand moved between her thighs. She instinctively stiffened, then shifted her weight to give him better access.

Her mouth pressed eagerly against his, her breath coming in harsh, rapid pants as she felt the heat of his skin, the rough brush of calluses against skin never touched by anyone but herself. She felt the slightest brush against the lace edging of her panties, her breath frozen in her chest as he slid one finger under the elastic.

BAM

She jumped at what sounded like a gunshot, followed by the roar of an engine whose muffler had seen better days. Tommy jerked his hand from under her skirt and they both sat there, statue still as they waited to see if their privacy would be invaded. A minute, maybe two passed. "I don't think they're coming down here," Kate said, turning back to Tommy.

She was just about to suggest they pick up where they'd left off when she heard the sound of the engine backfire again and the rumbling muffler. Then the metallic thud of the car hitting something, the sound of shattering glass or pottery. Kate was already pushing to her feet, her stomach turning with dread even before her brain registered that the crashing sound was coming from the direction of her house. She sprinted up the beach, barely hearing Tommy call after her to be careful.

She ran up to her house, but rather than going up the stairs to the deck, she ran around to the front. Sure enough, one of the giant terra-cotta planters that flanked each side of the driveway was smashed to bits, leaving a mountain of dirt and a pile of uprooted rhododendrons in the corner of the driveway.

"Probably just a drunk driver," Tommy said, breathing hard from his sprint up the beach. In the distance they could barely make out the red taillights of a pickup truck disappearing into the darkness.

She walked back to the house, a vague unease tickling at her brain through the haze of the adrenaline rush. When she opened the front door to the house and saw that it was dark except for the light she'd left on in the kitchen and dead quiet, she realized why the silence felt so wrong.

Michael should have woken up at the sound of the crash. She was pounding up the stairs before the thought had fully formed, the faint unease turning to acrid fear when she flung the door to her bedroom open, flicked on the light, and saw her empty bed. Her eyes did a quick, frantic inventory of the room. The TV was off. Lauren's bed was pristine, undisturbed, while her own bed looked like a tornado had hit it.

But empty. Undeniably empty.

"Michael?" she called as she raced across the room to fling open the closet. Nothing but her and Lauren's sundresses and light summer jackets. "Michael?" she called again, higher and more frantic as she headed for the bathroom that linked their room to his.

Again, empty. "Maybe he moved to his own bed," she said out loud, trying to convince herself nothing was wrong even though every cell in her body was screaming with the knowledge that it was.

"I'll go check downstairs," Tommy said when they found no trace of Michael in his room.

She heard the thud of Tommy's footsteps on the stairs as she went to her parents' room. Maybe Michael was just screwing with her. When he was little he was a master of hide-and-seek and regularly hid from their mother when it was time to go to school. "Michael, I swear to God if this is some kind of game, I will kick your ass when I find you." She was greeted by dead silence and nothing but clothes as she flung open her parents' closets. "Okay, I didn't mean that," she said, her voice tight with fear as she tried for a more cajoling tone. "If you come out I'll give you my allowance for the rest of the school year. Just get out here because you're scaring the crap out of me."

But there was no sound but the heavy thud of her heart.

After an hour searching every inch of the house and walking the neighborhood calling his name, Kate and Tommy were forced to face the reality that Michael was nowhere to be found.

———————

Her entire body went icy cold as her stomach twisted with panic. *He's fine. He's totally fine*, she said to herself over and over again. *We're going to find him and everything will be fine.* But she had an awful feeling in the pit of her stomach that nothing would ever be fine again.

Ignoring the late hour, Kate called the Burkharts, the Cunninghams, and every other friend of Michael's she could think of on the thin hope he'd snuck out. No one had seen him.

They called the sheriff's emergency number, and Kate gave them the few details they had and hung up to wait for the deputy to arrive. Then with shaking fingers she made the phone call she'd been dreading for the last hour and a half while they searched in vain for Michael.

Please let him not be able to get a signal, she thought as

she dialed the number for her father's notoriously unreliable cell phone. Or better yet, please God send a lightning bolt to strike me down right now so I don't have to tell my father what happened.

Suck it up, she mentally scolded herself. Michael was missing, possibly in danger, and she had to face reality and take responsibility, no matter how much she wanted to avoid her father's disapproval.

Her father answered the phone on just the second ring. His response, when Kate told him what was going on, was exactly as she'd expected and feared.

But nothing was worse than having to admit that she hadn't been in the house when Michael went missing. And having to admit why.

"I was out on the beach," she said, forcing the words through lips that had gone numb with cold. "I was with Tommy Ibarra."

Her father was silent for several seconds, the heaviness of it settling over Kate's shoulders like a lead blanket. "I will deal with you and your lack of morals and discipline after we find your brother," he said in an icy tone he'd never used with her before, raising goose bumps over every inch of Kate's skin.

The senator and his wife had to wait a couple of hours before their private jet was able to fly them back from Boise. By the time they landed in Sandpoint's tiny airport, the first pink of dawn was just peeking over the edge of the mountains.

Since she'd hung up the phone, Kate and Tommy had spent hours going over every detail of the little they'd seen and heard in the moments before they'd discovered Michael's absence.

"How long were you away from the house?" asked the sheriff, who had arrived on the scene quickly.

The kitchen and great room were teeming with people. In addition to the local law enforcement, the Burkharts had arrived shortly after Kate spoke with her father. Lauren, woken by the phone and worried when she heard Michael was missing, had come with them. They'd decided Hailey and John should stay back at their house, on the off chance Michael showed up there.

A few of the neighbors on the street had come over to see what the police cars and commotion was about, and now a deputy made his way around the room to ask if anyone had seen anyone or anything suspicious.

"I think it was about forty-five minutes, maybe an hour," Kate said, sniffing back tears as the guilt and shame gnawed at her from the inside. "I didn't—" She looked at Tommy, whose face was stark with worry and guilt that mirrored her own. "We didn't think it would be a big deal, we didn't go far."

Soft arms pulled her into a warm hug. "I'm sure everything will be okay." Kate recognized Sylvia Ibarra's voice as she blindly turned into the woman's fragrant embrace. Tommy had called his parents as soon as Kate had gotten off the phone with her father. Kate had known them only by sight before tonight, but now she was infinitely grateful for their solid, steady presence, the way they offered her and Tommy support absent of the accusation she could feel seething from the pores of everyone around her.

"Where's Kate?" Her father's voice cut like a razor through the room.

Kate lingered for one more second, her face buried against Mrs. Ibarra's ample bosom as if that could somehow give her the strength to face her father.

Slowly, reluctantly she turned to face him, her stomach twisting when she saw the look on his face. Accusation, of course, burning with such white-hot intensity it was a wonder she didn't turn to ash right there. But worse, disappointment, and beyond that disgust.

The small crowd parted like the Red Sea as he charged like an angry bull. As he got closer, Kate could see his forearms flex as his hands clenched into fists. Across the top of his forehead a vein pulsed. "What the hell were you thinking, leaving your brother in the house alone?"

She felt his booming voice like a blow and took an instinctive step back, afraid for the first time in her life that her father might actually hit her.

Tommy, who was looking frantically from one to the other, stepped forward. "It was my fault, sir," Tommy said. "I was the one who suggested we go outside for more privacy."

Her father wheeled on Tommy and grabbed him by the collar. Though Tommy was at least six inches taller and incredibly strong, he didn't resist as the senator propelled him until his back hit the paneled wall. "More privacy so you could rape my daughter while my son is left unprotected?" he shouted as he slammed Tommy back against the wall.

Tommy's father wasn't about to stand for that. He placed a firm hand on Senator Beckett's shoulder. "My son would never do anything to a girl unless she wanted it."

"Your son would seduce a sixteen-year-old girl who doesn't know any better than to leave her brother unattended in the middle of the night," the senator said as he turned his angry gaze to Leo Ibarra.

"Maybe you're forgetting there were two people involved here," Tommy's father said tightly.

"You implying my daughter's a whore?"

Tommy's dad backed up and held his hands up, signaling for peace. "Your daughter seems like a very nice girl—"

"No, you're right," her father said, turning a glare on her

so filled with rage he looked nearly psychotic. "Even though I tried to raise her right, she's nothing but—"

Tommy surged forward before he could finish, his fist cocked back. Kate jumped in front of him and planted her palms against his chest. "Stop it!" she shouted.

She looked around at the many stares focused warily on her. Then she looked at her mother and Lauren, huddled in a corner, their arms wrapped around each other, their eyes showing nothing but fear.

"Stop. Just stop," she said weakly, her hands dropping from Tommy's chest. She turned to her father, straightening her spine with all the dignity she could muster. "You can rage at me all you want, but that's not going to help us find Michael. Right now we have to focus on finding him before something awful happens to him."

Her father didn't reply. The rage in his face melted away as quickly as it came, his expression as hard and flat as cement.

"Kate." Tommy reached out to take her arm, but she eluded his grasp.

"You should go," Kate said, forcing the words around the softball-size lump that settled in her throat. "I can't really be around you right now."

The look of stunned hurt on his face barely penetrated the fog of fear and guilt surrounding her. After the Ibarras left, Sheriff Lyons tried to console them with the notion that the car accident in front of the house could easily be coincidental. "Kids Michael's age like to start pushing the boundaries, see what it's like to party with the big kids. He probably snuck out to one of the parties, got hold of some beer, and is at this very moment puking his guts out in the bushes somewhere or passed out on the beach."

"Or maybe he got drunk, wandered into the lake, and drowned, or got hit trying to cross the highway," Lauren snapped. "Even if he left on his own, there are a lot of ways he could get hurt." Her voice broke at the end, and that little sob was like a knife to Kate's stomach.

Though Kate clung to the faint hope that the sheriff was right, Sunday morning turned into Sunday afternoon, then Sunday night. Another night passed while Kate and her family kept a sleepless vigil.

Monday morning an FBI agent flew up from the Boise field office to help with the investigation. Kate listened mutely as Agent Martins explained that if Michael was the victim of a kidnapping for ransom, they should expect to get a call within thirty-six hours. Kate stared at the phone, clinging to the faint hope that Michael had been taken by a sick jerk who just wanted money rather than that he was somewhere hurt or, God forbid, dead.

While dozens of people canvassed every inch of town, Tommy, his father, and a handful of other ranchers rode out on horseback into the surrounding wilderness area to look for any signs of Michael.

As Monday turned into Tuesday and there was no ransom call and no other sign of Michael, the cold blanket of dread that had settled over the Beckett household grew so heavy and oppressive Kate felt it hard to breathe.

Reporters circled like sharks, thrusting microphones into the faces of family members the second they dared step outside. Kate hadn't left the house since her first devastating encounter with a reporter. The woman, with her dark hair styled into a helmet and her whiter-than-white teeth, had wheedled her way into the house for a sit-down interview with the family. Kate choked back tears as her parents expressed their grief and begged anyone who knew anything about Michael and his whereabouts to come forward with information.

Lauren had made a similar, tearful plea. Then the

reporter turned her attention to Kate. "You were the only one home besides Michael Saturday night, right?"

Kate nodded mutely, staring at her knotted hands resting in her lap.

"You didn't hear anything?"

Kate shook her head. "The TV was up too loud," she said, marveling a little at how easily the lie slipped off her tongue. "I didn't hear anything until the crash." Her father had managed to convince the sheriff to keep the part about Kate meeting Tommy out of the official report.

It was one thing for her family to know she was a slut. It was another for the world to know it.

Even so, within a few short hours, the world would know her brother was missing because of her carelessness.

Her father had ended the interview shortly afterward, and other than law enforcement, the only people allowed in the Becketts' house were the Burkharts. Phillip, his wife, Andrea, John and Hailey had hunkered down to help field calls, fend off the press, and make sure there was food to eat, even though none of them had much of an appetite.

"I know you feel terrible," John said to Kate early Tuesday morning when she wandered, zombielike, into the kitchen and poured herself a glass of orange juice. She startled, splashing juice over her hand and onto the floor. She hadn't even noticed him sitting at the kitchen table.

"And based on what you think of Tommy, I guess you think I deserve to," Kate said sharply as she grabbed a towel to blot up the mess.

"I stand by my agreement with your father that he's not good enough for you, but that doesn't mean it's your fault Michael's gone," he said gently.

"Of course it is," Kate said in a choked voice. "I was supposed to be here. I was in charge."

John rose from his chair and crossed to her. At first Kate resisted as he pulled her against him. But as she settled against his broad chest, felt his hand stroke her hair, it was impossible not to lean into him, absorbing the comfort. She realized, with a jolt, that this was the first time anyone had touched her in nearly three days. Since Saturday night, everyone had kept her at arm's length, meeting her eyes only briefly before skittering away.

Then there was her father, who hadn't so much as spoken to her or looked at her directly, as though she didn't exist.

Hot tears squeezed out of her eyes, and as she broke into sobs against John's chest, she felt a keen longing to be held by other arms, against another chest.

Tommy.

She hadn't seen him face to face since Sunday morning, and now she wanted to so badly it was like a physical ache.

Admitting that, even to herself, sent another blade of guilt stabbing through her core. Her need to see Tommy, to be with him, was what had caused this mess in the first place.

John held her as she sobbed harder, her guilt and grief swirling together with the faint pleasure of having someone, anyone, reach out to her in kindness even if she didn't deserve it.

They didn't get their first break until Tuesday evening. A local who'd gone camping Sunday morning and had been unaware of the crisis until he and his girlfriend got back to town on Tuesday afternoon said that he'd seen an older-model truck with a bad muffler turning onto Kootenai Drive around eleven thirty on Saturday night, which, once they pieced the timeline together, they figured to be about fifteen minutes before Kate and Tommy heard the sound of the engine approaching.

Though slight, it was something to go on. "Emerson Flannery drives a bombed-out F150, doesn't he?" the sheriff asked.

The deputy nodded. "Just got his license back after his DUI."

The sheriff shook his head. "Should have known, if there's trouble around here the Flannerys would have to be involved."

"Public intoxication, drugs, theft, sure," the deputy said. "But I never heard of them harming kids—not outside their family anyways."

The Flannerys were notorious in Sandpoint and the surrounding area, a family of drunks, addicts, and small-time criminals. But as far as Kate knew, none of them had ever been involved in anything like kidnapping. Still…

"Last week Tommy and I ran into Emerson down by the lake, near our house. He started following us down the beach," Kate offered.

"Did he threaten you at all, or give you reason to think he'd hurt your family?" Lyons asked.

Kate shook her head. "He was really drunk, calling us names, but I didn't think he had any idea who I was."

The sheriff called in an APB on Flannery's truck. "You come with me," he said to his deputy. "Even if he's not involved, I know better than to confront a Flannery without backup."

For several hours there was no word. Exhausted, Kate curled up into the overstuffed armchair in the great room and fell into a fitful sleep.

She didn't know what time it was when the phone jolted her awake, but it was pitch black outside and she could hear her parents' muffled voices coming from the kitchen.

Heart racing, Kate padded to the kitchen and hovered in

the doorway. Her parents stood close, their heads angled to the receiver so they could both hear.

Lauren joined her, slipping past Kate to go stand next to her parents. Kate strained but though she could make out the sheriff's voice, his words were unclear.

But Kate didn't need to hear the words to know that her worst fears had come true. She could see it in the way her father's face drained of color and his skin slackened, aging him a full decade in seconds.

She could hear it in her mother's frantic "No, no!" and the way she buried her face in her hands as she slid to the floor.

Kate rushed forward. "What—what is it?" She knew the answer. But something inside her needed to hear the words spoken out loud.

"Michael's dead," her father said in a voice that sounded ripped from his chest. "Flannery killed him, then killed himself."

Kate felt like a giant fist had closed around her lungs, robbing her of breath. No, no, the denial echoed in her head, but all she could do was sink to the floor and struggle to breathe. Her mind raced with a million simultaneous thoughts, wishes, prayers.

Let me go back and do it over again and I'll make sure nothing happens.

Please, God, let this be a mistake.

Take me instead. Let him come back and take me instead.

She didn't know how much time had passed before she heard a car approach and a knock on the door. Her mother sprang to her feet and raced to the door. Her father followed more slowly, as though he could delay facing reality.

As the door swung open, Kate saw the broad shoulders of Sheriff Lyons. Photographers snapped frantically from behind, bathing him in a strobe of light. He stepped inside, his face pulled into a solemn mask of grief.

Kate's mom backed away until her knees hit the couch and she collapsed back onto its cushions. Her father sat beside her. Sheriff Lyons took a seat in the armchair and rested his elbows on his knees, his back bowed as though he bore the weight of the world on it.

Kate and Lauren hovered anxiously in the doorway. Kate reached out blindly with her hand, her eyes filling with fresh tears when she felt her sister's cold fingers twine with her own.

"We found Flannery's truck parked in front of his trailer about a hundred yards from where the fire road dead-ends into a hiking trail. About thirty yards in is a small cabin that the forest service and hunters still use. We found Flannery and Michael inside. Michael was tied to the woodstove."

"How—" Her mother's question choked off on a sob. "How did he die?"

The sheriff hesitated. "You sure you want to do this right now?"

"I need to know everything," her mother said, her voice rising. "He was my baby, and I need to know exactly what happened to him."

If her father felt the same, he didn't show it. He sat statue still, his gaze locked on a point somewhere over the sheriff's right shoulder.

The sheriff's gaze flicked to Kate and Lauren.

"Go upstairs, girls," her father said, barely audible.

"No, I—" Kate started.

"Get the hell upstairs!" her father roared, and sprang to his feet so quickly Kate jumped back a foot. "After everything you've done, the least you can do is listen to me!" The vein in his forehead was back, along with the rush of florid color in his cheeks.

Kate and Lauren sprinted up the stairs to their room. But no sooner had they shut the door than Kate carefully pushed it open and slipped out into the hallway. Lauren joined her, and soon they were perched on the third step from the top, hidden from view but able to hear everything.

"Michael was shot at point-blank range twice, once in the chest, once in the head," the sheriff said, unable to keep the quiver out of his voice. "Flannery then turned the gun on himself. He left a note," the sheriff continued, "apologizing for what he'd done, explaining that he was going to put himself down to keep himself from hurting anyone else."

Kate's mother made a sound like a wounded animal that shook Kate to the bottom of her soul.

Kate felt like she was being sucked into a black hole. She must have made a sound, because her father's gaze snapped up to the gallery to where she and Lauren listened. The white-hot anger in his eyes was so fierce, Kate was sure there was going to be nothing left of her but a pile of ash.

When he spoke, his voice, though quiet, seemed to echo through the room. "It should have been you."

Chapter 1

Sandpoint, ID
Present day

As Kate Beckett steered her rented sedan off Highway 95, she felt her stomach clench with dread. Though she'd had nearly an hour and a half during the drive from the airport in Spokane, as she pulled off the highway and headed for the center of Sandpoint, Idaho, her heart rate doubled and the lump in her throat threatened to choke her.

While her dashboard display claimed it was a toasty eighty-three degrees outside, typical for the end of August, even in the mountains of Idaho, Kate felt like ice water was pumping through her veins, her fingers numbly clutching the steering wheel as she glanced down at her phone to double-check the directions.

Her route took her through the center of town and past Sandpoint's City Beach. Fourteen years had passed since Kate had been here, and she felt she was seeing the town as though through a dream. Everything at once searingly familiar yet oddly different as she cataloged the changes the town had undergone in a decade and a half. First Street was still crowded with tourists, as it always was in summer, families enjoying the last gasps of summer on the lake before school started.

The shop that had once sold beautiful hand-sewn quilts was now occupied by a Starbucks. But there was still a line trailing down the block in front of Ike's ice cream store. Kate watched two teenage girls and a boy, tanned and water-logged from a day on the lake, towels draped around their necks, emerge from the shop. As they laughed and jostled each other around licks of enormous soft-serve cones, Kate felt her chest pinch and a burning behind her eyes.

How many times had she, Lauren, and Michael finished up a day of water-skiing and suntanning with chocolate dip cones from Ike's? They had been that carefree, that joyful, completely unaware of the asteroid hurtling toward them, moments away from blowing life as they knew it to smithereens.

Kate gave herself a mental shake and continued along the lakeshore. She needed to keep a sharp eye out for street signs, not lose herself in wallowing in the past.

The truth was, anything and everything in Sandpoint—from the way the piercingly blue sky competed for brilliance with the azure of Lake Pend Oreille, to the scent of the air—sunbaked earth mingled with crisp pine—to, yes, something as simple as the sight of an oversize ice cream cone—could send her hurtling back into the black hole if she let it.

But right now there was no time for that. Now she had to be strong, focused. Another girl, another family needed her and her expertise. She needed to be completely focused on getting her back to safety. To save the girl who still had a chance and waste no time grieving over the one who was long gone.

Kate turned down Kootenai Bay Road and tried to calm the trembling in her stomach. She knew this road, which wound its way through one of Sandpoint's most luxurious developments, all too well. She knew so many of these houses, houses occupied by her "lake friends," as she, Lauren and Michael had called them. Families who, like Kate's, had rented the same houses at the same time every year, until they'd formed something of a community, albeit one that only lasted a month or so out of every summer.

Once Kate and her family had been deeply entrenched in that community. But after the tragedy—as Mother called it—it was as though the previous seven summers hadn't existed, as though she and her sister and brother hadn't spent eleven months of the year anticipating the one they would spend here. This part of their lives—all the joy, friendships, everything—had been excised from their existence like a cancerous tumor.

She'd often wondered if their little community had gone on without them. She knew some had reached out to her parents and tried to keep in touch, but only because Kate had found cards and letters unopened in the trash. Put there by her father's social secretary as per his and her mother's instructions.

Did the Michaelsons still rent number 293? she mused as she drove by a familiar, massive post-and-beam house that edged up onto the lake.

There was another, even more impressive log home two houses down. Did the Burkharts, who lived most of the year outside of San Francisco, still own what they loved to call "their little lakeside retreat"? Did teenagers still gather around their bonfire before pairing off into the darkness to make out?

At the thought, a face flashed in her brain. Dark eyes sparking with amusement, a flash of white teeth against tan skin. Tempting her to sin even as she knew there would be hell to pay if she ever got caught...

She gave herself a mental smack, sent the image fleeing.

She pulled up in front of number 540, which, had been rented by the Cunninghams the last summer she'd spent here. Kate hadn't spent much time there since the Cunningham kids were a few years younger. But her brother,

Michael, had made fast friends with the oldest, Billy, the summer they were both eleven and had spent the next two summers having sleepovers here when they weren't watching movies and camping out in the Becketts' spacious rental about a quarter mile away.

She noticed the sheriff's car parked along the curb as well as the news van and the small throng of reporters and felt an eerie sense of déjà vu. Though she dealt with reporters all the time, seeing them in this setting was unnerving. Reminding her, reminding the world, that even in an idyllic setting such as this, evil could still lurk in the shadows.

She pulled into the driveway and braced herself before knocking. The noise from the crowd hit her like a wave as she marched determinedly up the front walkway. The press, anticipating her arrival, came at her like a swarm. She pushed her way through, ignoring their questions and saying only "I won't be making a statement until I meet with the family and the local authorities."

She barely had time to knock before the door swung open, revealing a middle-age woman dressed in khaki shorts and a light blue polo shirt. "It's good to see you again, Kate. Come on in." The woman gestured her in with a sweep of her hand. "Though I wish it could be under better circumstances," she quickly added.

Kate cocked her head at the woman's greeting. Kate was on television often enough that occasionally she was recognized, but the familiarity in the woman's voice and smile said that she should know her. She studied the woman's face for a moment, and then she got it.

Trade in the salt-and-pepper hair for dark brown and erase a decade and a half's worth of lines from the woman's face, and Kate recognized Tracy Albright who ran the quilt shop—now Starbucks—down on Main Street. "It's nice to see you too, Mrs. Albright," Kate said, smiling automatically though it felt strained at the edges.

She waved a hand. "Oh, call me Tracy. You're not sixteen anymore, and having a grown woman call me Mrs. Albright makes me feel about a hundred years old!"

"Are you a friend of Mr. Fuller's?" Kate asked as she followed Mrs. Albright—Tracy—through the slate-tiled entryway to the great room that adjoined the kitchen.

"Not exactly," Tracy replied over her shoulder as Kate took stock of the house where Michael had spent so much time that last summer. Though Kate herself hadn't spent tons of time here, she'd visited often enough to notice the changes. The layout of the house was the same—a massive great room with a stone fireplace adjoined the kitchen and was the center of the main floor. A wooden staircase led up the hall to the second floor with a gallery looking over the great room and two bedrooms on either end. A hallway off the great room led to two more rooms.

Two sets of sliders offered an unimpeded view of the lake and the Bitterroot and Selkirk Mountains above. Outside, the house was surrounded by a wooden deck with stairs that led down to the communal dock reserved for the houses clustered along this stretch of beach.

And across the lake, Kate could see dozens of Jet Skiers and power boats. In two weeks the lake would be virtually empty, no one left but the locals to enjoy the mountain paradise.

The mission-style couches and tables Kate remembered were gone, replaced with an overstuffed leather sectional and love seat. The kitchen, she noticed, had been completely remodeled. The terra-cotta tiles she remembered had been replaced by hardwood floors, the appliances all shiny stainless steel, the kind you'd find in a restaurant kitchen. Yet more evidence that life here had continued after the Becketts had left.

"After I sold the shop last summer, I thought I'd spend my retirement kicking back on the boat in the summer and cross-country skiing all winter," Tracy said as she led Kate down the hallway off the great room. "But turns out after working my tail off every day for thirty years, I don't have much patience for sitting around on my duff dangling a fishing pole over the side of the boat. I was bored stiff after just two weeks. Not to mention Art—my husband," she clarified, "thought that since I was home all the time, it meant I was going to turn into his personal servant. Got all ticked off when I wouldn't cook him a hot lunch every day. Thirty-five years of marriage and I've never made him a hot lunch, and suddenly I'm supposed to be Betty Crocker?"

Despite the circumstances, Kate felt the corner of her mouth quirk up at the woman's exasperated yet affectionate tone. She'd forgotten that about this place, how friendly the people were, inviting you into their homes and sharing confidences as if you were lifelong friends even if she hadn't set foot in the town in fourteen years.

Not to mention, they—her father, in particular—hadn't left on the best of terms with several of the locals.

"So anyway, instead of staying home thinking up ways I could kill Art without getting caught, I realized there are a lot of renters here with extra cash who might want to spend it on someone who can help with the grocery shopping, the cooking, the boat rentals, all that kind of stuff so when they get here they're all set up to enjoy the lake. So now the rental agency hires me out as sort of a personal concierge for renters who request it."

"That sounds like a great business," Kate said politely, though as she heard the low rumble of male voices coming from behind the closed door at the end of the hall, she felt a surge of anxiety, a need to get down to business. In the back of her mind she could hear the clock ticking with every beat of her heart, each second forward more foreboding than the last.

"These last couple of days I've been putting in some extra time here with the Fullers," Tracy continued, her face now somber. "I don't want Jackson and Brooke to worry about anything as silly as cooking dinner. I'm sure you can relate," she said, a sad smile tugging her lips as she reached out to pat Kate's arm.

Kate nodded, resisting the urge to yank away from the other woman's touch.

She knew the other woman meant nothing but kindness, but to this day, she couldn't help her violent, gut-deep resentment of such empty gestures. The sympathy, the pats on the hand or shoulder, the look of false understanding.

No one who hadn't gone through it could really understand. And even then, each person experienced the loss in a different way. Each family endured their unique crisis in their unique way.

She masked all of this behind the bland smile she'd perfected for the cameras and whispered a quiet thank-you to Tracy.

"That poor family," Tracy said with a sorrowful shake of her head. "First they lose the mother to cancer, and now this happens."

Kate's heart squeezed in sympathy, thinking how unfair the universe could be. Jackson's wife, Suzanne, had died of cancer less than a year ago. To face the possibility of losing a child...

She swallowed back the lump in her throat and followed Tracy down the hall to the office. As Tracy knocked on the door, she straightened her shoulders and brought her focus back on the here and now. The past was the past. Now nothing was more important than to make sure the people behind the heavy wooden door did not become one of the people in the world who could truly relate to what Kate had gone through.

The door opened to reveal a tall, broad-shouldered man in his late forties. His face was haggard—Kate couldn't imagine that he'd slept in the past thirty-six hours. Deep lines were carved into either side of his mouth, and his silver-dusted blond hair looked like he'd run his hand through it a thousand times. Still, he was handsome, with his square jaw, sharp cheekbones, and blue eyes that glimmered with intelligence behind their strain.

Kate held out her hand. "Hello, Mr. Fuller," she said, unsmiling, her gaze locked on his. "Under different circumstances I would say it's nice to meet you, but I wish you didn't need my help here."

There was a faint twitch of his lips, a ghost of a smile. "Thanks for that. I have to say I agree. But I'm glad CJ was able to get in touch with you—any support we can foster in the community and the media will help."

At the mention, Kate smiled at the man who was lingering behind Jackson Fuller. Though she'd dreaded coming back to Sandpoint, she couldn't deny the flash of warmth she'd felt when she'd heard CJ—short for Cody James—Kovac's voice on the line yesterday morning. She'd met CJ when she was twelve, when his family had rented a house a few doors down from the Becketts. Two years later, his father decided to cash out of his successful software business and moved the family out to the lake full time.

Kate and Lauren had joked that with his sun-streaked brown hair and tanned, muscular—and usually shirtless—torso, CJ would have looked more at home on the beaches of San Diego than on a mountain lake in rural Idaho. With his quick smile and easy charm, CJ had taken it on himself to be their ambassador in Sandpoint. Once he'd earned his official townie status, he started taking them to all the cool parties none of the tourist kids ever got invited to.

Now she couldn't help noticing that his once-smiling green eyes had a somber cast. Partly due to the reason she was here, she was sure. But she knew most of the shadows had to do with the last year of his own life and the circumstances that led him to leave a promising career with the FBI and return home to Sandpoint.

It was funny seeing the boy who'd once smuggled a six-pack of Coors Light under his sweatshirt dressed in the brown and tan of the Bonner County Sheriff's uniform. And as she stepped forward to give him a hug, she couldn't help notice that he'd gotten a few inches taller and the muscular torso had filled out solidly enough that it strained the fabric of his uniform shirt.

"You look good, Kate," he said simply as he engulfed her in a hug. "I see you on TV all the time, but I'd forgotten how pretty you are in person."

Kate felt a flush of heat in her cheeks. At one time, CJ had made no bones about the crush he was nursing on her. But then Kate had only had eyes for another local boy.

She pulled away from CJ, turning her attention back to Fuller when she caught a movement from the shadows of the office from the corner of her eye.

"You—" The word got stuck halfway up her throat, and she took a step back as though punched by an unseen fist. Tommy Ibarra stepped fully from the shadows, and her mind spun with a thousand memories, a thousand questions. She stood there, dumbstruck, as one managed to squeeze its way to the surface of the quagmire. "What are you doing here?"

"Jackson asked me to join you," he replied.

Every cell in her body came alive at the familiar rumble of his voice, deeper now than it had been at nineteen. Yet there was nothing familiar in the flat, stony stare that met her own or the tight, grim line of his mouth.

Even as he looked at her with none of the warmth or tenderness she remembered, flashes of hot and cold tore through her and her stomach dove for her feet.

Get it together, she scolded herself. She'd known damn well when she decided to help with the Fuller case that she ran the risk of running into Tommy. She didn't know if he still lived here or not—it wasn't like she kept tabs on him. No matter how strong the urge to Google him sometimes became.

However, as his parents had lived here for generations, their sheep ranch one of the oldest in the area, their roots were so deep and so strong she couldn't imagine them ever leaving.

Apparently Tommy hadn't either. Maybe he'd given in to his parents' pressure to take over the ranch.

Looking at him now, he didn't look much like a rancher. Sure, his body was as lean and fit as it had ever been, as it would be if he did hard physical labor every day. But the boy she'd remembered as tall and lanky had packed on several inches—he now towered nearly a foot over her own five foot six inches. And judging from the way the muscles of his chest, shoulders, and arms stood out against the soft cotton of his button-down shirt, he'd put on at least twenty-five pounds, and not the kind you got from eating too much of Ike's soft serve.

And his face...God, it had fared just as well as the rest of him. The last time she'd seen him, his nose and chin were still a shade too bold for his lean face. Now that he'd filled out, the strong, chiseled features and deep-set dark eyes that told of his Basque ancestry had created a face that, while not classically handsome, was so compelling she couldn't imagine any straight female would be able to tear her eyes away.

The only hint of softness was his mouth. Even now, with his full lips pressed into a grim line, she couldn't stop the tide of memories rushing forth. Memories of how that mouth had felt moving over her own. Touching, tasting, tempting her to sin.

Tempting her to disaster.

Just like that, the memories crumbled to dust, a harsh reminder of why she was here. And it wasn't to take a walk down memory lane with Tomas Ibarra.

"What is he doing here?" she repeated to CJ, struggling to keep her voice steady so as not to upset Mr. Fuller. She didn't know whether he knew about her past with Tommy, but she didn't want him to have any doubts about her abilities to help him deal with the frustrating tangle of logistics, law enforcement procedures, and media relations he would have to face in the coming days—or, God forbid, months.

"I work as a professional security consultant," Tommy broke in. "Jackson is one of my clients."

"You're his bodyguard?" Kate asked, her brows knitting in concern. From the information she'd received about Jackson Fuller and his family, she learned that Fuller had done well since he'd moved from government work into the private sector seven years ago. However, she didn't realize he'd amassed the kind of wealth that might create a need for fulltime personal security. That could put an entirely different spin on what was going on here.

As though reading her mind, Tommy said, "It's not like that. While I provide both physical and cybersecurity for my clients, I also help them manage the flow of information and help them identify leaks in cases of corporate espionage. I met Jackson years ago in the Army, and he's been a friend as well as a client since I started my business. I'm currently consulting for him on a new company he's starting."

Tommy joined the Army, she mused to herself, tucking

away that information as she pasted on a smile that was as genuine as Pamela Anderson's breasts. "I see. Well, I'm sure Mr. Fuller appreciates your support, and of course we appreciate any help that we can get from volunteers, but right now if you could excuse me so I can talk with him and the sheriff in private—"

"I want him to stay," Fuller said gruffly. "Tommy's the best in his field—"

Kate felt the skin on her upper back and neck prickle. "I'm sure that's true, but I'm not sure how much value he'll add right now in the information-gathering phase—"

"I'm staying," Tommy said curtly, folding his arms across his chest in a way that made him look as formidable as one of the granite peaks jutting into the sky around them. He gave Fuller's shoulder a squeeze with his big hand. "After everything he's been through in the past months, I'm not leaving him to deal with this alone. Not even if it means leaving him in the hands of one of the country's foremost experts on missing children."

Was it just her, or did she hear a tinge of derision as he uttered the word "expert"? Or was she just paranoid, imagining criticism whenever people spoke of her? Well-deserved criticism, a soft inner voice hissed. Kate swallowed back a surge of guilt and grief and resolved herself to spending at least several moments in Tommy's overwhelming presence.

"Fine," she said. She perched on the edge of an armchair positioned on the other side of the desk—more leather—and took out her iPad and pulled up the notes she already had about the case. "Now tell me everything about the night your daughter disappeared."

Chapter 2

Kate listened intently as Jackson recounted the events leading up to Tricia's disappearance approximately thirty-six hours before. Most of what he told her she already knew from the police report CJ had sent to her and from broadcast media coverage.

Kate had sucked up every bit of information—scant though it was—after receiving a phone call from a producer at CNN asking if she would comment on the case of fourteen-year-old Tricia Fuller who'd gone missing in Sandpoint, Idaho. Revisiting Sandpoint and everything that had happened here was the last thing on earth Kate wanted to do, but she knew she couldn't say no.

Her own notoriety and the fact that the media had connected her to Tricia's case meant that Tricia and her family would receive more coverage than 99.9 percent of any of the other hundreds of thousands of kids currently missing in the United States.

It was horribly unfair, Kate knew, that some children were headline fodder for weeks, even months, rallying the public around the families and galvanizing the search.

The reality of it gnawed at her conscience for the families and kids who were ignored, whose faces she wasn't helping to keep on the TV screen or the front pages of the news. But she couldn't let that keep her from seizing on the tragic connection she had with this case and this town and the media's desire to exploit it, not if it could help get Tricia home safely.

—‿m‿—

"Brooke, her sister, had gone out," Jackson said, "some party on the lake. I'd gone to bed early, around nine," he continued. "At that point Tricia was watching a movie on the great room TV."

He reached up and scrubbed a big, blunt-fingered hand across his face. "Goddamn pills. I didn't hear a goddamn thing when she left, I was so out of it."

Kate gave CJ and Tommy puzzled looks. She hadn't heard anything about Jackson being under the influence. "Pills?"

"Goddamn sleeping pills," Jackson clarified. "My doctor prescribed them because I haven't been sleeping more than an hour or two at night, ever since Suzanne..." He broke off, pressed against his eyes with his thumb and forefinger.

Kate's heart squeezed in sympathy as Jackson took a shuddering breath and tried to compose himself. Shortly after the New Year, Suzanne Fuller, his wife of twenty-five years, had been diagnosed with pancreatic cancer. Despite attempts at treatment, she'd died within six weeks.

"I keep thinking, if only I hadn't taken it, I would have heard her sneaking out. I would have been able to stop her."

She couldn't imagine the man's pain, first losing his wife, then having to deal with the horror of having his young daughter disappear.

"She followed her sister to the party?"

Jackson nodded. "More to spite Brooke, I think, than

because she really wanted to go. They haven't been getting along well lately. When Tommy suggested we come out here, I was hoping that a change of scenery..." His voice trailed off as he gazed out the windows across the lake.

Tommy shifted on his feet and his eyes met hers. There was no missing the guilt that flashed across his face.

"Brooke was the last one to see her," CJ offered.

"What time was that again?" That bit of information was already seared into Kate's memory banks, but she wanted to make sure everyone was sharing the same information. Inconsistencies led to mistakes, false leads, and confusion when keen focus on the details was essential.

"A little before eleven, Brooke said," CJ replied. "It's in the police report I sent you. She indicated they argued, and she told Tricia to ride her bike back to the house."

But when Brooke arrived home a little after midnight, Kate knew, Tricia was nowhere to be found.

"Can I speak to Brooke?"

CJ and Jackson exchanged glances. "She's not up to talking to anyone," Jackson said tightly. "As you may imagine, she's struggling with all of this."

She could so easily imagine. Again her gaze was drawn to Tommy as though by a tractor beam, as her own guilt and grief formed a tight knot in her chest, threatening to cut off her breath. "Maybe later. At some point, it would be good if we could get her in front of the cameras."

"Jesus, that's cold," Tommy interjected. "That's all you can think about?"

Kate felt her hackles rise at the notion of having to defend herself, especially to him. "She may be able to relay other information that didn't come across in a written police report—no offense, CJ," she said, and he held up his hands to indicate none was taken. "Not to mention, there's always the chance that if someone took her and sees her grieving sister—"

"What do you mean, *if*?" Jackson asked in a low voice.

Kate knew to tread carefully. "I'm sure you know that there is some speculation that Tricia might have left on her own accord—"

"Tricia would never do that! She's a straight A student, played on the varsity tennis team as a freshman. No matter how difficult the last year has been, she would never run away. Brooke, on the other hand..." His voice trailed off, his mouth compressing into a thin line.

Every instinct in Kate's body screamed at her to let it go. Jackson was in enough pain without her calling his daughter's character into question. But it was imperative that they explore all the possibilities. "Kids hide a lot of things from their parents," she said quietly. "If Tricia is sneaking out to go to parties, isn't it possible she's doing other things you're not aware of?"

"Kate," Tommy said in a warning tone. Jackson's shoulders were rigid, his face grim.

"If she's a runaway, it will affect how we approach things in the media—"

"Right, so they can portray her as an ungrateful brat who's wasting time and resources—" Tommy snapped.

Kate continued as though he hadn't spoken. "—and how much of our efforts will go to working with organizations that focus on runaways and troubled teens."

"I get your point," Jackson said, "but our family's been through the wringer this year, and I don't believe for a second Tricia would do this to us."

Kate looked at CJ. "You reported it as a stranger abduction case. You still believe that?"

CJ gave a grim nod. Kate wouldn't completely dismiss

the possibility that Tricia was a runaway, but CJ's opinion was enough to convince her until they found evidence to the contrary. Part of her would always see CJ as the flirty teenage wannabe stud, but the years had lined his face with experience and brought depths of knowledge to his eyes. She'd checked around with her contacts and knew he had been on the fast track to making Special Agent at the Bureau before he left for personal reasons. She'd trust his instincts. "Then we'll make sure the press portrays it that way."

"Glad we got that settled," Tommy said, and even if Kate couldn't hear the disdain in his voice, she would have seen it in the curl of his lip.

"Then again," he added, "I guess you've had enough experience with the press that you must know what you're doing."

Kate's fingers curled involuntarily at the emphasis he placed on the word "experience." That snide undertone and the way his lip held its sneer let her know loud and clear he wasn't talking about the many interviews she'd done over the years and the appearances she'd made on CNN, MSNBC, Headline News—you name it—on behalf of the St. Anthony Foundation.

No, it was clear Tommy had heard about her failed engagement to a news anchor that had ended so disastrously her broken heart was the least of the damage.

Kate's spine pulled tight and she fixed Tommy with the bland stare she'd spent more than a decade perfecting so no one would ever suspect the turmoil constantly churning and raging beneath the surface. "Yes, my work with St. Anthony's has resulted in a lot of time with the various media outlets. While it may seem cold and calculating to be worrying about spin control, I've learned it's important to control the message right from the get-go, so people stay focused on finding Tricia rather than wasting time speculating on what motivation she might have had to leave of her own accord."

"Whatever you say," Tommy said without so much as a flicker of emotion. "All we want is to make sure Tricia gets home unharmed."

"That's all any of us want." Kate turned to Jackson, unable to stop herself from reaching out to take his hand. "I know this sounds trite, and nobody will ever know what you're going through, but after what my family experienced, know that I'm going to use everything I've learned in the decade I've worked with the foundation to find Tricia." Jackson nodded stiffly and swallowed hard, his big hand closing around hers with almost desperate strength. He was doing his best to remain stoic, but Kate could feel the pain and anxiety emanating from his body, and her own eyes stung with tears. She swallowed them back, cautioning herself to push her own emotions aside.

It would be too easy to let herself sink into the dark hole of empathetic grief. It was a struggle with every case the foundation worked on; it was nearly impossible to learn about these kids, meet with their families, and see what they were going through and not let their sadness bring her own screaming back to the surface. But her job was not to grieve with them, it was to maintain a clear head at a time when emotions were beyond overwhelming. She was the linchpin, connecting the family with law enforcement, volunteers, and the media.

And usually with any outside investigators brought in to help. But Jackson had brought in Tommy himself, and though they seemed to have entered into an uneasy truce, she was more than happy to let Jackson deal with him directly.

"CJ, can you bring me up to speed on the investigation? How many people are involved?"

"I'm heading up the investigation myself, as you know," he said, gesturing with his chin at the report on the table in front of Kate. "But our resources here are limited. I made some calls to the state police district office, but so far they've only made contact by phone."

"Hopefully the additional media exposure will give them a kick in the ass," Kate murmured. "Support from the community is critical. The first thing we need to do is coordinate the volunteers. We need to set up central headquarters—"

"Tracy helped us print up some flyers and has been taking the calls here," Jackson said.

Kate shook her head. "We're talking about coordinating dozens of people—you don't want to have that many people in your house. Not to mention, while we like to think everyone would be helping out of the pure goodness of their hearts, there are a lot of twisted people who are attracted to cases like this, attracted to victims. You don't want those people to have access to your personal space."

Kate felt a knot in her stomach. She of all people knew that. She had spent years protecting herself, and even she hadn't been smart enough to spot the wolf in sheep's clothing she'd ushered through her own front door.

"We need to find a print shop in town that will help print flyers and set up a tip line and get people to man the phones. CJ, maybe you can put me in touch—"

"I'll help you with that," Tommy said impatiently. "CJ needs to keep his focus on the investigation itself, not deal with logistics a high schooler could handle."

Every cell in her body rejected the idea. She needed someone who knew the local business owners, someone to make introductions, someone who would be her constant companion for at least the next couple of days.

No way was she spending that kind of time in close contact

with Tommy Ibarra. "But CJ knows the town and as the sheriff he's got the respect—"

Tommy made a scoffing sound. "And the fact that my family has been here for five generations and that I still live here more than half the year doesn't count for anything."

Even before he said it, Kate knew how stupid her protest sounded. Of course Tommy was connected with the local business owners as well as—if not better than—CJ was.

"And despite your father's opinion of me," Tommy bit out, "I'm still pretty well liked around here."

For a brief moment she saw a crack in his stony facade, enough to let his real emotions shine through. What she saw didn't put her any more at ease, as Tommy's eyes glittered at her with resentment that had been simmering for more than a decade.

Shame and the knowledge she deserved every bit of his resentment burned like acid in her chest. The sixteen-year-old girl still lurking inside her wanted to jump to her defense. *I had to go along with it. I couldn't say anything, not if I wanted to make it up to my father for everything that had happened.*

But they both knew the truth. One call to the dean at the University of Idaho, one call to the press to expose her father's strong-arm tactics against Tommy and his family, and his life at least would have returned to normal. Instead, in a last, futile attempt to regain her family's favor, she'd stayed silent, unwilling to create a media scandal that would alienate her from her family once and for all.

What Kate hadn't realized, until it was too late, was that no matter what she did, her father was never going to forgive her. He was never going to love her again.

I'm sorry, Kate wanted to say, but she couldn't push the words past her lips.

CJ cleared his throat and lowered his gaze spotted something really interesting on the b tips of his boots. Jackson's brow knitted in confu had a problem with Senator Beckett?"

Kate swallowed hard and opened her mouth to answer when Tommy cut her off. "It's old news and, like I said, never really amounted to much." Kate watched as the resentment faded, Tommy's expression turning flat and emotionless once again. So different from the Tommy she'd known, whose every emotion showed in the depths of his eyes. He could brush it off, but Kate knew the truth: The senator's manipulations and the life Tommy had lived since then had turned him into a hard-eyed stranger she barely recognized.

"We should get going then," she said to Tommy. As she pushed to her feet, she added, "The reporters are going to want to talk to me about my involvement. Are you comfortable with me giving them a statement?" The question was as much for CJ as for Jackson.

Jackson nodded. "That's a big part of why I contacted you. I don't want to be in front of the cameras any more than I have to, and I certainly don't want them bothering Brooke."

CJ added, "As long as you don't divulge details we don't want leaked—and as of now there are none—I'm hoping for as much media attention as we can get."

"Good." The four of them walked to the front door. She said goodbye to Jackson while CJ and Tommy followed her outside. As expected, the reporters were gathered on the front porch in a buzzing knot. The second the door swung open, half a dozen microphones were pointed at their faces. CJ quickly took his leave.

Tommy hung back and gestured with one big hand as though to say "It's all you."

Kate mentally braced herself. She'd done enough interviews

to be comfortable in front of the cameras, but she knew the press for this case would be different. She was used to rehashing her own past. It was, of course, why she'd majored in criminology at NYU.

She'd originally planned to go into law enforcement. But after a summer spent interning at the St. Anthony's Foundation, named for the patron saint of missing people, she'd realized she could do more good leveraging her own notoriety to draw national attention to cases that might otherwise linger in obscurity.

This time, she knew, the rehashing would be worse. Because this time when she was talking about her past, she would be in the same town, breathing the same air, seeing the same familiar places she'd seen that night long ago.

And not only that, she was surrounded by people who had been there. Who remembered what had happened that horrible night, who had lived through it with her.

People like Tommy, who had also been damaged in the aftermath.

She fielded the first few questions easily.

"Do you have any leads on Tricia's location?" This from a grizzled, middle-age man who was scribbling his notes on an old-school steno pad.

"We have no new information, but we'll be setting up a tip line soon for people to call with information," Kate replied.

"What about speculation that Tricia is a runaway?" asked a petite brunette who looked like she was still in high school.

"Right now there's nothing to indicate that Tricia left on her own. She was last seen heading in the direction of home on her bike, the ATM card her father gave her for emergencies hasn't been used, and she hasn't been seen at any of the area bus terminals or along the major roads."

"At what point will the search shift its focus to looking for a body?"

This was from a slim blonde whose perfectly applied makeup didn't do anything to hide the hard glint in her eyes. Kate knew her type well, the kind of reporter who gained notoriety by provoking her interview subjects into anger or an overly emotional response. "We of course hope it never comes to that. Right now we're working on the premise that Tricia is alive, and we're hoping that anyone who has any information about her whereabouts will come forward as soon as possible."

Another reporter tried to get a question in, but the blonde's sharp voice drowned him out. "What makes you think you'll have any more success helping to get Tricia Fuller back than you did with Madeline Drexler?"

Kate braced herself against the pain spearing her chest at the mention of eleven-year-old Madeline, the memory of her small broken body covered by nothing but a pile of wet leaves. "I have to be optimistic with every case we get involved in," she said, hoping the fact that the question had her crumpling inside wasn't obvious on camera. "I couldn't do this job otherwise."

With Kate's defenses already weakened, blondie decided to go in for the kill. "Of course, but you've had to overcome other tragedies where some would say you had some culpability. Starting with your own brother right here in Sandpoint."

Kate felt like she was about to fly apart, like a glass crashing to the ground to shatter into a million shards. She wanted to lash out at the reporter, take her to task for taking the sucker punch. But she knew that while she had to tread carefully with the press on every case she worked on, this time it was particularly important.

Just the memory of her meeting the day before with Ron

Weaver, the chairman of the board of St. Anthony's, was enough to make her cheeks burn with shame.

After what happened with the Drexler case, we can't afford to have even a hint of misconduct. Because of your carelessness, we've had major donors threaten to pull their funding. If you make even one misstep, Kate, it will be disaster for us and for you.

She didn't let the camera pick up any of her turmoil as she forced her stiff lips to form a reply. "Of course I will never get over what happened to my brother and my own guilt for not keeping a closer eye on him that night. But I'm here now to focus on giving Tricia and her family the happy ending mine will never have."

Chapter 3

For the last fourteen years, Tommy Ibarra was convinced that if he never laid eyes on Kate Beckett again, it would be too soon. Now, as he pulled his truck into the space next to hers and watched her climb out of her rented sedan, he was still reeling from that first moment he saw her when she walked into Jackson Fuller's den.

It was like being punched in the face, addling his brain, making his head ring with the impact. Even though, unlike Kate, he had several hours to prepare himself to see her again, he still wasn't ready for his first in the flesh encounter with her.

Probably never would be.

He didn't know what it was about her—had never really known. With her blond hair tinged with the barest hint of red, her pale skin, and finely sculpted features, she was classically beautiful but hardly striking. And her body didn't sport anything close to the outrageous curves that had caught his eye in the past.

But there was something about her, always had been, from the first time he'd met her, that hot, sunny July day when he was fifteen. He'd been mowing the lawn at one of the big mansions on the lake, drenched with sweat as the sun beat down on him. He'd cursed a blue streak when he went to the cooler in his truck only to realize he'd forgotten to restock it with cold drinks.

Then she'd appeared, a skinny little girl with big blue eyes and a wide smile that took up most of her face, pressing an icy cold soda into his hand and introducing herself. That moment had sparked an unlikely friendship where Tommy had taken the sheltered senator's daughter under his wing like a surrogate kid sister.

Until the summer she turned sixteen, and new feelings cropped up that were anything but brotherly.

As he climbed out of his truck, he let his gaze rake over her as she waited for him on the sidewalk. In her close-fitting jeans and sleeveless white button-front shirt, she was nearly as slim as she'd been when she was sixteen. Her hair in its ponytail was a little darker. But damned if she didn't still have that smattering of freckles across her nose and that keen intelligence in her clear blue eyes that had inexplicably fascinated him from the first moment they'd met his.

And still, always, there was that composure, that aura of untouchability that compelled him to reach out, to touch, to see if he could break through the wall of reserve she wore like an invisible cloak.

Today that reserve was mixed with a heavy dose of discomfort, her body practically vibrating with tension as he joined her on the sidewalk. "Where to first?" she asked in a too-chipper voice that grated on his nerves.

"You said we needed a volunteer headquarters. Tim Greaves manages several of the properties downtown, and I know he has some vacant storefronts," he said, starting down the sidewalk in the direction of the Realtor's office. "I called him on the way, he's expecting us."

Kate nodded and fell in step with him, her legs moving double time to keep up with his long-legged strides. In spite of himself, he snuck looks down at her, for some reason fascinated by the brisk swing of her pale, bare arms, the subtle flex of her leg muscles under her jeans.

The hot sun beat down on them, and as her skin heated he caught the scent of her shampoo.

A jolt of heat hit low in his belly as he was immediately transported back fourteen years, that same mix of floral and fruit saturating his senses as they lay on a blanket on the beach, arms and legs in a tangle, heartbeats and breath coming hard and fast as they kissed and caressed while his body demanded so much more.

He wondered if she still tasted the same...

He shook the memories off, shoved them back in the mental vault where they belonged. What the fuck was wrong with him? The last time he'd tangled with Kate Beckett, his entire world had been turned upside down.

"How's your father?" Tommy asked to reinforce his point.

Her mouth tightened almost imperceptibly as she walked. "He's well. Gearing up for another election year—"

"Be sure to tell him he can't count on my vote," he muttered.

Her pace faltered. "Tommy," she said. He paused. She reached out with one pale, slim hand as though to touch him, then pulled back before she made contact. She swallowed hard, and as Tommy watched her throat work, he tried not to remember the shuddering, sighing sound she used to make as he flicked his tongue down the pale, slender length.

She cleared her throat and he jerked his eyes back up to her face. Her full pink mouth was pulled down at the corners, and there was a storm brewing in her wide, pale blue eyes. "I know this is fourteen years overdue, but I owe you an apology for what happened after Michael—"

The mention of Kate's little brother brought a stab of

guilt and sadness so fresh it was like it was happening now. And along with it, all the anger, resentment, and helplessness he'd felt at having his entire world go ass up because he was too dumb to stay away from Kate Beckett. He'd done what he could to make the best of a bad situation, but there was no denying that the senator's revenge had changed the course of his life, changed him in ways he never would have seen coming. And he had no interest in dredging up the rage, the humiliation, and the gut-wrenching pain of Kate's rejection and ultimate betrayal.

"This is Tim's office," Tommy said, cutting her off as he indicated the glass door that read "Greaves Property Management LLC" and reached past her to push it open.

This time she did touch him, putting her hand on his chest to stay him. It sent a pulse of heat straight to his groin, making him go heavy and thick as he imagined her hand elsewhere. "Please, you have to know that I hated what my father did, and I felt—feel—terrible about how much trouble he caused for you and your family. I should have done something."

Tommy looked meaningfully down at her hand, then back at her face to pin her with a hard stare. Hot color flooded her cheeks as she snatched her hand away and took a couple awkward steps back. "Like you said, Kate, it was fourteen years ago. Water under the bridge. And I landed on my feet eventually." He should have left it at that. But a little demon inside urged him to go in for just one dig. "Really, the only person to blame is myself. I should have known better than to mess with a sixteen-year-old virgin who wasn't worth the trouble."

Her only reaction was a tightening of her lips, a flush of hot color to her cheeks. Nevertheless, Tommy felt mean and small. Swearing under his breath, he pulled the door to Tim's office open and ushered Kate inside.

Within an hour Tim had them set up in an empty store-front on First Street, nestled between Ike's and Mary's Cafe. Tommy hooked Kate up with the print shop down the block to produce thousands of flyers with Tricia's information, then left to gather special communication equipment from his house and swing by the rec center to retrieve the folding chairs and tables they would need for the volunteers who would man the phones.

By the time Tommy returned two hours later, the crew from the phone company was already on-site installing several phone lines. No small feat considering it often took days, sometimes even a week to get a phone line installed around here.

But Kate's arrival had immediately raised the profile of the case, and the guys at the phone company knew they'd get nothing but bad press by dawdling.

Jackson Fuller showed up and helped Tommy unload the tables and chairs from his truck bed. "You should be home," Tommy said.

He responded with a curt shake of his head. "I can't just sit at home and do nothing but stare at the front door, hoping Tricia will walk through it."

Tommy balanced one side of the table and backed his way in the door while Jackson took the other. "What about Brooke? Shouldn't someone be home with her?" he asked.

Jackson grimaced and helped Tommy unfold the legs and set the table upright. "She won't come out of her room. Tracy says she hasn't touched her food. She blames herself."

"Do *you* blame her?" Though Kate's voice was pitched low, it cut like cold steel through the din of men working and metal chairs sliding around.

Tommy turned to face Kate, and he wondered if Jackson could sense the tension in every fiber of her body.

"No," he said tiredly as he ran a hand through his hair. It was already sticking up all over his head, as though he'd run his hands through it dozens of times already. "Of course, I wish she'd been more considerate of her sister and not told her to leave the party alone. It's not her job to protect her. It's mine, one I failed when I didn't stop her from sneaking out because I was too fucked up to hear her."

Kate crossed to him and put a consoling hand on his arm, her expression measurably more relaxed at Jackson's reply. "It's not your fault either," she said. "If someone is determined to take a child, they'll find a way. You can't let guilt drain you when you need all of your energy focused on finding her."

He didn't look convinced. He scanned the room, his gaze catching on the tables where the phone boys were busy connecting half a dozen or so phones.

His brow furrowed. "That's a lot of phones."

"I expect to field a hundred or so calls within the first hour after we announce the hotline number," Kate said briskly as she placed the metal folding chairs around the tables. "Especially once we announce a reward for information."

"Reward?" Jackson said.

Kate stopped her flurry of activity. "Did we not discuss the reward? I'm sorry, I thought we went over that—"

He shook his head. "It's highly possible we did. Everything's been a blur. How much do you think we'll need?"

Kate's gaze flicked uncomfortably to Tommy's. Finding nothing there to calm her, she swallowed hard and looked back at Jackson. "It fully depends on your resources. I'm not sure I'm comfortable giving you a price outright—"

"Give him a ballpark, Kate," Tommy snapped.

"If they're able, families usually offer at least twenty thousand."

Jackson swore. "Normally that wouldn't be an issue, but between Suzanne's treatments and start-up costs for the business, I've eaten through our cash buffer. The money is there, but it could take awhile to—"

"I'm happy to offer up whatever you need," a masculine voice boomed from the doorway. Though Tommy hadn't heard the voice in years, a reptilian part of his brain recognized it and was immediately repulsed. The muscles in his shoulders immediately bunched.

"John," he said before he'd even turned around.

"Tommy Ibarra," John said. "I'm surprised you recognized me, it's been so long since we've seen each other."

I never forget a douchebag. Like it or not, Burkhart's voice was forever etched in his memory banks.

Tommy remained silent as John offered his hand to Jackson, who, despite the animosity Tommy didn't bother to hide, shook his hand and introduced himself.

"And Kate," John said, a big grin spreading across his face as he opened his arms wide.

It took all of Tommy's restraint not to insert himself between them as Kate stepped readily into his embrace. A sour feeling twisted his gut as he compared her warm hug for John with his own reception.

It wasn't jealousy, he told himself harshly. Besides, what else did you expect from Kate? Under what circumstances would she possibly have been happy to see him, after what they'd been through?

And the feeling, he reminded himself, was absolutely mutual.

Still, as Burkhart released her, it was all Tommy could do not to plant his fist right in the middle of his smug face.

"I was at Tim Greaves's office going over some paperwork for a property rental and he mentioned he'd set you up here to coordinate the volunteer effort. I thought I'd come by and see what I can do to help."

"I was wondering if you'd be in town," Kate said, sounding way too delighted for Tommy's taste. "I didn't get a chance to email you before I flew out."

"And it's not as though you were coming out here to catch up with old friends," Tommy bit out, irrationally angered by the fact that Kate and Burkhart had apparently kept in touch all these years while he himself had been left to dangle, waiting for a response that never came.

"You said you wanted to help," Tommy said, angling his chin at him. "If you two are finished with your little reunion, Jackson here has a missing fourteen-year-old he'd like to find."

Kate's blue eyes narrowed into a glare. "I know exactly why I'm here."

"And I'm here because I want to help, and from what I heard when I was walking in here, the first way I can do that is by putting up cash for the reward," John said.

"That won't be necessary," Tommy started. While Jackson would have trouble getting access to a sizable sum of cash any time soon, Tommy had done well enough for himself that he could put up a decent chunk without it hurting too much. "I can—"

"How about a hundred thousand?" Burkhart offered as though Tommy hadn't spoken.

Kate's eyebrows arched up to her hairline. "A hundred?"

"Not enough?" he asked. "Make it two hundred thousand."

Tommy hid a wince. A hundred he could have managed. Two would involve more effort and time to liquidate than they had.

Jackson shook his head. "That's very generous, but I can't ask you to do that."

Burkhart held up a silencing hand. "You didn't ask, I'm offering."

Jackson scrutinized him with the same steely gaze that had made dozens of enemies of the United States squirm. For a moment the hard-as-nails operative Tommy had known broke through the mantle of the father overcome with grief and worry as he tried to discern the other man's motives.

Apparently Jackson decided they were sound because he nodded his head once and held his hand. "I'm in your debt and will do whatever I can to pay it back once my little girl is home safe."

Burkhart shook his head and schooled his face into a mask of humility that Tommy didn't buy for a second. "You don't need to pay me back. Cases like this, a young girl missing in our community…" He turned his gaze to Kate. "I remember what it was like when Kate's family lost Michael, how it tore their family apart. If I can do anything to keep another family from going through that…"

Tommy looked at Kate, felt a stab of disgust when he saw that Kate was eating up his line with the gusto of a large-mouth bass gulping a fat, juicy worm.

Then the disgust turned toward himself when he saw the tears in Kate's eyes, the way her expression seemed suddenly haunted. Help was help, and if Burkhart's money could help get Tricia back safely, Tommy would kiss the douchebag's ass himself.

"This is great news," Kate said, struggling to compose herself. "We'll announce it to the press as soon as the tip line is up and running."

The sound of a phone ringing pierced the air. Burkhart pulled his cell out of his pocket and offered a sheepish apology. "I have to take this," he said, already headed for the door. "I'll check back in later."

Kate called CJ to fill him in on the latest development and then sat down and pulled out her laptop to prepare her statement for the press.

Jackson stood in the middle of the room, looking a little dazed and at a loss for something to do.

"Why don't you go home and tell Brooke the good news in person," Tommy offered gently. "I'll call you when the flyers come in and we can start distributing them."

Tommy walked him out and retrieved a box of equipment and his laptop from his truck. He pulled six small black boxes from the box and tried to keep his gaze from snagging on Kate. But it was damn hard to keep from getting distracted by the way she sucked her full bottom lip between her teeth as she tried to concentrate. Almost impossible not to remember how the plump, pink curve had felt between his own teeth, how it had tasted when he traced it with his tongue.

"What are you doing?" she asked, frowning pointedly at the black box he was hooking up to the first phone.

"Tracing equipment," he said matter-of-factly.

"The police will put a trace here if they think it's necessary. Until then the phone company will track all the calls."

Tommy shook his head. "All they can tell us is the number the call came from. It can't give us the immediate, exact location of the caller. And I don't know if you've noticed, but the local law enforcement isn't exactly overstaffed. CJ does the best he can with what he's got, but they're not exactly brimming with technological expertise. By the time they decide you need a trace and get one installed, it could be too late."

Kate came over and bent her head to take a closer look. "I've never worked with one of these."

Tommy shook his brain out of the red fog that settled in

as her scent enveloped him. He craned to look up over his shoulder at her. "You've never worked with *me* before."

She turned to him, her face mere inches from his. So close he could see the thin line of pale lashes before her mascara took over, feel her warm breath feather over his lips. All she had to do was lean in just a little bit more and her mouth would be on his.

She froze in place. As though she didn't know if she wanted to close the distance between them or fling herself away.

Her eyelids flickered, and that was enough to break the spell. She surged to her feet, stumbling a little as she straightened. "You're right, I haven't, which is why I'd appreciate it if you consulted me before tampering with the phone lines."

"I'm installing state-of-the-art tracing equipment. I'd hardly call that tampering."

"What if it malfunctions, or interrupts the calls—"

"Kate," he snapped, "I'm a communications and security expert. One of the things I'm paid—and very well, I might add—to do is design and test equipment like this. Jackson isn't just my client, he's one of my oldest friends. Do you really think I would do anything that would interfere with getting Tricia back safely?"

"Of course not," Kate said, contrite, and turned back to her laptop screen.

CJ came by just as Tommy was wrapping up, trailed by a pack of reporters who had already sniffed out the location of the volunteer headquarters.

The minute Tommy declared the phone lines ready, Kate readied herself to talk to the press gathered on the sidewalk outside.

Tommy watched, inexplicably fascinated as she gave herself a quick primp. First she smoothed her hair back from her face. As he watched her slim fingers comb through the reddish blond waves, he could practically feel their silky weight against his own fingers.

And the way she smoothed lipstick over her surprisingly lush mouth made him want to pin her down and not stop kissing her until every bit of color disappeared.

The thought made his cock twitch behind the fly of his pants, and he winced at the sharp physical reaction. Christ. How hard up did a guy have to be to spring a woody from watching a woman put on lipstick?

As he dragged his gaze away, it snagged on CJ, who was staring at Kate with his own look of lust.

For the second time in as many hours, Tommy had to force himself not to punch a man.

The only one who deserves to be punched is you, dumbass, he scolded himself. CJ was his friend—no way would Tommy ever get in a sword fight with him over a woman, especially not Kate.

Kate and CJ stepped outside, leaving Tommy alone. With the phone equipment installed, there wasn't much else for him to do here.

A fact Kate made a point of noting as she and CJ stepped back inside after the press briefing. "Hopefully the phones will start ringing soon," she said. "Tommy set it up so all the calls can be traced—"

"Let me guess, you can triangulate on a caller's location with a margin of error of less than ten feet," CJ broke in.

"Yeah, if you're living in the dinosaur age," Tommy said. "Try less than ten inches."

CJ shook his head and muttered "Army prick," but his words held no real heat.

"Not my fault you Marines are inferior."

"I'm sure you have a lot of work to catch up on," Kate

said pointedly to Tommy. "Thanks for all of your help this morning, but I can handle things from here."

He had no doubt that was true. With her years of experience with St. Anthony's, he had no doubt Kate could coordinate a platoon of volunteers with her eyes closed. But her obvious discomfort in his presence, her clear desire to be rid of him, rankled him just enough to want to mess with her.

"Like I said before, finding Tricia is my number one priority. There's nothing else that requires my immediate attention."

Giving her a smile that didn't quite reach his eyes, Tommy pulled his laptop from its case and settled in one of the metal chairs to dig through Tricia's correspondence leading up to the night she disappeared.

"You find anything yet?" CJ asked, wandering over from Kate's side to look over Tommy's shoulder.

"Nothing beyond what I can only assume is the typical teenage girl back-and-forth.

"What are you looking at?" Kate's shoes tapped briskly along the hard linoleum floor as she too came to stand behind Tommy's chair.

"Tricia's email and online postings from Twitter and Facebook."

"Didn't you take custody of the laptop?" she asked CJ.

Tommy and CJ exchanged a look. "Jackson did give us the computer," CJ said. "We also decided that, in the interest of expediency, Tommy should have a copy of the hard drive."

"Remember what I said about cops being strapped for resources and not exactly on the cutting edge of technology—no offense," Tommy said to CJ.

"None taken. Wave your nerd flag high."

"It applies here too," Tommy said. "Bonner County doesn't

have its own cybercrimes division, so right now Tricia's computer is hanging out in Boise, waiting its turn to be analyzed unless it gets bumped up in priority. Which it might, what with you opening the floodgates on the press coverage."

"Even then," CJ pointed out, "we need to go through all the hoops with the service providers, get warrants to access the accounts. All of which will cause critical delays."

"Of course. I've worked with private investigators in other cases."

"Tommy's one of the best in the country. And the best thing," CJ continued, "is that Tommy's giving us his services for free. If you knew how much he could make—"

"It's the least I can do," Tommy cut him off. He didn't know why he was so uncomfortable bragging to Kate about his success, even if he wasn't doing the bragging. He didn't have anything to prove to Kate, her father or anyone, and unlike Burkhart, he didn't need to make a big public show of how well he was doing.

Kate's expression softened a bit, as though she picked up on his discomfort. "Having worked to raise money to pay people like you, I appreciate you donating your time. Plus, it's good to have someone familiar with the family and the situation on board, so thank you." This time Tommy could tell Kate wasn't just paying lip service. He didn't know if it was CJ's endorsement or if she'd just resigned herself that he would be working closely with her until they found Tricia.

All he knew was that tentative smile of hers gave him that same twisty feeling in his gut he'd gotten the first time he'd noticed it that summer fourteen years ago.

"No problem," he said gruffly, and focused his attention back on his computer.

An electronic trill rang through the air. CJ pulled his phone out of his pocket and scowled at the screen. "Time to pick up Travis. The sitter can't be at my place until four—I'll be back as soon as I can."

"Take your time," Kate called.

She made a *tsk*ing sound as the door closed behind him. "So sad about Kelly," she said. "She was so young. And his poor nephew."

A little over a year ago, CJ's older sister, Kelly, was killed in a hit and run by a drunk driver, leaving her eight-year-old son behind.

"CJ's taking good care of him," Tommy said.

"He had to give up so much," Kate said. "His career with the FBI, his life in Denver. One day you're a single guy, the next day you're a single father—"

The admiration in her voice raised his hackles. "If you're looking to take on the role of Mrs. Sheriff Kovac, get in line. Every single woman—and some married ones—under the age of fifty has her eye on CJ."

"So when you cast them off, you send them his way?" she said wryly.

"Oh, they don't sniff around me too much," he replied, unable to keep the sly grin off his face. "I'm too mean."

Kate settled back in her chair in front of her own laptop, but she couldn't keep her lips from quirking up at the corner. "Only because you want them to think so. I remember how sweet you can really be."

"Don't kid yourself that you know me anymore," he said, too harshly, but Kate's little smile and the misty look in her eyes summoned his own memories of that summer. Memories he'd shoved down deep and had no interest in dredging up. "Anything soft, or sweet, or nice about me disappeared when your father did his damnedest to ruin my life."

Her cheeks flooded with color and, just like that, the fragile connection was gone. *Good.*

Kate was a colleague, an ally in the quest to get Tricia home safe. Tommy couldn't afford to see her as anything more.

And if that were true, he'd get up right now, head back to his home office, and churn through the data on Tricia's hard drive in peace and quiet. Isolated from the distractions of the sound of her slim body shifting in her chair, the sound of her delicate fingers tapping on the keyboard, the way the fragrance of her shampoo drifted over on the breeze when she ran her fingers through the red-gold strands of her hair.

Instead he stayed exactly where he was, unable to make himself leave.

Chapter 4

Kate almost jumped out of her chair in delight when the door swung open about fifteen minutes after CJ left. She didn't care who it was. After sitting in uncomfortable silence with Tommy, she would welcome any distraction. She looked up to see a young man who could have been anywhere from his late teens to his early twenties. "Are you here to volunteer?" she asked after he stood silent for several seconds, looking uncertain.

"Uh, yeah, I guess so," he said. "My name's Ben, Ben Kortlang," he said as though she might recognize the name.

After a few seconds she did. From the police report CJ had forwarded to her. "You were with Brooke the night Tricia went missing."

"I feel awful," Ben said, the words pouring out of him now that Kate had acknowledged his involvement. "When Brooke told her to leave, I should have driven her home. But I was already buzzed," he admitted sheepishly. "And then Brooke and I—well, she...you know," he said, his cheeks reddening as he trailed off.

"We can fill in the blanks," Tommy said.

"And Brooke is so...Well, I really like her and...I kind of forgot all about Tricia until the next day when I heard she didn't make it home."

Kate could understand the distraction. Combine raging adolescent hormones and the fact that—from what Kate had seen in the pictures anyway—Brooke was a seventeen-year-old knockout, she could see how Ben would be quickly distracted.

And as she took in Ben's rangy form, sun-streaked brown hair, and green eyes, she could see how a girl like Brooke might find him equally distracting.

"And now Brooke won't talk to me. I've called her like twenty times and texted her a bunch of times, but she doesn't answer. It's so messed up. I feel bad and all—I know I should have walked Tricia home if I couldn't drive, but Brooke's treating me like somehow it's my fault."

Kate could feel Tommy's gaze burning a hole in the back of her neck. "I'm sure she doesn't blame you," she said, her throat tightening as she forced the reassuring words out of her mouth. "I haven't talked to her myself, but I imagine she's struggling with her own feelings of guilt right now, and it's probably really hard for her to face anyone or anything that has to do with that night."

Ben shoved his hands into the pockets of his cargo shorts and looked down at his brown-and-white skater sneakers. "Yeah, that's what Mr. Fuller said when he answered her phone."

"It was nice of Jackson to give you an update," Tommy said. "At least you know he doesn't blame you too. That's a heavy burden when you're already carrying plenty of your own guilt."

Ben looked curiously between the two of them, aware as Kate was that Tommy's words weren't meant expressly for him. "Right. Well, when I saw the news that you were looking for volunteers I figured I should come down, do whatever I can to help."

"Once the flyers get here, we'll need help distributing them around town—" Just then the door opened, and Kate saw a female figure balancing a large box. Backlit by the afternoon sunlight, the woman's features were obscured as she stepped over the threshold.

Kate felt her smile slip as she recognized the woman.

"Mom," Tommy said sharply. "What are you doing here?"

"I brought the flyers," she said, raising the box in front of her as though the answer was obvious. "I ran into Sherry on her way over here, and since I was heading here anyway, I told her I'd take them for her." She set the box down on a table and turned to Tommy. "Stop glowering at me and give me a hug."

Kate couldn't help smiling at the way Tommy rolled his eyes as he heaved himself to his feet and walked over to his mother. Despite his reluctance, there was no mistaking the genuine warmth as he embraced her. No matter what he said or how he felt about Kate, the warmth and sweetness were still in there somewhere.

Tommy's mother returned his firm squeeze and stepped back. Though she must have been in her late fifties, Sylvia Ibarra's shoulder-length hair was barely streaked with gray, and though the lines around her eyes and mouth had deepened, with her warm brown eyes and bright smile, she was still a lovely woman. Dressed in knee-length shorts, a short-sleeve striped T-shirt, and woven leather sandals, she was tall, fit, and ready to take on the world with the energy of a woman half her age. Kate couldn't help but compare her to her own mother, who, from the time of Michael's death, had seemed to shrivel more and more each year.

One day Kate expected to hear that her mother's assistant had gone to wake her and found a grasshopper in bed instead, like that obscure Greek myth.

"Hello, Ben," Sylvia said. "I won't ask you if you're having a good summer, given the circumstances," she said after the young man returned her greeting.

"No, ma'am," he replied solemnly.

Kate braced herself as Sylvia turned her attention on her.

But instead of the expected animosity, Kate read only friendliness, mixed with a bit of sadness in the older woman's eyes. "Kate," she said softly. "You're looking well. Of course, I know from TV you've only grown more beautiful, but really, the cameras don't do you justice."

Kate thanked her and rose to greet her properly. To Kate's surprise, rather than taking her proffered hand, Tommy's mother pulled her into a hug so warm it brought tears to her eyes, enveloping her in the scents of clean laundry and fresh-baked cookies. "I never did get to say goodbye to you properly after everything that happened," Sylvia said, when she finally broke the embrace.

Kate stepped back, sniffing back tears as discreetly as she could. "I would have expected you to greet me with a slap in the face."

Sylvia shook her head and made a disdainful sniffing sound. "What happened wasn't your doing," she said, arching a dark eyebrow at her son. Her dark gaze turned back to Kate. "Just as what happened to your brother wasn't yours, no matter what your father said."

Just like that, all the guilt and grief Kate worked so hard to keep at bay came surging to the forefront. If her emotions had a color, they would be bilious green, pumping through her bloodstream, gnawing at her guts, poisoning her with their toxins.

"I—" Kate struggled to draw breath, much less form a reply.

Sylvia patted her gently on the arm, "It's okay, dear, of course we don't have to talk about it. I just wanted to say my piece, clear the air first thing. Ah, there's my book club," she said, smiling and gesturing to whoever was outside. "I called everyone and told them to come as soon as I saw the press conference." Kate gathered her composure as Sylvia introduced the half a dozen middle-age women who had come down to volunteer.

She brought Sylvia and two of her friends up to speed on working the tip line, explaining what questions needed to be asked and how to log calls.

She dispatched the rest along with Ben to paper the town with flyers, then set to work setting up a bulletin board with a map of the area so they could pinpoint any sightings called in. As the afternoon progressed, a few dozen more volunteers arrived, and soon Kate had enough people signed up to cover the tip lines twenty-four hours a day for the next week.

Kate prayed that they would have answers by then. In her experience with missing person cases, after the initial burst of enthusiasm from the volunteers, interest in the case waned after a couple of weeks. Kate hardly faulted them. They had their own lives to lead and their own families to tend to.

Only the families of the victims, the ones dealing with the constant, agonizing pain of wondering where their child was and if he or she was safe, could muster the dogged determination to keep the mission going until they had answers. For better or worse.

Right now she had to channel all of the local enthusiasm into getting as much information as quickly as possible.

"What's out here?" Kate asked the owner of the hardware store, pointing at the map to one of the many roads leading away from the lake and up into the mountains.

"That's a forest road that connects with Route 2. A few people have seasonal cabins out that way, but it's pretty thinly populated."

"No stores, gas stations?"

A thickly muscled arm reached past hers. "There's the Gas and Go about ten miles in—right about here," Tommy said, tapping a spot on the map with the blunt tip of one long finger.

Since Kate had thrown herself in with the volunteers, she'd managed to keep her awareness of Tommy at a level where she could still function. Now just the sound of his voice was enough to send a curl of heat down her spine— forget the fact that he was standing close enough that she had only to lean back and she'd be nestled against the hard wall of his chest.

"Along with hitting everything along the major trucking and bus routes in a fifty-mile radius," she said, trying to move away from Tommy quickly without being conspicuous about it, "we also need to plaster all the smaller local places."

Tommy went back to his computer while Kate began assigning the different routes to the waiting volunteers. Satisfied that the phones were covered by the remaining people, Kate gathered up a stack of flyers and planned to go out herself. Not only were they short on drivers, Kate was still keenly, inappropriately aware of Tommy sitting across the room, her senses still addled from the experience of having him standing beside her, close enough she could feel the heat of his body radiating off him and pick up the scent of laundry soap mixed with the unique musk of his skin.

"Wait," Tommy said as she reached for her purse. "I think I found something."

Kate's protest died in her throat as she hurried to stand behind Tommy, whose heavy brow was knitted into a fierce look of concentration as he studied his computer screen.

She leaned in, squinting a little as she focused in on what she quickly realized was a chatroom dialogue.

"This wasn't just deleted, it was shredded," Tommy said.

That meant that Tricia hadn't wanted to risk the logs being found if someone wanted to restore her deleted files. It was something she meant to keep well hidden.

When can we actually meet IRL? the person with the handle RJRED asked.

My dad has us at this stupid place in Idaho, Tricia with the handle TRIFULL97 replied.

That sux.

Then the conversation abruptly ended when Tricia indicated that her "nosy bitch of a sister" was coming and she didn't want to get busted.

"Wonder what that's about," Kate said.

"Don't know," Tommy muttered. "But I think we need to get somewhere more private to discuss this." Kate looked up, and, sure enough, several volunteers were looking curiously at them.

"Right," she said tightly, mentally kicking herself for being so stupid, so careless.

"Christ, I'm an idiot," Tommy said, echoing her own thoughts. "I shouldn't even have this here. One person sees it, leaks it to the press."

Kate winced. She knew all too well the disasters that ensued when the wrong reporter got hold of the right information.

"We can go into the office," Kate said, using her thumb to indicate the small room in the back corner of the storefront.

Tommy shook his head. "Even with the door closed, it's too easy to listen in. We'll go to my place. Call CJ and tell him to meet us there," he said as he packed up his computer and started for the door.

"Why not go to CJ's office?" She was so not comfortable with the idea of going to Tommy's house.

Alone.

He answered with a curt shake of his head. "Sheriff's office or not, this is still a small town," he said, his voice pitched low so no one else could hear. "Everyone knows we're both involved in the search. If we show up and lock ourselves in his office, they'll know something's up and next thing you know the press will be talking. I don't want Jackson to see it and think I'm keeping anything from him, but there's no need to get him in the loop until we know what we're looking at. Or if there's anything I need to prepare him for."

Kate nodded grimly. Parents were often shocked at what their children's communications revealed; sometimes there were direct communications with their predators. She packed up her laptop and picked up a stack of flyers to distribute after she finished up at Tommy's house.

"Where do you live?" Kate asked when they were outside and Tommy was heading for his truck.

"Just follow me," he replied. He kept a reasonable speed that allowed her to easily keep pace as she followed him down First Street, down the lakeshore, and then right off a road that led up into the hills and onto the same road that led to his parents' ranch.

Did he still live with his parents? Kate felt a prickle of unease. Maybe he wasn't nearly as successful as he tried to portray himself to be. Maybe he was some hack who'd conned his way into working with CJ and managed to get a couple decent clients.

After all, when she'd Googled Tomas Ibarra or Ibarra Security Services earlier, she hadn't found any information about Tommy whatsoever.

Was she once again putting her trust into someone who didn't deserve it? Who was using her only to raise his own profile?

She'd barely completed the thought before she followed

Tommy's truck down a gravel driveway. About a hundred yards in was a massive wooden gate attached to a ten-foot-high wall that stretched out on either side of the driveway as far as the eye could see.

As Tommy stopped next to the console that would unlock the gate, Kate's phone buzzed.

"Make sure you get a little speed going through," Tommy said on the other end. "For security reasons I have the gate programmed to shut a lot faster than normal."

"Okay," Kate said, watching as Tommy's arm extended out of the truck. Instead of typing in a key code, it looked like he pressed his thumb to the console.

The gate swung open and Tommy took off, his truck tires spitting gravel as he shot through the gate. Kate followed suit, barely making it through before the gate slammed shut.

Any doubts she might have had about Tommy's success disappeared as she got her first look at his house. Though it had modern lines, the heavy wood beams and glass helped it blend almost seamlessly into the landscape. It wasn't a massive home by any means, but even from the outside Kate could see the attention to craftsmanship and the careful detail of the structure and the landscaping.

As she followed him up the walkway, she felt a burst of shame for doubting his motives. When had she ever known Tommy to ever be anything but honorable? Even at nineteen, with her practically begging him to take her virginity, he'd held her off, determined to do the right thing.

He might have good reason to resent her and her family, but that was no reason to suspect he'd lost his character. Too many years in Washington, she mused. Though she hadn't lived there in over a decade, growing up watching her father and his colleagues change positions and turn allies into enemies and back again had taken its toll.

Away from her family, she'd done her best to quell her instinct to question everyone and their motives. She'd mostly succeeded, only to learn that sometimes people's motives did merit questions.

Sometimes people who claimed to care about her really *were* just using her.

But not Tommy. It was clear when she walked through the heavy wooden front door that if Tommy's business had paid for this house, he didn't need any help from anyone to raise his profile.

The door opened into a great room with high, beamed ceiling and a multicolored slate floor. Huge windows opened up onto breathtaking views of the mountains, giving the house an open feel even as the wood frame and wide beams gave an impression of sturdiness and security.

"So, yeah, this is home," Tommy said, and she didn't miss the hint of pride in his voice.

"Tommy, this is gorgeous. How long have you lived here?"

There was no missing the satisfaction in his eyes at her compliment, and maybe a little relief? Had he been worried about what she'd think of his place?

The thought that Tommy might still care about what she thought gave her a little tingly sensation she had no business feeling.

"I bought the land seven years ago. The house was finished four years ago. It took me awhile to get the design worked out."

"You designed this yourself?" She didn't bother to keep the admiration out of her voice. "Now that I look, I can tell, this house is so very...you." There was no other way to describe it. The house was a reflection of Tommy himself, with its heavy, sometimes harsh lines and startling beauty.

And with all the wood and the slate and the leather furniture, it was undeniably masculine.

In fact, as she followed Tommy down a wide hallway, she noticed that there wasn't a trace of a feminine touch anywhere. There was no reason for her to care about that one way or the other, but she felt the tightness in her chest ease.

The hallway was flanked by two closed doors on the right and one to the left, and at the end the heavy carved door was ajar. Through it Kate got a partial view of a carved wood bookcase and massive platform bed with a simple white comforter spread over the top.

Unbidden, Kate got a flash of being in that massive bed, Tommy's huge, muscular form coming down over her—

"Here's the office," Tommy said, and opened the door to the left.

Once again Kate damned her fair complexion. She didn't need a mirror to know her cheeks were beet red, that they went even redder when she sheepishly met Tommy's gaze.

The look in his dark, deep-set eyes said he knew exactly what she'd been thinking when she looked at his bedroom. And the underlying heat there made her nipples pull tight against the silk cups of her bra.

For once in her life she was happy to be small chested, so there was no way for Tommy to see her body's almost desperate reaction to nothing more than a heated look.

"Let's get started then," she said, pushing past him into his office. The office was as magnificent as the rest of the house, with one wall made entirely of glass. A huge carved teak desk was at the opposite end, and she counted no less than five computer towers on top of the adjoining table.

Four separate flat-screen panels were mounted on the walls. Tommy crossed to the desk and picked up a remote that brought all four to life.

One screen was tuned to CNN, two displayed rows of indecipherable code, and the last flickered to life as soon as Tommy opened up his laptop and pushed a few buttons.

She looked up at the flat screen as Tricia's chat log appeared. She barely had time to read a sentence before one of the CNN talking heads distracted her.

"Many people have questioned the family's decision to involve Beckett after what happened in the Madeline Drexler case."

Kate's stomach dropped to the floor, her blood going icy as eleven-year-old Madeline's face with her gap-toothed grin appeared on the screen. Her throat closed as it did every time she saw the photo of the little girl with bright blue eyes and a tousled, light brown bob. Even in the picture you could see the spark in her eyes, hinting at mischief and laughter.

The screen cut back to the studio, and Kate felt her lip curl in distaste as she recognized Ramona Walker, a former prosecuting attorney who appeared frequently on the news as a legal analyst. In Walker's view, people like Kate and organizations like St. Anthony's were getting too involved in some of these cases and ended up hindering the investigations more than they helped.

As a result, she and Kate were often brought in on the same programs and pitted against each other.

Walker had dyed black hair styled into a helmet and thin lips painted a dark crimson. Those lips were currently pinched in disdain. "As your viewers are no doubt aware," she said in her slight British accent that she couldn't possibly have gotten growing up outside of Pittsburgh, "Kate Beckett leaked information the family gave to her to reporter Graham Hewitt, who she was involved with at the time. Now, you can blame the family for trusting someone who isn't law enforcement with information critical to the case, but how

Kate could choose to bolster her boyfriend's career over the safety of a child is unfathomable."

"I'm not sure that's exactly what happened," the anchor said as they flashed a picture of Kate and Graham, taken of them at a black-tie fundraiser for the foundation last fall. Seeing herself smiling, so happy, so clueless about the snake she'd chosen to lie down with brought a surge of nausea so fierce for a second Kate was afraid she was going to hurl all over Tommy's handwoven Mexican rug. "Beckett claimed she didn't purposely leak anything—"

The screen went suddenly dark. "Sorry," Tommy muttered. "You don't need to see that."

Kate shook her head and walked over to the bank of windows. She stared out at the mountains, but in her head all she could see was Madeline. And not the Madeline in the photo who was smiling so wide you could see most of her tiny white baby teeth but the girl they'd found three days after Graham had delivered his exclusive update on the case, tipping off the suspect before the police were able to arrest him.

"It doesn't matter. I've already heard it, and worse. It's nothing I don't deserve."

Tommy's grave expression wavered, and she saw a flicker of compassion there. "We all make mistakes, Kate. But it wasn't your fault Madeline died. She died because some sick fuck who gets off on hurting kids stole her from her family."

"Tell that to her dad, who for the first time in a week had hope that the police were going to find his little girl alive. Maybe they're right. Maybe Jackson is an idiot for asking for my help."

"You've helped a lot of kids, Kate," he countered.

"Not enough," she protested. "Nothing will ever be enough to make up for my mistakes."

He moved to stand beside her, his arms folded across his chest. "We could have both made better choices the night Michael died," Tommy said, not bothering to pretend he didn't know what she was really talking about. "But that doesn't mean it's your fault he died. You didn't put the gun in Emerson Flannery's hand."

"But I wasn't there to stop him either," she said in a voice thick with tears.

"You might have been hurt too."

"You don't know how many times I wish it had been me instead," she murmured, and her father had too.

Beside her, she could sense Tommy's muscles coil tight. "I sure as hell never did."

Kate risked a glance at him the moment he turned to her. His eyes were dark with sadness, and something else. Something warm and deep, making her feel safe and breathlessly excited all at once.

She got a strange, twisty, falling-off-a cliff sensation. It was as if she'd fallen through a time warp and the last fourteen years had disappeared. She was once again a sixteen-year-old girl/woman in the heated throes of first love...and first lust.

That time of hope and joy and the kind of wild happiness that came only from having a guy like Tommy Ibarra seek her out, pursue her, tell her she was beautiful as he drove her out of her mind with his lips and hands.

She wanted to feel that again, remember that time when she knew what it was to be happy. Remember what it was like before...

There was a sharp, shrill buzz, and then CJ's voice boomed through an unseen speaker. "Ibarra, you going to grant me entrance to the fortress?"

Kate jolted back to reality and retreated to the opposite

corner of the room. Tommy stalked to the door and pressed a button on a small box mounted to the wall of the office that Kate hadn't noticed before.

While she could feel her face turning beet red again, Tommy seemed to be oblivious to the little moment she was having. And thank God for that.

Her entire body felt flushed, hyperaware. If she was honest with herself, she had to admit that if Tommy made a serious attempt to seduce her, she wasn't sure she'd be able to resist.

And that could only lead to disaster. While Tommy was a living reminder of one of the happiest times in her life, he was also a living reminder of how a seemingly small lapse in her judgment could have tragic consequences.

Kate had been stupid for a guy exactly twice in her life, and both times with horrific results. She needed to remember that even as her body tempted her to go in for round two with Tommy Ibarra.

Chapter 5

Tommy strode down the hall, grateful for the chance to get away from Kate and get his shit together. He was on the verge of losing control.

Which was pretty fucking ridiculous, considering his time in the Army had taken him to some of the worst hell-holes on earth that required him to sit stock still, hours on end, no matter that a bullet might scream by your head or the mosquitoes might chew you to hamburger. But Kate, with her big sad eyes and soft, trembling mouth, had him straining against the urge to pull her into his arms, kiss her mouth until the sadness was gone and all that remained was pure heat.

He flung open the door for CJ, who gave him a wary look. "Did you hear something?"

Tommy shook his head, confused. "No, why?"

"You look like someone just fed you a shit sandwich. I was afraid somewhere between the car and your door someone found a body."

Tommy ran his palm down his face to smooth out the scowl he hadn't even realized was there. "We're still going through Tricia's chat logs," he said, and started back down the hall to his office. CJ's heavy work boots *thunk*ed on the slate floors as he followed. When he entered Tommy's office, he let out a low whistle. "Shit, this really is like command center at the Bat Cave," he said as he took in the multiple computers and monitors.

He and Kate exchanged quick greetings while Tommy worked his way back through the chat log archives.

"What is this site, anyway?" CJ said as he read an exchange Tricia had with another person three months ago. "*'My dad is so messed up. Sometimes I wish he was the one who died. Not because I don't love him but because I think Mom could have handled it better,'* " he read, frowning.

"It's a chat room for kids whose parents have died," Kate said, her voice tight. "Tricia started going on there about seven months ago, a couple of months after her mother died." She looked to Tommy for confirmation.

They were quiet for the next several minutes as they read through Tricia's cyberconversations. After her initial posts, she interacted primarily with two different users.

Mari1999's profile said she was a fifteen-year-old from Nashville whose father had died last year. Coldust20 was a seventeen-year-old boy from Miami whose mother had committed suicide eighteen months ago.

To Tommy, the conversations, while sometimes heartbreaking, looked harmless. "I'll get their IP addresses to make sure they check out," he said, "but none of this strikes me as a predator posing as a lure."

Kate nodded. "Usually in cases of online stalking, the sexual innuendo escalates pretty rapidly. And usually you'll see requests to meet in real life happen quickly if that's the predator's end game."

"Isn't that always the end game?" CJ asked.

"No," Kate said. Though her voice was soft, there was no disguising the note of disgust. "Some sick freaks get a thrill from the interaction, imagining the underage girl or boy on the other side of the conversation while they describe deviant sexual acts or send them explicit pictures and videos."

Revulsion tightened Tommy's stomach. "Jesus, I've seen some bad places and bad people, but I can't imagine how sick you have to be to get off on something like that."

"There are people so sick you almost believe they're another species, not even human," Kate said, her eyes flashing with emotions. And she was determined to hunt down every single one. Tommy could see it in her face, in the way her soft mouth pulled into a tight line, in the set of her shoulders. In the way she seemed to cast off the horrible images that were no doubt flooding her mind and focused on the task at hand, motioning him to continue scrolling through the logs.

Tommy felt an unwelcome tug of admiration in his gut. Sure, he'd admired the way she'd given herself to a cause she was passionate about. But his opinion had always been colored by their past, by the way she'd turned her back on him to save her family from a scandal.

Wealthy, snobbish, image conscious. Though he couldn't deny that Kate had helped a lot of children and a lot of families, a small, petty voice had always whispered that she'd become the spokesperson for St. Anthony's for her own selfish reasons. To keep up a positive image of herself as a do-gooder and boost her family's profile by association.

To help wash away the stain of the guilt she no doubt felt about the night Michael was murdered.

Even if all that did play into her motivation, he couldn't deny that Kate was far more than just a talking head, the pretty mouthpiece they trotted out onto the TV shows to help boost press coverage for a case. If Tricia's case was anything to go by, she dug into every single case with dedication and tenacity.

And she didn't shy away from the gory realities of what the victims were subjected to.

Kate was tough. It wasn't a word he ever would have imagined using to describe her. Certainly not the beautiful but reserved teenager he'd been so determined to coax out of her shell.

And not the girl he'd seen after Michael died, broken down, teetering on the brink of destruction from her brother's death and her family's accusations.

Kate hadn't just grown up, she'd grown strong. She would have had to, dealing day in, day out with the victims, sharing the soul-numbing grief of the families.

And, he thought, recalling the earlier news report, dealing with the guilt when things went horribly wrong.

Great. Now on top of everything else, you're starting to admire her. As if it wasn't enough that the inexplicable chemical reaction his body had to her was as intense now as it had been at nineteen.

"Tommy?" Her voice snapped him out of his daze. His eyes locked on hers, and he realized he'd been staring at her for who knew how many seconds, leaving Tricia's conversation with Mari1999 up for far longer that it would have taken her and CJ to read it.

Tommy quickly paged to the next screen. He cleared his throat, hoping his olive complexion hid the fact that he was blushing like a goddamn schoolgirl.

Nearly an hour later, CJ started pacing around the room. "If someone was cyberstalking her, it sure as shit wasn't through this forum," he said. "I say we move on. Read back through her emails, go back over her Facebook—"

"Wait," Kate said, and Tommy's finger stilled over the mouse.

The room was silent as they read through a three-page-long

conversation between Tricia and a user they didn't recognize. It was from five days ago.

"That's a new friend," Tommy said.

"Scroll back, see when the first contact was made."

"A week ago." Moto98 had joined the bulletin board that day and immediately tried to start off a conversation with Tricia and her friends.

"The day after Jackson and the girls got here," Tommy said. The conversation was innocent enough, as Moto98 introduced himself as a fifteen-year-old from Boulder whose father had recently died of leukemia. There was nothing in the conversation to make Tommy suspect he wasn't who he claimed to be, but he couldn't deny that tingling feeling between his shoulders, that strange gut instinct that told him something just wasn't right.

He continued to read as the new member tried to engage Tricia. Not that she had taken to the new friendship immediately. After a few polite exchanges, Tricia continued her lengthy exchanges with her regular crew, with Moto98 interjecting occasionally, only to be ignored. At one point, Tricia and Coldust20 pointedly excused themselves to go chat privately.

The new guy didn't push it but continued to follow Tricia's conversations and comment over the next couple of days. Then, five days ago, Moto98 made a comment about how his older brother was being a total dick, partying all the time and not even seeming to care that their mother had just died.

At that, Tricia unleashed the floodgates, telling him how awful her sister had been to her, especially in the last week since their father made them go to some dumb lake house in Idaho so they could bond.

My dad is so clueless. Like forcing us to leave our friends is going to make us actually like each other.

The conversation ended abruptly, as Tricia wrote *Speaking of, I gotta bail because bitchface just got home from the lake. Can't let her catch me on here—not after I left my computer logged in here and she put a bunch of stuff on Facebook.*

"That's cold." Tommy winced.

"Sounds like typical big-sister behavior," CJ said with a shrug. "Kelly used to torture the hell out of me," he said with a wistful half smile.

"I remember the time she pantsed you in the middle of Derek Swanson's birthday party," Tommy replied, and felt a pang of sadness for the beautiful, wild young woman who loudly claimed that getting knocked up was the best thing that ever happened to her.

"Lucky for you she didn't have Facebook or Twitter to share the pictures with the entire planet," Kate said as she continued to read down. "'*She still snoops, but I know better than to leave anything for her to find,*'" Kate read aloud.

"That explains the shredder program for deleted files," Tommy said.

The last conversation with Moto98 was on Thursday evening, the night she disappeared.

I hate being here, Tricia complained. *And get this. I met a guy at the beach yesterday—his name is Ben and he is OMG so hot. Like that guy from Vampire Diaries but with blue eyes. And he was totally flirting with me! And then you-know-who comes along with her boobs practically falling out of her bathing suit—she was wearing the one I told you about, the one where the bottom practically goes up her ass crack, the one Mom never would have let her buy, much less actually wear. So anyway, yeah, she shows up, flipping her hair like she's having a seizure, and next thing I know Ben's practically got drool running down his chin.*

He's going to be here in like five minutes to take her to one of those dumb bonfire parties they have all the time. And I'm going to spend the night here on the computer all night like a loser.

Who are you calling a loser? ;-)

Sorry. You know what I mean. At home I have friends, stuff to do. Before, I didn't want to go out and do anything, but now I want to be with people.

So go out.

Right, I'm going to just go wander the streets and try to find a friend.

No, dummy, go to the party.

I can't go. My sister will kill me.

Who gives a shit if your sister gets mad? Wait, I've got it. You wait till she leaves, and then you put on the sluttiest thing you can find and you go to that bonfire and give that man-stealing bitch a run for her money. :) :):) :)

OMG, I totally should!

"And that's exactly what she did," Kate said softly.

Tommy felt like a boulder had settled in his stomach.

"You think he targeted her?" CJ asked.

"We won't know until I go back through the chat logs and get a lock on Moto98's location when the conversations took place. But this is all looking a little too coincidental to me," Tommy replied.

"Check to see if he's been on the board since that night," Kate said, her voice tight.

A few quick keystrokes was all it took to verify that he hadn't. Tommy's mouth pulled tighter. "It's going to take me awhile to get into the accounts and figure out where that user was when these conversations took place."

"How long?" Kate pushed.

"Depends. If we're really dealing with a calculated predator who knows anything about covering his tracks, could be several hours at least."

Kate rubbed a weary hand over her face. "I don't know if I can last that long." The words had barely left her mouth before her stomach let out soft roar.

"You eat anything today?" CJ asked.

Kate's brow furrowed and she looked up at the ceiling as she went back through the day.

"I think I had a piece of toast before I went to the airport this morning," Kate said after several seconds.

"I need to talk to Jackson about this," CJ said. "Why don't you come with me and afterward we'll grab a bite."

Kate nodded and rose from her chair.

"I should go with you," Tommy said, rising too. "Jackson will want to know all the details—"

"And as the lead investigator on this case, I think I'm capable of giving him the information," CJ said. Though they'd known each other most of their lives and had always been friendly, there was no missing the challenge in the sheriff's voice.

Tommy struggled to keep the bite out of his reply. "He might ask some technical questions that may be beyond the skill set of a county sheriff."

"I might have only spent two years there, but I think the FBI gave me a better foundation than most guys in my position. I appreciate your help with this, Tommy, I really do, but I can't have you inserting yourself into every aspect of this case." So back the fuck off. No misreading the subtext there.

Even as he told himself it wasn't worth it to get into a pissing match, Tommy felt his chest spread, his stance widening as he squared up against CJ.

"Neither CJ nor I have the ability to get into the user information," Kate said, flicking her glance nervously between the men, tuned into the tension fogging the room.

"So it makes more sense for you to keep digging while we talk to Jackson, right?"

"Right," Tommy said. Of course she was right. But that still didn't take the sting out of watching her head for the door, CJ at her side.

And it damn sure didn't keep his hands from clenching into fists at the way CJ guided her to the front door with a proprietary hand on her back and the way Kate seemed to have no problem with it.

Kate paused before she stepped out the door, looking over her shoulder as she asked, "You'll let us know as soon as you find out anything?"

"Of course," Tommy replied. He should have been proud of himself for keeping his voice neutral, his expression impassive.

Instead, as he watched CJ walk her to her car, say something that made her smile as he opened her door and got her settled inside, he was disgusted with himself and the wave of resentment he couldn't keep at bay.

—⁓—

"What was up with that?" Kate asked after Tommy shut his heavy wooden door behind them with enough force for her to feel the vibration in the poured-concrete steps.

CJ shook his head with a grimace and guided her down the walkway, his hand resting companionably on her shoulder. "Tommy's a great guy, and I really do need his help, especially with this computer shit. But he needs to back off."

"From what I remember Tommy's pretty forceful," Kate said, flashing back to the way he'd pursued her years ago. "A lot about him seems to have changed since I saw him last, but not that."

"No, he's still about as subtle as a battering ram." CJ grinned.

Kate couldn't help but return the grin as she climbed into her rental. As she followed CJ out of the gate, she couldn't help thinking there was something more than standard male posturing going on. Though Tommy had become a master at keeping his thoughts from showing on his face, Kate could feel a subtle shift in the room when she and CJ started to leave.

Together.

It wasn't anything major, a sharpening of his features, of the energy coming from his big, broad body. An electric crackle that something was going on that he didn't like.

Almost like he was jealous.

Jesus, Kate, get over yourself, she thought, and tried to convince herself the idea didn't thrill her a little.

Maybe you had a little moment back there, but that doesn't mean Tommy gives two shits if you go off with CJ or anyone else.

Not to mention, you have far more important things to worry about. Tommy was probably just concerned for his friend and client. No doubt he felt responsible, not just because of their relationship, but because they'd come to visit at Tommy's suggestion. Kate understood all too well how that overdeveloped sense of responsibility could make you want to be involved at every level, take in every detail as it unfolded, whether that was the most useful way to spend your time or not.

Whatever frustration he felt, she was flattering herself if she thought it had anything to do with any lingering spark on his part.

Twenty minutes later, Kate parked her car behind CJ's cruiser in Jackson Fuller's driveway. Tracy answered the door. "I'd ask if there was any news, but I'm sure Jackson would be the first to hear if there were."

CJ nodded. "Nothing substantial, but we wanted to give Jackson a quick update on the search efforts." Tricia's online activity needed to be kept out of the press for now.

Tracy motioned them toward the office. "I'm heading out now, but there's lasagna in the oven and a salad to go with it. If you could convince Jackson and Brooke to eat some of it, you'd be doing them a great service."

Kate followed CJ down the hall, and as she passed the kitchen the mouthwatering aroma of the lasagna made her stomach lurch with hunger.

"Maybe we should have stopped for a sandwich on the way," CJ said with a smile as he raised his hand to knock on the closed door.

He opened the door when summoned. Jackson stood in the middle of the room, in front of the window facing the lake. The late-afternoon light shadowed his blunt features, making him look more haggard than he had just a few hours ago.

They sat down and CJ quickly explained what they'd discovered in Tricia's deleted files.

Jackson buried his face in his hands. "Jesus, Tommy offered to put spyware on the girls' computers and phones ages ago. My wife was against it—she didn't think it was right to invade their privacy. And now this sicko was tracking her—"

"We don't know that for sure," CJ broke in. "The conversations themselves aren't suspicious, but we'll know more once Tommy is able to ID the computer address and the network."

Jackson's mouth tightened into a grim line. "So it's either a break in the case or nothing," he said, frustration making his voice tight. "Goddamn it, when are you going to come to me with something real?" His fist crashed down on a side table, sending the chess board that had been set up there crashing to the floor.

"I know it's frustrating," Kate said. "And I wish we could give you more answers, but we thought it was important to let you know what we've found out so far."

"Right," Jackson said tightly. "It's just driving me crazy, not knowing. After I left you I drove clear to Coeur D'Alene and stopped at every store and gas station in between to put up flyers and see if anyone had any information. But it's like we're just spinning our wheels and she's still out there—"

His voice broke and he squeezed his eyes shut against the tears. Kate felt her own eyes burn in sympathy as she crossed to him and placed her hand on his arm. Under his skin, she could feel the muscles vibrating with effort to hold his emotions in check. She wanted to tell him to let go, that it was okay to break down.

But she sensed that like the man Tommy had become, Jackson Fuller wasn't one to give free rein to his emotions, especially not in front of an audience.

"Tracy left dinner for you. Why don't you go get Brooke and see if she'll come sit with us. I think we could all use a bite to eat."

Jackson shook his head. "I'm not hungry."

"That doesn't matter," Kate said, taking his arm in her hand and tugging him firmly to the door. "Right now you're going on nothing but adrenaline and anxiety, and that will only get you so far. You need to keep your strength up. Not just for Tricia—you have another daughter too," she reminded him a little too forcefully.

Jackson gave a heavy sigh but allowed Kate to shoo him out of the office. He paused on the way to the kitchen at the foot of the stairs and called up. "Brooke, come down and have some supper."

Silence.

As he trudged heavily up the stairs, Kate and CJ went to the kitchen and busied themselves getting dinner out and setting the table. From upstairs, she could hear the rap of Jackson's fist on the door and the low murmur of voices.

She wasn't entirely surprised when Jackson returned alone. "She won't come down."

They ate in silence, and after Kate was satisfied Jackson had eaten enough to keep him going, she and CJ cleared the table.

"When did Tommy say he'd have news?" Jackson asked as he walked them to the door.

"He said it could take several hours," CJ said. "You should try to get some rest. We'll call you as soon as we know anything more."

"Rest?" Jackson said with a snort of disgust. His shoulders straightened, and for a moment Kate got a glimpse of the harassed military man he once had been. "Think you'd be able to rest if your fourteen-year-old daughter disappeared and you had no idea where she was?"

Two slashes of red appeared on CJ's cheekbones, and he unconsciously straightened to attention. "I'm sure I wouldn't, sir. I apologize for suggesting it."

"We'll speak soon," Kate said, and impulsively reached up to give Jackson a hug. He jerked a little in surprise at first, then returned the embrace, his arms almost desperately tight around her as though trying to absorb whatever comfort he could get. By the time he let her go, Kate's eyes were wet again, thinking about the long, sleepless night he would spend.

She and CJ bypassed the press with curt "no comments." But when Kate got to her car, she realized she'd left her purse in the kitchen. She waved CJ off and hurried back up the walkway.

She knocked lightly and tried the knob. It was unlocked so she let herself in. There was no sign of Jackson, who must have retreated to the office once again.

As she went to the kitchen, she saw a girl sitting at the kitchen table, staring sightlessly out the window, a plate of salad sitting untouched in front of her. Dark, straight hair hung to the middle of her back, and her slim, tanned arms were shown off by a bright green tank top. Kate immediately recognized Brooke from the pictures that had been flashed around the news.

Kate said her name and got no response. As she walked closer to the table, she saw the telltale white cords coming out from under her ears and realized she was wearing earbuds.

Kate waved, trying to catch her attention.

Brooke let out a little shriek and jumped about a foot, knocking over her chair in the process. "What are you doing here?" she said as she fumbled with her iPod. She stood with her arms folded around her stomach, as if she was trying to keep herself from flying apart.

"I'm Kate Beckett," Kate said, and held out her hand. Brooke accepted, and though her hand was small and chilled, her grip was surprisingly firm.

"I know," Brooke said simply. "I've seen you on the news."

Kate nodded.

"I was obsessed with the Madeline Drexler case," she said. "You were all over that."

Kate's shoulders tightened. "Yes, I got very involved with the case and Madeline's family."

Brooke cocked her eyebrow and studied her in the way only a teenage girl could, with the kind of utter disdain that came from the false confidence that you knew everything.

"A lot of people think it's your fault she was killed," she said.

No matter how many times Kate heard it, it never failed to stab her straight through the chest. "I made a mistake and trusted the wrong person. But I never purposely did anything to hurt Madeline. I did everything I could to get her back safe. That doesn't mean I don't feel guilty though."

Brooke blinked and, when she opened her eyes, the teenage arrogance was gone, giving way to an expression that could only be described as tortured. "I didn't think it was your fault—what happened to Madeline. It's nobody's fault but that sick pig who took her. He's the one who took her. He's the one who killed her, right? Not you? Right?"

Brooke's voice raised in pitch with every syllable, and Kate could tell by the desperate look on her face she needed something, anything, to help convince her that it wasn't her fault that her sister was kidnapped, hurt, possibly even dead.

Despite Tricia's description of Brooke's mean-girl antics, Kate's heart ached like a big bruise in her chest. She knew exactly how Brooke felt, knew that no matter whether deserved or not, she would always blame herself, always have the guilt eating away at her like acid. And she knew that even if she didn't believe it, she needed someone to tell her it wasn't her fault, she wasn't a horrible person who allowed her sister to be hurt.

"Of course he was ultimately to blame. Just as whoever took Tricia is to blame for whatever happens to her."

Brooke nodded, but the look in her eyes told her she didn't believe Kate for a second. "Have you found anything else about where she could be?" the girl asked.

Kate debated the wisdom of revealing their latest findings to Brooke and decided to go for it. "We found chat logs from a bulletin board for kids who have lost their parents."

Even guilt and grief stricken, Brooke couldn't restrain from rolling her eyes. "I told Tricia she should get some real friends instead of hanging out online with a bunch of whiny losers."

"Did she ever talk about any of the people she chatted online with?"

Brooke shook her head. "No, especially not after I—" She clamped her mouth shut.

"After you hacked into her account and put her conversations up on Facebook?"

The girl's face blushed beet red. "You probably think I'm a total bitch, just like my dad does—"

"I'm sure your father doesn't think that."

"He does! Before this all happened, before we even came here, he told me how disappointed he was in me and how disappointed Mom would be if she saw how mean I was being to Tricia."

She squeezed her eyes shut, but that couldn't stop the tears pouring down her face. Kate didn't speak, sensing a dam had just been breached, unleashing everything Brooke had been holding inside.

She didn't hear the sound of heavy footsteps on the floor until they were right next to her. She looked up, startled, to see Jackson standing there, looking confused at the sight of his daughter sobbing on the shoulder of a virtual stranger.

"What's wrong? Did something happen?"

Kate shook her head. "I was just asking Brooke about some things—"

"What did you do to upset her?" he demanded. "Don't we have enough to deal with without you sending my daughter into hysterics?"

"I didn't—" Kate started to defend herself.

"She didn't do anything," Brooke said. Before anyone could stop her, she turned and ran from the room.

Jackson stared after her for a moment, then shook his head. "Will you excuse me?"

"Of course," she said, while inside she was screaming at him to go to her, to comfort her. As she heard his footsteps retreating down the hall, she couldn't help thinking of the night Michael died. How she had retreated to the corner, alone, dying for any bit of comfort.

She went back to the volunteer headquarters to check in, compulsively checking her phone to see if there was any word from Tommy.

Finally, exhausted and gritty eyed, she drove to the townhouse she'd rented in a complex near the lake and made a beeline for the master bedroom. Though her body ached with tiredness, she couldn't still her brain, the thought and worries fluttering around like a swarm of moths.

They were going to get Tricia back. They had to.

Chapter 6

She lay still across the bed, one fragile wrist thrown across her forehead. Her breath was heavy with sleep, and he watched, mesmerized by the gentle rise and fall. In the dim light cast by the candle he'd lit, he could see that her cheeks were flushed and covered in a light sheen of sweat. Even with the fan going the little room was stifling. He felt his own skin get sticky under the layers of his shirt and hooded sweatshirt.

He grimaced, hating the thought of her suffering any discomfort. But there was no help for it. For now, she would have to suffer the overbearing heat, just as others had had to suffer the elements, whether it was freezing cold or bone-chilling damp.

She shifted in her sleep, and a metal *clang* drew his attention to her slim right wrist. Tucked halfway under the pillow so you couldn't see the cuff around it, or the chain that attached it to another cuff that was locked around the bars of the headboard.

Looking at her like this, he could almost believe she was here because she wanted to be, a willing lover sleeping in their bed, dreaming of the moment he would join her.

Soon. Soon she would smile and open her arms in welcome instead of cowering back in fear or lashing out in anger.

She was the one. He knew it, in the very depths of his soul. He'd known it from the first moment he'd seen her, standing in front of Ike's, her big blue eyes taking everything in, her small pink tongue licking at her soft-serve ice cream cone with the kind of innocent sensuality that only the truly pure possessed.

She was so beautiful, he marveled, the most beautiful one yet. With her long, wheat-colored curls that spilled across the pillow, her blue eyes now hidden under lids so heavily lashed they cast shadows on the curve of her cheekbones. Her features were delicately sculpted but still had a hint of girlish roundness. Her soft, parted lips were still a childish deep pink, not yet needing any color to enhance them.

And her body . . . just blossoming from a girl to a woman. Her breasts were small mounds pushing against the soft cotton of the T-shirt he'd dressed her in. Her legs and arms had that long, coltish look that never failed to drive him crazy.

So long and tan and lean, inspiring a thousand fantasies of what it would feel like to have them wrap around him as he kissed that pink mouth, drove himself into the depths of a body untouched by any man but him.

He felt a heat and heaviness between his legs, his blood running thick and hot at the images that filled his mind. He shoved them angrily aside. He was not going to sully her with such thoughts. She was pure and fresh and beautiful and deserved to be treated like a queen. He wouldn't allow himself to dishonor her with his filthy lust, not until she came to him willingly, in love, accepting him as her husband before she accepted him as her lover.

He willed his body back into submission and took a seat in the chair he'd set next to the bed, taking care to pull the hood of his sweatshirt closer to his face. He reached out and brushed her hair back from her cheek, closing his eyes as he breathed in the sweet scent of her hair and skin.

Even the close, musty air couldn't disguise her fresh, floral scent. Her hair was like silk between his fingers, her skin satin smooth.

Every inch of her absolutely perfect.

"Wake up, my love," he whispered. She shifted against the covers and turned her face away, her brow furrowing as she tried to hold onto sleep.

He gave her shoulder a little shake. She made a snuffling sound but didn't open her eyes.

"Come on, Tricia love," he said with another gentle shake. She shouldn't be completely out—the dose he'd given her earlier was small enough that he should be able to rouse her.

Slowly, as though weighted, her eyelids lifted, revealing beautiful eyes still blurry with sleep and the drugs he'd had to give her to keep her quiet while he was out. Her eyes scanned the room, and he saw the moment she realized this wasn't a dream. She was awake, and this was her reality now.

"What's going on?" she asked. She tried to jerk away from his touch, but her moves were clumsy and she was stopped short when she reached the end of her chain. "Why are you doing this?" she cried, her voice high and hysterical as she jerked at her chain over and over.

Thin streams of crimson leaked from her cuffed wrist, and his stomach clenched at the sight. He grabbed her arm and yanked her close. "You have to stop it! You're only hurting yourself!" he said tightly. "And you'll understand why I'm doing this soon enough. Just be a good girl, a sweet girl, and I'll give you everything you ever wanted." He stroked her cheek, trying not to let the way she cringed away bother him, reminded himself they always did at first. Some of them never stopped.

But Tricia, sweet Tricia, she would eventually love him back, given enough time. "I just want to go home," she said with a soft sob.

His fingers curled into a fist and he pulled his hand away, tamping down his disappointment as he retrieved the bags he'd brought with him. "I brought you some food," he said as he arranged the cartons on the small table in the center of the room.

"I'm not hungry," she said sullenly, her voice muffled by the pillow she'd buried her face in.

"It's the chicken panini from Mary's," he said softly. "I know it's your favorite."

"How do you know that?" she said, her eyes wide and wary as she rolled over to look at him.

He smiled patiently. "I know everything about you, remember?"

She swallowed hard, and the sight of her throat bobbing up and down under the delicate skin made him want to taste it with his tongue. "How?"

"Does it matter?" he asked as he placed half of her sandwich on a plate, along with some potato chips. He sat on the edge of the bed and offered her the plate, carefully keeping his face turned from the light. She scooted as far away from him as she could go.

The fury he held so carefully in check tried to rear its ugly head. He fought it back, reminding himself he couldn't take it personally. Of course she was wary. This was all new to her. Unlike him, she didn't see, she didn't know yet how gloriously happy they were going to be. She needed time to get used to the idea, get used to him.

Once that happened, she would gladly accept him into her heart, into her body.

And if she didn't... He shoved away the images of the others who had come before. The defiant ones. The lying, cheating bitches who only pretended to love him.

They were nothing, insignificant, he told himself. Bugs

he'd crushed once he'd realized his mistakes. And he was disrespecting Tricia by letting them even slip into his thoughts while he was with her.

"Here." He picked up the sandwich and waved it under her nose. "You've only had a little juice since I brought you here. I know you must be hungry."

As if on cue, her stomach let out a low growl. Her cheeks pinkened and her eyes dropped. He put the sandwich right to her lips. Her lips parted and her small white teeth closed over one corner as she reluctantly took a bite.

Watching her chew and swallow, he felt a surge of pride to see her eat the food that he'd provided. Call him old-fashioned, but this was what he truly felt he was made for. Caring for, providing for the woman he loved.

After a few bites she took the sandwich from him to feed herself. "Barbecue is my favorite flavor too," he said as she ate her chips. "See how much we have in common?"

Her gaze flicked warily to him but she didn't say anything as she pushed the last bite of her sandwich into her mouth.

"Soon you'll see," he said, unable to resist reaching out and running his hand up her bare, smooth thigh. "We are going to be so happy together."

She froze midchew. Then, with a look of disgust that cut him to his very core, she reared her head back and spit a half-chewed mess of chicken and bread at him and flung herself across the bed, crying out as the chain stopped her momentum and dug the cuff deeply into her wrist.

"You're a fucking psycho. You're totally whacked if you ever think I would ever want to be with a creep like you."

This time there was no stopping the beast as it roared free inside of him. He saw nothing but red as he leapt across the bed, grabbed her, and threw her back down onto the mattress. "You will not speak to me like that!" he yelled as his hand connected with her cheek. "You will treat me with respect or it will go very badly for you."

He slapped her again, hard enough to whip her head to the side. The red fog faded and he sat back, trembling, his hands clenched into fists. Her left eye was swollen and her bottom lip was puffy and bleeding. "Look what you made me do," he said, running his fingers gently over the bruise blooming on her cheekbone. "I don't want to hurt you, but I won't allow you to disrespect me. Now apologize for saying those things and spitting your food at me."

She was silent, her eyes locked on a spot just past his shoulder.

His mouth tightened as he fisted his hand into her hair and jerked her up from the bed. She sat up with a cry, her head twisted to the side as his fingers tightened.

"Apologize," he said through clenched teeth.

At her continued silence, he reached out with his other hand and covered her breast. He clamped his fingers over it, squeezing until she let out a whimper of pain. "Apologize, or this is just the beginning of your lesson in good manners."

"I'm sorry," she whispered almost inaudibly.

"Louder," he said, pinching her nipple and twisting it hard.

"I'm sorry," she yelled. "Please don't hurt me."

He felt a warm glow at the look of submission in her eyes. The first step. He released her and sat back. "I promise I'll never hurt you, Tricia," he said, his voice gentle once again. "Not unless you make me. What's most important now is for you to accept the fact that you belong with me now. And I will never let you go."

Chapter 7

The flames of the bonfire cast harsh shadows over the sharp edges of Tommy's cheekbones and jaw, brought out golden-brown streaks in his dark hair, and highlighted the crinkles at the corners of his eyes as he smiled at something the girl next to him said.

Despite the roaring fire, a chill settled over Kate's skin at the realization that while she'd spent all of last year looking forward to seeing Tommy again, he couldn't care less that she was here.

Tommy's a sophomore in college and star of the football team. Of course he doesn't have time for a silly, up-tight high schooler like you.

Logically, she got it. She was three years younger than him, and their friendship had always been an unlikely one. Even last summer he'd spent less time with her, more interested in older girls and partying with his friends than taking her on hikes and showing her the best out-of-the-way swimming spots on the lake.

Just because Kate recognized the truth didn't make it hurt any less.

She'd gotten the first inkling yesterday, when Tommy had shown up to mow their lawn, as he had every summer since they'd started coming to the lake. Kate had bounded out of the house, two ice-cold sodas in hand, eager to catch up.

But when she'd gone to hug him, he'd been awkward and stiff, practically pushing her away. Kate tried to tell herself she was imagining it. But she didn't imagine him putting his earphones in and cranking up his Walkman. And there was no mistaking the way he packed up his mower and lit out right after he was finished, claiming he had too much work to do to stay for a quick swim.

Nor was there any mistaking the way he barely spared her a nod when she and her sister arrived at the party tonight. As if they hadn't spent hours over the past several years together, laughing and talking about their different lives, confessing dreams for the future that didn't align with the paths their parents envisioned for them.

Kate felt her heart crack open in that moment, the way his gaze caught, then drifted over her as though he barely knew her. Worse, like he didn't want to know her.

Music blared, laughter rang out as dozens of people gathered around the bonfire. Kate couldn't hear any of it as she watched Tommy bend his head to whisper into the ear of the girl practically plastered to his side.

A fountain of jealousy erupted in Kate's stomach as Kelly Kovac tilted her head back in laughter, sending her long blond hair spilling over her shoulders and making her boobs test the holding power of her halter top. She was everything Kate wasn't: tall, curvy, gregarious.

The kind of girl every nineteen-year-old guy, including Tommy Ibarra, dreamed of having at his side at a summer bonfire.

She glanced down at her own modest curves pressing against the bodice of her sundress. Humiliation burned like acid in her stomach as she thought about how carefully she'd gotten dressed tonight, how she'd fantasized about Tommy seeing how much she'd grown up in the past year and realizing she wasn't a kid anymore.

Her gaze locked on the smooth skin of Kelly's cleavage, the skin glowing golden in the firelight.

As if your baby B cups could ever compete with that.

Kate gave them fifteen minutes before they snuck off to go fool around.

She took a sip of beer from her plastic cup and nearly gagged. Kate wasn't a big drinker in general, and tonight the jealousy gave it an extra-bitter taste.

She dumped it into the fire, listening to the hiss and sputter with a pang of regret. Tonight would have been a good night to finally develop a taste for alcohol. But she couldn't even count on that crutch to take the edge off the hurt.

She dragged her eyes from him and looked around for her sister. Kate's heart sank when she spotted her. Lauren was cozied up to David Crawford, her latest crush. Lauren was turning on the charm big-time in a way, looking up at him through her lashes and tossing her dark mane of hair in a way Kate could never seem to master. David was eating it up, and Kate knew there was no way she was getting her sister out of here any time soon.

And there was no way she was going home without her, not unless she wanted an earful from her father about how selfish and irresponsible she was. Kate was the more serious, responsible twin. Kate could be trusted not to get drunk and sneak off with boys and to make sure her sister didn't either.

She heard Lauren's loud peal of laughter and watched her bring her cup to her lips. To be fair, Kate rarely prevented Lauren from having a good time altogether. She just made sure it never went too far.

Which had inspired Lauren last summer to start calling Kate the funsucker 2000.

Maybe that was why Tommy had gotten sick of her.

The thought made her eyes burn, and she realized with horror she was about to start crying. Even if Tommy wasn't paying attention, she couldn't just stay here crying like an idiot.

She pushed to her feet and started down the beach, wishing with everything she had that she could go home to lick her wounds.

But no, Kate could never bail, Kate had to be responsible and make sure her sister stayed out of trouble. She swallowed back her sobs and took deep breaths of the cool night air, wondering how she was going to make it through an entire month in Sandpoint, running into Tommy while he pretended she didn't exist.

"Kate!"

She stopped short at the call, a thrill shooting down her spine at the sound of the familiar voice. She turned slowly, half afraid she was imagining it. But no, even with his face shadowed by darkness, Kate recognized Tommy's lanky frame and broad shoulders silhouetted by the fire as he trotted down the beach after her. "You're not leaving, are you?"

Warmth burst in her chest at the concern in his voice, as though he really cared. Maybe—she smacked the thought down as the hurt, confusion, and no small amount of anger welled up at the way he'd treated her for the past two days. "What do you care? You're too busy with Kelly bigboobs to talk to me."

"Katie, I'm sorry," he said taking a step closer. He held out his hand awkwardly and let it drop.

Kate held up her hands. "Look, I get it, I'm not beautiful, or built, or even any fun, so I get why you don't want to

*hang out with me. But I don't see why you don't even like
me—"*

He moved so fast one second she was midsentence and
the next his mouth was covering hers, his arms lifting her up
off the sand as he plastered her to his body.

Her lips were parted in surprise, allowing his tongue
to sweep inside. It took about five seconds for the shock
to wear off and for Kate to realize that Tommy Ibarra was
actually kissing her.

And just as she'd dreamed, it felt really, really good.

Though Kate wasn't nearly as active on the dating scene
as her sister, she'd been kissed a handful of times before.
But nothing could have prepared her for the rush of heat
that blew through her at the first touch of Tommy's mouth
on hers.

It was almost overpowering, the new sensations rushing through her. His tongue stroked against hers, exploring, and soon Kate's breath was coming in hot, shaky pants,
her hands trembling so much it was embarrassing but she
couldn't make it stop.

But at the same time she couldn't get enough of his taste,
the warm, musky scent of his skin, the feel of his muscles
rippling under the smooth skin of his arms as her fingers
clutched him for balance.

He sank to his knees onto the sand, pulling her with him.
Rolling to his back, he pulled her down on top of him, holding her so most of her weight landed on his chest and her
bare legs tangled with his.

With a groan he tore his mouth away from hers, his own
breath coming hard and fast. "This is why, okay? This is
why I've been such a dick."

"What?" In Kate's kiss-addled state, the explanation
made no sense.

"It started last summer, and I knew you were too young. You're still too young—"

"I'll be seventeen next month!" Kate protested.

Tommy gave a helpless chuckle and slid his hands up and down her back. "And you're still jailbait. That should be reason enough for me to keep my hands off." His hand came up to curve around the nape of her neck and guided her mouth back down to his.

She parted her lips eagerly, reached up her hands to thread in his thick, dark hair. Hardly able to believe any of this was happening as heat like nothing she'd ever felt before sizzled through every nerve.

"I spent the last month telling myself I wasn't going to touch you," Tommy murmured between hot, drugging kisses, "that I could be around you like always and nothing would happen. Then I saw you, and you looked so pretty, and I just knew..." His hands swept down her spine, coming to rest at the small of her back, his fingers curling into the tender skin. "I know you're not experienced."

The heat of embarrassment momentarily chased away the heat of young lust. Was it that obvious?

"...but I want you to know I won't pressure you into anything you're not ready for."

Kate's breath hitched as he sucked her bottom lip between his, doubt creeping around the edges of her pleasure. He said that now, but what if he got impatient? Or worse, bored? What if he decided wasting his time with a Goody Two-shoes like her wasn't worth it?

As though reading her mind, Tommy broke the kiss and cradled her face in his hands. "I don't know what it is about you, Katie, but something about you drives me a little crazy. I just can't seem to stay away from you."

Kate jolted awake, heart pounding, the feel of Tommy's

lips on hers so vivid she swore she could still taste him. She closed her eyes, clinging to the threads of the dream. Trying to hold onto that feeling of happiness, that moment of feeling like everything she ever wanted in life was falling into her hands.

But the dream faded, disappeared, as quickly and completely as the happiness of those few weeks with Tommy had disappeared.

Where had that come from? she wondered as she swung her legs over the side of the bed and made her way to the bathroom.

She hadn't allowed herself to think of that night in forever, and so far her subconscious had cooperated. Why now? She sighed as she stepped under the hot shower spray. Why was the universe taunting her with the memories of that night, the magic of their first kiss, the way his arms had felt so safe and strong around her?

As the dream faded, the Tommy of her memories merged with the cold, stony warrior she'd encountered yesterday, a man hardened by that one horrible night and the life he'd lived since.

As though she needed any more reminders of how different everything was now. Of everything she'd lost.

It was still early, just after six, when Kate arrived at headquarters. Despite the early hour, the blond reporter from the day before was waiting out front.

"Maura Walsh, KITV News," she said. "Kate, can you tell us if there have been any new developments since you've gotten involved with the search?"

Nothing I'd share with a vulture like you, she thought as Walsh shoved the microphone practically up her nose. Unlike Kate, who was foggy headed from her restless night, Walsh was positively beaming with energy, makeup flawless, not a hair out of place in her helmetlike coif. Kate schooled her features into a neutral expression. "We have nothing to share right now, but hopefully some solid leads have come in through the tip line, and the sheriff and his deputies will be conducting another search effort today."

Kate tried to step around Walsh, but the woman moved with her and blocked her path. "Are you concerned that the forty-eight-hour mark has been passed?"

The coffee Kate had drunk on her way in curdled in her stomach at the reference to the critical time window. "Of course. I'm concerned with every minute that passes without us finding Tricia."

"You are aware, though," Walsh persisted, "that statistics say that in the case of an abduction, after forty-eight hours the likelihood of finding the victim alive is cut in half."

Of course I'm aware, she wanted to shout. One didn't work closely on over a hundred missing children's cases without being aware of the statistic that the media loved to throw out there. And don't think the dread hadn't hit her hard last night at around eleven p.m. when that forty-eight-hour mark had passed and they still didn't have a single clue to Tricia's where-abouts. "I'm well aware what statistics say, but for now—"

Walsh didn't let her finish her thought. "At what point do you think the investigation will shift from kidnapping to homicide?"

Kate clenched her hands into fists. "I can hardly specu-late on how Sheriff Kovac will handle the investigation on an ongoing basis. Right now there is no evidence that leads us to believe Tricia is anything but alive. We're all focused on finding her and getting her home safe. Now, if you'll excuse me." Kate pushed past, taking petty satisfaction at the reporter's grunt when Kate's shoulder knocked into her.

At this hour the volunteer headquarters was empty

except for the two middle-age women—more friends of Sylvia Ibarra—who had volunteered to pull the graveyard shift on the tip line.

Kate smiled a good morning and asked how the night had gone.

"We got nothing from midnight to four," said the one with a salt-and-pepper bob. "Then, just in the past two hours, we got dozens."

"People have called all the way from Chicago," the other woman said. "We logged everything into the database, just like you showed us."

"Great, I'll take a look." Kate opened her laptop and logged in. Of course CJ would have the final say on which leads he pursued, but Kate had enough experience to do a first pass and filter out the truly useless calls.

She looked at her screen and sighed heavily as she took in the amount of data she had to sift through. Of course, it was great that people had responded to the pleas for information. But Kate knew from experience that most of the calls would gain them nothing. Some were merely mistaken, thinking they'd seen the victims when they hadn't. Others were certifiably insane, calling in with crazy stories of alien abductions and demonic possessions.

And then there were the real sickos, the ones who called in with lurid, disgusting stories about what they were doing to the victim, getting off on sharing their twisted fantasies with people who were unlikely to hang up on them.

Those were all the ones who called when there was little or no reward offered. With the money John had put up, likely a lot more people were thinking they saw something of interest if it would net them nearly a quarter of a million dollars.

"Let's see if we can find a needle in a haystack," she said softly to herself, and began to read.

As Kate scrolled through the log, she was relieved to see that while there were two alien abduction stories and one alleged sighting of Bigfoot near where Tricia was last seen, there were no psycho fantasy calls.

She marked one call, from a woman in Missoula who thought she'd seen Tricia last night at an all-night diner. Over the next hour and half she pored over the data, trying to keep disappointment from overwhelming her when nothing promising materialized.

She wondered if Tommy had discovered any more information about Tricia's cyberfriends. She damn well hoped so, since John Q. Public didn't seem to be coming forward with anything useful.

Her phone rang and she answered it on the first ring, hoping it was Tommy with an update.

But instead of Tommy's deep rumble, it was John's voice on the other line. "I wanted to check in and see if there was any news."

"There's good news and bad news," Kate said, telling herself the only reason she was disappointed it wasn't Tommy on the other line was because she wanted information, not because after fourteen years his voice still made her stomach do cartwheels. "The good news is that the reward you offered has generated a lot of calls. The bad news is that some of those callers think Tricia has been carried off by Bigfoot."

He let out a guffaw on the other end. "I'm sorry," he said, quickly stifling the laugh. "I guess there are a lot of crazies out there."

Kate gave a weary chuckle. "You have no idea."

"I'm sorry I won't be able to join the search party today," he said. "I'm working on a development up in Bonner and have a bunch of fires to put out."

"Don't worry, we have fifty volunteers registered to participate."

"Good, I just hate sitting around doing nothing."

"You put up several hundred thousand dollars for a reward. That's hardly nothing."

"It's easy to throw money at a problem when you have a lot of it," John said with the casual arrogance of someone who has never been anything but extremely wealthy.

"That may be so, but it means the world to the family, and to me too. I don't know how to thank you."

"Thank me by having dinner with me tonight," he said. "You remember Magda, our housekeeper? She's still an amazing cook, and I've moved half of my wine cellar up from Denver."

Kate had an uncomfortable image of a candlelit table and crystal goblets filled with red wine. Though he hadn't given her any overt signal that he was attracted to her, Kate couldn't help wondering if whatever crush he'd had on her all those years ago might still be there.

She hoped not, because her lack of feelings in that direction hadn't changed. She hated the idea of injecting that kind of awkwardness into their otherwise drama-free friendship. "I don't think dinner is a great idea, given the circumstances—"

"Lunch then. Come on, you'll need a break."

"Lunch," she agreed. They settled on a time, and though Kate didn't feel a hundred percent right about the idea of having lunch with an old friend when she was supposed to be helping with the search for Tricia, if a meal with her was the only thanks John wanted for ponying up the reward, she couldn't be so rude as to refuse him.

CJ and two of his deputies arrived shortly after she hung up. They didn't have time for more than a quick hello before the volunteer searchers began to arrive. Kate and the deputies were busy registering everyone, checking IDs, and making sure everyone looked into one of the surveillance cameras Tommy had installed.

CJ was about to lead the first team out when the front door opened.

"I don't think she'll want to see you."

The hardness in CJ's voice cut through the din of the crowd like a knife, stealing Kate's attention away from the deputy who was giving her an overview of the search areas they would be focusing on today.

At first she didn't recognize the slight, dark-haired woman who was pushing her way through the crowd toward her despite CJ's attempts to stay her.

Her hair was dark, almost black, and cut in short, pixie layers that framed one of the most beautiful faces Kate had ever seen. Dark eyebrows arched over large, thickly lashed gray eyes. Her nose was small and slightly tilted at the tip, giving her an almost elfish look. Her full lips were pressed together, her look uncertain.

"Erin," Kate said, her stomach flipping over as she matched this lovely young woman with the thirteen-year-old girl who'd tromped down the beach in scraggly cutoffs and a stretched-out tank top selling cookies to whoever would buy them. "It's been a long time," she murmured for lack of anything else. What did one say to the niece of the man who'd murdered her brother?

"Erin, come on, why do you have to show up where you know you're not wanted?" CJ said.

Hurt, raw and deep, flashed in Erin's eyes at CJ's cutting voice. She shot CJ a snide look. "Why do you always have to push your way into my business?" she shot back.

The hurt gone in an instant, and Kate was sure she was

the only one who saw it. Sympathy momentarily overrode her bad memories of Erin's family. Kate hadn't known Erin well, but she remembered a scrappy, smart girl who was doing what she could to outplay the awful hand she'd been dealt by being born into the notorious Flannery family.

Her only involvement with Michael's death was being unfortunate enough to be related to the man who'd killed him. "Who says she's not wanted?" Kate said.

Erin flashed her a quick, grateful smile.

"I brought some pastries and coffee from the restaurant," Erin said, drawing Kate's attention to the bags she held in each hand. "It's too busy right now for me to help with the search effort, but at least I can offer up free food."

"Thanks," Kate said with a smile, clearing a space on the table for Erin to put out the food. Kate hadn't woken up with much of an appetite, but when Erin opened the first box and the scent of fresh-baked croissants wafted through the room, she couldn't resist.

Her eyes closed in ecstasy as she bit into a still-warm chocolate croissant. "This is amazing, Erin."

Erin's smile brightened. "Thanks. The croissants are kind of my specialty."

"You make all of this?" Kate asked, impressed at the variety of pastries packed into the four pink boxes Erin had brought.

"Yep, every day, from scratch, ever since I took over for Mary."

"I didn't know you were running the cafe."

"Mary had me take over a couple years ago," Erin replied with a faintly challenging air. "When she died she left me the deed to the building as well."

"Based on the line you had out the door yesterday at lunchtime, I'd say Mary made the right choice."

The search volunteers were similarly enthusiastic about
the free food and coffee, crowding around the table and
good-naturedly elbowing each other aside to get to their
favorites as they sang Erin's praises.

Only CJ, she noticed, hadn't eaten a bite. "You're not
having any?"

"I'm not hungry," he said impatiently.

Erin was restocking the napkin supply, but Kate saw her
shoulders stiffen. Something was going on between those two.

"I need to get back," Erin said. She turned to CJ and held
out a small box emblazoned with the restaurant's name.

"What's this?" CJ took the small white box gingerly, as
though it might contain a rattlesnake.

"It's for Travis. Raspberry cream cheese croissant. It's
his favorite."

CJ grunted something that could have passed for thanks.

Erin stared at him hard for a beat, then turned back to
Kate. "I'll bring sandwiches by this afternoon."

"That won't be—" CJ began.

"That's extremely generous of you," Kate replied, and
shot CJ a hard look.

Erin shrugged. "It's the least I can do," she said, and
held out her hand tentatively, as though she was afraid Kate
would refuse it.

Kate clasped it in both hands. "Thank you."

Erin smiled, though her eyes were suspiciously damp,
and Kate felt her own eyes burn with emotion.

After Erin left, Kate turned on CJ. "What was that all
about?"

"What?"

"You were really rude to her."

He stiffened. "I'm sorry if you saw it that way. I was just
looking out for you."

"How do you figure?"

"You really want her dropping by, hanging out, reminding you of what happened?"

Her shoulders tightened with irritation. She didn't know why she felt so compelled to defend a woman she barely knew and who came from the same family tree as the man who had murdered her brother. Maybe it was because she recognized something in Erin's stormy gray eyes: a deep sadness mixed with guilt that wasn't hers to bear but was no less keenly felt. A wariness that came from years of being judged and having people you love push you away.

"The moment I pulled into town, those memories have been front and center," Kate said ruefully. "I appreciate the concern, but it's going to take a lot more than Erin Flannery's offer of muffins to push me over the edge."

CJ shrugged, having the grace to look a little ashamed. "Sorry."

"I'm not the one you should apologize to."

CJ gave a noncommittal grunt.

"It's not her fault she was born into the trashiest family in the county. Looks like she's managed to turn her life around in spite of that. Maybe you could give her a little credit."

"I do," he said defensively. "But a lot of people in this town have long memories and strong opinions. And I hate to see her get hurt."

Kate shook her head and gave him a quizzical smile. "Seems like you'd accomplish that better by being a little nicer to her."

"Tried that once," CJ said curtly, his mouth pulling into a grimace. There was a flash of something on his face—a combination of guilt and regret that told Kate something must have happened between the town's golden boy and the feisty daughter of the family responsible for most of the crime in a fifty-mile radius. Whatever it was, CJ didn't seem inclined to elaborate, though there was no mistaking the fact that the memory caused him obvious distress.

Without thinking, Kate reached out and pulled him into a quick hug. "I know you're a nice guy, CJ. Sometimes people who haven't had a lot of kindness in their lives have a hard time accepting it."

Chapter 8

Tommy stood in the doorway of the volunteer headquarters feeling his jaw clench as he looked over the heads of the volunteers milling around and saw Kate and CJ tucked into a cozy corner, their heads close together as they spoke, acting like they were the only two people in the room.

Unbidden, his stomach burned with the unfamiliar, unwelcome sensation that had overtaken him yesterday when she'd left his house with CJ. The same feeling that had eaten at him every time she smiled and spoke easily with CJ. A sharp contrast to how she eyed Tommy like a nervous cat circling a junkyard dog.

Christ, he was jealous, uneasy in a way he hadn't been since he was a goddamn clueless teenager, working up the nerve to talk to a girl. Working up the nerve to make a move on Kate when she could have her pick from a crew of good-looking guys her age who were richer, more polished, and way more likely to be approved by daddy dearest than he was.

Part of him—a cowardly, yellow-bellied part of himself he didn't even realize was in his makeup—wanted to back out the door. He was a fucking idiot for coming here in the first place. Every bit of information he'd discovered could have been easily given over the phone or, hell, even email.

Would have been better if he'd done that if he wanted to keep it safe from prying eyes and curious ears.

But no, for some stupid reason this morning he'd woken tortured by images from his sex-soaked dreams—starring Kate, natch—and an undeniable compulsion to see her in the flesh.

And damned if she didn't look good, he thought with no small amount of irritation. Not that she was trying that hard, wearing jeans and a green-and-blue plaid shirt, her red-kissed blond hair pulled into a low ponytail that fell midway down her back. Still, Tommy felt his gaze drawn to her bare neck, the pale skin of her throat and the hint of collarbone revealed by her collar.

"Excuse me," a male voice said, jostling into the back-pack slung over Tommy's shoulder as he passed and jerking him out of his daze. Christ on a stick, this was not the time to indulge in memories of how sweet and smooth the skin of Kate's throat had been against his lips.

As his gaze locked on the flyer clasped in one of the vol-unteer's hands, he fixed his mind on the image of Tricia Fuller and reminded himself that he had an important rea-son to be here, one that didn't involve alternately ogling Kate Beckett and indulging in adolescent angst because she seemed to enjoy the handsome sheriff's company a bit too much for his liking.

He wove through the crowd, nodding in greeting to the volunteers, most of whom he knew. As he got closer to Kate, he picked up on the snippets of their conversation.

"Nice, huh?" CJ was saying. "That's exactly how guys like to be described."

"What's wrong with nice?" Kate asked.

CJ laughed. "Nice is the kiss of death for a guy. It's like saying a girl has a nice personality."

Despite his resolve to be all business, Tommy felt his hackles raise and his fists clench as Kate gave CJ a playful swat. "Based on what I've seen out there," she said, "you could do a whole lot worse than nice."

"You two look cozy," Tommy said, regretting the words and his peevish tone the instant they left his mouth.

Kate looked up, her smile dissolving as she met Tommy's hard stare. "I wasn't expecting you this morning."

"I managed to ID Moto98 based on the IP address—"

"You could have called me. No need to come all the way down here," CJ said, one dark eyebrow cocked as though he knew exactly why Tommy had gone to the trouble.

"There were other developments I wanted to go over in person," Tommy said, schooling his expression into an impassive mask.

CJ made a quick announcement that his deputies would lead the first two search teams out as scheduled, while his team would be delayed.

The three went to the small office in the back of the space, ignoring the curious stares and whispers from the volunteers.

"So?" CJ said, his arms folded across his chest, his feet spread apart.

The office didn't have any furniture except for an empty bookcase in the corner, so Tommy pulled his laptop out of his backpack and set it on top.

"I traced the IP address on the account back to a Roger Frankel of Grand Junction, Colorado."

"I'll call the local authorities and see if they can find him for questioning."

Tommy shook his head. "Roger Frankel is seventy-eight years old and in a wheelchair."

"That doesn't mean he can't be making inappropriate contact with underage girls online," Kate pointed out.

"But it does make him an unlikely candidate to physically carry off a healthy, able-bodied girl like Tricia," Tommy said. "Besides, Frankel has no record or arrests for sexual misconduct. And then there's the fact that his house was robbed over six months ago and the computer was among the items stolen."

"You could have told us that to start," Kate said. "How did you get all this anyway?"

Tommy gave her a pointed look.

"Right, you have your ways," she said, exasperated. "I hope we never need to rely on any of this in court, because none of it will ever stand."

"You can have a trial or you can have Tricia back safe."

Kate recoiled from his harsh tone, and Tommy tried to ignore the pinching feeling in his chest. It wasn't his job to make her feel good. "But here's the really interesting bit I uncovered," Tommy added, pulling a map up onto the screen. "When I look at the activity log on the wireless network at Jackson's rental house, look what comes up."

"Holy shit, that's the same IP address," CJ breathed. Tommy didn't say anything, letting them read through the logs so they could reach the same conclusion he did. "He was using their network."

"How close would he have to be to pick up the signal?" Kate asked.

"The network there has a range of about three hundred feet," Tommy said.

Kate shivered beside him, and he could feel it ripple through every nerve. "He was so close, and no one ever saw anything."

"There's that pretty densely wooded area close to the house. Easy enough to hide, especially when he was there mostly after dark," CJ pointed out.

"He was lurking on their network for two days before he made any contact," Kate said. "Was he monitoring her, figuring out how she spent her time online? Is that possible?"

Tommy nodded. "It would take a sophisticated user, but it's definitely possible."

"So he stalks her online, befriends her, and encourages her to go out so he can be sure she'll be alone and vulnerable," Kate said, her voice tight with emotion.

"It's a good bet he was watching her in person too," Tommy said.

Kate nodded. "She might have even seen him, Brooke and Jackson too, and not even known it."

"What else did you find out about Frankel?" CJ asked. "Any adult children who fit the profile who would have access to his computer?"

Tommy shook his head. "No children, no relatives that came up on the first search, but his insurance records show payments to a home healthcare service. I was planning to pull up records on anyone who visited his house in the past year."

CJ nodded. "That would be great, and in the meantime, I'll call the locals down there and make sure we get their cooperation in case we need to go and question anyone."

Kate shifted uncomfortably. "I don't know if it's such a great idea for you to be hacking into the files of a private corporation—"

"It is if it leads us to whoever took Tricia," Tommy snapped.

"If it somehow gets out to the press that we're using illegal methods to get our information, it could ruin the case, not to mention my reputation and the image of St. Anthony's—"

"I don't see how it will get out to the press unless one of us leaks it," Tommy snapped. "And from what I've seen, you did a damn good job of trashing your reputation long before I ever came back on the scene."

Kate's face went white, and the look of devastation there hit him like a punch in the gut.

"Shit," he said, "I'm sorry. That was uncalled for—"

Kate held her hand up. "No, you're right. As long as I can trust you two to keep this quiet we'll be fine." She looked at her watch and swore softly. "Speaking of the press, I'm scheduled to give a statement in twenty minutes and I need to prep."

"We can meet back at my place," Tommy said.

Kate shook her head. "John is expecting me at his place for lunch."

Tommy couldn't have stifled his snort of disdain if there had been a gun to his head.

"What's your problem with him?" Kate snapped. Tommy was happy to see the color in her cheeks, the fight back in her after his cheap shot.

"He's an entitled, self-important prick," Tommy said, "who thinks his shit doesn't stink."

"He's being very generous with the reward money."

"Money he inherited from Daddy," Tommy muttered.

"The business has been very successful since he took over, even in a recession. He must be doing something right," Kate snapped back.

Tommy shrugged. "He always acted like the locals were beneath him, and that hasn't changed a bit no matter how he thinks he's going to come back and help the little people."

"That's not true—"

"It is kind of true," CJ said. "Don't get me wrong"—he backpedaled as Kate's eyes narrowed—"I'm grateful for what he's done for the town and the help he's providing, but you have to admit he's kind of a tool."

Kate rolled her eyes. "You can think whatever you want of him, but I will always remember him as one of the few people who reached out to me at a time when most of the people I cared about wouldn't even look at me, much less speak to me."

Her barb hit its mark, catching Tommy square in the chest even as he bit back the urge to correct her. Jesus, it shouldn't hurt so much. He hadn't let it hurt in years. She was just a kid, he'd told himself. They both were. She barely had any more control over the situation than he had.

Yeah, he could tell himself that all he wanted, but that didn't keep the memory of the gut-twisting pain he'd felt all those years ago from trying to claw back to the surface. The memory of how he *had* reached out. And it had been Kate who had left him twisting in the wind after he'd opened up a vein and poured it onto a page, then stood by silently while her father did his damnedest to destroy his future.

—⁓—

She didn't give a crap what Tommy Ibarra thought of her. No matter how many times Kate repeated it to herself, she couldn't shake the sting of his words, the bone-deep hurt at the way he'd lashed out, striking her in what he knew to be her weakest point.

Of course his anger was to be expected. But it was still hard to reconcile the good-natured, smiling Tommy of her memories with the cold-hearted stranger who cared nothing for her and her feelings.

As he'd told her so bluntly, he wasn't the same person he'd been. None of them was, and she'd do well to watch her back. Kate's anger at Tommy disappeared as she pulled up in front of John's lake house, overpowered by the wave of nostalgia that washed over her at the sight, so keen it stopped her breath in her chest.

When she'd agreed to have lunch here, she hadn't realized how fast and hard the memories would hit her. She climbed out of the car and started up the walkway, only to stop in her tracks as she experienced a sharp, twisting vertigo. How many times had she parked in this driveway, walked up the front steps of the huge home built from logs and river rock? Caught the sweet smell of Andrea Burkhart's peonies drifting in the hot summer wind?

The last time she had been here had been with her family as they all gathered for yet another crush of a barbecue. Her father's hand had rested absently on her shoulder as she said hello to the Burkharts before he went off to the bar to get drinks for himself and her mother.

Lauren had waited for her father to turn his back before she rolled her eyes exaggeratedly in the direction of her latest crush.

Michael barely passed go before he took off down the beach to play football with a group of boys, his skinny tan arms pumping as he ran, his wide smile showing off the braces that were to come off when they got home, just in time for school to start.

Two days later he was dead.

Somehow, the fact that Michael had died without getting his braces off set free a new, fresh wave of grief so keen Kate barely made it to the front steps before her legs gave out.

Sometimes it hit her like this, unexpectedly, the pain so cutting she couldn't even cry, so sharp she nearly blacked out. All she could do was sit with her head between her knees, struggling to breathe as she fought to beat the pain back before it consumed her.

"Kate?" The voice sounded like it came from the bottom of a deep well.

She squinted up at the dark shape silhouetted by sunlight.

Though she couldn't make out his face, she recognized the familiar set of John's shoulders. She tried to answer him, but her voice was frozen in her throat.

"Kate," John repeated, the urgency in his tone breaking through the fog. "Are you okay? Do you need something? Some water?" He sank down on the stoop next to her and put his hand on her shoulder, but the warmth of his touch did little to chase away the cold that seemed to have settled deep in her bones.

"I'm sorry," she managed to choke out between gasps. "Sometimes I—" Her heart felt like it was going to beat out of her chest, and his face started to swim in front of her.

"Here," John said, guiding her head between her knees. "Just relax and breathe."

Kate struggled to do exactly that as he rubbed slow, gentle circles on her back and slowed his own breath to a steady, deep cadence.

Soon her heartbeat had calmed and her breath matched his. She lifted her head.

"You okay?"

Kate nodded, and he blew out a relieved breath. "Jesus, you scared me. For a second I thought you were going into anaphylactic shock or something." Though he was smiling now, his blue eyes were still worried behind the thin lenses of his glasses.

"More like a combination panic attack and flashback," Kate said. "It hasn't happened in a long time but, being here, seeing this place..."

He grimaced. "Christ, I didn't even consider that being here might bring back bad memories—"

"It's okay," Kate said. She pushed herself to her feet, immediately regretting it when her knees buckled under her.

John stood and caught her under her elbow, and she mustered

up a grateful smile. "It's really not the bad memories that got to me. More like I got out of the car and suddenly remembered how happy we all were. Then it hits me all over again how we're never going to get that back."

She was grateful when John didn't offer stupid platitudes about finding happiness again or how she couldn't let what happened to Michael still affect her so deeply after so many years. Instead he just gave her a quick, sympathetic hug.

"You okay to come inside?"

Kate nodded and let John guide her through the front door. Once again it was like taking a step back in time, walking into the Burkharts' lake house. Though John had made a few changes in the great room, like replacing the old TV with a new flat screen and swapping out the glass coffee table for one made from hardwood, it looked almost exactly as it had fourteen years ago.

"You still have the leather couch," she said with a half smile, running her hand across the back. Another memory hit her, one that made her grin spread wider.

"What?" John asked.

Kate pressed her lips together but couldn't stifle the giggle. "Michael called it the fart couch, because any time someone shifted in their seat it sounded like someone ripped a huge one. I remember one time, your mom—" She broke off into an uncontrollable fit of giggles. "She was wearing this short dress, so when she moved—" She broke off again, tears streaming down her face. "She looked horrified, and your dad—" She struggled to compose herself, remembering John's father, Phillip, rowdy, raucous, and always ready to joke. "He goes, 'good lord, honey, next time use the bathroom.'"

"I don't remember that particular incident, but that sounds about like my dad." John chuckled.

"Your poor mother was mortified"—Kate laughed—"and I thought Michael was going to wet his pants he was laughing so hard. After that we used to have contests to see who could make the loudest sound."

"I must have missed that," he said dryly.

"You used to leave so fast you practically left skid marks when we all came over. Way too immature for a college man like you. Not that I blame you, now that I remember the kind of ridiculousness we were up to," she said, and wiped a tear from under her eye.

"I thought I was too cool." He nodded. "I clearly had no idea what I was missing."

The last of Kate's giggles faded. "We had a lot of fun here, in this house, on this lake." She looked at John and felt her smile falter at the corners. "It feels good to talk about Michael, to remember him with someone who knew him too."

"He was a good kid," John said, giving her another quick, sympathetic squeeze. "And you're right, there are so many good memories in this place. Best memories of my life, that's for sure. Maybe that's why I never get around to redecorating. Though you do have me reconsidering that couch."

Kate let out a watery chuckle and followed him through the archway to the kitchen. "This doesn't look anything like I remember," she remarked. Cream Formica counters had been replaced with a pale stone and the matching Formica cabinets were now made of hardwood the color of butter. The layout had changed to include a huge, butcher block island, and the appliances were all new.

"While there's a certain value to nostalgia, I could hardly expect Magda to replicate her kitchen magic using a fifty-year-old electric range," John said, nodding toward the tiny, dark-haired woman who was bustling around the kitchen.

She paused when John said, "Kate, you remember Magda, don't you?"

"Of course," she said, holding out her hand to the woman whose dark, deep-set eyes flickered nervously in John's direction before she gave Kate a tentative smile and took her hand. Magda had worked as the Burkharts' housekeeper and nanny for over two decades. When the Burkharts had come to Sandpoint in the summers, Magda had accompanied them.

"It's very nice to see you again, Kate," Magda said in her thick eastern European accent. "You look beautiful as always."

Kate smiled and thanked her. "When I decided to move here full time last year, I brought Magda out with me," John explained. "She's going to set up lunch for us on the deck, if that's okay."

Kate nodded and followed him through the sliding glass doors and stepped out onto the wraparound deck. Like all the houses on this street, John's sat right on a private beach and offered breathtaking views of the lake and the mountains beyond. The Burkharts also had a dock that extended two hundred feet into the lake. At the end was a boathouse that was big enough to house both a ski boat and a small motor yacht as well as store kayaks and Jet Skis.

John must have noticed her wistful look as she watched the boaters speed by and listened to families setting up on the beach to picnic in the distance. "You must have missed it here," he said.

Kate nodded. "I missed what we were in this place. The time we spent here was the only time my family seemed normal—well, when my father was normal," she corrected herself. "When he hung out with your parents and our other friends, it was the only time he wasn't 'Senator Beckett,' you know?"

"My dad kept trying to convince them to come back, you know."

Kate nodded. "He might have, but my mom was—" She swallowed hard, her throat clenching as she thought about the silent wraith that had replaced the beautiful vibrant woman in the weeks after Michael's death. "He mentioned it to her, and she didn't get out of bed for two weeks. Even my father knew better than to ask again."

John's reply was lost as Magda softly called that lunch was ready.

Kate took a seat at the large teak table shaded by a canvas umbrella and tried to redirect her brain from the maudlin course it was taking. No small feat. As she'd pointed out to CJ that morning, every breath she took here in Sandpoint brought back memories. All of them—even the good ones— came with a measure of pain.

The memories made it difficult for Kate to do more than pick at her salad, gorgeous as it was, made of fresh local greens and grilled Idaho salmon. She pasted a smile on her face, one that became more genuine as John seemed content to let the past go for a while in favor of easier subjects, such as work and TV.

"So it's not like *Law & Order*, these cases you work on?" he asked. "Nothing seems to get wrapped up in a neat little package."

"Sadly, no," Kate said. She set down her fork, admitting defeat in the face of the gnawing sensation in her stomach, one that never seemed to quiet. "A lot of times it's like the kids just vanish into thin air. The families go months, years even, without any information. As horrible as it was losing Michael, I imagine not knowing what happened to your child is its own level of hell."

John was about to reply but was distracted by the fall of

heavy footsteps on the stairs leading up from the beach. Kate looked up and saw a young man in his late teens or early twenties. Tall, broad shouldered, with coffee brown hair and equally dark eyes, he showed promise of being a real heartbreaker one day if he hadn't earned his stripes already.

He stopped short when he saw them at the table. "Mr. John, I finished stacking the wood under the deck like you told me to." Something about the way he spoke, the way his hands curled awkwardly, signaled something wasn't totally right with him.

"Christian," John said, an edge to his voice. "Do you see that I have company and that you're interrupting?"

"I'm Kate," she said with a smile as she stood and offered her hand.

"Christian Lazlo Goragus," the boy said, his gaze aimed at the redwood boards of the deck as he pumped her hand once, his grip just shy of too hard. Kate sat back down and Christian's gaze followed, his head cocked to the side as he studied her.

"Christian," John started to warn.

"I know you!" Christian burst out, pointing enthusiastically. "You were on the TV, talking about that girl."

"Yes, I was talking about Tricia," Kate said, straightening. "Do you know her?"

"No." He shook his head emphatically. "I saw her a few times. She's pretty, really pretty. And sad sometimes."

"Why was she sad?"

"Kate—"

Kate shot John a silencing look. People tended to tune out kids like Christian, treat them like wallpaper, but if he'd been around Tricia, it was possible he'd seen or heard something important. "Did she talk to you about why she was sad?"

He shook his head. "No. She won't ever talk to me. I just hear her crying down by the lake sometimes."

The hairs on Kate's neck stood up. "What do you mean? Where do you hear her?"

John put his hand over hers and gave his head a little shake. "He gets his tenses mixed up. It's a language problem associated with his condition," he said quietly. "He also has a difficulty with the concept of time. Christian," John said more loudly, "when did you hear Tricia crying?"

"The other month ago?" he said uncertainly.

John gave her an I-told-you-so look. "Christian, since you're finished with the chores, why don't you help your mother in the house."

"Okay," he said, his big, hightop-clad feet slapping against the boards as he went inside. As he left Kate heard him singing tunelessly. She wasn't sure, but she thought it sounded like "All the pretty girls go away."

She gave John a puzzled look. He shook his head with an exasperated air. "I've had the news on too much lately. I sometimes forget how easily he gets obsessed with certain things. It's even worse with this because he's familiar with Tricia."

"I never realized Magda had a son," Kate said when Christian closed the door behind him. "I didn't know she was married."

"She wasn't," John said. "She got pregnant my sophomore year of high school. She never said who the father was, and by that time she was part of the family. There was no way we were kicking her out on the street."

That would explain the handful of summers Magda didn't join the family at the lake, Kate thought.

"I believe the current favored term is 'mentally disabled.' But as I heard it, Magda had a very difficult birth, and as a result Christian was deprived of oxygen long enough that he suffered some brain damage," John said gravely.

"That's awful," Kate said.

"He's done very well, considering, and of course our family always made sure he had the best care available."

"She was lucky your family is so generous," Kate said, and took a sip of her iced tea.

John nodded. "Even with our help, though, it hasn't been easy for her. It really makes me question sometimes if I'll ever have kids. So much can go wrong. Jennifer and I were trying but..."

Kate's heart squeezed at the mention of John's wife, who had committed suicide two years before.

"I know this sounds sick, but I think sometimes it might have been a good thing that we didn't pass on her genes." He shook his head sadly. "But my next thought is that I'm sad that I don't have a piece of her still with me."

"I'm sorry I never got the chance to meet her." Kate had heard about the marriage months after it happened, through one of her infrequent email exchanges with Lauren. Lauren hadn't been invited to the wedding either—no one had, as they'd eloped after John met Jennifer while he was in Florida for business. She'd met Jennifer in Aspen when Kate's family and the Burkharts met to ski over New Year's.

All Lauren had said about Jennifer was that she was gorgeous, seemed young for John, and didn't talk much.

"I think you would have liked her," John said sadly. "She was smart, very intense. But troubled. She had a very bad childhood, and even though I thought I could help her, she was never able to leave her demons behind." He shook his head, hard. "Enough going on about our sad pasts. Just because we lose someone we love doesn't mean we can't still live, right?" he said, and his hand came over to cover Kate's.

Her heart sank a little at the look in his eyes, the first and only indication this entire time that he felt anything other than friendship for her.

"Kate, I was wondering—"

When her phone rang it was hard for her not to let out a gusty sigh of relief. She held up a finger and pulled her phone out of her bag. It was Tommy. "I have to take this."

Of course, it could have been the cable company doing a customer service survey and she would have taken it.

"How's lunch? Did he serve you on gold plates with diamond-encrusted silverware?"

Maybe figuring out how to let John down easy would have been more pleasant. "Do you have something you want to tell me, or are you just calling to be a pain in my ass?"

John's eyebrows shot up and Tommy let out a reluctant chuckle. It sounded rusty, coming from his throat, like he didn't laugh very often. Kate felt an inordinate shot of pleasure at the sound. "I got a few hits from the home healthcare service and some from other service providers who were in and out of Frankel's house leading up to the robbery."

"So is CJ going to follow up?"

Tommy paused for a few seconds, then: "We were hoping you could help us narrow them down, based on the information we have on them. Give us some pointers on where to start."

"I'm not a profiler. The FBI—"

"We'll send the information to the FBI, but they'll take at least a couple of days to respond. I know you're not a pro, but as you like to point out, you have enough experience that your eye will be better than mine or CJ's. We all have our areas of expertise in this, and it would be nice if you could help out. Now if you're too busy having lunch with Mr. Wonderful—"

"Of course I'll help out," Kate snapped. Jackass. "Where do you want to meet?"

"CJ's office. I'll bring all the information there."

Kate hung up her phone and gave John an apologetic smile that she hoped didn't betray the excitement buzzing through her body. She told herself it was due entirely to the fact they might be closing in on a lead and not because Tommy, in not so many words, might be starting to respect her as more than just a talking head. "I'm so sorry to eat and run, but I have to go."

John stood from the table. "Something about Tricia?"

Kate nodded. "I can't get into details, but Tommy thinks he might have found something worth looking into."

The muscles around John's mouth tightened. "Tommy?"

"Ibarra," Kate clarified.

"Oh, I know which Tommy you're talking about. I didn't realize you two were getting so chummy again. I can never get a break when he's around."

The butterflies of excitement sank like rocks in her stomach. "That's inappropriate, and completely unfair. Tricia's father asked Tommy to help with the investigation. It's in Tricia's best interest that Tommy and I put aside whatever differences we have in order to find her. I think you should do the same."

John grimaced. "You're right," he said with a sheepish look on his face. "Something about that guy rubs me the wrong way."

Kate didn't think it was wise to tell him the feeling was mutual.

"And I'm sorry for saying that. I know you're here as a professional and your only focus is on the case. In fact, it was probably unfair of me to insist you have lunch today with so much going on."

Kate gave him a noncommittal shrug.

John leaned down, a sly smile on his face. "Even so, I'm

not going to apologize for it. I had too much fun catching up with you. But I promise not to force my company on you until this mess is all over."

"It's hardly torture," Kate said, and leaned up to give him a quick kiss on the cheek. She waved to Magda and thanked her for lunch as John walked her to the door.

Chapter 9

Kate arrived at the sheriff's station ten minutes later. The dispatcher, a woman Kate recognized as one of the volunteers from the day before, directed her to CJ's office. "CJ's running a little late—he had a domestic violence call clear over by Priest Lake that he had to respond to, but Tommy's already back there."

Kate thanked her and walked back to the office, trying to ignore the knot tightening in her belly as she anticipated spending any time alone with Tommy in a small enclosed space.

She took a bracing breath and pushed the door open. He was sitting at the small table in the corner, his tall, muscular frame managing to make the furniture look like it had been built for children. He gave her a cool nod in greeting. She did the same, trying not to notice the way the sun streaming in from the window made his thick, short hair come alive with a riot of red and gold highlights or the way his biceps strained the sleeves of his black polo shirt.

She joined him at the table, and he pushed a stack of papers toward her. "You can start with that," he said, not bothering to look up as he spoke. "I'm still gathering additional info about a few more potential leads."

Okay, so no small talk. And why should there be? They were both professionals, working on this case, and whatever had happened between them in the past was dead and buried and had no relevance in their lives now.

She'd never had a colleague so studiously ignore her as Tommy was doing now, his eyes locked on the computer. He'd been the one to call her there, she thought. And now he wanted to pretend she didn't exist?

As she sifted through the papers, she felt a little devil tap her on the shoulder, the one she'd never known existed until she met Tommy Ibarra. The one that urged her to do things that were totally out of character. Who convinced her to lie, and sneak, and offer her virginity up on a platter to the first boy who made her secret parts tingle.

Now that devil urged her to ignore all the leave-me-alone signals Tommy was putting out there. "So how did you get all this information?" Kate asked as she began looking through the papers.

Tommy looked up, his expression stony. "Some of it's public record. The rest you probably don't want to know."

Kate scanned what looked like someone's medical chart from a Boulder area hospital. "Don't you worry about getting caught?"

"It's my job not to get caught. That's why my clients hire me."

Kate wrinkled her nose. "But couldn't you be arrested? Can't they?"

Those acre-wide shoulders lifted and lowered in a shrug. "I don't worry about it much."

"But don't you worry about what your clients are doing with that information?" she pressed.

His dark gaze met hers, deadpan. "Many of my clients hire me to find pieces of information no one else can find. I give them what they want, and they pay me well for it. What they do with that information is their business."

Kate stared blankly at the sheet of paper in front of her until the letters started to swim. Despite his behavior over the last two days, it was still hard for Kate to wrap her head around how the Tommy she had known had become so cynical, so cold. She'd done this, she realized. She and her father, when he'd tried to rip Tommy's world apart as much as their own had been.

"How did you get into this?"

Tommy arched a dark brow in question.

"This business. I thought you'd end up taking over the ranch, like your father wanted. I never knew you were even into computers."

Tommy's mouth quirked to the side, the first crack in his stony expression she'd seen. "Me neither, until I got into the Army. I'd studied a little computer science in college, but when I joined the Ranger Corps I was assigned as the lead communications specialist for my regiment. Turned out I also had a knack for surveillance, both the physical and cyber kind. After I got out I had enough contacts who were familiar with me and my skills to start my own business."

"I know Sandpoint has grown, but it doesn't seem like it would generate the kind of demand that would pay for that house of yours."

Finally, a little smile glimmered in his eyes as he looked up from his computer screen. "As long as I have access to the Internet and a phone line, I can work anywhere. But I also have an office and a place in Seattle, and I work with several larger firms that hire me as a contractor. I only spend about half my time here."

"And the rest of your time jet-setting around the globe," Kate prodded.

"Mostly just around the States. I got my share of jet-setting in my Ranger days."

"I never would have imagined you in the military, much less special forces," Kate mused. Not then, anyway. Now Tommy's military experience seemed to have seeped into every cell in his body. It was in his steady, impassive gaze, the way he held his body, perfectly still yet vibrating with readiness.

This time when he looked at her his dark gaze was sharp, challenging. "Oh, yeah? How did you imagine I turned out after what happened?"

Kate swallowed hard as she realized her mistake in admitting that she'd thought about him at all. She felt her face heat as she remembered some of what she'd imagined, the fantasies she'd spun. Her very favorite had been the one where she left school one day to find Tommy's truck parked outside. He'd be leaning against it, wearing a T-shirt and worn jeans, a sly smile on his face and a knowing glint in his eye. He'd pin her up against the truck and kiss her like he'd been dying for the taste of her.

Then...oh God, just thinking about it made her want to melt into a puddle of embarrassment, though he couldn't possibly read her thoughts...Then he'd pull an engagement ring out of her pocket and ask her to marry him. Of course she'd say yes and drive back to Idaho with him.

"I imagined you here, working with your father on the ranch, most likely married with a couple kids," she said simply.

"There was a time in my life when it easily could have gone that way, though I don't know that my father and I could ever see eye to eye enough to work that closely together. As it is, he can only stand me coming around to help a couple days a week."

Kate gave him a little smile and went back to her reading.

After a few moments Tommy broke the silence. "You know, I never spent much time imagining what happened to you."

The knife dug deeply into her chest and just as quickly withdrew. "I didn't have to, not with you popping up on the news all the time. I couldn't get away from you no matter how bad I wanted to. Apparently I still can't."

And back in went the knife.

Why should it matter, she scolded herself, especially when the feeling was mutual. Wasn't it?

She didn't have much time to stew on it before CJ burst in the office, his brusque "What have we got?" a sharp reminder that she had a job to do.

And once again Tommy was proving too much of a distraction.

Tommy hit a key on his computer that made the printer start humming and spit out several more pages. "Here's some more info on the shuttle driver." Tommy gestured with his chin. "He's already in your pile."

Kate grabbed the pages, and while Tommy gave CJ the highlights, Kate focused all of her attention on parsing the data Tommy had gathered.

He was thorough, no doubt about that. He'd collected school, driving, employment, and medical records for over half a dozen possible suspects.

Two hours later Kate had arranged all of the information in order of priority. "The top three are the handyman, Robert Walford, his roommate, Dillon O'Brien, who helped him out at Frankel's sometimes, and Vitaki Korcu, the son of the overnight nurse who drove his mother to and from work."

As CJ made phone calls to the local law enforcement in Boulder, Tommy went to work tracking down any information he could find about the top three men's recent credit card activity to see if there was any evidence that they'd headed this way.

Though nothing was solid yet, Kate couldn't suppress

excitement bubbling through her blood along with the slight easing of the knot in her stomach as she felt one more nudge of optimism thanks to the information Tommy had gathered.

She didn't want to get her hopes up, but as she drove back to the townhouse, she couldn't keep from thinking that maybe, just maybe they were about to get a break.

———⚊———

The envelope was on her windshield the next morning when she went outside. She instinctively looked around, even though it could have been placed there any time in the last twelve hours. At this early hour, there still wasn't much activity. Kate picked up the envelope carefully and with no small amount of trepidation.

Being a marginally public figure, Kate had gotten her share of harassing notes and phone calls.

Then again, it could be nothing but a marketing brochure, although she noticed none of the other cars parked along the street had anything tucked under their windshields.

She opened the envelope to find two pieces of paper inside. The one was plain printer paper, the message typewritten in black text: "They didn't find her in time. Will this time be any different?"

A jolt of adrenaline shot through her as she pulled out the second page. It was a photocopy of a news article. The headline read "Local girl, 16, Missing." The accompanying photo showed a pretty girl with big eyes and a wide smile. Her long, light hair—it was hard to tell the exact hue from the black-and-white photo—was held back from her face by a headband.

Kate went on to read the article describing how Ellie Cantrell, a sixteen-year-old from Omaha, Nebraska, went missing on her way home from cheerleading practice. She looked at the dateline of the article. October 12, 2001. Nearly ten years ago. At the time the article had been written, the girl had been missing for three days.

Goose bumps broke out all over her body as she read her mother's reply to speculation that the girl had run away. "Ellie is a straight A student. She volunteers as a Candy Striper at the hospital." The statements from Ellie's friends matched those of her parents, describing her as a nice girl, a studious girl, not big into partying.

No one who knew her could point to anything in her life that would motivate her to run away. "Ellie's really tight with her parents," said one friend. "Running away isn't something she would do."

Kate took the article and went back into the townhouse. Within minutes she had her laptop going and had logged into the St. Anthony's Web site to access the comprehensive database of missing persons.

It took her only a few seconds to pull up Ellie's record. And to find out the young girl's fate.

Her throat tightened as she looked at the field marked "Status." It was filled with the single word: "Deceased."

Kate brought up her Web browser and did a search on Ellie Cantrell, which led to thousands of results. Kate clicked on the headline that read "Missing Omaha Teen's Body Found."

Thirteen days after her disappearance, Ellie Cantrell's body had been found in a shallow grave in a wooded area less than five miles from her house. The cause of death, Kate read, her eyes burning with unshed tears, appeared to be blunt force trauma to the head and face, though final determination would be known after the autopsy.

She'd been beaten to death.

Kate clicked back to the results page and then followed the links through to half a dozen follow-up articles. The medical examiner's report revealed that she'd also been sexually assaulted. Though it came as no surprise, it nauseated Kate nonetheless.

But even more interesting were the reports that authorities believed Ellie's case was connected to at least three others in Colorado, Utah, and Montana. Kate pulled up all of the information they could find on the man the press had dubbed the Bludgeoner.

All were pretty girls between the ages of fourteen and seventeen. All were good students who enjoyed active social lives but weren't described as partiers. Not the kind of girls to put themselves in risky situations.

No arrest was ever made, but the FBI did question Arthur Dorsey of Ogden, Utah. Two days after he was taken in for questioning, Dorsey hanged himself. When they found a baseball bat with traces of blood matching one of the victims among Dorsey's personal possessions, the FBI quickly concluded he was responsible for the murders.

The strongest evidence was that no cases with similar patterns were flagged after his death.

Dorsey was described as a loner who, despite the fact that he was well educated, had no permanent residence. He worked as a carpenter and a handyman, moving from place to place as the mood struck him.

He'd been placed in all of the victims' cities near the time of their abductions and deaths.

Kate's stomach knotted as she read how it was believed Dorsey targeted his victims and stalked them for several days, even weeks, before he took them. Learning their patterns, finding out where they went, when they were likely to be alone and vulnerable.

Just as Tricia's stalker had monitored her.

Dorsey was dead. But that knowledge didn't stop the hairs on the back of her neck from prickling or the warning twist in her gut that told her she needed to pay very close attention to this.

Kate grabbed her phone and without thinking dialed Tommy's number. It didn't even occur to her that she should call CJ first until Tommy's curt greeting crackled across the line. "Kate."

Kate didn't bother with any social niceties and quickly filled Tommy in on the envelope, the news story, and the connection to the other missing girls. "All of them were murdered roughly two weeks after being taken," she said. "He beat them to death."

"And you think there's a connection? It says here the guy they think did it hanged himself." Of course Tommy had logged on and pulled up the information faster than she could speak.

"Someone obviously wants me to think so, if they left the article on my car."

"What does CJ think?"

Kate was glad Tommy couldn't see her cheeks flush as she admitted, "I haven't called him yet."

As Tommy was silent for a few seconds, Kate blurted, "Ibarra comes up before Kovac in my contact list."

His soft grunt told her he could smell the bullshit through the phone line. "I'll be over in ten. I'll call CJ on the way and have him meet us."

"Shouldn't we go to the sheriff's station?"

"I want to see if there's any way we can figure out who left you that note. In the meantime, don't handle it any more than you need to."

Right. If the person who left the note was serious about

keeping his or her identity a secret, there weren't likely to be any prints, but it was worth a try.

Kate hung up, and while she waited for the guys to arrive, she pulled up everything she could find on the Cantrell case.

The FBI had been brought in after Ellie Cantrell's murder. She was the third victim, and by that time there was an unmistakable pattern: Girl is kidnapped on her way home from a normal activity in the early evening. Ten days to two weeks later, the body is found in a shallow grave close to the victim's house.

Dorsey was questioned after it was uncovered that he'd worked on construction sites close to all four of the victims. His mother protested loudly that her son wasn't capable of such heinous crimes, that any evidence against him was purely coincidental. She'd even gone so far as to try to sue the FBI agent in charge of the investigation for driving her son to suicide.

Despite her efforts, the media widely believed Dorsey was the killer.

The families of the victims agreed, even when another set of fingerprints was found on the bat in Dorsey's rented room. "Investigating a dead man isn't going to bring my daughter back," said one father from Billings, Montana. "The monster who killed my little girl is rotting in hell. The only way I'd feel better was if I'd sent him there myself."

But as the note on her desk caught her eye, Kate couldn't help wondering if maybe Arthur Dorsey's mother had been on to something.

Chapter 10

Nine and a half minutes after he'd hung up the phone, Tommy was knocking on Kate's door. He called himself five thousand kinds of idiot as his skin seemed to tighten in anticipation at the sound of her footsteps approaching the door.

He couldn't stop his breath from hitching for a split second before she opened it, as if he were bracing himself for the first sight of her of the day. And God help him if he didn't feel a little sucker-punched as he met her anxious blue eyes as she ushered him inside.

"There's the note." Kate gestured to the desk. Tommy nodded, set his laptop case on the floor, and tried not to notice the creamy length of her legs stretching out from the hem of her shorts or the soft curve of her breasts pressing against the thin cotton of her long-sleeve T-shirt.

Tommy pulled a pair of latex gloves out of his pocket and walked over to examine it.

"You always carry those around?" Kate said, eyeing his hands suspiciously as he picked up the typewritten note.

He cocked an eyebrow at her, and no matter how much common sense told him not to flirt, not to tease, not to react with anything but complete indifference, he couldn't stop himself from saying "Latex comes in handy. I always make sure I'm carrying."

He could tell she caught his meaning from the magenta stain in her cheeks. It took a force of will to keep the smile from his face. Goddamn, he'd forgotten how much fun it was to make her blush, make her eyes drift silently to the floor. With her red-gold hair spilling over her shoulder, her cheeks pink, she didn't look a day older than that sixteen-year-old he'd loved to tease.

She'd been so innocent then, it hadn't taken much.

That it didn't take much more now sent his thoughts drifting in a wholly inappropriate direction, such as wondering exactly how innocent she still was. How many lovers had she had in the past fourteen years, and did they make her skin get that rosy flush all over?

He shoved the thought away and along with it the acid burn that accompanied the thought of another man touching her, running his hands over her smooth, pale skin..."Where's your car?" he asked, a little too gruffly, judging by the startled look she gave him.

"Out front."

He followed her out the door and about halfway down the block where she'd parked her rental. "It was tucked under the windshield when I came out this morning."

"You didn't hear or see anything unusual." It wasn't a question. He doubted anyone else had seen anything either. The townhouses were popular rentals, being both on the lake and close to downtown, and also cheaper to rent than the larger lakeside houses. Dozens of people were in and out at all hours of the day, and anyone could have waited till Kate parked and went inside and slipped the envelope under the wiper without being remarked on.

He cursed under his breath, kicking himself for not trying harder to convince the owners to install security cameras. Two years ago Tommy had installed a new alarm system across all the units after several homes nearby had been broken into. But the owner had balked at the cost of a state-of-the-art video surveillance system, and Tommy hadn't been able to get him to budge.

All it would have taken was one street-facing camera, and they might be able to see who was passing Kate the information. But unless that person made him- or herself known, his identity would remain a mystery. Along with the motivation for writing the note.

The skin of his shoulders pulled tight at the thought of someone watching her, tracking her moves without her knowing, of possibly leaving the note to fuck with her. He'd always had that protective instinct when it came to her. Apparently it was still there, no matter how many years had passed or how much damage they'd managed to do to each other.

They went back upstairs and Kate showed him all the material she'd found online about the cases.

Tommy scanned through several articles. "You realize someone could just be doing this to mess with you."

Kate nodded. "Of course. But something in my gut is telling me we need to pay attention to it." Tommy nodded and took his own laptop out of his bag. He was damned familiar with the feeling, and most of the times he'd gotten in trouble was when he'd ignored it.

Except, he reminded himself, for the summer when his gut convinced him that beautiful, innocent, too-young-for-him Kate was the only girl in the world for him.

So much for his gut, but he had to agree that the Bludgeoner case begged for more investigation.

By the time CJ showed up with his own stack of papers, Tommy had managed to access information from the state and local law enforcement systems where the victims had lived and also had a copy of Dorsey's interrogation transcript and the report from the medical examiner who'd done his autopsy.

"You got the files?" Kate asked, her voice eager as CJ put his papers in the middle of the small dining table.

"This is what they could send electronically," CJ said. "The rest will have to be pulled and sent hard copy. And there's no guarantee we'll get all of it."

"I'm just glad you still have enough friends in the Bureau to have access to this," Tommy said. "I may be the best, but hacking into the FBI's files is something I like to save for only the most special occasions."

Kate gave a little snort but didn't say anything.

"I don't think my limited influence would get you very far if you got caught," CJ said. "I had to call in most of my favors just to access these files, and to be honest, I'm not convinced it was worth it. Tying Tricia's disappearance to a serial case closed ten years ago just doesn't make sense."

"It made sense to whoever left me that note," Kate pointed out.

"Any whack job with access to a computer and a printer can leave you a note," CJ retorted.

"Well, on the bright side," Tommy broke in, "if it is the same guy who has Tricia, and he's holding to his pattern, we probably have an entire week until he snaps and beats her to death."

They pulled out chairs around the dining table and started sifting through the files, searching for any kernel of information that might link these cases to Tricia's.

"It says here that there was some argument over whether Dorsey committed suicide," Tommy said as he read through the medical examiner's report. "One of the assistant medical examiners questioned whether the abrasions on Dorsey's neck were consistent with the type of rope he used."

"Did he suspect foul play?" CJ asked.

"All it says here is that the assistant thought it was worth additional investigation. Who knows? Maybe the real killer set Dorsey up to take the fall and faked his suicide."

"That sounds a little far-fetched," CJ said.

"Oh, trust me. Stranger things have happened. Remember my friend Sean?"

Kate half listened to their conversation as she pored over the pages. She was at once nauseated yet unable to look away. *You have to keep it together*, she kept reminding herself. *You deal with this kind of thing every day. You're strong. Stuff like this doesn't shock you anymore.*

Yet as she read paragraph after paragraph of the injuries inflicted on Stephanie Adler, the girl thought to be the Bludgeoner's second victim, she couldn't keep the horror at bay. Couldn't imagine how terrifying and unbearably painful the last minutes of her life must have been.

How excruciating it was for her parents to learn that their child was not only dead but that she'd died an agonizing death.

She swallowed hard and flipped the page, only to lock eyes on a picture that sent her hurtling over the edge. It was a close-up picture of Stephanie's face, so battered her parents had to identify her by a unique birthmark on her right thigh. Her skin was a cold gray where it wasn't mottled with dark bruises. Her nose, once small and turned up at the tip, had been broken so badly it looked like a blob of clay stuck to her skin. Her cheekbones had been crushed. Finger-shape bruises ringed her throat, but that wasn't what killed her.

The medical examiner had determined that the cause of death was from repeated blows to her face and head with a heavy object, eventually damaging her brain so badly that her frontal lobe had been virtually turned to soup.

Kate had seen evidence of worse, done to younger victims, but telling herself that didn't stop her vision from swimming, didn't stifle the sensation that if she didn't get out, now, she was likely to claw out her own eyes to avoid seeing another gruesome image, reading about another vile act.

She sucked in a shaky breath and put the photos aside for a moment to read the details in the medical examiner's report. It took a moment for her to focus on the small print, but soon she was able to absorb additional evidence the body revealed.

Thin cut on the victim's neck, most likely left by a chain or necklace. Likely inflicted as assailant twisted the chain tightly around the victim's neck. Kate absently lifted her fingers to her own throat, feeling her own skin tingle at the imagined sting of a chain digging into her neck. The wounds were consistent with those found on the other bodies.

Also in keeping with the other victims, Stephanie had been found with the residue of a skin cream with an iridescent ingredient that gave the girls' skin a subtle sparkle. What kind of sick monster coated his victims' skin in sparkly skin cream before killing them?

She skimmed down and was about to turn the page when her gaze locked on a piece of evidence that wasn't included in the other victims' reports.

She didn't realize she'd made a sound but suddenly Tommy and CJ were both there, peering over her shoulder.

"What?" Tommy asked.

Kate licked her suddenly dry lips. It took her a couple of tries to get the words out. "Beaute D'or," she finally managed, and was met by confused grunts. "The skin cream. Stephanie Adler had enough of it on her skin that they were able to identify the brand. It's this really fancy stuff, with real gold powder mixed in."

"And that freaked you out why?" Tommy said.

Kate closed the folder with shaking hands. "My mom used to use it, and Lauren and I were always sneaking it—we liked the way it made our skin sparkle. So when we turned sixteen she got us our own for our birthday." Silence hung thickly over the room as they absorbed the information.

"You were wearing it that night," Tommy said, his voice tight. "I remember the way..." He cut off his words, and Kate heard his heavy footsteps as he crossed to the window.

It meant nothing, she was sure. "It's just a coincidence," she said, hoping that saying the words aloud would alleviate the tight, tingly feeling creeping up her back and shoulders. "You can get it anywhere, any department store," she said through the tightness in her throat.

But she couldn't stop the roll of nausea as she remembered how she and Lauren had so treasured that little jar of gold-flecked cream, used it so sparingly to make it last. The way she'd so carefully smoothed it on her skin that night, anticipating how Tommy would see it shimmer, touch the silky smoothness himself.

For the victims, it had been just one more step in the killer's sadistic ritual, one more violation as he'd rubbed it over their skin.

She stood abruptly, swaying a little as Tommy and CJ looked up, startled. "I need—I need to get out," she stammered. "I need air."

Fueled by her need as much as the humiliation of having them see her break down, Kate darted for the front door, pausing only long enough to grab her keys, a light jacket, and her cell phone.

She walked quickly, blindly down the sidewalk, ignoring

their calls to stop. "Please don't follow me," she called in a choked voice. "Please, I just need some space."

She didn't check whether they obeyed, just kept going.

Her phone rang several times in a row. Kate powered it off with a twinge of guilt, unable to even have it vibrating in her pocket. She needed to be cut off for a little while.

At home in L.A. she often went on long hikes in the hills to clear her head. Today she instinctively strode to the edge of town where the trails wound their way up into the mountains.

Though she hadn't been there in years, her sneaker-clad feet automatically followed the path she'd taken dozens of times in her youth even as she struggled to clear her mind and pull herself together.

There was no reason for her to fall apart. But she was forced to admit that no matter how she tried to keep the emotions at bay, being here, in this town, working so closely with Tommy and CJ was a constant reminder of Michael, that summer, that night.

Even if she could keep the memories and rough emotions out of her conscious mind, they were there, lurking. Like toxins seeping into her system, slowly eating away at her, sapping her strength until she broke.

The trail angled up sharply and Kate charged up it as though the hounds of hell were chasing her, as though she could purge the weakness and the sadness from her body through her sweat and fast-moving breath.

And tears, she realized as she felt them rolling down her cheeks.

She walked for miles, barely noticing their passing. As she sifted through her memories of this trail, she guessed she was about four miles from the townhouse, about three and a half miles from where she'd picked up the trail. She crested the ridge where the trail topped out and looked at the mountains surrounding her and the gorgeous view of the lake.

She took a deep breath, feeling somewhat better. The hike had its usual effect of calming her down, taking her mind away, reminding her that even in a world where people could be so ugly, there was still an awful lot of beauty.

She continued over the ridge, remembering that there was another fork she could take up ahead that would loop her down and around and back to town.

She felt a twinge of unease as she watched a bank of gunmetal gray thunderheads moving in from the south. Soon the wind picked up, whipping her hair around and cutting through the thin cover of her jacket.

When she'd left the house, the sun had been shining and the temperature had been in the high seventies. Now it felt like it had dropped at least fifteen degrees. Kate quickened her pace to a jog as goose bumps broke out over her bare legs.

She was only a few miles out of town, and it was all downhill. If she ran, surely she could make it back before the storm hit. Her gaze drifted to the other trail going off to the right, the one that, if she remembered correctly, met up with the fire road in less than a mile. Then it was only another mile back to town. Every cell in her body revolted at the thought. She wouldn't take that trail if someone held a gun to her head.

Because to get to the fire road, she would have to pass a hunting shack, the same shack where Michael—

A bolt of lightning streaked down from the sky, so close it made Kate's hair stand on end. The boom that accompanied was so loud she felt the concussion through her entire body.

—m—

Tommy stared out his wall of windows. He never got tired of watching the weather change in the summer, the way the heavy dark clouds would blow in over the mountain with stunning speed. The thunder and lightning that accompanied it was better than any pyrotechnic display he'd ever seen.

The rain came down in sheets, streaming down the panes. He opened them, and some of the water leaked through the screens onto the floor of his office. He didn't care, closing his eyes to inhale the smell of wet dirt and grass, the electricity of the storm giving the air a slightly metallic edge.

During his time as a Ranger, he'd been deployed twice to Iraq. Baking in the desert sun, every inch of his body coated in a fine layer of sand that never seemed to wash away, he'd spent hours, days, fantasizing about the summer thunderstorms in his mountain home. But today the storm didn't soothe him. Not when he couldn't get the image of Kate's pale, pinched face as she fled from the townhouse out of his head.

Seeing her distress so close to the surface conjured up all kinds of urges he didn't want to deal with, like the urge to pull her close, chase all her demons away.

But he also knew from experience that sometimes when you got to that state, the last thing you wanted was company or comfort. Sometimes you just needed to get away as fast and far as you could and have a little breathing room before you dove back into reality.

He'd forced himself to let her go, and they'd stayed at her place a little while longer before CJ got called away to deal with a situation thirty miles away. Tommy packed up and went back to his own home to make phone calls and put out several fires that had flared with the other clients he'd been ignoring.

And, if he was going to be honest with himself, after looking at those crime scene photos, reading the reports of what those girls had been through, and discovering the random coincidence with the skin cream, he was ready for a breather too. Helping a client come up with a strategy to identify the corporate spy in his research and development lab had been a welcome distraction.

But after another hour passed without a word, he called the volunteer headquarters, praying Kate had turned up. Tension curled in his gut when they said there had been no sign of her.

The next call was to CJ. "Have you heard from Kate?"

"No. Not since she left," CJ said.

"Maybe she's back at her place and just not answering the phone," Tommy said.

"I'll get someone to drive over and check," CJ said, his own voice tight with unease.

The next ten minutes crawled by as Tommy waited for CJ to call back. His adrenaline spiked at CJ's next words. "Her place is empty, and her car is still out front."

"She's probably fine," Tommy said, as if that could stop the voice screaming in his head to find her now. Christ, the worst-case scenario was that she was caught out in the rain somewhere.

Lightning crackled in the meadow outside his window, and a boom of thunder vibrated through the house, as though to drive home the point that this wasn't just a little rain shower they were experiencing.

"I'm still over in LaClede," CJ said.

"I'll find her." Tommy was already off the phone before CJ could say another word.

In an instant, he was in mission mode, all fear shoved aside for clear, cold rationality. Kate had her phone with her. As long as the battery wasn't dead, finding her would be easy.

A few minutes, a few clever keystrokes into her cell phone service provider's Web site, and he was able to pull up a map with a little blue dot that showed the location of Kate's phone and presumably Kate herself.

He took one look at the map and swore.

He shoved away from the desk and headed for his bedroom, where he stuffed a couple of shirts, sweatpants, and fleece jacket into a backpack. Then he pulled a waterproof GORE-TEX shell over his T-shirt and cargo pants and headed out for his truck.

—᙮᙮᙮—

The rain was falling so hard and so heavily Kate could barely see. It didn't help that once she got over the ridge, the trail maintenance tapered off dramatically. While she knew generally the direction she needed to head, several times she'd found herself off the trail, bushwhacking her way through thickets of chokecherry trees and sagebrush. Her bare legs stung with dozens of cuts and welts.

And she was cold. Mind-numbingly, bone-jarringly cold. Her jacket didn't have a hood so her hair was soaked, strands clinging to her neck in sopping ropes. Not that a hood would have helped, she grumbled to herself. The damn thing was so flimsy it didn't offer up the least defense to the cutting wind, and the so-called water-resistant fabric proved to be anything but.

She was soaked to the skin, her entire body shaking with cold as she struggled back to the narrow dirt line she hoped was the trail. Lightning continued to brighten the sky around her, making her heart pound with as much fear as exertion. This section of trail, coming down from the ridge, was all grass and shrubs, leaving Kate the tallest object for several hundred yards. Once she found the trail, she kept her head down, walking as fast as she could toward the outcropping of trees on the other side of the meadow. With the wind and rain whipping in her ears, her gaze intently locked on the trail in front of her, she didn't hear the male voice calling her name until she was only a few feet away.

"Kate!" the voice shouted.

She looked up, shocked, to see a man standing in front of her. Even with the hood of his navy-colored shell shadowing his face, Kate recognized Tommy instantly. There was no mistaking the broad span of his shoulders, the way every muscle was coiled for action.

"What are you doing here?" she yelled above the rain.

He let out a harsh laugh. "Saving a clueless tourist from freezing to death or getting struck by lightning. Come on, we've got to get out of this." He grabbed her hand and tucked her behind him so he bore the brunt of the wind and rain. Under other circumstances she might have questioned the wisdom of getting too close to Tommy Ibarra, but right now she reveled in the warmth that soaked through her palm where it was pressed against his. She pushed herself as close to his back as she could get without tripping both of them.

His pace was quick, much faster than hers as the trail that had so confounded her seemed to reveal itself to him. Within a few minutes, they were in the relative shelter of a grove of pine trees.

She followed him silently, too tired and cold to speak as he led her through the woods. After about half a mile the trail forked and the terrain opened up. Once again they were completely exposed.

Kate bit back a protest when Tommy took the fork going to the right. Even though every cell in her body recoiled. The shack wasn't visible yet, but Kate knew it was there, just over the rise in front of them.

A voice in her head screamed at her to jerk her hand out of Tommy's hold and flee in the opposite direction. But she knew the safest thing to do was to follow him. She would have to pass the shack, yes, but Tommy's truck was no doubt parked on the fire road just a couple hundred yards beyond. She forced herself to focus on the warm grip of his hand on hers, his size and strength, as though that could protect her from everything, even her own horrible memories.

They came up over the rise. Kate squeezed her eyes shut and burrowed her head harder against Tommy's back, determined not to look.

Lightning flashed to her right, turning her vision red behind her closed eyes. Tommy's swear was muffled by the accompanying thunder. The wind picked up again, whipping so fiercely now Kate knew she wouldn't be able to see even with her eyes open. Tommy sped up the pace and Kate forced her frozen body to keep up, knowing the faster they moved, the faster she'd be in Tommy's truck with the heater going full blast.

Tommy stopped and Kate stumbled into him, confused. Though she hadn't hiked these trails in years, she didn't think they'd been moving fast enough to make it to the road.

She realized, as she opened her eyes, her stomach twisting with dread, that they hadn't.

Instead of leading her to the road, Tommy had led her right to the shack. The greenish gray structure was humble but sturdy and gave no clue to the horror that had happened inside one long-ago summer night.

Kate shook her head, a litany of nos falling from her frozen lips. She didn't even realize she was backing up until she stumbled and would have fallen on her butt had Tommy not wrapped his hand around her arm at the last second.

He pulled her against him, bent his lips close to her ear. "Kate, I know you don't want to go in there," he said in a low, soothing tone she hadn't heard him use in fourteen years. Now it did little to calm her. "I don't either," he continued, "but we have to get out of this storm."

As though to prove his point, a bolt of lightning rocketed down not ten yards away and buried itself in the stump of a cottonwood tree. The smell of charred wood and ozone filled the air.

"No," Kate said again. "The road is right past it. I remember—"

Tommy shook his head. "There was a washout two years back and the road was never repaired. My truck is parked almost two miles away."

Every muscle in her body cried out in protest. Still, she shook her head. "I can't," she choked. She squeezed her eyes closed but couldn't shut out the images of Michael, slumped against the wall, his T-shirt soaked with blood from where the bullet from Emerson Flannery's gun had slammed into his narrow chest.

Tommy cupped her face in his hands and tilted her head back to meet his gaze. "I know, Kate, I know what it's like," he said, his dark, deep-set eyes burning with emotion. "I once had to stay in a four-by-four cave for eight hours after a buddy of mine got his head blown off. I had to do it, because it was the only thing that was going to keep me safe. And you're going to do this. I know you; you're strong enough."

Kate started to shake her head then winced as she was suddenly pummeled by what felt like dozens of icy marbles.

Hail. Hurling down on them in chunks varying in sizes from BBs to golf balls.

You have to suck it up, she told herself. *It's just a building where something very bad happened.*

Squaring her shaking shoulders, she brushed by Tommy to the front door of the hunting cabin and shoved it open.

Chapter 11

Tommy couldn't suppress the surge of pride he felt as Kate walked through the doorway of the shack.

He knew how hard it must have been for her to step inside. He hadn't been lying about being trapped in a cave with the body of one of his best friends. He knew what it took to resist the urge to run in a situation like this. And though she did a good job of keeping up a resilient front, he knew how much she'd loved her brother.

Being forced to enter the scene of his murder was like torture. But he didn't see much choice. If it had just been rain, he could have run the two miles with Kate on his back, no problem, and he would have warmed her up in the truck.

But the lightning storm that raged outside made a run too risky.

He closed the door behind him and shrugged off his dripping shell. The high-tech waterproof fabric had done its job. Though his pants were soaked from midthigh down, his long-sleeve T-shirt was bone dry.

Kate, in contrast, stood shivering in the center of the small cabin, rainwater dripping off to form a puddle around her feet. The dirty windows didn't let in much light, but he could see her shiver, her face ghost pale as she kept her gaze fixed to a spot on the floor.

Any admiration for her courage evaporated as he took in her sorry state, anger flaring at her for being so foolish to put herself at such risk.

"What the hell were you thinking, Kate?" he asked sharply as he flung his backpack onto a tattered wicker chair and yanked out the dry T-shirt and fleece jacket he'd packed. "I know you haven't been here for a while, but you know better than to go out in the mountains without the right gear." He tossed the shirt and fleece at her. "Put these on."

"I d-d-didn't kn-know I w-w-would be out this long," she said, struggling to close her violently trembling fingers around the zipper tab of her useless jacket.

"It doesn't matter if you go out for five minutes or five hours," he snapped. "You know how quickly the weather changes here. For Christ's sake, you were here the summer those hikers got caught in a blizzard the first week of August!" His voice was raised, too loud for the tiny space, but he couldn't help it. Not when his brain was spinning with images of Kate, her slender body blue with cold. And hell, the cold was just the start. She could have been crushed under a limb of a tree blown down in the high winds. "Dammit, Kate, you're lucky you didn't get struck by lightning and turned into a charcoal briquette."

"I know!" she cried. "And I'm sorry I wasn't exactly thinking about the weather when I left. I made a stupid move, and I'm sorry you had to be inconvenienced!"

An idea flared in his head with a way for her to pay him back, sending a rush of heat through him that chased away any chill that might have settled into his skin.

Kate, however, was another story. Lips blue, convulsing with cold, so far she'd only managed to take off her jacket.

"You need to get out of those wet clothes," Tommy said hoarsely.

"I'm trying," she said through chattering teeth. Her shirt clung to her like a second skin, outlining the soft curves of her breasts and slim line of her waist.

Tommy's mouth went dry as he caught the outline of her nipples poking through, the cold pulling them into hard little points. Another shudder and she lost her grip on the hem of the T-shirt. Cursing, Tommy walked the two steps to her side and yanked the shirt up over her head, leaving her naked from the waist up except for the cream silk and lace contraption that passed for a bra.

He knew better than to look, but his gaze locked on her breasts as though drawn there by a tractor beam. His cock instantly thickened at the sight.

The silky fabric had gone all but transparent, and through it Tommy could make out creamy skin and the deep pink of her nipples. Lust hit him like a punch to his gut. His hands itched at the memory of her soft skin under his hands, the firm buds of her nipples between his fingers.

He wanted to peel the straps down her shoulders, push the filmy fabric aside, and run his tongue inside the soft curves before he took her into his mouth, sucking and licking until she moaned with need.

Instead he tore his gaze away and shoved the dry T-shirt at her. "You probably want to take the bra off too," he said, his voice sounding thick. "You'll get the shirt wet otherwise."

She nodded shakily, turned her back to him, and reached for the back closure on her bra. It took her three tries but she finally managed to unhook it, Tommy noted with relief.

If he'd had to undo it for her, he couldn't be held responsible for what happened next.

As it was, he was practically shaking with lust as his eyes locked on the slender line of her back, the deep curve of her waist, the lush curve of her ass filling out the shorts that clung damply to her curves.

She pulled the dry T-shirt over her head and the throaty sound of pleasure that came from her made him feel like she'd reached out and cupped his balls.

Over that went the fleece, and then Tommy handed her the sweats.

She thanked him and again turned her back, shifting a little as she reached up under the layers of cotton and fleece to fumble with the button and zipper of her shorts. *Look away*, he told himself. *Look the fuck away*.

Yeah, fat chance. Kate Beckett was undressing in front of him and there was no way in hell he was missing it.

Though he couldn't see anything with both his T-shirt and the fleece hanging nearly to her knees, that didn't stop his cock from rearing to full attention as Kate shoved the shorts down her legs. Tommy followed them hungrily down the sleek, pale length of her legs. The fact that they were covered in scratches and bristling with goose bumps didn't stop him from imagining how they'd feel wrapped around his waist.

He put a mental clamp on that image, reminding himself of the thousand or so reasons why it was a bad idea for him to let any woman—but especially Kate—get under his skin. He tore his gaze from the smooth lines of her calves and focused on the floor, only to have it snag on the crumpled mound of her shorts. And there, peeking out of the mound of olive green, was a scrap of cream-colored silk edged in lace.

Jesus Christ.

He jerked his gaze back up as she dragged the sweatpants on and ordered himself to get a fucking grip.

"Better?" he asked.

Kate nodded and wrapped her arms around herself, her

body still shaking with cold. His clothes were ridiculously large on her, hiding every inch of her slim curves. Her hair hung in wet ropes over her shoulder, and her lips were tinged grayish blue.

She should have looked ridiculous, comical even. There was nothing about her appearance right now that should be filling Tommy's head with fantasies that started with him peeling off the yards of fabric and ended with him sliding himself as hard and deep inside her as he could possibly get.

He bit out a curse and stalked across the small dirt floor. Desperate to get away from her, impossible though it was in the tight quarters. Even across the room, he couldn't escape the floral scent of her damp hair, combined with the smell of his own laundry soap from the clothes she wore.

His clothes, which she was wearing with not even a thin barrier of underwear between the fabric and her skin.

Was it possible for a man to be jealous of a pair of sweatpants?

He scrubbed at the dirt-encrusted window and peered outside, willing the storm to let up enough so they could make a break for it.

Lightning crackled and the rain crashed harder on the wood-shingled roof, taunting him.

"How long do you think it will last?" Kate asked, her voice still shaky.

Tommy turned and faced her. "Hard to tell. Usually these things blow over quickly, but sometimes the storms get caught on one side of the mountain."

But even if the lightning stopped in the next five minutes, Kate was in no way ready to go back into the elements, he acknowledged grimly. She perched on a rickety bench that fronted an equally rickety-looking table, her knees folded into her chest and her arms wrapped around them. Still, there was no way he could miss the way her body still convulsed with cold.

He knew that kind of cold, how it could settle into your bones and wrack your body until nothing short of a steaming shower or some quality time in front of a roaring fire could warm you. Since he was lacking both, he came to the unfortunate realization that he was going to have to take matters into his own hands.

He took a deep, bracing breath. He could do this. He'd spent the last fourteen years learning how to push away all emotions and keep an iron grip on his baser urges. He didn't let anything rule him.

He damn sure wasn't going to be felled by a hundred fifteen pounds of damp, freezing woman, no matter how badly she could fry his circuits with one soft look of her blue eyes, one innocent flick of her tongue across that plump mouth.

Bracing himself as if for battle, he marched over to Kate. Ignoring her startled look, he snatched her up in his arms, sat back down on the bench, and settled her into his lap, his arms wrapped tight around her.

—◆◆◆—

Kate didn't think she was ever going to get warm. The piles of fleecy fabric Tommy had brought offered some relief, but even as she sat huddled in on herself, it wasn't enough. She was still shivering so hard it was as if she were having a seizure. And though the dilapidated shack bore no evidence of the violence that had occurred here, the thought of what had happened sent a wave of cold through her that had nothing to do with the icy rain that had soaked her.

Tommy's attitude didn't help, his tension rippling off him in waves, his body language conveying quite clearly that he would rather be anywhere in the world than stuck here with her.

So why was her head suddenly full of long-forgotten memories of the way he smiled at her, the way he laughed at her? The way he made her feel so special and wanted with a mere look.

Seeing him now, every muscle pulled tight across the back turned to her, the grim look he wore, it was hard to believe that boy she knew ever existed. The life he'd lived in the last decade and a half had stripped all the light out of him. Stripped away any hint of softness.

It had started with Michael's death, she knew. But more had happened since then. Things she would never know.

And the fault for that was squarely on her shoulders, she knew. If she hadn't let her father take away Tommy's scholarship, would he have joined the military, seen and done the things that had morphed him into the hardened warrior he'd become?

She'd never know. She'd lost that right the moment she decided to side with her father and keep the truth to herself.

She saw him shift in the corner of her eye and looked up, startling when she saw him headed straight toward her, his mouth pulled into a grim, determined line.

She wasn't sure what she was expecting, but it wasn't for him to pull her up off the bench like she weighed nothing and settle her into his lap.

She stiffened for a second, but any thought of discomfort fled at the delicious warmth that seeped through the heavy fabric of her borrowed clothes. It didn't seem possible given how chilled she was, but immediately everywhere her body touched his began to pulse with heat.

She burrowed closer, tucking her hands between their bodies and burying her head against the wall of his chest.

His arms wrapped around her, warmer than a down comforter, and she could feel the heat of his palms through the layers of clothing as they swept up and down her back.

Within minutes her tremors stopped, her teeth quit their chattering as the heat of him radiated through her skin and pulsed in her blood. She became acutely, intensely aware of him, his huge, muscular arms wrapped around her, the spicy, musky scent of him.

She opened her eyes, flicking them up from his chest to the hard, tan column of his neck. Her lips tingled at the memory of trailing soft, sucking kisses down its length. Her mouth watered at the remembered salty taste of his skin on her tongue.

Cheeks flooding with heat, she forced the thoughts from her head. Whatever chemistry might linger between them, he'd made it more than clear he wasn't interested in any replay of the past.

She wasn't ready to separate herself from her human furnace, but this position was too close, too intimate, too reminiscent of the times she'd draped herself over his hard body and explored the hard planes, starting at his neck, trailing across his shoulders, down his chest but never going any farther.

Too shy and inexperienced to give him the pleasure they both craved.

She shifted, turning in his arms to try to face outward.

Tommy let out a sharp grunt and tightened his arms around her. "Dammit, will you stop squirming around like that?"

"Sorry," she snapped, shifting again, "I'm just trying to get more comfortable—" Every muscle froze as her butt ground into the cradle of his hips.

She swallowed hard, her entire body flushing as she felt

the unmistakable heat and hardness of him pressed into the flesh of her hip.

"Shit," he breathed, barely audible.

"It's okay," she said, her voice high and annoyingly breathy. "I know it's just friction, like a reflex."

"Yeah," he said, his voice crackling with an electric heat that drew her eyes up like a magnet. His own were so full of heat she was surprised her borrowed clothes didn't start to smoke. "Just reflex."

In the next breath his mouth was covering hers, his big hand cupping the back of her head, holding her still for his kiss.

Kate's lips parted eagerly at the first thrust of his tongue. She'd told herself she imagined it, that her memories of kissing Tommy Ibarra had been exaggerated, overblown. Her brain, soaked in the throes of first lust, followed by the worst trauma she'd ever known, had infused the memories of that summer with a kind of intensity that couldn't have existed.

She couldn't have been more wrong, and the realization shook her to the core. Her memories of Tommy's kiss, his touch, didn't come close to what she was feeling now. It was like being thrust into a vortex full of heat and light, where nothing mattered but the taste of him, the soft rasp of his tongue against hers as he tasted every corner of her mouth. She opened her mouth wider, pressed her lips harder, sucked his tongue into her mouth like she was starving for the taste of him.

This. This was the reason she'd broken the rules, defied her father, been willing to give Tommy anything and everything he wanted, even if he was too much of a gentleman to ask for it.

He wasn't a gentleman now, cupping his hands under her ass and shifting her so her knees fell on either side of his thighs, straddling him. A harsh, animal sound came from his throat as she settled against him, her gasp echoing his as the rock-hard column of his erection pushed against her core.

She twined her arms around his neck, threaded her fingers through the thick silk of his hair as she rocked against him. A hollow ache opened up inside her, a soul-deep hunger she'd only ever felt with Tommy. That feeling that made her fingers clutch and her lips devour, as if she could never get enough.

Desire was a tight knot between her legs. Every brush of his body against hers made that knot pulse, pulling the muscles of her belly tight. She loved the way he touched her, his strong fingers curled into the slim curve of her hips, holding her tight, pressing her closer.

One hand stole up under the hem of her shirt, and she moaned against the silky skin of his throat, at the feel of his callused palm against the bare skin of her back, around to her rib cage, sliding up to swallow up the curve of her breast.

Another cry bubbled up from her throat as his thumb brushed the tight point of her nipple. The soft touch sent a rush of heat and wetness between her legs, the pleasure pulling so tight it bordered on pain.

The storm, the surroundings, the bone-jarring cold, everything fell away. There was nothing in her world but heat and need and that endless hollow ache that was created by Tommy, his touch, his taste, and could only be soothed by the same.

"Tommy," she whispered, taking the lobe of his teeth between her teeth. "Tommy," she repeated, in that single word telling him everything she needed.

He groaned and started to pull the hem of her shirt up her back. Kate felt a strange vibration against her inner thigh.

Tommy stilled. "Son of a bitch, what the hell am I doing,"

he muttered, pushing Kate back so he could fumble in the pocket of his cargo pants.

Kate scrambled off his lap, feeling like she'd been doused by a bucket of cold water as Tommy put the phone to his ear.

What was *he* doing? What was *she* doing? was the more important question. She crossed her arms over her chest, willing her body to calm down as she listened to Tommy greet CJ. She closed her eyes and gave silent thanks to her friend, whose phone call had stopped her from doing something very, very stupid.

Though it shamed her to her core to admit it, she knew that if Tommy's phone hadn't started buzzing, Kate would have let him pull her to the floor and have raw, down and dirty sex right there.

In the very place her brother had been murdered.

All traces of desire fled, chased by shame and self-disgust.

And a small dose of fear. Because Tommy had just proven to her that he was just as dangerous to her today as he'd been to a naive sixteen-year-old caught in the throes of her first love.

She swallowed hard, tugged her sweatshirt back in place, and smoothed a hand over her damp hair.

"Yeah, I'm with her right now." His gaze caught hers, and she saw that the flames had disappeared. Once again his expression was flat, hard, as though he hadn't had his hand up her shirt, squeezing her bare breast mere seconds before.

But the hot color slashing his cheekbones told a different story. That and . . : Kate couldn't keep her eyes from drifting down the front of his body to the front of his pants. Her mouth went dry at the sight of him, his erection clearly outlined against the worn fabric.

She quickly turned away. The shack suddenly seemed to shrink in size, the walls squeezing in. There didn't seem to be enough oxygen for both her and the huge, hard man who could steal her reason with one touch of his lips.

She didn't turn around as he ended his phone call. She heard the door open and shivered at the rush of cool, damp air.

"The storm's let up," Tommy said gruffly. "I think it's safe to get moving if you're up to it."

Kate nodded sharply and pulled her shoes on. She followed Tommy out, keeping up with his brisk pace, ignoring the way her shoes were squishing around her feet and rubbing her heels raw.

The urge to address what had happened bubbled up, but every time she opened her mouth to speak she caught herself, the right words never seeming to form.

The silence grew heavier until it felt like a force field between them. Tommy's expression was closed, hard, leaving no doubt to his mood.

Kate climbed silently into his truck. Though her insides were roiling with a mass of confusion and questions, instinct told her to keep them to herself. Trying to talk to Tommy now would be like poking at an angry lion, and she wasn't prepared to handle the claws.

There was nothing to gain by dissecting what had happened. The smartest thing to do was to follow his lead, close herself off, and act like nothing had ever happened.

Chapter 12

The squeak of the hinges made Tricia's blood run cold. Followed by heavy footsteps on the floor. One, two, three, four, five steps to her door.

Going by the sliver of light that appeared and disappeared at the bottom of the boarded-up window across from the bed she was cuffed to, she was in her third full day of captivity. In that short time certain things had been seared into her brain. The squeak of the door hinges. The number of times hard-soled shoes would *thunk* on the floor before she heard the creak of the doorknob.

The feel of his palm exploding across her cheekbone, slamming into her lip.

The door started to ease open, her heart thudding in her chest like a wild bird was trapped inside. A scream bubbled up in her throat, but she held it back. She'd already learned the hard way that wherever she was, it was far enough from others that no one could hear her, no matter how loud she screamed.

The door swung open, and his shape was momentarily backlit by the light in the hallway. But other than a general outline of his body, to her frustration she couldn't make out his features. The room she was in was kept dark, and though he always brought a candle with him, with his hood pulled up over his head and his face obscured by shadows, she was unable to get a clear look at her captor.

Part of her was comforted by this. In movies and books, if the bad guy let a victim see his face, it usually meant he was going to kill her.

The thought was like a drop of gasoline added to the rapidly dwindling flame of hope that he would eventually set her free.

"Hello, sweetheart." His voice called softly through the darkness as he closed the door behind him. The gentle, almost tender tone made her stomach flip with nausea. She heard him shuffling in the darkness, smelled sulfur as he struck a match and lit the candle that sat in the middle of the little table across from the bed.

"Aren't you going to greet me?" Though his tone was still soft, cajoling, now there was an edge to it.

Her lips, swollen and sore from yesterday's beating, pressed mutinously together.

"Tricia," he said, a warning. "You know what will happen if you don't treat me with courtesy and respect."

She wanted to be tough, like Katniss from *The Hunger Games*, and not give in so easily to this sick creep. But fear that he might beat her again, or worse, compelled her to obey. "Hello, sir," she choked through a throat burned raw from her own screams.

"I brought you another special treat," he said, and placed a grocery bag on the table along with a cardboard drink holder with three drink cups nestled inside.

I don't want anything to do with you or any of your treats, freak, she thought, but didn't dare say the words out loud.

She swallowed hard, watching in silence as he removed the cups from their cardboard holder. "I brought you a milk shake from Ike's," he said. His smile gleamed at her from the shadows and did nothing to reassure her. "I wasn't sure what flavor, so I got one of each."

Oh, God, the thought of a strawberry milk shake, cold and sweet on her tongue, made her mouth water and her empty stomach clench. He hadn't fed her in what must have been a couple of days, not since she'd spit the sandwich in his face and gotten the crap beaten out of her.

"I don't like milk shakes," she said, hating the way her voice quavered. She wanted to show him she was strong, defiant, that she would never give in. Instead, she sounded exactly how she felt: tired, weak, and very, very scared.

"Now, now, don't lie." The edge was back, and she didn't miss the way his fingers curled into a fist on the table. "I saw you there just last week with your sister and your father. I heard you tell them it was the best milk shake you'd ever had."

Bile choked her at the thought of this person—no, he wasn't a person, because human beings didn't steal people away, hide them in dark rooms, and punch them repeatedly in the face when they didn't get their way—this awful creep stalking her, watching her, listening to her conversations, and, oh God, being so close to her family.

"I would have brought you another sandwich," he said mildly, "but I figured your jaw was still pretty sore."

Though she couldn't see his eyes, she could feel his stare on her, flat, menacing, so cold it sent a shudder through her.

She realized then what she'd probably known all along. Though her favorite books and movies featured kick-ass heroines who would die before they showed any sign of weakness to their captors, Tricia was *not* a badass.

She could read all she wanted about girls who were trained to protect vampires or play all the war games she wanted on her computer. But when push came to shove, even the self-defense classes her father had insisted she and Brooke take hadn't been any use. She hadn't been able to stop him from grabbing her. She'd fought her hardest, but he'd easily overpowered her.

Though the thought made her empty stomach roil, she realized that if she wanted a chance in hell to survive, she was going to have to be nice to him. "It is sore," she said, rubbing her jaw with her free hand. "Thank you for being so considerate."

She could see the lines of his shoulders soften. "You're welcome, sweetheart. Which flavor? Strawberry, vanilla, or chocolate?"

"Strawberry," she choked out. Followed by "please," when she saw his shadow stiffen. "Please may I have the strawberry one," she added quickly for good measure.

"One strawberry milk shake, coming right up," he said with a weird, childish giggle that made her skin crawl.

He crossed to the bed and handed it to her. She took it in her free hand.

He settled on the edge of the mattress, his head turned away from her as he lifted another of the cups. "Strawberry is my favorite too," he said, as though confiding some wonderful secret. "But I'll settle for chocolate today if it makes you happy."

The nausea roiling in her stomach at his proximity was no match for the hunger that had all but gnawed at her. Her hand shook as she closed her lips over the straw, her eyes closing involuntarily as the sweet, creamy flavor hit her tongue, thick and cold, chasing away the stifling heat of her prison. She sucked it down as fast as she could, ignoring the pain of brain freeze as she savored the delicious cold drink. For a moment, she could pretend that she was magically transported back to Ike's, squabbling with Brooke about whether they should get a pint of vanilla or chocolate to take home.

Like none of this had ever happened.

"All I want is to make you happy," he said softly, and like that Tricia came thudding back to reality. She opened her eyes and saw not the gleaming black-and-white tiles and highly polished wood tables of Ike's but the dark, dirty shadows of her prison.

Stuck here with a man ready to turn on her at any moment.

"You know that, don't you?"

She nodded hesitantly, and the milk shake started to curdle in her stomach. She put it aside.

She forced herself not to flinch as he reached a hand to her face.

Willed herself to sit utterly still, not let any sign of her revulsion show as he traced his fingers over the cheekbone that still throbbed from his blows. "I didn't like having to hurt you. You know that, right? I never want to have to hurt you again."

Tricia nodded again, not sure what he expected her to say.

"When I touch you, I only want you to feel pleasure." His hand moved from her cheek to her hair, stroking down its length in a caress that was eerily tender.

Loverlike.

The milk shake churned in her stomach. Cramps seized her and her mouth filled with saliva as the little she drank threatened to come spewing back up. She forced herself to keep it down, afraid of what he might do if she threw up all over him.

Though another beating would be more welcome than what he had in mind.

"Can—can I go to the bathroom please?" she asked in a

small, shaky voice. "It's been awhile and I really need to." It wasn't a lie. Though he'd limited her water, Tricia's bladder felt like it was about to burst. He'd provided a plastic bin as a bedpan, but the few times Tricia had tried to use it, awkward and one-handed, she'd ended up peeing mostly on the bed and the floor.

His hand froze on her shoulder and he was quiet several seconds. No doubt contemplating if her need was real or a ploy to get away from his unwelcome touch.

"Please," she said, infusing her plea with a desperation she didn't have to fake.

"You were so mad the other day when you had to change the sheets," she said, a shudder going through her at the way he'd berated her when he'd walked in and been hit by the unmistakable odor.

"You're like an animal, wallowing in your filth and stink," he'd said. With her face throbbing and head pounding from the recently delivered beating, it hadn't been hard to bite back a sniping comment that if he'd uncuff her, she might make it to the small bathroom more than once a day.

He nodded and she felt a tremor of relief as he twisted his body and fumbled in his pocket. Forced herself not to scramble when his weight pressed into her as he leaned over to unlock the cuff from the metal bed frame.

Once free, she swung her legs over the side of the bed and scrambled to her feet, only to have her limbs turn to water underneath her.

Her head swam, her vision dipping and diving about the room, her head suddenly fuzzy as she struggled to remember what she was doing, why she was in the dark with a shadowy figure holding her upper arm in an iron-hard grip.

He's drugging me, she thought in a brief moment of clarity as she shuffled across the room at his urging. Something powerful and fast acting, if she was able to feel it so quickly after consuming less than half of her milk shake.

She wavered a little as he pushed the door open to what looked like a small closet, her vision tunneling as she tried to process what was going on.

Right, the bathroom, she remembered, becoming acutely aware of her body's urgent need.

"Go ahead." The voice came out of a void, echoing and bouncing around her head like when she had gas at the dentist's office. He gave her a little shove and pushed her into the small room.

She started to reach for the waistband of her shorts then stopped, the drug not enough to wipe away all shreds of basic modesty and outright revulsion at the thought of taking her pants down in front of this creep.

"Privacy" was all she could get out of lips that felt rubbery and not of her body.

As he had done the last time, he shook his head. "We have to build trust, my love. Until then I have to keep an eye on you."

Hot, embarrassed tears ran down her cheeks as she pulled down her pants and sat on the toilet. He turned his head slightly away. The heat of anger and embarrassment cut through the fog of the drug enough for her to take advantage of the fact that he wasn't watching her closely.

Before, she'd been too terrified, her eyes unused to the dark, to pay any attention to this part of her prison. Now her eyes scanned the shadows eagerly, looking for any means of escape, anything that could be used as a weapon.

The drugs took hold again, swirly gray fog deadening the brief surge of adrenaline. She tried to keep it at bay, her brain struggling to catalog every detail.

"Finish up," he said harshly.

She flushed the toilet and pulled her shorts and under-pants up with clumsy fingers, then let him lead her back to the bed.

She offered her left hand without protest and didn't even flinch at the metallic *snick* of the cuff closing over her wrist.

When she lay back against her pillow, she didn't turn her face away from him when he pulled a chair up to the side of the bed, as though the way he sat there and just stared at her didn't freak her out. The drug tried to pull her under, a leaden gray wave. She tried to fight, one coherent corner of her brain imagining what he could do to her vulnerable, unconscious body.

Panic at the thought made her heart flutter even as she felt like she was floating out of her body. As the last threads of consciousness slipped away, she locked on the one thing that gave her even a shred of hope.

In the bathroom, right next to the vanity, a crack in the floor showed straight through to the dirt outside. If she could get through that floor, she could get to freedom.

All she had to do was convince him to trust her.

Chapter 13

Kate spread the case file in front of her on the table, but after two paragraphs, the words blurred in front of her eyes. She stood up, went into the kitchen and poured herself a glass of water, then went to the living room and switched on the TV, her thumb twitching as she scanned through all five hundred channels in record time and found nothing to hold her interest for more than a few seconds.

Up again, to pace to the window, staring out at the darkness of the lake, the mountains like black, craggy shadows against the night dark sky.

Back to the table, to try to read the police report on Stephanie Adler. The coincidence with the skin cream nagged at her, but there was nothing in the report to show that it was anything more. She read through all of the files again to see if she'd missed something the first several times and found nothing. Twenty minutes later, back on her feet to start another restless cycle.

It had been like this for hours, from the moment she'd returned home. Over Tommy's protests, Kate had insisted he drop her at volunteer headquarters once they got back to town.

She hadn't given her drowned-rat appearance much thought until she ran into the small group of reporters hardy enough to brave the elements huddled under the awning outside.

Still, somehow appearing in the press looking like a drowned cat wearing clothes that threatened to fall off her seemed a better option than having Tommy accompany her back to her place. Alone.

Because even if he apparently had no problem shutting himself off and pretending nothing had happened, Kate had a bad feeling that if he walked her to her door, she would grab him by the collar, drag him inside, and not let him go until he damn well finished what he'd started.

The bad weather had forced them to call off the search parties, and the phone lines were covered through the night. Kate had given in to CJ's urging to go home and get some rest after her stressful afternoon.

And he didn't know the half of it, she thought as she made another foray to the kitchen. Or maybe he did, she thought, remembering the sidelong look he'd given Tommy when he'd met them at the volunteer headquarters.

This time, instead of water, she reached for a bottle of wine, desperate to get rid of the itchy, uneasy feeling that had taken over her body. Like everything was pulled tight, her skin two sizes too small for her body. Maybe a glass of cabernet would help her mellow out.

Half a glass in, she realized her mistake.

The wine took the edge off, sure. But it also sent her defenses crumbling, and now the reason for her restlessness took center stage in her brain.

That kiss.

She walked over to the couch and sank down. This time she didn't turn on the TV. Instead, she took another sip of wine and closed her eyes. Her lips, the tips of her breasts, her entire body tingled at the memory. Of his lips on hers, his hot, callused hands on her skin, closing over her breasts, his long, thick fingers plucking at her nipples.

And, God, the feel of him nestled against her sex. So thick, so hard, leaving no doubt of how much he wanted her. Her own body, hot and wet, leaving no doubt how much she wanted him.

Now the mere memory of it was enough to pull her nipples into hard points against the soft cotton of her tank top, make her sex swell and throb between her legs. She shifted again, trying to will the ache away.

This was not her. This was not how she operated. She'd had lovers—good lovers—but no one had ever made her hot and ready with just a kiss. No one had ever made her ache at the memory of his hands on her skin.

No one but Tommy, a wicked little voice whispered.

She took a sip of her wine, trying to dull the memory of this afternoon's kiss as it melded with all of the kisses and touches they'd shared that summer. How she'd walked around, her body literally aching for him, a giant void of need inside of her that she was convinced only he could fill. An ache she was still too young and scared to fill until that last horrible night.

For fourteen years, she'd convinced herself that the only reason he'd felt so special was because he was the first guy to make her feel real desire.

And that seemed to be true as she went on in life and her true, sexual nature became clear. While she enjoyed sex, there was none of that bone-deep ache for the other's touch, no ravenous craving for the taste of him on her tongue. And none of her handful of skilled lovers had ever made her forget his mouth and hands on her. All it took was the feel of Tommy's lips and hands on her and she was willing to have sex with him right then, right there.

In the very room where her brother was murdered.

Her father was right. There *was* something deeply, terribly flawed in her.

She drained her wine and got up to get a second glass and face the stark reality. No matter what she told herself, Tommy was like her own personal form of meth. Just like the first time, one hit and she was hooked.

Worse, the man she was dealing with now was not the Tommy she'd once fallen in love with.

The nineteen-year-old she'd fallen for was full of laughter and easy smiles, and he looked at her like she'd hung the moon.

This new Tommy, with his hard stares, harder body, and stony silences…Kate was pretty sure he didn't even like her. And judging from his attitude after CJ's call interrupted them, he was pissed as hell that he'd given in to the combustible chemistry that simmered between them.

It was better this way, she reminded herself, even as she felt a pinch of disappointment, and maybe a little hurt, in her chest. She and Tommy had never been anything but trouble for each other, and they had no business stirring up trouble when the stakes were so high.

She started back for the couch. The mellow buzz of the wine didn't do much to soothe the tightness between her legs or in her breasts, but it slowed her thoughts down enough she thought she might be suitably distracted by a movie.

A sharp rap on her front door froze her midstride. She glanced at the clock and frowned, wondering who would come over after nine without calling first.

She headed for the door, setting her glass on the breakfast bar on her way. She leaned up onto her toes to peer through the peephole.

Though the overhead light cast his features in shadow,

there was no mistaking the strong cut of his jaw, the sharpness of his cheekbones, not to mention those acre-wide shoulders.

She flipped the dead bolt, the metallic *thunk* echoing the thud of her heart as it threatened to beat out of her chest. "Tommy," she said as she opened the door, her voice coming out all breathy and raspy. "What are you doing here? Did something happen? Did they find something?" Her stomach plummeted to the floor. *That had to be it*, she thought as she stepped aside and ushered him into the entryway.

There was no other reason for him to be there than to deliver horrible news, too horrible to deliver over the phone. She closed the door and tried to brace herself for the worst.

But Tommy, who stood, arms folded, feet slightly apart, didn't look like a man who was preparing to deliver devastating news. He looked grim, sure, but these days Tommy always looked grim. As she met his gaze, she got that funny feeling she always got with him, like he could see right through her. Like he knew exactly what she was thinking.

Her face went hot at the memory of what she'd been thinking right before he knocked on her door.

"What's going on? Did you find something?" Kate said again.

Tommy shook his head. "Nothing new." His gaze raked her from head to toe, taking in her knit pajama bottoms, her thin tank top. It lingered on the hard points of her nipples pushing against the soft cotton and Kate felt her entire body sizzle.

"Then what are you doing here?"

"I think you know the answer to that."

Before she could react, he closed the distance between them, pulled her to him, and covered her mouth with his.

Kate didn't even think. Her lips parted instinctively to take him in as he thrust his tongue inside.

He kissed her like he wanted to consume her, one hand cupping her head, the other spread against her back, holding her so tight she could barely breathe.

Kate didn't care. Just as before, one touch of his mouth and her entire universe shrank down to this, his lips on hers, the rasp of his tongue against hers, the hard wall of his chest crushing against the softness of her breasts.

One kiss, and he had her wanting him so badly she was nearly shaking with it, his effect on her so profound it scared her.

That tiny kernel of fear allowed what was left of her common sense to wave in feeble protest. "We can't do this," she said, even as she took his bottom lip between her teeth and swiped her tongue along its curve. "You know this is a bad idea."

"You don't think I've been telling myself that since the first goddamn moment I laid eyes on you?" There was no mistaking the anger in his voice. At him? At her? Then Kate didn't care about the answer as he roughly shoved his hand up under her tank top and closed his hand over her breast. His mouth trailed over her jaw, down her neck, and Kate couldn't stifle a moan as he cupped and kneaded her breast, his thumb rasping back and forth across her nipple. "I've spent the last fourteen fucking years making sure no one ever got in, no one ever made me lose my head and do something stupid again. I told myself whatever I felt for you was dead and buried and I'd never be dumb enough to let anyone get to me the way you got to me."

His mouth came over hers again in a deep, claiming kiss as his fingers closed over her nipple in a pinch that danced on the line between pleasure and pain. "And then one goddamn look at you and I'm fucking lost. And all I can think about is how you used to taste." He slid his tongue against hers. "How you used to feel." His other hand slid down to squeeze her ass.

Kate gave a little whimpering cry as the knot of desire between her legs pulled tighter, threatening to unravel with nothing more than his hand on her breast and his mouth on hers.

"And the way you used to kiss me, like you couldn't get enough. The way your hot little body was practically begging for me and I was too much of a good guy to do anything about it. For all the good it did me."

The undercurrent of anger cut through the haze and made her pause. She pulled her mouth from his. "So are you saying I owe you?"

He stared at her a few seconds, his eyes glittering with a mix of heat, desire, and pent-up frustration. His breath came in harsh pants, and she could see the thrum of his pulse in his neck. As out of control as she was.

The realization sent a fresh wave of heat coursing through her, a slick rush of moisture soaking the silk of her panties.

"I tried to be so good," he whispered, almost pained as he kissed her again. "I tried to hide the fact that every second I was with you—hell, even when I wasn't with you—all I could think about was stripping you naked, sucking your tits, licking your pussy until you came in my mouth. Sliding my cock as deep inside you as I could get and fucking you until you came so hard you passed out."

His words were crude, deliberately so, and she should have been offended. But her body reacted to them like gasoline on a fire, raising her desire to a level she'd never experienced.

He yanked his shirt off, then hers, and she didn't think to protest as he pulled her against him. They both gasped, nerves jumping at the first contact of skin on skin.

"I never stopped wanting that, wanting you," he murmured against the tender skin of her neck. He gave her a firm nip under her ear that sent a shudder through her body. "I thought I could keep it under control. I never should have touched you. I shouldn't be touching you now, but I can't fucking help myself."

Kate could relate, her body trembling, every nerve alight with sensation as her hands roamed every inch of his bare skin, delighting in the ways he was familiar, the ways he'd changed.

"And how the hell am I supposed to resist when I know you want me too?"

Kate didn't bother to try to deny it. Even if she had, he would have found out her lie the instant he slid his hand down the waistband of her pajama bottoms, down the front of her panties, and cupped the swollen mound of her sex.

His eyes locked on hers and he parted her slick folds.

Her fingers dug into his shoulders and her lips parted on a cry as he circled her clit, his gaze still locked on hers. "Do you have any idea how many times I dreamed about touching you like this? Feeling you?" Her eyes squeezed shut as he slid one finger deep inside her.

He kissed her hard, his finger pumping, thrusting inside her, his thumb flicking her clit. Kate let out a high-pitched cry. Then, just as he was about to hurl her over the edge, he pulled his hand away with a whispered curse.

Kate's cry of protest died in her throat when Tommy cupped his hands under her butt and lifted her from the floor. She eagerly wrapped her legs around his waist and let him carry her upstairs, loving the feel of his cock, hard and throbbing through the fabric of his pants as it nudged against her sex. His mouth never left hers as he made his way down the hall and pushed open the door to the master bedroom.

Earlier she'd turned on the lamp on the bedside table, and now its light cast a golden glow across the tawny skin of his chest and shoulders. He laid her down across the bed, hooked his fingers in the waistband of her pants, and pulled them and her underwear off in one fell swoop.

For several seconds he just stood there looking at her, and her face heated as a wave of self-consciousness washed over her. She'd never had a problem with her weight, but the trade-off to that was a set of breasts that barely filled his big hands. And her fair complexion required a near-compulsive use of sunscreen, which left her skin pale as milk, in sharp contrast to his tawny hue.

"Christ, Kate, you're gorgeous," he said, his voice low and raspy.

Any anxiety that he looked at her and would dismiss her as pale and flat chested and infinitely undesirable fled at the almost-reverent tone in his voice, the way his eyes greedily moved over every inch of her pale skin. Her nipples hardened under his stare. As his gaze roved down her belly to the patch of curls that was a shade darker than the hair on her head, she felt her sex swell and pulse in anticipation.

Never much of an exhibitionist, Kate surprised herself by stretching her arms up over her head, arching her back against the mattress in invitation. She angled one leg out to the side and pulled her knee up, offering him a view in between so he could see just how wet, just how ready she was for him.

One look and it was like a switch went off, the last thread of Tommy's control snapping. He came down over her with an animal growl, settling himself between her legs, hips grinding against hers as he bent to take her nipple in his mouth.

He sucked, hard, and she let out a sharp cry at the heat

and pressure tugging between her legs. He cupped her breasts, sucking and tonguing her nipples in turn, and her hips rocked up off the bed to rub herself against the irresistible hardness straining against the front of his pants.

It wasn't enough, not by a long shot, and within seconds Kate was fumbling with his belt buckle, desperate to feel the hard, thick length of him inside of her.

She'd never felt anything like this, a need bordering on desperation, as though she would have a psychotic break if Tommy Ibarra didn't get inside her in the next ten seconds.

Her shaking hands finally managed to loosen his belt and unbutton his pants, but he brushed her aside before she could start tugging at his zipper. The metallic zip seemed to echo in the dim room as he worked around the massive bulge now contained only by the soft cotton of his boxer briefs.

Kate couldn't wait, shoving his pants and underwear down his hips and reaching out to touch him, his heat and hardness spilling into her hand.

Her mouth went dry at the sight of him. Tommy was a big man, as big here as everywhere else, she realized as she drank in the sight of him. Even longer and thicker than she'd imagined, the head dark and swollen, glimmering with a bead of pre-come, so hard she could see his pulse throb in the thick vein that ran down its length.

Unable to resist, she wrapped her fist around him and stroked him from base to tip. His breath hissed between his teeth and she did it again, loving the way the muscles in his arms jerked and stood out in stark relief as he braced himself above her. Again she pumped him, her own body clenching as he pulsed in her hand, anticipating the feel of his whole hard length buried inside of her.

She circled her thumb around the tip as he shuddered against her.

"Enough," he rasped, wrapping his fingers around her wrist in a firm grip as he pulled her hand away. He sat back on his heels, his chest bellowing in and out as he fumbled in his back pocket.

A wallet appeared and then a foil packet. *I always carry latex protection*, he'd said. Kate felt a little pang as she wondered how often he did this that he felt he always needed to be prepared.

Then she couldn't think about anything as her gaze locked on the sight of his big hand rolling the condom down the thick length of his cock. She'd never imagined such a sight could be arousing—in fact, she had always been a little embarrassed at such moments.

But now she was riveted by the sight of him stroking himself, his cock straining against his grip, wondered what it might be like to watch him stroke himself to pleasure.

Then he was over her, kissing her hard before he reared up on his knees. Kate drew her knees up, opening herself wide as he guided himself to her with one hand. She cried out as he ran the head of his cock along her clit and rubbed himself against her. Electric pulses spread from between her legs through her entire body, and for a brief second she was afraid she was going to come before he even got inside her.

Then he was there, squeezing inside.

She gasped at the feel of him pushing inside, pleasure mingling with pain as her body stretched to accommodate him. He sank farther, and she gave another high-pitched cry, her body stiffening in pleasure.

He paused, chest heaving in and out as he panted, "Am I hurting you?"

She shook her head against the comforter. "No, it's okay—"

"You're so tight." He groaned as he pushed deeper. He hooked her knee over his elbow and opened her wider. Then he was there, as deep as he could go, deeper than any other man had ever been.

Tommy Ibarra is inside of me.

That was all it took to send her careening over the edge. Her orgasm hit her with sudden, stunning force. He didn't even have to move—just the feel of him, buried deep, so big and hard her body could barely contain him, was enough to make her shudder and clench around him as waves of pleasure like nothing she'd ever known poured through her. Stars exploded behind her closed eyes as electric pulses wracking her body until even the tips of her toes tingled with it.

When she came back to herself she felt Tommy, still rock hard and deep inside her. He was propped up on his elbows and his face hung above hers. Pulled tight with desire, he nevertheless looked a little stunned. She suspected it matched her own expression. "Did you seriously just come?"

Kate's face flooded with heat at her body's unexpected, over-the-top response, her body still trembling with the aftershocks. "I'm sorry," she said. "I don't usually—"

He gave a low groan and bent his head to kiss her. "Jesus, don't be sorry." He rocked his hips, the thrust and drag sending another burst of pleasure through her core. "It was amazing. You're amazing." His words trailed off into a groan as he withdrew almost all the way and pushed all the way back in one sleek move.

She threaded her fingers through his hair and drew his mouth town to hers, sucking and nipping at his lips as he took her in hard, deep thrusts that pushed her across the bed.

Harsh, guttural moans she barely recognized as her own rose in her throat, echoing his deep groans. She'd never had sex like this, so hard, so fast, almost primitive.

Tommy took her wrists in his hands and pinned them to the bed. Kate had never felt so taken, so dominated.

So wanted.

The thought sent another burst of pleasure through her, and unbelievably she felt herself building to another peak. She never would have believed it, not so close on the heels of that first mind-bending release. Her body tightened and rippled around him as she rocked her hips against him, spreading her legs wide so that he stroked the center of her pleasure with every thrust.

He was getting close too, she could feel it in the way he sped up his pace, pounding into her with no restraint as he seemed to swell even larger inside of her.

"Kate." Her name sounded like dark magic on his lips as he slid his hand between their bodies and found her with his fingers. He circled her clit once, twice, and she flew apart into a million shards of light.

As though from far away she heard his own deep moan, felt him dig his fingers into her hips in a grip that should have hurt as he held himself deep inside of her.

She drifted back to earth as the last of the shudders wracked him, her body clenching instinctively against the thick hardness still pulsing inside her.

He collapsed onto her, burying his face against her shoulder as his breath sawed in and out of his chest like he'd just run a four-minute mile.

As the seconds passed, Kate became acutely aware of the reality of her situation. She was naked on her bed with a half-dressed Tommy Ibarra still inside her after giving her the two most mind-blowing orgasms of her life.

What the hell had she just done?

Chapter 14

What the hell had he just done? Tommy silently asked himself as he lay sprawled on top of Kate. He struggled to catch his breath, his body still shaking from an orgasm so intense he felt like he'd been turned inside out.

Jesus, he was an idiot, coming over here, letting this happen. No, scratch that, *making* this happen.

Because he didn't have enough goddamn self-control to keep away from Kate. Maybe if he'd been able to keep his hands off her earlier, he would have been able to keep the last thread of control from snapping.

But it was like that kiss had opened the floodgates on everything he'd bottled up and stuffed away fourteen years ago. The overwhelming need to touch, to taste, to just be with Kate that he'd boxed up and buried so deep he convinced himself he'd never really felt it came spewing to the surface at the first taste of her lips.

And maybe, just maybe, he would have been able to put the lid back on had she not returned his kiss with that sweet, eager hunger he'd tried so hard to forget.

God, he loved the way she kissed him, like there was nothing in the world more delicious than his taste, like she could kiss him forever and never get enough. She always had a slightly disoriented look on her face after she kissed him, as if she didn't quite understand the overwhelming need pulsing through her.

He'd loved it because it always echoed how he felt.

After she'd left him, he'd bitterly told himself it meant nothing, that he was just the first guy who got her tinder to flare up but he wouldn't be the last. She'd lose that stunned look soon enough.

Except she hadn't. At least not with him.

He didn't want to think about what had gone on with her other lovers. All he knew was that this afternoon in that little shack, after he'd come up for a much-needed gasp of air, she'd had that same starry-eyed look of wonder on her face that he'd never been able to completely purge from his memory.

And then, oh Christ, the way she'd licked her lips, like she was savoring the taste of him...

All of that pent-up, unfulfilled desire came raging back to life. After that torturous ride back to town, forced to endure the fresh, damp scent of her skin and hair, her usual floral aroma sharpened by the dark scent of her need, he'd done everything he could to keep his own urges at bay.

But nothing—not the ten-mile run through the cold downpour, not the icy shower that followed or hours of monotonous paperwork that he'd decided to tackle after avoiding it for weeks could dull the edge of his desire.

Finally, he'd left his house in defeat and headed into town. Though Sandpoint was full of families this time of year, there were plenty of young, single women vacationing here too. He knew several of them would be gathered at Roxy's, the closest thing to a hot spot Sandpoint had to offer. A couple of drinks, a few spins around the dance floor, and he had little doubt he'd find a woman willing to help him with this latest challenge.

He pointed his truck toward town, not proud of his plan to go find some woman for an anonymous, meaningless fuck. But there was nothing else to be done for it.

Except when he'd come to the intersection of First and Pine, instead of turning right toward Roxy's, he'd turned left. Instinctively, inevitably pulling up outside of the complex that included Kate's townhouse.

Even then he hadn't immediately gotten out of the truck, told himself to turn the goddamn engine back on and get the hell out of there. Though his keys remained in the ignition, he couldn't get his fingers to turn them.

He stared up at her window for what could have been minutes or hours, watching her flit around the top floor, a restless ball of energy offering faint glimpses of rippling strawberry blond hair and pale skin smoother than satin to the touch.

As though under a spell, he'd found himself climbing out of the truck and up the stairway leading to her door. Though he'd never considered tank tops and knit pants particularly sexy, the sight of her, her hair spilling over her bare shoulders, the hard, eager points of her breasts pushing against the fabric of her top, the way the pants clung to the sleek curves of her legs...

Christ, she might as well have been wearing garters and stockings. There was no going back.

Now he lay on top of her, his dick still hard inside her for all that he'd come less than a minute ago, probably crushing her with his much greater weight.

He needed to get the hell out. That would be the smart thing. And he'd bet good money she was thinking it too, with the way her body was stiffening against him, her own regrets at their rash behavior starting to churn in her head.

He shifted, meaning to pull away, but stopped as his lips

brushed against the soft underside of her jaw. God, he loved the feel of her skin, smooth and soft against his roughness.

He opened his mouth over the spot, heard her soft sigh as he sucked the delicate skin between his lips. He should leave, but he didn't want to.

Didn't want to leave this moment, this place, where all of the darkness of their shared past and current realities ceased to exist. Where there was nothing but them, nothing but the crazy heat stirring up between them and the pleasure their bodies could share.

"Tommy," she said, a feeble protest. He silenced it with his mouth over hers, once again catching her wrists in his hands and pinning them lightly to the bed. Her lips parted on a low moan and he felt her inner muscles twitch around him.

That was all it took to bring him back to full, raging hardness inside her. His kiss deepened, his tongue sliding and tangling with hers.

She shifted her legs restlessly against him, and as he heard the rasp of cloth he realized he'd never managed to get his pants off.

He pushed away, loving her faint moan of protest even as his cock twitched to register its displeasure. He consoled himself with the reminder that he would be right back inside her as soon as humanly possible. But it was suddenly very important that he was completely naked with her. Every bare inch of his body sliding up against every bare inch of hers.

He sat on the edge of the bed and quickly took off his boots, socks, and pants, but not before he retrieved another condom from his pocket.

As discreetly as possible, he switched out his protection and turned back to Kate, his cock so hard he thought it was going to stretch out of his skin at the sight of her.

He paused, one knee resting on the bed, and just looked

at her, savoring the sight of her naked body. When they were together before, it had seemed like the holy grail. All those places he'd touched but never seen, now laid bare, more beautiful, sexier than anything he'd ever been able to imagine.

Her pale skin was flushed, abraded in places from the too-firm pressure of his lips and the scrape of his heavy beard. Every inch of her pale as cream and just as smooth. Except for those beautiful tits, small and firm and topped with hard nipples the same pink as her mouth.

Reclining against the bed, her hair spread across the pillow, her plump bottom lip caught uncertainly in her teeth, she looked like some kind of virgin sacrifice waiting for him to come claim her.

It did something to him, the way she looked at him, all uncertain and innocent, while she'd just proven to him once and for all what he'd always suspected.

Behind that buttoned-up, ice-wouldn't-melt-in-her-mouth proper exterior, Kate was a raging sea of sexual desire. Just remembering how hard she'd come and how quickly made his balls pull tight.

And her soft, unsteady "I'm sorry," as though having her come, shaking, around his cock could be anything to apologize for.

Just like when they kissed, she'd had that surprised look, as though her body's reaction to him had caught her completely off guard.

He felt a strange pressure in his chest, like a mass of something trying to break free from its confines. He was struck by a sudden familiarity, and he started a little at the memory of the last time he'd felt it.

Fourteen years ago. Kate's mouth hot and wet under his, her skin warm and soft under his hands. Her breathy moan in his ear as she whispered that she wanted him to be her first.

That same bundle of tenderness combined with an insane level of desire tried to burst free. Tommy ruthlessly pushed the tenderness aside. It had no place between them, not anymore.

Tonight had nothing to do with tenderness. Tonight was about scratching a long-suffered itch once and for all so he could finally free himself of the inexplicable hold she still had on him, despite everything she'd cost him.

Still, that didn't keep his hands from shaking as he ran them up the length of her legs or his mouth from watering as she parted them at his urging. Offering him an unimpeded view of the tidy patch of red-gold curls at the juncture and the gleaming pink folds underneath.

She was as beautiful there as she was everywhere, a wet, exotic fruit beckoning him to take a taste. He bent his head, slid his lips up the inner curve of one thigh. The taste of her, the scent of her, musky and mysterious, made his cock throb painfully.

He parted her with his thumbs, loving the hitch in her breath as he closed his lips over the throbbing bud of her clit. Loving even more when she moaned his name and rocked her hips, urging him closer.

Heaven, he thought as he licked, sucked, and stroked. She was as delicious here as she was everywhere, her salty-sweet flavor washing over his tongue, her high-pitched moans vibrating through him, sending sparks of need straight to his cock.

He felt her stiffen against him, her fingers knotting into his hair. She was so close, on the razor's edge.

He reared up over her at the first tremor and sank into her in one smooth thrust. He threw his head back, his eyes squeezed shut at the feel of her squeezing around him like a tight, wet fist.

He rocked in and out, barely able to move, she was so tight around him. He held himself deep inside her until the last tremors faded, then rolled to his back so she was sprawled on top of him.

He could feel her breath coming in soft, hot pants against his throat, feel her heart thudding in time with his behind her delicate rib cage. He ran his hands up and down her back in a slow caress, feeling his cock swell even bigger inside her as a wave of purely masculine pride washed through him.

He had done this to her. From the first moment he touched her hand, felt the heat spark between them, he'd fantasized about this. Breaking through her cool, composed facade to find the heat and need that raged inside.

For him. Only for him.

For tonight, anyway. Tonight he wasn't going to worry about consequences. Tonight he was going to steal this scrap of time with her like a starving man stealing a crust of bread.

And just as a mere crust of bread couldn't fill a yawning void created by months of deprivation, he had a bad feeling that a couple hours in Kate's bed weren't going to do much to scratch his itch.

He shoved the thought aside. It would be enough. It had to be.

He threaded his hand in the silk of her hair and tilted her head up for his kiss. Though his cock throbbed insistently, urging him to take her fast and hard again, Tommy kept an iron grip on his desire as he savored the taste of her, the feel of her.

He explored her mouth in slow, lazy kisses, ran his lips down her neck, over her ears, rediscovering all of the secret spots that made her shift and sigh and squeeze around him.

She rediscovered him in turn, sucking on his earlobes, nipping at the juncture of his neck and shoulder, making him surge deeper inside of her.

They stayed like that for endless minutes, kissing, touching, stroking, his cock buried deep inside her, savoring every squeeze and ripple of her delicious body around him, the slide of her smooth skin against his.

He felt her breasts against his chest, her nipples firm little points pressing against him. He broke the kiss, lifting her until he could capture one between his lips. He sucked hard, groaning as her body spasmed around him. Again he sucked her, hard, pulling a moan from her throat as her inner muscles clamped down tight.

Kate braced her hands on the mattress and started to move, sliding up and down the thick column of his erection as he sucked and licked at her breasts. Slowly at first, then gaining more urgency as he sucked and teased.

A high, keening cry came from her throat and her body went tight against his. She came with his name on her lips, sinking down on him until he was as deep as he could possibly get.

Tommy let out a guttural cry as she milked him hard. His balls pulled tight against his body, and the muscles of his thighs went rock hard as his orgasm bore down on him. His eyes squeezed tight, red sparks flashing as his body shook with a climax that was even more intense than the first.

He didn't know how long he lay there in a daze, absently stroking Kate's back as she sprawled across his chest. Half of him was screaming to get out, now, before he got pulled even deeper under her spell.

The other half wouldn't have moved if someone had put a loaded gun to his head. He'd never felt this way after sex. Shaken to his core, as if he'd been blown apart and put back together. Like nothing could ever go wrong as long as he held this woman in his arms. Like he was exactly where he needed to be and he never wanted to leave.

The thought sent a spike of panic down his spine. It was crazy emotional shit like that that had screwed up his life in his first go-round with Kate. And while he wasn't a clueless kid who was at the mercy of a vengeful father, Tommy knew that if he let Kate get under his skin again, there would be hell to pay.

Let her get under your skin? a snide voice asked. *Look at you—one kiss and all of your resolve to stay away from her crumbled to dust. You with your so-called iron-clad control, couldn't even last a week with her. I'd say she's pretty firmly embedded there.*

All the more reason to make an escape.

Yet he couldn't make himself pull away from her just yet. It felt too damn good—*she* felt too damn good. The soft weight of her on his chest, the warm puff of her breath against his throat. The silky strands of her hair tickling his wrist as his fingers circled the unbelievably smooth skin of her back and shoulders.

Several minutes passed and she stirred against him with a little sigh. He tensed as she propped herself up on her elbows, her brows knitted in a quizzical look.

Crap. Here come the questions about what does this mean and where do we go from here and all the other shit he never wanted to deal with after sex.

To his surprise, Kate didn't ask for a debrief on what just happened. "How did you know where the bedroom was?"

"All of the units have the same layout. If you've been in one, you've been in them all."

"Oh," she said, and he felt her stiffen against him, her mouth, swollen and red from his kisses, pulled tight.

He knew immediately what she thought, that he'd been in at least one more bedroom in this complex. While technically it was true—he'd been in all of the bedrooms of all of the townhouses when he'd done the wiring for the security system—it wasn't in the way she thought.

He didn't correct her. "I should go," he said, seizing the chance to get out, even as his conscience pricked at hurting her.

"Right," she said, and rolled off him, scrambling to get under the covers. He pulled on his clothes and turned to see her hunched against the headboard, her hair hiding her face as she stared at the bedspread.

"You okay?"

Her gaze snapped to his, and the look on her face made his stomach clench. Gone was the misty glow, the look of surprised delight she'd had on her face as he sent her over the edge. Now she looked disappointed, her mouth pulled in a rueful smile. "I'm sure this is all routine for you. I'm not exactly up on proper etiquette after a one-night stand. That *is* what this is, isn't it?"

Tommy stayed silent. He felt like a jerk but couldn't think of anything to say that wouldn't give her the wrong idea. Or, God forbid, let slip that while he'd come here tonight hoping to satisfy his craving for her once and for all, he was afraid all he'd accomplished was ripping down the last barriers of defense he'd had against her.

Even now he could feel it all bubbling up inside him, everything he'd felt from practically the first moment, the summer she was sixteen, when he realized that Kate was no longer a little girl. There had been lust, sure, but also a fascination. A curiosity, a need to know everything about her, inside and out, and a knowledge that he could spend a lifetime learning her and still discover something new.

And then there was the drive to protect her, to keep her safe and wipe away all the hurt the world might pile on her. Like he was piling on now.

Her eyes snapped with anger. "That being the case, I'll spare you the part where you lie and say you're going to call me and that we should do this again sometime. And I'll spare myself the part where I dissect everything that happened and try to determine what it all meant, because in the end, it meant nothing, right?"

Yes. The lie stayed locked in his throat. "Kate—" he began, then trailed off. There was nothing he could think to say that wouldn't dig him into a deeper, more dangerous hole. He'd already shown himself to have changed from the love-struck boy he'd been into a cold, unfeeling jerk. Best to let her continue to believe that.

She waved a slender hand at him. "Don't worry about it. I get it. We never got to experience what it would be like to be together. Now we know. Curiosity satisfied. We can move on."

But as he took one last look at her, clutching the sheet to her like armor, her posture forlorn despite the hard look on her face, Tommy felt his own heart squeeze in his chest. Far from satisfying anything, he was afraid what had happened here tonight had only rekindled a need in him that went beyond lust, beyond sex.

A need that made him weak, vulnerable in a way he promised himself he'd never be weak again.

Chapter 15

Kate was so tired she almost felt drunk the next morning when she walked into the volunteer headquarters. She greeted the women who were manning the phone lines and made a beeline to the coffee station that had been set up in one corner.

As she took a drink, she made a mental note to stop by Mary's and thank Erin, who continued to replenish the coffee and pastry stores like some kind of coffee elf.

Kate finished her coffee quickly but didn't hold much hope that it would do much to clear the cobwebs in her brain. Contrary to what she'd said in her lame attempt at bravado, she'd stayed up most of the night going over every second, every detail of what had happened from the second Tommy walked through the door until the second he left.

What he said. What he didn't say.

And, dear God, the things he did. Even with her heart and pride bruised by his callous exit, her body clenched and flooded with heat at the memory of his mouth and hands on her, his thick hardness buried deep inside her.

She'd fantasized about it endlessly, what it would be like to actually have sex with Tommy. To be naked, skin to skin, taking him inside her, as deep and close as two people could be.

None of her imaginings could even come close to the reality of the pleasure.

But she hadn't bargained for the pain, which had settled in her chest and wouldn't go away. No matter how much she scolded herself that she was a big girl. Lots of people—men and women—had sex without any expectation of it going any further.

Logically she knew what happened last night didn't mean anything.

And yet the way he'd kissed her, the way he'd touched her, it was like something had broken free inside of him. Gone was the stone-faced warrior he'd become. For a while, it was as though she'd held in her arms the Tommy she'd fallen in love with. All the passion, the tenderness, the way he touched her like he couldn't get enough of her.

The way he looked at her, seemed to revel in her pleasure as he pushed her over the edge. Naively, for a fleeting moment Kate thought he felt it too, that crazy, undeniable connection she couldn't seem to shake. The pull between them that was so strong it was like gravity, hurling her into his arms time and again.

But then it was over and he'd gone silent and distant, hadn't offered up any soft words to reassure her that it was anything more than two bodies coming together to satisfy a long-held curiosity.

Even as the memory stung, she knew she had only herself to blame. For all that he'd stormed in like a bull in a china shop, thrilling her with his loss of control, he hadn't made any bones about how he felt about the situation.

He didn't want to want her. Didn't even seem to like her, she was forced to admit, despite the few times he'd shown any sign of softening toward her.

Yet she'd let herself get caught up in the blind, stupid

hope that maybe she still meant something to him besides being the girl who had nearly ruined his life. Because like it or not, Tommy Ibarra still meant something to her.

The admission made her burn with shame. What was wrong with her that she completely lost control—not just physical but emotional too—when it came to him?

And when was she ever going to learn that no matter what she did, she was never going to get back what she'd lost?

But isn't that what your whole life is about? Trying to make up for something you'll never, ever be able to fix?

She shoved the maudlin thought aside along with her adolescent musings about Tommy and pulled out her laptop to log into the tip database. Within an hour she concluded there was little of value in the dozen or so calls they'd received, but she flagged the few that had any promise and was just about to send them to the sheriff's department when her phone rang.

Her heart jumped at the sight of Tommy's number on the screen. She quashed any hopes that he might be calling about anything other than the case before she thumbed the "answer" button.

It was a good thing, because Tommy barely offered a gruff greeting before he dropped the first bomb of the day. "CJ talked to the agent in charge of the Bludgeoner case. He doesn't think Tricia's disappearance is at all related."

Ten minutes later, Kate stormed into CJ's office, grateful to have anger and frustration to seize on. It made coming face to face with Tommy's stony stare a little less devastating.

"How can they not at least consider it?" Kate exclaimed. "They didn't have enough evidence to arrest Dorsey before he died. They have to consider the possibility that he didn't do it."

CJ shook his head. "As far as the Bureau is concerned,

Dorsey's arrest was imminent. Offing himself saved them a lot of time and tax dollars."

"And the victims' families? They're satisfied with this?" Kate asked.

"The ones who would speak to us at all are, yes."

"But if they knew—"

CJ cut her off with a raised hand. "Look, Kate, these people went through a horrible tragedy. They don't have much, but they do have closure, and you know damn well how much that's worth. Do you really want the FBI to reopen the case, dredge up all that ugliness for them on the very slim chance that the cases are related?"

"I have all the sympathy in the world for those families, but Tricia's life is worth more to me than their peace of mind."

CJ's mouth pulled into a tight line. "Of course her life is more valuable, but the Bureau is overloaded as it is, and they're not willing to allocate resources to reopen a case they considered closed almost a decade ago."

"You're still going to look into it, aren't you?" Kate asked CJ. "I think you should talk to Dorsey's mother—"

She broke off as CJ shook his head. "We can only afford to follow up on the highest-priority leads, and right now that means tracking down the leads in Boulder. I've got one of my deputies headed down there this afternoon."

"So you're just going to let this go? Ignore the fact that someone deliberately brought my attention to the Bludgeoner case like it means nothing?"

CJ's big palm slammed down on his desk with a metallic bang. "Hell no, I'm not going to ignore it. But I have limited manpower and I have to prioritize, and you said yourself it could easily be someone screwing with—" The phone on his desk rang. CJ snatched up the handset. "What?" He was silent a couple seconds, listening. "Son of a bitch. I'll be out as soon as I can."

Kate gaped as he strode to the door and grabbed his hat from the stand. "Where are you going?"

"Priest River. A trailer exploded and two people were killed. We think it's a meth lab tied in with a ring that distributes across the Northwest."

"But—"

"Look, Kate, I'm doing my best here," CJ said tightly. "Right now we're going to focus on the most likely leads."

He closed the door and she whirled to face Tommy. "What do you think? Am I crazy to think we should be on top of this?"

Tommy was silent a few seconds, and despite her resolve not to let him get to her, she felt her skin heat under his steady gaze. "I think a lack of resources is a piss-poor reason not to take this seriously."

Kate nodded, even as uneasiness twisted in her stomach. "He's right though—the three leads in Boulder are more logical." She wasn't an investigator, and it was possible— probable even—that whoever had brought the Bludgeoner case to her attention had done it as a sick prank. Still... "But there's something there. I can feel it in my gut."

Tommy nodded. "Then you should trust it. If CJ's going to put it on the back burner, it's up to us to pick up the slack."

"So you'll help me?"

Tommy pushed himself away from the wall he was leaning against and slowly approached. Kate forced herself to keep her eyes locked on his face instead of straying down to his chest and stomach, which she knew now was ridged with hard muscle and bisected by a line of soft, dark hair. "Of course I'll help you. I promised Jackson I'd do whatever I could to get Tricia back. That sure as hell doesn't include sitting back and doing nothing while we wait for CJ to 'prioritize,' " he said, eyebrow cocked sardonically as his fingers made air quotes.

"CJ's right, though," Kate said, her brow furrowing as she sucked in her bottom lip. "I don't think we should approach the victims' families until we have more to go on. Having to relive it all again…" She trailed off, thinking of how with every case, with every press appearance, she had to revisit and discuss what happened to Michael. "It's like ripping off scar tissue every time. I don't want to put them through it."

Tommy nodded, and something flickered in his eyes. Sympathy? She wasn't sure, but it was the first bit of softness she'd seen in his gaze since he'd left her the night before. "I can relate a little—God knows I don't like to talk about what happened when I was deployed with a bunch of strangers. I can't imagine what it's like when it involves your kids." He paused a beat. "Or your brother."

This time there was no mistaking the sympathy.

"Victims' families are out, and only one person is interested in opening the case back up," Kate said, "and that's—"

"Dorsey's mother," Tommy finished for her. "I've already got her information." He pulled out his iPad and pulled up an address in Spokane.

"She moved," Kate said.

Tommy nodded. "Six years ago. She lives with her daughter, Judy, Dorsey's older sister, who's a nurse at Sacred Heart Medical Center. Since Arthur's death, Mrs. Dorsey has had episodes of severe depression, apparently so severe Judy had concerns about her living on her own."

"You've been busy, ferreting this all out."

He caught her gaze with that unfathomable stare of his. "I didn't sleep much last night."

"That makes two of us," Kate replied before she could think better of it. "Okay, so let's call her."

Tommy's mouth tightened and he ran his hand over his thick, short hair. "Unfortunately, it's not that easy. From what I could tell, Judy canceled the phone line four years ago—"

"What about her cell?" Kate interrupted. "I thought you were the investigative mastermind who could do that in his sleep—"

"She doesn't have a cell phone, at least not one with a permanent number and account."

"How in the world are they getting by without a phone?"

Tommy shrugged. "How do I know? Maybe she has a pay-as-you-go from Wal-Mart. Point is, no way to call her. Good news is we're less than two hours from Spokane. We can get there and back before dinnertime."

Kate suppressed a frustrated sigh. Hours alone in a car with Tommy was exactly what she needed. "Let me get my stuff out of the car."

As soon as they stepped out into the parking lot, Kate had a microphone in her face. Startled, she took a moment to compose herself, irritated that no one had mentioned that any reporters had gathered outside. In the past three days, their ranks had thinned and they'd been less of a constant presence. As much as Kate wanted to keep the case front and center in the media, she was less than excited to see Maura Walsh, the blonde from KITV, smiling her too-white smile from the other side of the microphone. A smile that did nothing to disguise the calculating glint in her eyes.

Kate recognized the look all too well. And as she watched the woman's gaze track Tommy's broad back as he brushed by without making eye contact, a knot settled in Kate's stomach as she thought of all the dirt the woman might be able to dig up if she looked hard enough.

And if Kate wasn't careful with Tommy, Walsh wouldn't have to dig at all.

Kate shook off her anxiety, determined to let none of it show as she pasted on her game face, a look she'd perfected over the course of thousands of news appearances. Her expression serious but not so grave as to be uninviting, her concern for the victims apparent but not melodramatic.

"Ms. Beckett, we were unable to get a statement from the sheriff earlier. Perhaps you can give us an update on how the search for Tricia Fuller is progressing."

"The sheriff's department is coordinating the ongoing search efforts, and additional volunteers are expected to arrive later today."

"At this point, with Tricia missing for five days without any sign of her, how optimistic are you about the chances of finding her alive?"

An image flashed in her head, a picture of Ellie Cantrell's body, her face beaten beyond recognition, and Kate felt a cold sweat break out. "Very optimistic," she said tightly. "Now if you'll excuse me—"

"Do you have anything to say to your detractors?" Walsh said as Kate started to step away.

Kate halted midstep. "I wasn't aware I had any." The lie slipped through her lips as smooth as silk.

"Just this morning Ramona Walker accused you of being a quote 'pathetic, attention-starved young woman who feeds her narcissism with the pain and suffering of victims' families.'"

Kate stretched her mouth into something she hoped resembled a smile. "Ms. Walker doesn't mince words, does she? But in a way, she's right. I *am* all about getting attention—for the victims and their families, and to the plight of all the children who disappear every day in this country."

"But what about the accusations that your involvement is not just ineffective, it can also be detrimental, as in the Drexler case?"

It wasn't the first time Kate had heard comments like that. It had gotten worse in the past few years when so many competing news outlets turned to sensationalism to draw viewers. She'd built a tough skin, but it had weakened in the fallout of Graham's betrayal and Madeline's death. But she'd be damned if she'd ever let Walsh see her crack. "What happened to Madeline was a horrible tragedy, one that will haunt me for the rest of my life. All I can tell you is that I'm doing everything I can to make certain that won't be the case with Tricia."

Somehow she managed to keep her shoulders straight, her expression composed as she strode across the parking lot. She waited until she was around the building and out of the other woman's view before she let the facade collapse.

By the time she reached Tommy, who was waiting for her next to her rented sedan, her hands were shaking.

"You know, it wouldn't hurt if you stopped and spoke to the press every once in a while," she snapped. She was lashing out irrationally, but sometimes the pressure of having to maintain her composure while bitches like Walsh dragged her name through the mud made her feel like her head was going to explode.

Tommy scoffed. "No thanks. I'm happy to do my work in the background and keep as low a profile as possible. Unlike some people who can't seem to resist jumping in front of a camera every time it's pointed in her direction."

Four days ago she'd been able to brush off a similar barb from him. Not today. Not after last night. Not after having the cold hard truth of how little she meant to him laid out in front of her.

To her utter humiliation, she burst into tears.

Chapter 16

S hit," Tommy said. The expression of horror on his face as
he frantically looked around the parking lot would have
been comical if she hadn't been so hurt.

"I do what I can, okay? I've lived my life in the public
eye, and I try to use that to help these families."

"I know, Kate," he said, his voice pitched low. "It was a
low blow—"

But the sleepless nights, the pressure of the case—not
to mention Tommy's hot and cold routine—pushed her to
a breaking point. "You think I enjoy getting emotionally
involved with families, feeling their pain as they imagine
what might be happening to their kids? Having to go on TV
and calmly talk about it when the truth is worse than they
ever imagined?"

Tommy wisely stayed silent.

Kate flung her arms up in the air. "Like it's so fun for me,
to go on national television and be reminded, every single
time, that I'm the girl who left her brother alone the night
he was kidnapped and murdered. And now I get to be the
media whore who leaked information that got Madeline
killed." Like most men when confronted with a sobbing
woman, Tommy looked pained, willing to do whatever it
took to make it stop. He put his hands on her shoulders and

gave her a squeeze. Impossibly, she felt herself start to calm at his touch. "Kate, I know how hard it is, to do what you do. You do good for these families, and none of what they say is true."

Kate swallowed back another sob, guilt churning in her stomach as she admitted out loud what she barely liked to admit to herself. "No, some of it is true," she said ruefully. "Part of the reason I do this is that I feel like if I keep showing the world how sorry I am, it will somehow erase the giant black mark on my permanent record."

"You weren't the only one there that night," he pointed out, his voice gruff as his fingers tightened around her shoulders. "I—"

"No," Kate cut him off sharply. "I was supposed to watch out for him. I should have known better. I should have done better. That night and after." She sniffed one last time and shook her head, stepped out of his grip, trying not to notice how her arms felt suddenly cold. "I'm sorry," she said, embarrassment surging as she pulled herself together. Of all the people to break down in front of. It could only be worse if she'd done it in front of the camera. "I shouldn't have unloaded on you like that."

"I get it," he replied. He leaned closer, his expression grave. "We're all under a lot of pressure. Sometimes you get a little crazy and do stupid things."

She wondered if he was talking about what happened last night and felt her heart squeeze, her eyes sting with a new threat of tears at the thought. "We should get going," she said briskly. "I just need to get a couple things from my car—"

"Mind if we take yours?" he asked, gesturing to her car. "My rear right tire has a slow leak, and I don't want to risk it blowing out on the road."

Kate shrugged. "Sure," she said, and immediately regretted it once she was buckled in, closed up in what felt like a tiny capsule with Tommy. The truck would have been bad enough, but Kate's standard rental had roughly half the room of his truck cab.

He seemed even huger than normal, taking up all the space. His shoulders were so wide they nearly brushed hers. His hand draped over the center console, so close she was sure she could feel its heat on the skin of her waist. Every breath she took was saturated with his scent, shampoo and shaving cream mixed with his own musk.

Kate nearly swerved into a parked squad car in her eagerness to get a window down.

"Jesus, watch it," Tommy snapped.

"Sorry, it's just hot in here," Kate said, wincing at the breathless tone of her voice.

"You're telling me," he muttered, so low she wasn't sure she heard him right. "We need to stop by Jackson's first," Tommy said. "I haven't given him an update, and I don't want to tell him about the Bludgeoner over the phone."

Kate nodded and turned the car down Route 200. Despite her humiliation over having Tommy witness her mini-breakdown, she felt lighter, calmer than she had for days. Maybe a good cry was exactly what she needed.

Now if she could just flip a switch and stop the cells in her body from humming in pleasure at Tommy's closeness and the memories of everything they'd done last night, she'd be golden.

They pulled into Jackson's driveway and Tommy waited, if somewhat impatiently, as Kate did a quick once-over to repair the havoc her crying jag had played on her face. Eye drops for the red eyes, concealer around the nose, a whisk of blush on her pale cheeks. Topped off with a swipe of lipstick and she was good to go.

"You know, Jackson doesn't give a shit if you wear lipstick," Tommy said as he ushered her up the walkway.

"I care," she said coolly. "Besides, I don't want him to see me like this. I'm supposed to be the one who keeps a cool head when the rest of the family can't." She felt her game face slip into place automatically as Tommy rang the doorbell.

"That's a talent," Tommy mused as they waited for Tracy to answer the door.

"What?"

"The way you can be totally out of control one moment and the next it's like butter wouldn't melt in your mouth."

"Okay, fine, I cried and ranted a little, but I wasn't totally out of control."

"I've seen you out of control," he said, his voice low and laced with a heat she had to be imagining. "And I'm not talking about the crying." Her gaze flicked up to his and she saw the unmistakable gleam of heat in their dark depths.

Was he actually flirting with her? As they prepared to tell his friend that his daughter's disappearance could be connected with a string of brutal murders?

Her game face cracked, giving way to a violent flush as she stammered, "Th-this is so not appropriate to bring up right now."

"I know," he said angrily as footsteps approached.

Whether he was angry at himself or her she didn't know, and the door swung open before there was time to find out.

Tracy greeted them with a smile that was slightly dimmed around the edges. "Hello, Tommy, Kate." She paused, two deep grooves forming between her eyes as she stared at Kate. "It must be hotter than I realized for you to be so flushed, Kate."

Though there was no way the other woman could guess

at the images careening through Kate's mind, she felt her blush burn brighter.

"I'll get you both something cold to drink," she said, and led them to the kitchen.

"That would be lovely," Kate replied. But as they followed Tracy through the great room, the heavy, somber feeling of the house chased away any inappropriate thoughts.

Kate was all too familiar with the feeling, as if the despair and helplessness had seeped out of the residents to create its own atmosphere. It grew heavier as each day passed without knowing.

Sometimes it continued to grow long after the truth of what happened came to light. In Kate's house, it had grown so thick it nearly suffocated her.

She pushed her own heaviness aside and focused on this house's primary source. Jackson Fuller stood outside on the deck, staring out over the water. His broad shoulders slumped under his navy knit shirt. His arms were folded across his stomach, and he was slightly hunched as though in pain.

He straightened at the sound of Tommy's voice, and when he turned there was no mistaking the dark circles under his eyes and the deep grooves of worry carved into his cheeks. He gestured for them all to take a seat around the teak patio table while Tracy came out bearing a tray holding a pitcher of iced tea and glasses. She poured a glass for each of them, and while Jackson thanked her, she noticed he didn't take so much as a sip.

She wondered if he'd eaten anything since the lasagna they'd shared. It already felt like a lifetime to Kate. It must have felt like infinity to Jackson.

She listened as Tommy quickly filled Jackson in on the note Kate received and the reasons they believed Tricia's disappearance could be linked to the other victims.

"The FBI thinks Dorsey, who killed himself shortly after he was questioned, was the culprit, but I don't think it's as cut and dried as they want us to think," Tommy said.

"But the murders stopped after he died," Jackson said.

"True," Kate said, "but it's not unheard of for serials to stop for years, even decades before starting up again. Remember the BTK killer in Kansas? He killed for over fifteen years, then stopped. They manage to get the impulses under control, and then one day something triggers them and they're back at it." Jackson nodded, his mouth pulled into a thin line. "At this point we need to consider every possibility. But I hope to God there isn't anything here."

"The bright side, if it can be called that," Tommy said grimly, "is that the girls were all believed to be held within a five-mile radius of where they were taken. So if it's the same guy, it means she's most likely close."

"And he didn't kill them right away," Kate said. "He waited at least a week after they were taken." The lump in her stomach echoed the dread in Jackson's expression. As reassurance, it was pretty piss poor.

"And what is he doing to her in that week?" Jackson choked. "And what if we don't get to her in time and she's beaten to death?"

There was a sharp gasp. Kate turned and locked eyes with Brooke Fuller's horrified gaze. She wasn't alone—Ben Kortlang stood next to her, his expression equally shocked. "Oh my god, she's dead? She was beaten to death—"

Kate pushed from her chair and cut her off. "No, you came in at the end. We were just telling your father about a potential connection to another case—"

"Where the guy kidnaps girls and beats them to death?" Brooke's already-pale face went gray. Sobs choked in her chest and she buried her face in her hands. A keening wail came from her and she tried to flee, only to be caught by Ben's hands on her shoulders.

"It's okay," Ben said, pulling her resisting form into his chest. "They didn't say she's dead. You have to think positive—"

"Leave me alone!" Brooke screamed, and shoved at Ben's chest. "How can I think positive when it's my fault she's gone in the first place. You stupid idiot, you have no idea what you're talking about!" Hurt flashed in the young man's eyes and he let her push past him to flee back down the steps to the beach. A squeezing pressure in Kate's chest made it hard to breathe. She looked at Jackson, still seated at the teak table, his shoulders slumped as he cradled his head in his hands.

Kate listened as Brooke's sobs trailed off into the distance, her stare locked on Jackson's bent head, willing him to get up, go after her. Didn't he see that if he didn't act soon, he was going to lose what was left of his family?

"Aren't you going to go after her?" Tommy asked finally.

Jackson shook his head. "She won't talk to me anyway."

"You have to keep trying," Kate said. "She's dealing with a lot of guilt, a lot of pain—"

"Well, that makes two of us!" Jackson said, and slammed his hand down on the table. "And right now I'm too fucking exhausted and scared to deal with a bratty teenager who had a part in getting us into this mess. And don't think I don't blame you too," he said, pointing an accusing finger at Ben. "You two are older, you should have taken more responsibility."

"I'm sorry, sir. I don't know what else to say," Ben said helplessly.

Jackson shook his head, turning his gaze back to Tommy. "And I'll appreciate it if you keep your advice about my family dynamics to yourself. I brought you on to help find my daughter." He stood from the table and stalked back into the house.

"Right," Tommy said, disappointment deepening his voice as he watched his friend's back retreat through the sliding glass doors.

Kate watched Ben's throat bob as he swallowed hard, his face a mask of guilt and shame. She reached out and put her hand on his arm. "You can't take what he said to heart. Emotions are running high, and he's saying things he doesn't mean." At least, she hoped that was true. But she remembered trying to tell herself the same things about her own father, her own family. And then the pain, as sharp today as if it had happened yesterday, when she realized they meant every single word.

"He's right," Ben said, his voice thick with emotion. "I should have looked out for her that night. We both should have."

"You can second guess yourself to death and spend the rest of your life wishing you'd done something different," Kate said. "But right now, I suggest you go after Brooke. No matter what she says, I know she needs a friend right now."

Ben shook his head. "It's my fault she was even at that party. She blames me as much as her father does."

"No," Kate said. "Trust me, right now she doesn't blame anyone but herself. She's lashing out, but I know it would mean everything in the world if you just let her know you are there for her." She could feel Tommy's gaze on the back of her neck, her throat tight as she remembered how desperately she'd wished Tommy could have seen past her rejection all those years ago.

"If nothing else," Tommy said darkly, "someone should go make sure she doesn't do anything to hurt herself."

Ben started a little at that. "You really think she

might…" He turned and jogged down the stairs to the beach and headed off in the direction Brooke had taken.

Kate's eyes flicked to Tommy and she unconsciously covered the fine white line on the inside of one wrist. Did he know? Kate's father had been so careful to keep any whiff of scandal out of the public eye. Then again, Tommy had demonstrated his ability to unearth supposedly unattainable information enough for her to realize she couldn't count on anything being private.

His gaze was blank, revealing nothing. "We should get going."

Kate nodded, following him out to the car on legs that felt stiff and clumsy.

"You want me to drive?" Tommy asked. "You look a little…off."

Kate nodded and gratefully handed the keys over. She was afraid in her current state she would drive into a tree or wander over the yellow line.

She is not you, and Jackson is not your father, she tried to remind herself as she buckled herself into the car. Though she wanted to believe he didn't mean it, Jackson's comments about Brooke hit her like a knife through the heart. The only consolation was that Brooke had already run too far to hear it.

But what else had she already heard?

Her heart throbbed in her chest like one big bruise as she thought of how Brooke must be feeling, five days into her sister's disappearance. The guilt, the grief, clawing at her until it was eating her from the inside out. And nothing—not the warmest hugs or words of reassurance could make it go away.

Kate knew that. But Kate also knew what it was to crave any small bit of comfort from the people around you, some sign that you were loved despite your thoughtless actions and horrible mistakes. And she knew the urge to lash out, push people away. Only to realize the mistake after it was too late.

"I'm worried about them," Kate said as they pulled onto the highway.

"Jackson will come around," Tommy said. "I've known him for a long time, since the girls were little. He's a great dad. It's just the stress talking."

Kate shook her head. "Situations like this, a family is either pulled closer or it's torn apart. Their mother is already gone, and if we don't find Tricia…" She blinked away the tears burning her eyes. "Even if he does blame her on some level, if he doesn't reach out to Brooke and make sure she understands he loves her, no matter what, I'm afraid of what might happen. To both of them."

Chapter 17

Out of the corner of his eye, Tommy saw Kate's thumb sweep across the faint line on the inside of her left wrist. Only a couple millimeters thick, its silvery color blending in with her pale skin, it was almost imperceptible. Tommy wouldn't have even noticed it had he not run his tongue over the smooth skin and seen it up close.

It hadn't registered in the moment. It was only after he'd gone back to his place, spent the night torturing himself by replaying every second, every touch, every taste, every brush of skin on skin.

That moment created a skip in the playback as the long, thin scar on the inside of her wrist finally registered.

He didn't want to think about what that might mean, tried to tell himself it was nothing. Kate had been devastated by her brother's death, but she wasn't the type to try suicide.

After all, she'd never want to cause another family scandal, he thought, and then felt like an asshole for even thinking it. No matter how much he'd spent the last fourteen years trying to convince himself that Kate was a spoiled girl who shared her family's obsession with public image, deep down he'd always known there was so much more to her.

And the thought of her trying to snuff it out made him feel as if his guts were being ripped out.

His grip tightened on the steering wheel and he forced the thought away, wondering when the hell he'd gotten so damn melodramatic.

"You all ended up okay," he said gruffly.

"What do you mean?"

"You, your family, you all managed to pull together."

Kate responded with a harsh laugh. "Right."

"I saw the pictures in the magazines, the Beckett family Christmas, vacationing in Florida—"

"You actually believed that?" Kate said incredulously. "Jeez, Tommy, I always gave you credit for being so smart, but I may need to rethink that. You know my father is a master at manipulating the press into seeing only the image he wants them to see. Where do you think I get my on-camera skills from?"

"So what really happened?"

"You know what happened," she said tightly. "Michael died. They all blamed me."

Guilt bubbled through him like acid. "There were two of us there that night," he reminded her. "I should have—"

"No," Kate interrupted harshly. "I was supposed to take care of him. I was supposed to know better. But I was so gung-ho on losing my virginity that night, I didn't care about anything else. No morals, just like my father said."

"Don't talk about yourself like that," he said, his voice harsher than he'd meant. But he couldn't help remembering Kate as she'd been that night, so sweet, so eager. How her whispered "I love you" had sent a pulse of joy through him like nothing else he'd ever felt. He didn't want anybody talking about that sweet girl that way, not even herself.

"Anyway, they were never able to move past it. Not that I ever expected them to get over it, but part of me felt like I carried around enough guilt that I don't need them reminding me that it was all my fault."

Unable to resist, Tommy reached over and covered her hand with his, his heart squeezing when she gripped his fingers like a lifeline.

"I haven't been home for more than a few hours since I left for college. That spread in *People* magazine, the one that caught up with us five later?"

"The one with you all in front of the Christmas tree?" Tommy remembered it well—the issue was months late by the time he'd received it in a care package on base in Afghanistan. He'd been about to discard it when his eyes snagged on the cover, his fists clenching on recognition.

The Becketts were positioned in front of a Christmas tree in the massive living room in their mansion in Boise where they spent the holidays. Senator and Mrs. Beckett stood behind their daughters, who were seated on leather stools wearing matching red sweaters. The senator had his hand on Kate's shoulder while Lauren reached over her shoulder to hold her mother's hand.

Tommy remembered being pissed off at the scene, all the trappings of wealth on display.

And the Becketts smiling amid all that luxury while he was stuck in one of earth's smelliest armpits, dodging bullets in the air and IEDs on the ground, alternately freezing cold or burning hot, depending on the season.

And then there was Kate herself, looking as beautiful as ever with that smile on her that had just a touch of sadness—this was a feature highlighting their triumph over tragedy, after all.

After the way Kate had so wholeheartedly rejected him and retreated back to the family fortress, he hadn't even considered that the smile, the image of the once-again happy family, hadn't been real.

"An hour after that picture was taken, my parents and

Lauren took a private jet to Aspen to go skiing. My parents told everyone I was busy at work on a research project and couldn't join them, but the truth was I went back to New York and spent Christmas in my apartment."

The knot in his gut pulled tighter. "Your mother let him get away with that?" Tommy had his issues with his mother and her tendency to poke her nose too far into his business, but he knew if he and his father ever had a falling out, for whatever reason, she would never coldly stand by and let him be all but banished by the family.

Kate gave another chuckle, this one a little watery. "Mom wasn't about to stand up to him about anything, or anyone else for that matter. After Michael..." She trailed off for a second. "He was her favorite, her baby. When he was killed, it was like she ceased to exist. With the right meds she can still pull off a couple public appearances a year, but otherwise she barely leaves the house."

That left Lauren, her twin. He almost didn't want to know.

"Lauren and I are still in touch, but it's never been the same."

His heart squeezed in his chest as he thought of Kate, grieving, in pain, receiving no comfort from the people who were supposed to love her most.

"Jesus, that's awful." Tommy had suffered too, from his own guilt and how Senator Beckett had systematically upended all of his plans for the future. But at least he'd had his parents and sister around to remind him that they loved him and that they believed in him.

That had helped him survive all of it, even the heartbreak. And by the time he joined the Army, he'd convinced himself that he should count himself lucky that Kate never answered that pathetic, pleading letter he'd sent. By the time her father finished with him, he knew he'd fallen in love with a fake. He convinced himself the Kate he thought he'd glimpsed in those rare moments she let her guard down never really existed. Nothing they'd had was real, because the girl he'd dreamed her up to be wasn't real.

But in the past four days, he'd seen too many signs of that girl to ignore. It was in the way she cried when she first met Brooke Fuller. The way she warmly greeted Erin Flannery whenever she saw the other woman, even as many of the locals continued to shun her and her family for their past crimes.

It was in the way she came apart in his arms, holding nothing back, taking everything he had to give.

The memory made his hand tighten around hers, made the blood thicken in his veins. From the second she'd walked into Jackson Fuller's house, he'd felt something crack inside, and every second he spent with her created another fissure, spidering out from his core.

Last night had been a major breach. Another like that and it was all going to blow to pieces.

There was something real, something big between them. But fuck him if he knew what to do about it.

His thumb brushed across the thin line striping her arm from her wrist to the middle of her forearm. "This?"

Kate tried to pull her hand free but he wouldn't let her. "What, you didn't tap into my medical files?"

He couldn't deny it hadn't occurred to him to do a deep background check a time or two. "I don't do that for personal gain."

"Well, if you did," Kate said, her voice falsely bright, "you would have discovered that one night the summer after Michael was killed, I sliced a three-inch gash into my left wrist."

"Jesus." He winced.

"We were supposed to go to Florida the next day, and I overheard my dad and Lauren arguing over whether I should go. I remember my father saying 'I can't stand the sight of her. Every time I see her, I wish she was the one who'd died.'"

Tommy's throat went tight and there was a strange heat behind his eyes. Fuck, he wasn't going to cry. "I'm sure Lauren defended you?"

Kate's mouth pulled into a mirthless smile. "She said she understood how he felt..."

Tommy sucked a breath through his teeth at that.

"...but that it would probably look strange to leave me alone. After what happened to Michael, people expected they would want to keep us close for their own peace of mind." She turned her gaze back to the window but didn't let go of his hand. "It was the moment I really got it, that they were never going to forgive me. I did everything I could, I even went along with it when he got your scholarship yanked and threatened your parents' ranch." Her fingers squeezed convulsively around his, and he felt an answering squeeze in his chest. "And I know it's not worth much, but I'm sorry I never spoke out against the lies my father told about you."

"I know you were just as trapped as I was." Though he'd acknowledged that a thousand times in the past, for the first time it actually rang true.

"In the end none of it mattered. Nothing I did or said mattered. I was nothing but a walking reminder of what my mistakes had cost them, and they all wanted me to just disappear." She turned back to him, her blue eyes swimming with the kind weary sadness that comes only when your heart has been ripped from your chest and put back wrong. "I decided I'd give them what they wanted.

"Luckily I didn't get very far," Kate said. She tried to make her tone light, but it came out brittle. "I opened up one vein, saw the blood coming out and passed out. The house-keeper found me a little while later, and I got to spend a week at a psychiatric facility while the rest of them went to Florida."

"Jesus," Tommy said, his fingers tightening convulsively around hers, imagining her in a hospital all alone. "That's awful, that they treated you that way."

Kate gave his hand another squeeze and gently disen-gaged hers. Tommy fought the urge to snatch it back, every instinct in his body screaming at him to hold onto her and never let her go.

"I didn't tell you so you'd feel sorry for me," she said qui-etly. "I told you so you'd understand why I'm so worried about Brooke, and Jackson too. I know how bad it can get."

He was silent for several seconds, glad they were driving on a straight stretch of highway. It was all he could do to keep the car under control when he felt like he'd just taken an ax to the chest. He felt so many things right now, but feeling pity for Kate wasn't at the top of the list—not even close.

Anger, yeah, at her family for taking their grief out on her. And at himself too, for all those years he spent resenting her. Sure, the logical part of his brain had told him over and over that what happened to him wasn't really her fault. She'd just been a kid too, experienced a horrible tragedy. When it came down to it, it made sense that she would be angry with him for being the one to suggest they leave the house that night, that in the end she would side with her father.

Yet that wounded nineteen-year-old had lurked inside of him all along. Hurt, humiliated, betrayed by the girl he loved and believed loved him back. Even worse was the helpless-ness. Though Tommy knew the truth and could have spoken out against the senator with or without Kate's support, he'd been warned that if he did so, or said a word publicly about his relationship with Kate, the senator would make sure that the bank that held the mortgage on his parents' ranch would call it in immediately.

Everything he felt for Kate had twisted into an ugly black mass that he'd shoved to the darkest recesses of his soul, never to be revisited.

Since then Tommy had done everything in his power to make sure he was never that weak again. Never at the mercy of anyone, physically, emotionally, financially.

But he felt weakened now. From the force of the sadness pulling at him, a deep cavernous ache as he thought of all the pain she must have been in to do something like that.

There was something else there, an ache in his chest he couldn't put a name on. All he knew was the idea of Kate being hurt, by herself or anyone else, made him feel like he was going out of his mind. And the idea that she could have died...

He'd lost her a long time ago, he reminded himself, and he'd been convinced he was over the breakup almost as soon as it happened.

What if he'd gotten a call, seen the news, that Kate had died? Because no one was around to love her and take care of her.

He got an urgent, gut-deep feeling that somehow that person should have been him. He shoved it away. "I'm sorry, I had no idea—"

"No reason you should have," Kate interrupted. "My father did a damn good job making sure no one had any idea," she said with a rueful smile.

She held her arm up to the window, examining it in the bright afternoon sunlight. "I'm surprised you even noticed it. The senator got the best plastic surgeon in D.C. to do the sutures, and now it's totally faded."

"I had to get really close," he said, shifting a little in his seat as he remembered exactly how close he'd been.

Kate's cheeks flushed as though she knew exactly what he was thinking about, and the atmosphere in the car changed abruptly.

The air got thick and close, the temperature seemed to rise about ten degrees. Tommy reached over and cranked up the AC, but it didn't do much to cool the blood pooling between his legs.

"Anyway, I'm sorry," he said, trying to bring the subject back around. As much as he didn't want to dwell on the idea of Kate trying to off herself, there was nothing like attempted suicide to take the edge off a boner. "I feel like I should have been there for you."

"Tommy," she said, her voice edged in regret, "after the way I pushed you away and especially after what my father did, there was no way I could have expected anything from you."

Chapter 18

Kate may not have expected anything from Tommy, but that didn't mean she didn't dream about him coming to her rescue. Every day and every night for that first year after Michael died. Every day of her senior year, the bell would ring and she'd imagine walking down the front steps of Sacred Heart Academy and finding Tommy's truck parked outside. He'd be inside, waiting to take her away forever.

Never in a million years would she admit that out loud. "And besides, like you said, you thought we were fine. Everybody did."

"Still," Tommy said. His shoulders were pulled tight and he smacked the steering wheel lightly with one big hand. "It's not right. It's not okay that you went through that and nobody did anything to help you."

"That's not true. After that, some of the best psychiatrists and therapists in the country did plenty to help me."

He shot her a glare, and Kate couldn't stifle the little thrill that shot through her to see a big, tough warrior like Tommy so angry on her behalf. "That's not what I meant and you know it."

He was silent a few seconds. Then, almost like he was talking to himself, he said, "I should have tried harder to get in touch, but when you didn't answer my letter...Maybe things would have gone differently—"

"What letter?"

Tommy's face took on that closed, stony look.

"Seriously, what letter?" Kate said.

Tommy pressed his lips into a rueful line. "You never got it, did you?"

She felt like snakes were coiling and uncoiling in her stomach. "I never got a letter from you, Tommy."

He slapped one big palm down on the steering wheel. "You're absolutely sure?

Was she sure? She'd spent days, months, wallowing in the impossible dream that by some miracle he didn't hate her, wishing with everything she had that he'd show up at her door. Call her.

Write her a letter. "I swear on my brother's grave," Kate said in a shaky voice. "If I had ever received a letter from you, I would have remembered it." She shook her head, her lips pursing around the bitter taste in her mouth as she realized the truth. "All of our personal mail was handled by my mother's assistant. I'm sure my father told her to make sure I didn't get anything from you."

Tommy let out a long, slow breath. "Well, doesn't all of this just hit the reset button," he muttered.

Kate wasn't sure exactly what he meant by that, but right now she had bigger concerns. "When did you send it?"

Kate watched as the muscles in his jaw clenched and unclenched. "Two days after you left. I told myself not to worry when you didn't answer right away. Two weeks later my scholarship was yanked, and I figured I had my answer."

Kate's stomach plummeted as she realized how hurt he must have been. "Oh, God, Tommy, I'm so sorry. You must have felt—"

"I got over it," he said stonily, the hard set of his jaw making it clear he wasn't going to go there.

"What did it say?" she said a few minutes later, curiosity burning too hot to contain.

"It doesn't matter," Tommy said, and just like that the steel doors slammed shut.

"Uh, it matters to me," Kate replied. "Since the fact that I believed you hated my guts was like a cherry on top of the shit sundae my life had become, hearing something from you to the contrary would have gone a long way toward making me feel like I wasn't a completely worthless human being!"

Tommy let out a startled laugh. "Shit sundae?"

She gave a soft laugh of her own. "That pretty much sums it up." When he stayed quiet, she prodded again. "So what did it say?"

He shifted in his seat, cleared his throat. He was uncomfortable.

"It didn't say anything about hating you, that's for sure," he muttered.

She gestured with her hand for him to elaborate.

He blew out a sharp breath. "I think I said something about how I was sorry and that I was there if you needed anyone to talk to, and hell, Kate, it was fourteen years ago. How the hell am I supposed to remember?"

But the dark slash of color on the cheekbone facing her and the way his fingers flexed and unflexed around the steering wheel told her differently.

She stifled the urge to press him further. It was clear from his face and his body language that he wasn't interested in going any deeper on the topic.

Just as it was clear he remembered a lot more of that letter than he claimed. Something important that he wasn't ready to share.

Too consumed with curiosity to muster up small talk,

Kate switched on the radio to quell the thick silence. Other than to ask her to double check Judy Dorsey's address, he stayed silent, closed up, for the rest of the drive to Spokane.

Yet Kate couldn't shake the feeling that with these latest revelations, something had shifted between them.

Reset button indeed.

—ᴍ—

As they pulled into Judy Dorsey's driveway, Tommy struggled to pull his tangled thoughts back under control.

She never got the letter.

She never got the letter.

The thought had been banging like a gong in his head for the last fifty miles, along with a twisted mess of stuff that bubbled up with the realization that when it came to Kate, he'd been wrong about a lot of things for a lot of years.

Of course, the possibility had occurred to him. The senator's disapproval of Tommy had been loud and clear well before Michael's death. Tommy wasn't stupid. When he didn't hear back from Kate, he'd known there was a possibility that the letter had been intercepted.

Yet the possibility that she'd read it, ignored it, and gone along with her father's plan to screw up his life had burned like acid in his gut for the past fourteen years.

He should be happy, he thought, or at least relieved. If she hadn't read—and ignored his letter—it meant he'd never humiliated himself.

He'd never all but begged her forgiveness for his part in what happened that night, begged her to call him or write him back. She'd never read the part where he told her that even if she didn't want to be with him, he still wanted to be her friend, that he'd take whatever she was willing to give as long as she didn't completely shut him out.

He'd never told her he loved her.

Yet more than relief, he felt a sharp ache. At the idea that things could have gone a lot differently for them if only the letter had reached her.

Maybe...

He smacked the thought down before it could even form. Really, idiot? Even if she had received the letter, you really think she would have welcomed you back with open arms? She was still the same girl who slammed the door in your face when you tried tell her you were sorry. She was still the same girl who had gone willingly with her father when he'd crooked his finger.

The same girl who had blamed him so much for his part in Michael's death that she'd willingly done her part to ruin his future.

Hearing something from you to the contrary would have gone a long way toward making me feel like I wasn't a completely worthless human being.

That didn't sound like someone who blamed him. That sounded like a heartbroken girl who was desperately grasping at any kindness thrown her way.

So what? Nothing would have turned out different. He slammed the door of the sedan and started up the walkway of Judy Dorsey's modest single-story house. *You were both a couple of dumb kids. Even without the tragedy, the relationship would have burned out as soon as you set foot back on campus that fall.*

Michael's death just sped all of that up and made sure the aftertaste was particularly foul for both of you.

Still, he couldn't get the picture of Kate, slumped on her floor, blood spilling from the milk-white skin of her wrist,

out of his head. Christ, he'd seen horrible things in his life—
bullet wounds, limbs blown off. Hell, he'd watched half of
his friend's skull get blown off and hadn't lost his cool for a
second.

But just the thought of Kate like that made him feel like
he was going to throw up.

If she'd known he was there, that he'd cared—no, loved
her—would she have felt so desperate?

He raised his hand to knock on the door, forcing the
thoughts aside. This was no time to wallow in their past and
wonder about what might have been.

They waited several seconds and he could feel Kate's
furtive, speculative stare. He'd felt it the entire remainder
of the drive, probing, trying to suss out the truth he had no
intention of sharing.

—⁂—

There was a sound from inside, the scrape of a chair
across the floor, followed by quick footsteps. Kate's gaze
snapped to the door, immediately on task as she pushed her
spinning thoughts about Tommy and his missing letter aside
for the moment.

The door opened to reveal a woman in her early forties.
She was dressed simply in a long-sleeve T-shirt and baggy
jeans, with dirty blond hair pulled back in a ponytail. She
had the kind of lines in her face that came more from fatigue
than age, and she had a tired, careworn air.

"Judy Dorsey?" Kate asked.

"That's me," she replied, her eyes narrowing on Kate's
face. No doubt trying to place her.

"Is your mother here?" Tommy asked.

Judy's gaze swung to Tommy and she got a wary look

on her face as she registered his size and stony expression. "What's this about?" She started to take a step back.

"Sorry, we should introduce ourselves." Kate pulled her face into her camera-ready smile and made quick introductions.

"Kate Beckett? The woman who's always on TV talking about missing kids?"

Kate nodded. "And Mr. Ibarra is currently helping with an ongoing investigation. That's why we're hoping to talk to your mother."

Judy's jaw clenched and she started to shake her head. "I'm sorry, my mother's not a well woman, and she really can't talk—"

The door started to close and Tommy caught it with the flat of his hand.

"I'll call the police!" Judy shouted.

"Please, that isn't necessary," Kate said. She pulled Tricia's picture up on her phone. "You've seen me on the news, talking about this girl?"

Judy's eyes flicked down to the screen and she gave a curt nod. "I'm sorry about her, but I don't see—"

"Without going into details," Tommy said, "we think there's a possible connection between Tricia's abduction and your brother's case. We know your mother did her own investigation, and we were hoping she might shed some light."

"No," Judy snapped. "My mother wasted too much time obsessing over my brother before she finally accepted what he did. I can't let you see her—"

"Judy? Who's at the door?" a thin voice called from inside.

"Nothing, Mo—"

But before she could get the words out, quick footsteps

sounded down the hallway and a gray head popped around Judy's shoulder.

Angela Dorsey wore her gray hair cut short, and despite her age her face still had a youthful look thanks to her small snub nose and wide, inquisitive brown eyes. Eyes that recognized Kate the second she laid eyes on her.

"What are you doing here?"

"Nothing, they were just leaving," Judy said.

Kate spoke quickly and loudly to drown her out. "We're looking into a link between the murders your son was accused of and a recent kidnapping. If there's a connection, it could prove your son's innocence once and for all."

That was all she needed to hear. Angela ushered them in over Judy's protests and led them down the hall to the living room. Though the house was small, from what Kate could see it was neat as a pin, its older but comfortable furnishings well cared for.

"Have a seat," she said, indicating a thickly padded couch covered in moss green ultrasuede.

"Mom, I don't think this is a good idea. You know how upset you get when you talk about this stuff."

"Judy, why don't you make yourself useful and offer our guests something to drink," Angela said in a voice that would cut stone.

No shrinking little old lady here, Kate thought.

"I keep all my files locked in the garage," she said. "Just let me go get them."

Judy made no move toward hospitality, instead glared at them, her plump arms folded across her chest. "The last time she wallowed in all of this, she got so depressed she wouldn't get out of bed for a month. I had to take off time from work—"

"And then we saw the doctor and adjusted my medication

so that is less likely to happen," Angela said. She made a shooing motion at her daughter. "Will you give us some privacy, please?"

"Just make sure you wrap up by six thirty." Judy said with an exasperated sigh. "My shift at the hospital starts at seven, and I'm not leaving you alone with her."

Angela watched her daughter leave the room, her expression troubled. "I will never understand why she was so quick to believe what they said about Arthur." She placed a folder on the coffee table in front of her. "She always thought I was crazy. Maybe I am."

"Or," Kate said, "maybe we'll stumble onto something that will finally prove you right."

—⁓—

Tommy watched quietly as Angela pulled a manila folder full of papers from a big accordion-style envelope.

"This is a copy of the FBI case file on my son," she said, indicating the smaller folder. "As far as I'm concerned, it's useless."

Tommy leafed through it while Kate read over his shoulder. It was essentially the same information they'd already seen, with a few additional notes. "They were able to put him in all of the cities where the girls were killed. They amassed sufficient evidence to bring him in for questioning. They found a baseball bat with one of the victims' blood on it," Tommy said.

"All circumstantial," Angela snapped, waving her hand as though to fan away a foul smell. "He traveled a lot, and he was in those cities working. He did finish work on new housing developments. He was usually hired by the same company and worked with a lot of the same men in different cities, but the FBI never bothered to look into it."

Tommy and Kate shared a look. That bit of information hadn't been in the files they'd seen either. Had other potential perps been at those same job sites with Dorsey when those girls were killed?

Angela opened up the accordion folder and pulled out a stack of papers. "I worked with a private investigator who cross-referenced and figured out who was on site with him in all four cities where the murders happened."

There were five names on the list.

"We gave the names to the FBI, but they never did anything with them," Angela said, her voice tight with frustration.

"Mind if I make a copy of these?" Tommy asked as he pulled a portable scanner out of his bag.

"Of course not," she replied.

As Tommy scanned the documents, Angela continued, her assessment of the FBI's handling of the case quickly ramping up into a rant. "So many things they didn't care about or dismissed out of hand," she said. "Our tax dollars at work, and they didn't even take into account the details."

"Such as?" Kate prompted.

"Like the fact that the last victim, Jessica Stiller, probably died after Arthur was already dead, God rest his soul."

Kate frowned and exchanged a look with Tommy.

"I don't remember seeing anything about that in the medical examiner's report," Kate said.

"That's because it wasn't," Angela said. "By the time they found the last victim, the FBI had taken over the case, and their medical examiner estimated the time of death to be before Arthur"—she paused, closed her eyes—"hanged himself. Although that's another can of worms, if you ask me."

Right, Tommy remembered. The theory was that Dorsey, knowing the FBI was closing in on him, killed the girl and then killed himself shortly after. Then again, Angela had gone on record many times with her doubt that the death was a suicide. While he felt for the woman, that was a can of worms he wasn't prepared to open right now.

"But the local authorities insisted on having their own examiner on the scene. Because of the condition of the body, he insisted that she could have been killed within a full twenty-four-hour period before or after Arthur died."

She pulled a report from the file and held it out for Kate. They read together, Tommy's brow furrowing as he read the local M.E.'s assessment of the body and time of death.

"It doesn't make any sense why this wouldn't make it into the file," he murmured.

"You know what else doesn't make sense?" Angela asked. "How in the world my son would get hold of that fancy lotion the girls all had on them."

"The Beaute D'or," Kate said, a shiver running down her spine as she remembered smoothing the cream on her own skin.

"Where in the world would Arthur have gotten hold of it?" Judy said, holding out her palms for emphasis.

Kate shrugged. "It's widely available."

"But it's ungodly expensive," Angela said. "Over $200 for a little jar. Look around you—this is the kind of life Arthur grew up in. He wouldn't know anything about fancy gold-filled creams or have the means to buy it. Where would he even get such a thing?"

"He'd have to buy it in an upscale department store, like Neiman Marcus or Barneys," Kate said, "or special order it like my mother did."

Tommy was struck by a sudden memory of that fateful night when Michael was killed. How less than an hour before he'd been out on that beach with Kate, enthralled by the way her sweet-smelling skin had seemed to sparkle in the moonlight.

Once again, the eerie coincidence made the skin on the back of his neck prickle.

As an argument for Dorsey's innocence, it was pretty light.

"If it was an integral part of his ritual, I don't think the cost would have been an issue," Kate said, echoing Tommy's thoughts.

"But if he had to special order it," Angela broke in, "it wouldn't have been possible. My house was his last permanent address. I would have remembered something like that showing up."

There were a thousand ways to poke holes in her theory, but Tommy resisted. The woman had suffered through that argument enough, and nothing was going to change her mind about her son. There was no reason for him to dogpile onto her pain.

They spent several more minutes going through the information Mrs. Dorsey provided, and Tommy scanned the most relevant documents.

"Please keep me updated on anything you find out," she said as she shook hands with Tommy at the door, "and don't hesitate to get in touch if you have any more questions." She quickly wrote down a number on a scrap of paper. "That's not listed anywhere so please don't share it."

"Of course." Kate nodded and held out her hand.

Instead of shaking it and releasing it as she had with Tommy, Angela clasped Kate's hand in both of hers, her expression turning somber. "I know I sound like an old crackpot grasping at straws, but I know in my heart my son didn't do what they think he did. Whoever did that to those girls is still out there, and if he's the one who went after Tricia, I pray to God you find her before it's too late."

—⁓—

It took Judy Dorsey ten minutes to find the old address book where she'd written the number. While part of her wondered if they even cared after all this time, she decided it was worth giving him the heads-up. If nothing else, maybe it would make life difficult for Little Miss Perfect and her overgrown companion, she thought with a grimace as she dialed.

The last time the press had dredged up Arthur's case, she'd barely been able to pull her mother back from the edge. Not that her mother appreciated any of it—not the fact that Judy took her in when it became clear she wasn't safe living by herself in Omaha. Not the sacrifices she'd made in her career and her personal life.

No, her mother still cared more about her dead, no-good, murdering brother than she did about her living, breathing daughter who had done more for her in the last week than her brother had done in a waste of a lifetime.

He answered on the third ring. "Hello?"

"Agent Fields?" Judy asked.

There was a slight hesitation and then: "Yes, this is Agent Fields. Who is this?"

Chapter 19

He didn't need to hear her name to know who it was. Judy Dorsey was the only one who had this number, and there was only one reason she would be calling.

His fingers tightened around the receiver, his stomach muscles clenching as he waited to hear what she had to say.

"I know it's been a long time, and it probably doesn't even matter at this point, but you said I should call you if anyone showed up wanting to talk about my brother's case."

He cleared his throat, determined not to let any of his apprehension show. He thanked her for calling. "It might not seem important after all this time, but we always like to be prepared to deal with the press or the victims' families should the need arise. Is it another TV show?"

No reason to worry if it was, he reminded himself. With all the investigation shows on cable these days, it seemed like every few years or so a producer was dredging up the Bludgeoner case.

"Not exactly," Judy said uncertainly. "I mean, Kate Beckett is on TV a lot, but that's not what she's here for."

His body flushed red hot, then went ice cold in a matter of seconds. His hand started to shake around the phone. "What does she want?"

But he knew before she spoke what Kate was doing there.

"She's here with a man—his name is escaping me right now—he's a private investigator helping her with the missing girl case. I'm sure you've heard about it—she was on vacation with her family over in Sandpoint?"

"We're monitoring the case, of course," he replied, hoping his voice didn't sound as choked as it felt.

"Well, they seem to think there might be a connection to my brother's case and this one."

He felt a spike of panic and tamped it down. There was nothing to worry about, he reminded himself. He'd been so careful, covered all of his tracks.

And then after Dorsey's death he'd finally found his true mate and hadn't needed to take such extreme measures until recently.

"You don't think it could be true, could it? Is it really possible that my brother wasn't guilty after all?"

He took a deep breath, forced the panic back. Kate and Ibarra could ask all the questions they wanted. Nothing would ever point them in his direction—nothing that could possibly connect him to those other girls. "I know it's hard to hear," he said, infusing his voice with false sympathy, "but all of our evidence points to your brother's guilt. Despite your mother's position, if there was evidence that contradicted that, I believe we would have found it by now."

Judy gave a heavy sigh. "I know. I accepted the truth a long time ago. I just wish Mother would."

He thanked her for her call and rang off.

His hand was shaking as he put down the receiver. When he scrubbed it over his face, it came back damp with his own cold sweat. It would all be all right, he assured himself. Ten years and no one had ever had even an inkling. He heard a soft footstep outside his office door.

Well, he corrected himself, there might be those who had inklings, but they knew better than to rat him out.

His breathing slowed to an even pace, and as he scanned the desk, his gaze snagged on the fabric bag sitting to the left of his computer.

Gifts for his beloved, along with some other necessities he'd planned to give her this afternoon.

But now...

No, he scolded himself. There was no reason to let that icy bitch and that gorilla who thought himself some security hotshot ruin his plans. He'd learned to cover his tracks before Ibarra even knew what a computer was, and Kate was nothing but a talking head.

He would go as planned, but not before he made a pit stop. It was time for him to do a little investigating of his own and find out exactly how much Kate and Tommy actually knew.

—⁓—

Kate thanked Mrs. Dorsey for her help and gently extricated her hand from the woman's grip.

As they walked out to the car, Tommy couldn't miss the dejected set to her shoulders. "Well," she said as she slid into the passenger seat and clipped herself in, "while she managed to raise some doubt about Dorsey's guilt, we have absolutely nothing that helps us with Tricia." She blew out a frustrated breath.

"First thing is to get in touch with the medical examiner," Tommy said as he pulled out of the Dorseys' driveway and headed for the highway.

Kate nodded. "That's very strange to me, that there could be such a potential discrepancy in the time of death and it wouldn't have been noted in the case file."

Tommy flexed his fingers on the steering wheel. "In any investigation you run across people with an agenda. The agent in charge clearly had it in his head Dorsey was their man. He would include whatever information supported that."

"But the defense would be all over that if it ever made it to trial," Kate argued.

Tommy shrugged. "Probably, but it was never an issue."

"Because Dorsey conveniently committed suicide," Kate said wryly. Her finger twisted and untwisted around a lock of her hair as she stared out the window. Tommy didn't interrupt her silence, knowing she was doing the same thing he was, taking what they'd just learned from Dorsey's mother, flipping it around in her head, trying to figure out if any of it could be of immediate use to them.

To his frustration, all Tommy was able to come up with was a hell of a lot more questions and pitifully few answers. None of which got them any closer to Tricia's whereabouts or confirmation she was even still alive.

His stomach clenched at the thought. Of course the possibility that they wouldn't find Tricia alive had been front and center in his mind from the second she'd gone missing.

But until today, until Kate had given him a firsthand view of what life was like after Michael's death—along with a couple more bombshells he didn't want to dwell on right now—Tommy hadn't thought too far into the future. About what might happen to Jackson and Brooke if they didn't find Tricia in time.

It was suddenly clear that he was on the hook for not just one life but three.

Tommy picked up his phone and dialed CJ to give him an update on what Mrs. Dorsey had told them.

"The price of the body cream and a highly disputable

discrepancy in the M.E.'s report isn't much proof of Dorsey's innocence," CJ replied skeptically.

Tommy agreed and hung up as they came up on the bridge that would take them into downtown Sandpoint. This stretch of highway curved along the side of a steep drop that offered stunning views of the mountains and the lake below.

"It's so weird," Kate said, her gaze still fixed out the window.

"What?"

"The gold dust cream." She gave her head a little shake and turned to face him. "I haven't thought of it in years. Now that I think of it, the last time I can remember using it was..." Her gaze drifted down to the floor.

"The night Michael died," Tommy said softly. "I remember."

"You noticed?" Kate's full lips quirked in a little half smile.

"I noticed everything," he said without thinking. And the way Kate's grin widened made him want to pull over and kiss it off her.

Nice, he thought. The sick fuck rubbed that gold shit all over the girls he killed, and your dick is getting hard remembering a heavy petting session a decade a half and ago. "It seemed strange when we first read the files," he said. "But when you think about where the guy lived and where he came from, it doesn't seem likely it would have come up on his radar. Regular old glitter lotion, sure—you see that on even your low-rent strippers—"

"You know from your vast experience?" Kate said archly.

"I wouldn't call it vast," Tommy said defensively.

Kate let out a soft laugh. "Maybe Dorsey became fascinated by a wealthy girl and got frustrated he couldn't have her."

"Someone like you?" Tommy said, and just the thought made the hairs on the back of his neck stand on end. *It was nothing but a coincidence.* Still, all of his senses flared to high alert as they crossed the bridge that spanned the lake into Sandpoint.

And when Kate dropped him off back at the sheriff's office to pick up his truck, he couldn't shake the feeling that he shouldn't leave her alone.

Not just because his protective impulses were firing off right and left. Though he was trying not to dwell too much on the heavy truths he'd discovered today, something in his chest pinched at the idea of her spending the night alone in that townhouse.

Kate had been left alone to deal with her pain too many times in her past.

Yet when she'd left him, there had been nothing close to invitation in her eyes. *Face it, dude, despite what happened last night, your chance to be the shoulder she cries on has long since passed.*

—◦◦◦—

To Kate, climbing the three steps to her townhouse felt like she was climbing Mt. Kilimanjaro. Right after she had dropped Tommy at his truck and turned her car toward the lake, a wave of exhaustion had hit her so hard she marveled she'd made the three-mile trip without passing out in the car.

Along with the exhaustion had been a need that bordered on desperation to keep Tommy by her side. To not let the tentative bond she'd sensed from this afternoon's revelations dissolve before it had a chance to form.

But she'd reminded herself harshly that just because

Tommy finally knew the truth about what she'd gone through didn't mean he automatically forgave her for her part in what was done to him. What had happened last night, along with a few hot looks he hadn't been able to conceal, proved that he was still sexually attracted to her, but just because he sympathized with her own sob story didn't mean he liked her any better.

That harshly sobering thought had kept her from embarrassing herself by begging him to come back to her place. To spend the rest of the night distracting her with his hot mouth, his strong hands, his big, powerful body until she forgot about all of the pain and sadness the day had dredged up.

If Tommy had come home with you, the first thing he would have done was read you the riot act for not setting the alarm, she thought with a rueful chuckle as she pushed open the door and saw the green light blinking on the panel.

The interior was dark, the thick drapes that kept late-afternoon sun and heat from overtaking the living room allowing only a line of light at their seam. Kate followed the narrow path of light to the sliding glass doors. She reached for the cord to pull the drapes and felt a chill creep up her back. There was a subtle movement, nothing more than a puff of air to warn her.

A hand closed over her mouth as the other went around her neck. Kate's heart leapt to her throat as the adrenaline spiked, sending her arms and legs flailing in every direction as she struggled to break free.

She tried to scream, but nothing came out but a harsh, gurgling sound as the hand around her throat tightened. She struggled harder, but the arm anchoring her to a large male chest was like a steel band, the long sleeves of his shirt making him impervious to the frantic clawing of her nails.

The already-dark room went darker, and Kate knew if

she didn't get away she was going to lose consciousness, or worse. Even more terrifying was the hard pressure she could feel growing against the small of her back. *He was getting aroused.*

The thought made her gag against the hand covering her mouth.

Forcing the panic aside, she racked her brains for the self-defense tips she'd received in one of countless training sessions St. Anthony's offered to the public. It had been ages since she'd attended as a student instead of an observer. She vowed to whoever was listening that if she made it out of this, she'd pay better attention next time.

She felt his foot kick against the outside of hers and had a flash of memory. After bringing her foot up, she stomped her heel against his instep with every ounce of power she could muster.

It wasn't much, but it was enough to elicit a grunt and make him loosen his grip just enough to give her the leverage to swing her elbow back into his ribs. She flung herself out of his hold. He was between her and the front door, which left the sliding glass doors off the downstairs guest room her closest escape.

She flung herself toward the stairs, crying out in pain as her knee met the corner of the coffee table. She was on the second stair when he tackled her from behind, sending them both tumbling down. All the breath rushed from her body as her ribs made contact with the wooden edge of the bottom step.

She managed to wriggle out of his hold and was pushing herself to her knees when she heard the air whistling behind her. There was a hollow *thunk*ing sound the split second before pain exploded in her skull and the bright flash of stars blinded her to everything around her.

—∿∿—

Tommy called himself all kinds of fool as he turned down Kate's street. After giving Jackson a quick update on their discussion with Mrs. Dorsey, in a move that echoed last night's actions, instead of turning right at the intersection of Kootenai Road and up the hill toward his house, he'd turned left.

To Kate's.

Last night he'd been driven by frustrated desire and long-simmering resentment. Right now he was a little afraid to look too closely at what was driving him.

Desire, no doubt. Need like nothing he'd ever felt pounded through him with every pulse. The memory of Kate, under him, over him, gloving him in her tight, slick body was so vivid he swore he could smell her in the air, taste her on his lips.

Lust, desire—that was easy to own up to.

It was the other stuff that had him feeling a little panicky.

But not panicky enough to turn his truck around and take his dumb ass home.

Anticipation sang through him as he parked his truck in front of Kate's rental. Not just for a repeat of last night's amazing sex—though he doubted he'd last thirty seconds before he had her laid out on the nearest flat surface. His chest was tight, his breath was short, at just the idea of seeing her.

He raised his hand to knock, his stomach clenching as he realized that right now, he didn't just want to fuck her, he wanted to *be* with her. He hadn't felt that way about a woman since...

Since Kate. No matter how hard he tried to fight it, she still had that inexplicable hold on him. Like a siren drawing him in.

Watch it you don't get smashed on the rocks again this time.

The warning froze his fist midway to the door. If he had a working brain cell left in his head, he'd turn and walk away. He started to turn when a crashing sound came from inside.

"Kate?" He knocked hard on the door. No answer. He tried the knob, his jaw clenching when it turned easily in his hand. He pushed the door open to find the townhouse almost completely dark, the drapes drawn tight against the afternoon sun.

"Kate?" he called again. There was a crashing sound from downstairs and a muffled curse.

Too deep to be Kate's. His blood curdled as he hurled himself down the stairs. As he rounded the corner, he saw the open sliding glass door that led outside and a masculine figure wearing a hoodie disappearing through it.

Instinctively Tommy gave chase, but he didn't make it more than two steps before he froze in his tracks.

That's when he saw Kate, crumpled on the floor like a rag doll, an angry crimson stain blooming under her head.

Still as death.

He could barely stop from laughing out loud as he darted between houses and through the forest. It had been so long since anyone had come close to catching him, he'd forgotten how exhilarating it could feel to run for his life. For so long, he'd been so careful, so controlled, he'd forgotten how fear could enhance the rush. Only when he made it back to the Zodiac raft he'd hidden behind some rocks in a nearby cove did the reality of what had nearly happened sink in. How unbelievably stupid and reckless he'd been. As he pulled out into the water, he railed at himself for being so foolish. Was he really willing to risk everything? For Kate?

There had been a time when he had been. But he'd botched that up but good, only to realize later that he should count himself lucky. Because it turned out Kate wasn't as good and pure as she pretended to be, not if she let white trash like Tommy Ibarra put his hands all over her.

He should have left before she realized someone was there. Yet when she interrupted his search of her townhouse—he'd sorely overestimated how long it would take them to drive from Spokane—instead of sneaking out the back, as he knew he should, he couldn't stop himself from grabbing her.

From wrapping his hand around her throat, covering her hand with his mouth. Showing her that no matter how many times she rejected him, he could still take her any time he wanted to.

The thought, combined with the futile struggles, aroused him unbearably, startling in its force. In that moment, he knew he had his solution. He would take her, keep her to satisfy his body's base needs while he waited for Tricia to accept him.

And finally Kate would receive the punishment she deserved for making him act so irrationally, so stupidly all those years ago. For making him act equally carelessly again now.

His hands shook as he grabbed the backpack from the motorized raft and quickly stripped off his hoodie and sweats, leaving him in a T-shirt and shorts. A guy boating with a hood pulled over his head in eighty-degree heat would cause suspicion. In a T-shirt, shorts, sunglasses, and a floppy-brimmed fishing hat, he looked like any other tourist tooling around the lake, soaking up the last of the sun's rays.

Still, he had to move fast. While Ibarra had unwittingly

saved him from himself—it was sheer stupidity to try to take Kate right then, right there, without making any of his usual preparations—he knew the cops would be at Kate's house in minutes.

He pushed the raft off the sand and used the oar to row himself out a ways before starting the motor. Within minutes he was buzzing through the water, pushing the thoughts of all the ways he was going to use Kate like the whore she was from his mind.

He was on his way to Tricia, his beloved. He couldn't bring this ugliness to her.

He would calm himself and make all the necessary preparations. He would save up all the ugliness to give to Kate.

—◆◆◆—

Kate could hear someone calling her name from very far away. But she didn't want to answer. She wanted to stay in this nice, comfy cocoon and sleep for days.

"Katie, Katie, wake up." The voice was deep, and there was no mistaking the hint of panic. She tried to tell him that no one called her Katie anymore, but she couldn't seem to make her mouth work.

There was more talking, but she only took in bits and pieces. "In the house...ran out the back door before I could see him...don't know how bad...ambulance, right away... lots of bleeding."

Kate finally recognized the voice as Tommy's and struggled to open her eyes, let him know she was okay. Her eyes opened, consciousness returned in a great rush. As the first wave of pain hit, she wished she could go back to that dark black cocoon.

Her head felt like someone was hammering a steel spike

into it. "Tommy." His name came out as a soft whimper that sent another hammer blow echoing through her skull.

She started to push herself up but was knocked back to the floor by a wave of pain so severe she was sure she was going to throw up.

"No, don't move." Though pitched low, Tommy's voice sent another spear of pain through her skull.

"My head hurts." Her voice came out as little more than a whimper.

"I know, I know." A gentle hand held her down. "Just try not to move until we can figure out how badly you're hurt."

She opened her eyes, unsure of where she was, unable to make out anything more than a large male form looming over her. Panic spiked through her with a sudden rush of memory. "He's here, in the house," she gasped, the words tearing at a throat that ached from the force of being crushed. She tried to sit up again but felt like she was anchored to the floor.

"It's okay. Whoever was in here is gone. I'm here now. I'm not going to let anything happen to you." Tommy took one hand in his and rested his other gently on her forehead. Inexplicably, though the throbbing in her head didn't abate, she felt a wash of relief course through her. She closed her eyes against the bright sunlight that sent daggers into her eyes.

It all came back in a flash, the man grabbing her from the shadows, his huge hand wrapping around her neck. Getting tackled on the stairs, the hollow echo of his blow connecting to the back of her head. "He was choking me," she whispered. "I thought he was going to kill me." Or worse, she thought, her stomach roiling as she remembered the revolting pressure of his erection pressing against her back.

"Shh, it's okay. I've got you now," Tommy said.

Instinctively she tried to sit up again.

"No," Tommy said firmly, his hand on her chest. "Wait for the paramedics."

As though on cue, the sound of sirens echoed in the distance.

Her fingers tightened reflexively around Tommy's fingers as the full force of what might have happened if he hadn't shown up hit her.

"Oh God, what if you hadn't come over?" Kate said, her voice high and thin. "He was going to—"

"Don't think about it right now," Tommy said, the gentle brush of his fingers over her cheek belying the undercurrent of rage in his voice. "You're safe now. That's all that matters."

The sound of sirens got louder. "I'm going to go upstairs and open the front door, okay? I want you to promise me you'll lie still and try not to move."

"Promise," Kate said. She winced at the pain of that single word, her eyes squeezed shut again. Immediately her grip on consciousness weakened.

As she drifted out again, she felt him lean closer, his lips right next to her ear as he whispered, "I'll be right back. Don't be scared."

Then there was a gentle touch on her forehead. A kiss? She was out again before she could be sure.

—⁂—

Tommy looked at Kate for a few moments, feeling that a softball-size lump was going to cut off his air supply as he watched her drift back to unconsciousness. Fear like nothing he'd ever felt before screamed through him at the sight of her, so pale and still. He'd nearly lost his mind when he'd seen her lying there, unconscious on the floor like a broken doll.

The moment she'd stirred, the soft sound of his name on her lips had sent a burst of relief and joy through him so fierce for a second he'd felt the burn of tears behind his eyelids.

But that did nothing to quell the rage that made him want to find the bastard who hurt her and tear him apart with his bare hands. He was going to find whoever did this and make him pay, he vowed.

For now, though, he had to shove the fury aside and put his energy toward helping Kate. And she was far from out of the woods. Just because she was awake didn't mean she was in the clear. Head injuries were tricky like that. A seemingly harmless bump on the head and you could end up with a brain bleed.

The blow Kate had taken had been anything but harmless.

You need to get upstairs and make sure they know where they need to go and that they don't waste any time. But everything in him rebelled against the idea of leaving her alone for even a second. An irrational, terrified part of him convinced that if he left her, she'd slip away.

On your feet, soldier! A voice that sounded an awful lot like his boot camp drill instructor screamed from within. *Focus on the task at hand and get your lily-livered ass upstairs.*

He shoved himself to his feet and marched up the stairs, pausing to open the drapes on the upstairs windows and allow early evening sunlight to flood the room. The sun-filled living room and kitchen showed nothing of the violence that had happened just minutes ago.

There was no hint of what had happened here, what *could*

have happened. A vision flooded his brain of Kate, her breath being choked off by a hand around her slender throat, her eyes wide with panic. Her slender body shoved to the ground. A man coming over her—he shoved the thought away, swallowed back the nausea that rose in his throat.

Jesus, he'd seen his best friends suffer the most gruesome wounds imaginable. Limbs blown off, intestines falling out of their abdomens. Horrific as it had been, as much as he'd loved his brothers, he'd always been able to do what needed to be done, whether that was to hold the enemy off or tend to his fellow soldiers with the kind of cold detachment necessary to make it through the situation.

But with Kate hurt, he couldn't seem to hold the anger and the fear at bay. It ripped at his guts and echoed in his head in an endless refrain: I can't lose her again. I can't lose her again.

He did his best to drown it out as he saw the flash of lights spin a pattern on the wall above the television. Tried to stay coherent as he described what had happened to both the paramedics and the sheriff's deputy who arrived seconds after.

All the while he felt like his heart was going to come out of his throat, his hands fisted to disguise their shaking as the paramedics quickly assessed Kate's condition, put a collar on her to stabilize her neck and head, then eased her onto a stretcher.

He let them do a cursory exam on him and climbed into the ambulance with her as she was taken to Sandpoint's main hospital, Bonner General.

CJ met them at the hospital, looking grim. "I heard the call go over dispatch. Did you get at look at the guy?"

Tommy shook his head. "All I saw was his arm and his leg as he took off through the doors that open to the lake.

Gray sweatshirt, dark pants. Gloves," he said grimly. "It will be awhile before Kate's in any shape to talk, but I don't know if she saw much of anything either."

He told CJ everything he'd seen and what Kate had told them, frustration twisting his gut at how laughably little he was able to tell them.

"Probably some tweaker who needs cash for a fix," CJ muttered. "Who else would break in in the middle of the afternoon?"

Tommy shook his head. "From what I saw the place hadn't been tossed."

"Maybe Kate walked in before he could do it."

"I'm not buying it."

"You think it has something to do with the case?"

"I think the timing is too damn close to be a coincidence."

CJ rubbed his hand across the back of his neck. "If that's the case, I'd love to know what he thinks we know."

He heard a clamor of voices and saw CJ grimace as he looked over Tommy's shoulder. Tommy turned to look, his expression quickly matching CJ's as he saw a crowd of a half dozen reporters, including, he noticed with a scowl, the blond bitch who had given Kate such a hard time earlier that day.

"What the hell are they doing here?" Tommy asked.

"Someone at the hospital must have tipped them off," CJ said grimly. He shoved his hat squarely on his head and strode across the lobby area. Tommy caught a camera swinging toward his face and pointedly turned his back. He heard CJ tell them he couldn't provide any additional details about Kate's condition, but assured them that a statement would be issued soon.

"What about Ms. Beckett's relationship with the man

who accompanied her to the hospital, Mr. Ibarra?" Tommy's shoulder's stiffened at the sound of the blonde's voice cutting through the others. "Mr. Ibarra?" Her voice rose to catch his attention. "You seem to be Ms. Beckett's constant companion. Is there a more personal component to your relationship?"

Christ, if that wasn't a loaded question. But Tommy wasn't about to take the bait. There was nothing about his relationship with Kate that he would offer up for public consumption. Without even turning around, he stalked down the hallway and into the men's room.

If the bitch decided to follow him into the john, he'd jump off that bridge when he came to it. By the time he came out, CJ had shooed the group back out the front door, but Tommy noticed that Maura Walsh's van was still parked outside.

CJ grimaced when he saw Tommy. "Thanks for the backup," he said wryly.

"You're the one in public office, man. I make it my business to keep my face out of the news."

"Yeah, well, I'm afraid this case has put you firmly in it, right next to Kate." He was silent a couple beats, a speculative look in his eyes. "So is she right? Is there something going on between the two of you?"

"Nothing you need to know about," Tommy said through clenched teeth.

CJ gave him a friendly clap on the shoulder. "I think it would be great if you got together again. Very Shakespearean, torn apart by tragedy..." He trailed off and his gaze turned serious once again. "I'm going back to the townhouse, take a look for myself and question the neighbors. Call me as soon as you talk to the doctor."

After CJ left, Tommy paced up and down the lobby area while the minutes ticked by at a snail's pace. How the hell long did it take to do a CT scan anyway?

Finally, when he thought he would spontaneously combust with impatience, the door swung open and the doctor emerged.

Dr. Schmidt was in his late fifties with receding gray hair and tired, kind eyes behind wire-rimmed glasses.

"Is she okay?" Tommy asked.

"Her scan looks clear," the doctor said. "No sign of hemorrhage or other trauma."

The wave of relief that ran through him was so strong it nearly took him out at the knees. Still, "I want to see her," he said, needing to see for himself in person that she was okay.

The doctor indicated the exam room, and Tommy went through the double doors without waiting to be invited. Dr. Schmidt's hard-soled shoes echoed on the linoleum behind him.

Kate was sitting up on the gurney, wrapped in a flimsy cotton hospital gown, her face tight and pale with pain.

"Hey," he said softly, his wince echoing hers as she turned at the sound of his voice.

He itched to pull her into his arms, breathe her in, soak up the relief that she was going to be okay. But from the look on her face, her head was still pounding with pain, and any jostling would just add to it.

Instead, he took her hand in his, curving his palm around fingers that felt too damn cold. "Can't you give her something for the pain?"

Dr. Schmidt shook his head. "Not with a concussion this severe. She needs to be monitored for the next twelve hours. Unless someone can stay with her, we'll have to admit her."

No fucking way was she staying in this hospital, not with the guy who did this to her running around free. CJ might think it was a long shot that the break-in and attack were connected to the case, but he wasn't taking any chances.

"She's coming home with me."

"You don't have to," Kate said weakly. "It's easier for me to stay here."

"The press has already found out about it, probably on a tip from one of the staff." He shot Dr. Schmidt a meaningful look. "Whoever did this to you knows you're here."

"The hospital has security. Besides, do you really think he'd come after me? It was probably just a random break-in." The way her voice went up at the end told him she hoped that was the case, but she didn't believe it any more than he did.

"It's possible, but I'm not banking your life on it."

Kate swallowed convulsively, the movement drawing his attention to the purple marks ringing her throat. Once again Tommy shoved back the murderous rage swelling in his chest. He was taking her to his house, where he could lock the gates, turn on the alarm, and monitor anyone approaching with his state-of-the-art surveillance system.

"Thank you," Kate said quietly.

"Not necessary," he replied, fear and anger making his voice harsh. He gave her hand a squeeze and made an effort to soften his tone when he spoke again. "I'll feel better once you're out of here."

"Okay," she said softly, and stared at him for several long seconds as though she knew there was more to it than he was letting on.

"I'll release her to your care then. Let's just get your discharge paperwork going and I'll send the nurse to help you dress," the doctor said.

Once the paperwork was handled, Tommy waited outside the exam room and made a quick phone call. When Kate emerged, he took her hand and guided her to the entrance the staff used. He breathed a sigh of relief when he saw the familiar blue and silver pickup idling right outside.

"Thanks, Dad," Tommy said as he helped Kate climb up and slide onto the bench seat.

"No problem, son," his father said, lifting two fingers to the brim of his straw hat and tipping it to Kate. "Now you just relax and I'll get you home as quick as I can."

Kate nodded and closed her eyes. Tommy winced at the evidence of strain from the short walk to the truck. Her face was even paler and tinged with green as though the pain was making her nauseated. Tommy tucked her against his side as though he could somehow take her pain and absorb it into his own body.

A surge of protectiveness, fierce and primal, swelled inside of him. He didn't understand its source, didn't understand why Kate had always brought it roaring to the surface, but he would be damned if he would leave her safety in anyone's hands but his own.

———⟊———

As he approached the grove where the single-wide was hidden, the chaos he'd created back at Kate's townhouse became a distant memory as anticipation welled inside of him, knowing Tricia was waiting inside. With his new plan set, a sense of peace like nothing he'd ever felt before washed over him, along with a surge of triumph.

But now wasn't the time to revel in all the ways Kate would be made to suffer. Now he was going to see his love.

And she was starting to love him back. He could feel it. Warmth bloomed in his chest at how sweet she'd been the last two times he'd visited. Thanking him for the food he brought, expressing her gratitude for his thoughtfulness, offering up a welcoming smile when he approached the bed.

She'd earned her gifts, he thought with a smile as he unlocked the door to the trailer and pushed it open.

"Hello, my darling," he called softly as he closed the door behind him and went, as always, to the small table in the middle of the room to light the scented candle. Soon the heavy vanilla scent masked the staleness of the air and the lingering odors that came from even one so lovely as Tricia being kept in an entirely enclosed space.

"Hello, sir," she said softly. "May I please have some water? I ran out awhile ago, and it's so hot—"

"Of course," he said, feeling a pinch of regret at having caused her to suffer. He rummaged through the food bags and pulled out a tall plastic bottle, still cold to the touch. He'd put his sweatshirt and pants back on before he'd set out for the trailer. Now he pulled his hood down to keep his face in shadow and went to her on the bed. He handed her the uncapped bottle and relished the sizzle of electricity that coursed through his body when her fingers brushed his.

"Thank you," she said as she eagerly took the bottle in her free hand and drank it down in greedy gulps.

"I'm so sorry I wasn't able to come sooner." He reached out and brushed her hair back from her face, and his heart thrilled when she not only didn't flinch but seemed to lean into his touch.

"I'm glad to see you," Tricia said softly, and set the empty bottle on the bed next to her.

"Are you hungry?"

She gave a small shake of her head.

"You sure? I brought your favorite sandwich from Mary's. You shouldn't have any problem chewing it."

"No, I'm okay right now," she said again.

"In that case I have something else for you." He pulled the small box out of his pocket and opened it up. "Here, let me light this so you can see." Careful to keep his face angled away, he lit the candle on the small bedside table and opened the box. Nestled inside was a delicate gold chain with a small charm, fine pieces of gold molded into the shape of a lily with a single diamond nestled in the center.

"It's beautiful," Tricia said.

"It once belonged to someone I loved very much," *or thought I did*, "and now I want you to have it."

He plucked it from the box, his fingers trembling with anticipation as he leaned forward to fasten it around her neck. He'd placed it on other necks before. Only one had ever worn it for more than a few days.

But in the end, she had died too.

He hoped from the very bottom of his soul that Tricia would wear it forever.

As he leaned closer to work the tiny clasp, he became aware of an unpleasant reality, one his nose couldn't ignore. His love, for all her beauty, was beginning to smell.

Fortunately, he'd thought to prepare for this too. "Today, my dear, I believe it's time for a shower."

She stiffened but didn't say anything as he retrieved a bag from the table. "Shampoo, conditioner, soap, even a toothbrush. And for after," he said, pulling out a small box, "this very special cream that will make you sparkle like the jewel you are."

She gave no response other than a little choking sound as he unfastened her cuff. "Come on now, let's get you to the bathroom," he said. But instead of getting up, she huddled against the headboard.

"Come on now," he said, an edge to his voice. "We've been getting along so well. You know I won't put up with this defiance." He reached down and took her arm in his grip and hauled her to her feet.

Only to discover she was shaking so hard her legs could barely support her. "I don't want to," she said, her voice shrill. "Please don't do this to me. I'm not ready, I'm not ready yet."

Realization dawned like a lead ball in his stomach when he realized she thought the shower was a prelude to him raping her. "Sweetheart," he said, ignoring her odor for a moment as he gathered her into his chest. "The last thing I want is to hurt you. And as much as I desire you, it's not something I want to take by force. I didn't lie when I said I would wait for you to come to me willingly."

Someone else won't be so lucky. He quickly shoved the thought aside, afraid the memory of Kate and her fear would push the bounds of his control. The last thing he wanted was for Tricia to be afraid of his needs.

Her trembling slowed. "You're not going to force me?"

"I won't hurt you unless you make me," he said, and stepped back, steering her once again toward the bathroom.

Once she was inside, he handed over the toiletries one by one. All except the special finishing touch. That he kept in his pocket. His fingers tingled in anticipation of smoothing the gold-flecked cream onto the long, slim length of her legs, her delicate shoulders and arms.

He reached past her and turned on the shower. The water was only lukewarm and came out in a feeble trickle, but it would have to do.

She hesitated again, plucking at the hem of her filthy T-shirt.

"What?" he said.

She shifted her feet uncomfortably. "It's just, there's no curtain or anything—"

"So? There's no one here."

"You're here! I've never been naked in front of a guy before," she blurted.

The reminder of her innocence sent a fresh wave of heat sizzling through his body. That more than anything made the blood heat in his veins and pool heavily between his legs.

Sweat bloomed on his skin at the thought of her naked in the shower, the water trickling over bare skin and slight curves. He swallowed hard, realizing if he stayed in there with her, he might not be able to control himself.

He studied her for several seconds, saw the fear in her eyes and knew she was attuned to his body's instinctive reaction.

He didn't yet know if he could trust her.

But for both their sakes, it was necessary to put her to the test.

"Okay." He nodded curtly. "You have five minutes."

Breath *whoosh*ed from her lungs, her relief palpable as he backed out of the bathroom.

"Thank you," she said, and started to close the door.

He stopped it with the flat of his hand.

"Please," she said again.

Trust was necessary to every relationship, he reminded himself. And if he ever wanted to earn hers, he had to give his. He nodded. "Five minutes," he repeated. "And no locks."

"Thank you," she said. The way she was practically crying with gratitude made him feel like the king of the universe.

—m—

Tricia's heart practically beat out of her throat as the latch clicked shut. She took a deep breath, willed herself to calm down. This was her one chance. She had to keep her head clear so she didn't blow it. She reached into the shower and fiddled with the faucet, cursing when she realized that the wimpy stream was all she would get.

Not much to cover the noise. Her belly knotted with tension as she carefully balanced on the toilet to reach for the window above.

It was boarded up from the outside, and on closer inspection Tricia wasn't certain she'd be able to fit her shoulders and hips through the narrow space, even if she did somehow manage to knock the board loose and pull herself up.

Not exactly a given, considering how weak she felt, even if her head was clearer than it had been in days. That was one upside to having gone so long without anything to eat or drink. Whatever he'd been dosing her with had pretty much cleared out of her system.

There was only one other alternative she could think of. She grabbed the candle from where her captor had placed it next to the toilet. Thoughtful of him, she thought snarkily.

She held the candle over the floor, looking for the slit in the cracked linoleum. It must be getting close to dark—there wasn't a crack of light leaking through the floor like last time, or from the thin seam at the window. Though it made it more difficult to find that key spot in the floor, it would be better cover for her if she managed to get out.

No, *when* you get out, she reminded herself fiercely. When the five minutes was up, he was going to come in here and find her gone, or...

A shudder ran through her at the thought. Failure wasn't an option.

She ran her hands frantically along the floor. Finally, she found the place she was looking for. A small crack, barely wide enough to get the tips of her fingers through. But she felt its promise in the feel of cool night air licking at her skin.

She pulled as hard as she could, bracing her feet against the lip of the shower for more leverage as she strained. Nothing.

She pulled again, muffled a cry as she felt a chunk of flooring give way. The hole was now as big as her fist. Another tug and she could fit both hands through.

"One minute."

She froze as the voice called through the door. Adrenaline surged through her, infusing her arms and hands with strength. One last, hard tug. There was a loud *crack*ing sound, one that made her simultaneously sick with fear even as the cool air rushed over her legs, signaling her freedom.

"Tricia?"

She scrambled for the hole she made, afraid her heart was going to explode as she slid her legs through even as the latch on the door rattled.

Her feet met the ground, wood, plastic, and metal scraping her legs and hips as she tried to squirm her way out.

The door flew open with such force it bounced off the opposite wall.

She didn't have a clear view of his face, but there was no mistaking the lightning-fast transition from concern to fury as he realized what she was doing.

With a roar he leapt forward and grabbed her under the shoulders. Tricia twisted and punched at him with her fists, tried to wriggle out of his grasp.

He was too much, his fury adding fuel to strength that was already far greater than hers. "You fucking little bitch!" he screamed, spit flying from his mouth as he yanked her back up through the hole.

Tricia cried out as something tore into her thigh, through skin and fat until it felt like it was gouging out a chunk of muscle.

Pain ripped through her as he hauled her up and slammed her into the wall so hard she could feel the cheap plaster crack under the impact.

He held her pinned there by her throat, her toes scrambling to make contact with the floor as the blood roared in her ears.

"You goddamn little bitch," he hissed again. "I give you a chance to earn my trust and this is how you repay me? By trying to escape, after everything I've done for you?"

Her vision started to tunnel, her thigh throbbed with pain, but even through that she could sense the anguish mingling with his rage. On some twisted level he was actually hurt, the psycho.

"I'm sorry," she said, but the words came out a choked whisper against the hand tightening around her throat.

"Sorry?" he roared, and released his grip on her throat.

She took a deep lungful of air, wincing at both the pain in her throat and the deep throb in her leg as her weight came down on it.

He grabbed her by her shoulders and shoved her through the doorway. She staggered, crying out as she fell to the floor. Tears stung her eyes as he fisted his hand in her hair and hauled her up by it to throw her back on the bed.

Through a haze of pain she saw his fist draw back. She tried to shift but still took the brunt of the punch on her cheekbone. Stars exploded behind her eyelids, her ears rang at a second, even harder blow. Her shoulders screamed in pain as her arms were jerked back, and the rattle of the handcuffs sent dread rippling through her. Though deep down she knew it was useless, instinct took over and she kicked and twisted, desperate to get away.

He pinned her legs down with his knees and she let out a harsh scream, nearly passing out from the pain as his knee ground into the gash in her thigh.

Her arms were stretched above her head and forced through the bars of the headboard, the cuffs snapped around her wrists so tight she could feel the metal already digging into the tender skin.

He sat back, breathing hard. "One thing I find I'm losing as I get older," he said through clenched teeth, "is my patience." His hand closed around her jaw, squeezing so hard she whimpered, expecting her jawbone to snap at any second. "I was willing to wait for you, but after that stunt you just pulled, I'm thinking I should just cut my losses and get rid of you like I did the rest of them."

Dancing on the edge of consciousness, Tricia prayed she would pass out so she wouldn't have to endure whatever came next.

But instead of his hands closing over her throat, she felt a stinging pain in her neck. Then nothing.

—⁂—

He staggered out of the trailer, gasping in lungsful of cold night air, trying to silence the voice screaming at him to end it all, right now. His hands curled into fists, aching to feel the crunch of delicate bone yielding to his knuckles.

Goddamn it, he'd been such a sap, he thought, his anger mixing with humiliation in a nauseating cocktail.

She'd played him, a supposedly innocent fourteen-year-old girl who'd tugged at his emotions with her sweetness and modesty, had totally fucking played him.

She was no better than Kate.

No, he wanted to roar in denial, thinking of her uncertain smile, her gratitude when she accepted the water he'd provided... it made his heart ache. It had only been five days, he reminded himself. That sweetness, that gratitude might become genuine eventually if he could just show her how much she needed him.

You kept the last one for over two weeks before she finally understood that her true place in this world was at your side, he reminded himself.

She left you too, another, bitter voice reminded him. It doesn't matter if it took years. She still wanted away.

No. He shook his head and forced his feet away from the trailer, through the grove until he caught the trail that would take him down to the lake. Sweat still clung to his skin despite the cool evening air. He stripped off his hoodie and tied the sleeves around his waist.

Tricia was different. He just had to give her more time. Have more patience. Part of what happened tonight was his fault, he realized. He'd been so impatient to move things forward, he'd trusted her too quickly.

He should have known she wasn't there yet. Hadn't he learned, over and over, that the truth that was so clear to him was much harder for them to grasp?

Some—most—never did.

And that was their undoing.

Chapter 20

By the time they got to Tommy's place, it was completely dark. His dad pulled the truck up the drive and watched, his face hidden in shadows as Tommy climbed out the passenger door and carefully eased Kate off the seat and into his arms. He didn't need to see his father's face to know it was drawn with concern, that his eyes were full of questions about exactly what was going on with his oldest child and this woman who had wreaked such havoc on his life all those years ago.

But all his dad said was "Have a good night, son. Kate, I hope you get better," before he leaned across the cab and pulled the door shut. As he shifted Kate in his arms and started up the walkway, Tommy was hit with a burst of gratitude that he had the kind of family he could count on to come to his aid, no questions asked—well, in his father's case at least, whenever he needed.

Whatever hardships he'd gone through, he'd always taken that security for granted.

"You can put me down," Kate grumbled against his chest.

"You barely weigh anything. Besides, I kind of like it," he said before he thought better of it. It was true though. Hell, "like" was too weak a word to describe how it felt to be carrying her into his house.

Her only reply was a soft "Far be it for me to deny you your he-man moment."

Tommy pushed the door closed with his hip and started down the hall.

A grin tugged at his lips. If she was perky enough to give him shit, her condition couldn't be that grave. Not that he wouldn't be watching her like a hawk for the next twelve hours.

His step hitched as he passed the guest room, but instead of pushing the door open to the very comfortably furnished room and tucking her into the queen-size bed, he continued down the hall to his own room.

This time he didn't even try to kid himself that he didn't know exactly what this was about.

He sat Kate on the side of the bed and went to his dresser to get out a T-shirt. "You can sleep in this," he said as he handed it to her.

"Thanks," she said, her gaze a little fuzzy as she looked around the room.

"I don't have anything here—"

"Once you're up to it I'll take you back to the townhouse to get a change of clothes. And there are plenty of brand-new toothbrushes in the bathroom. Just pick one."

Her plump mouth pulled tight. "You seem very prepared for overnight guests," she said, the bite in her voice diminished by her obvious exhaustion and pain.

Tommy sank to his knees in front of her and braced his hands on the mattress on either side of her hips. "I happen to like to buy in bulk." He gave her a pat on the knee and urged her toward the bathroom. "Let me know if you need help with anything."

He watched her shuffle away, some psycho part of him not wanting to have her away from his side for even the time it took her to brush her teeth and take care of any other business.

Part of him was glad to have a second alone to process everything, to absorb the significance of what he was doing even as she obviously had no clue. No idea that in the three years that he'd lived in this house, she would be the first woman to ever sleep in his bed.

Christ, up until now, the only woman other than his mother and his sister who had been in this house had been a Grace Kelly-esque blonde named Krista Slater. And that was only because he'd owed his buddy Sean Flynn a huge fucking favor, and he and Krista had come as a package deal.

Not to mention, Sean probably would have cut off his scrotum and fed it to him if he'd so much as breathed in Krista's direction.

This place was special, sacred. And the women he hooked up with casually had no place here.

He heard the water turn off and the door *click* open, and he turned in the direction of soft footsteps padding across the hardwood floor. His body kicked into gear as he took in the sight of Kate wearing nothing but an oversize olive green T-shirt with the word "ARMY" emblazoned across the front. The shirt settled over her like a tent, hanging almost to her knees as it completely swallowed all hint of the slim curves beneath.

But with her tousled red-gold hair spilling over her shoulders and the long, sleek length of her calves bare to his gaze, it struck him that women could spend thousands on supposedly sexy lingerie, but nothing was hotter than a hot woman wearing her man's shirt.

And by her man, are you referring to yourself, big guy? He shoved the thought aside and ordered his body back under control. She'd been attacked, for Christ's sake, and from the pallor of her skin and tight set to her mouth, still in a ton of pain. And you're leering at her like a goddamn pervert imagining what it would be like to hook the hem of that shirt and inch it up her legs, revealing inch after inch of pale, perfect skin...

He bit back a groan and hurried across the room to help her.

"Thanks," she said as he caught her when she swayed a little. "I thought it was easing off, but the headache came back with a vengeance while I was brushing my teeth."

The mention of her pain was like a cold shower, but he couldn't stop himself from moving in with a quick kiss on her cheek as he settled her against the pillows and dimmed the bedside lamp.

By the time he lifted his head, her eyelids were already drooping, her brow still furrowed against the pain.

"I'll be back in a couple hours to check on you. Otherwise, call me if you need anything."

She nodded almost imperceptibly against the pillow. "Thanks for taking care of me, Tommy," she said in a sleepy voice.

I'll always take care of you. But he couldn't get the words past the lump in his throat. He knew they weren't true. He might have shown up in the nick of time today, but that didn't make up for all the times he hadn't taken care of her.

As he left the room and retreated to his office, he tried to console himself with the reminder that back then, he'd been a naive kid himself. A nineteen-year-old from a ranching family who mowed lawns to pay for school wasn't any match for a shrewd U.S. senator with a massive grudge.

Yet as he detoured to the kitchen to grab a beer, that didn't stop the guilt gnawing away at him at the thought of all those years, all the pain she'd suffered, and he hadn't been there for her.

Hell, after he'd finished convincing himself he hated her, he hadn't let himself think of her at all.

The beer turned sour in his mouth and he pushed it aside. No good could come from kicking himself about what should or shouldn't have happened with Kate. But as he settled in front of his computer to write the summary he'd promised CJ, there was no getting around the fact that he still had feelings for her.

Big. Deep. And nothing to do with hate. He'd foolishly thought that whatever infatuation he'd felt for her was buried miles deep and covered up with scar tissue thicker than an elephant's hide.

But from the moment she walked into Jackson's office, it had become clear that the scar covering up whatever he felt for Kate was nothing more than paper thin, and every moment spent with her was another layer stripped away.

And underneath? Well, it was a hell of a lot more complicated than youthful infatuation.

Still, even succumbing to temptation and having mind-bending sex with her wasn't what delivered the death blow to the last of his defenses.

It wasn't even the sight of her, injured and unconscious, forcing him to confront the possibility of losing her—this time for good.

That moment came at about two o'clock in the morning when he checked on Kate for the second time. He was struck again at how right she looked, her hair spread across *his* pillow, her body covered by *his* sheets and blankets.

Her pale, sculpted features were relaxed now, the furrow between her eyebrows having disappeared. He hoped that meant the pain had eased. He leaned in close and whispered her name. She turned away from his voice, buried her head deeper in the pillow.

He couldn't resist the urge to run his fingers down her smooth cheek. "Come on, sleeping beauty, wake up and tell me your name."

Her hand came up to swat his away and he saw her eyes flutter. Like last time, she was unfocused at first, unsure for a moment where she was and how she got there. Then her gaze locked on him and a smile spread across her face that was so bright it was like looking into the sun.

"Tommy," she said, her voice saturated with a kind of pure happiness that hit him square in the gut and sent a warm glow rippling through every cell. "You're still here."

And Jesus, just like that, he was a goner. The last of the scab ripped off, and he was flying over the cliff. Chest cracked wide, diving into the abyss, and he didn't care if he ever came back.

It was like the first time he'd kissed her, but so much better—and worse.

Kate just smiled up at him, unaware of the tornado wrapped in a hurricane she'd unleashed inside him. "I'm so glad you're still here."

A still-functioning logical part of his brain knew she was probably still half asleep, not sure of what she said or what she meant. "Of course I'm still here," he managed to choke out. He eased down on the mattress next to her and pulled her against him, careful not to jostle her too much. "Of course I'm still here," he repeated, and buried his face against the crown of her head. "No matter what happens, I'll always be here with you."

—⁂—

The next time Kate woke up the sky was just turning light outside of the windows. She quickly became aware of three things. One, her head still hurt, but not to the degree that it had when she'd left the emergency room last night. Two, the bed she was in was unfamiliar, not one she ever remembered sleeping in before.

Three, she was not alone in the bed, if the large, warm, *hard* presence curled up against her back was anything to go by. Her hand drifted down to the thick, muscled arm that wrapped around her waist, holding her tightly against him as though he was worried someone was going to try to snatch her away.

Tommy. Her eyes snapped open as memories from the day before came screaming through her brain all at once. The attack, the hospital, the pain.

And through it all, the one constant was Tommy, never leaving her side, his eyes dark with concern, his deep voice whispering that he would always be there for her no matter what happened.

No, she had to have made that last part up, she told herself. Tommy was a stand-up guy who would help out anyone who needed it—even a woman who had at one point nearly ruined his life—but he'd made it clear that his feelings for her didn't go past common courtesy and whatever chemistry lingered from their disastrous teenage romance.

Still…She shifted, turning in his embrace to face him. The movement sent pain rippling through her back and legs, making her aware of the other injuries she hadn't noticed yesterday over the hammering in her head.

She tried but couldn't quite stifle the whimper working its way up her throat as she turned onto her right side. She felt Tommy's body stiffen a split second before his eyes flew open.

He was instantly aware, on guard, and Kate instinctively recoiled from the sudden intensity. But his gaze immediately softened as he focused on her face. Her heart jumped in her chest at his slow grin and the warm sparkle in his eyes.

His features were softer than usual, blurry from sleep. But more than that, there was none of that cool reserve she'd gotten so used to seeing on his face. With his full lips pulled into that smile that sent a tingle through her that made her temporarily forget about the various aches in her body and his dark eyes crinkling at the corners, he looked so different.

Happier. Younger.

Like the Tommy she'd known and fallen for so many years ago. Her breath hitched in her throat. It must be a side effect of the concussion, causing her to imagine things that weren't there.

But she couldn't dismiss the gentle touch of his hand as he brushed her hair back from her face, the way his hand curved around her neck and rested there in a touch that felt equal parts affectionate and possessive.

"How's your head?" he asked softly.

She shifted her head against the pillows to test the waters. A dull ache, but nothing close to the sledgehammer from the night before. "Not bad." She shifted, sucking a breath through her teeth as pain shot up her left side.

He winced in sympathy and carefully shifted her onto her back. "Is it your ribs?" He came up on one elbow and leaned over her, his face tight with concern. "The doctor said you had some bruising."

Kate's brow furrowed as another detail of the attack snapped into place. "That must have happened when he tackled me on the stairs."

"When I get my hands on the asshole that did this to you, he's going to be crying for his mommy by the time I'm done with him."

The ferocity of his words was at odds with his touch as

he ran his hand up over the sore area, the warmth somehow diminishing the pain. Instead, she became immediately, acutely aware of the intimacy of the moment. In bed with Tommy Ibarra, wearing nothing more than panties and a T-shirt that had ridden up over her hips. Under the covers, her bare legs brushed against his. Electricity shot through her at the feel of his hair-roughened calf slide against her own.

The fact that they hadn't had sex but had slept next to each other made it somehow more intimate. The last time she'd been in a bed with Tommy, he hadn't been able to get out of there fast enough after sex. And she'd been as relieved as she was hurt by his quick retreat.

But last night he'd tucked her into bed—his own bed, not the guest room. She hadn't been so out of it that she hadn't noticed.

He'd held her most of the night while they both slept, and now he seemed in no hurry to go anywhere.

His hand slid down from her ribs, to the curve of her waist, and came to rest on her hip. Her breath hitched as strong fingers curved around her and his big body shifted closer.

He'd worn a T-shirt and a pair of cargo shorts to bed, but there was no mistaking the subtle tension that overtook him, the wave of heat that radiated off of him. And there was no way she could miss the steely column of flesh pressing insistently against her opposite hip, branding her through layers of clothing with its heat and hardness.

"Kate." He groaned, bending his head to hers.

She reached her arm over to loop it around his shoulder and lifted her mouth for his kiss, then let out a sharp cry as a shaft of pain stabbed her in the side.

"Son of a bitch," Tommy muttered, and pulled away,

leaving the bed as quickly as he could without bouncing her around too much. "I'm sorry, Kate. This has got to be the last thing you want—"

"Don't apologize," Kate said, wincing again as she shifted herself up against the pillows. "I don't know if you could tell or not, but my spirit was pretty willing, if only my damn ribs would cooperate."

He shot her a rueful look. "And there's that little matter of a concussion."

"I think you could make me forget about my headache pretty quickly." She grinned back. "But the ribs—" Her breath caught as she tried to find a comfortable position.

He gave her a sympathetic nod. "Ribs are a bitch." He came over to her side of the bed and helped arrange the pillows around her, then went to the bathroom to get her water and ibuprofen. By the time she was settled semicomfortably, her head had started to throb again and her eyelids felt like they were weighed down with sandbags.

Even so, a prickle of heat sizzled through her when Tommy's lips pressed gently against her own.

"Get some more rest," he whispered. "You're going to need it for when you're recovered."

Any questions she might have had about his meaning dissolved at the feel of his teeth closing ever so gently around her earlobe, followed by a flick of his tongue against the sensitive flesh.

Chapter 21

By the time Kate woke again, the sun was glowing hotly through the crack in Tommy's drapes. The sun wasn't the only thing that was hot, she thought as she pushed herself into a sitting position. Thanks to Tommy, her brain had been torturing her with dreams of the two of them naked in a sweaty tangle, either in the middle of sex or about to get to it but somehow never managing to finish before she was struck down by a sharp ache somewhere in her body.

Unfortunately, the pain was real and not just part of the dream, a fact that was driven home as she pushed herself to her feet and felt a sharp ache in her hips and ribs. She sucked in a breath and took a moment to catalog her injuries. Her headache had diminished to a dull background ache, and after she took a few steps, the aches in her hip and ribs subsided somewhat.

She was nearly to the bathroom when the door to the bedroom flung open.

"What the hell are you doing up?" Tommy strode over, his brows knitted into a tight frown.

"I need to use the bathroom," Kate snapped.

"You should have waited for me to help you," Tommy chided as he wrapped his arm around her shoulders for support.

"You forgot to leave the butler bell when you left."

"Smartass," he muttered. "I'll wait out here until you're finished.

"Really, I think I can make it out to the kitchen by myself." Achy or not, she didn't like the mental picture of Tommy sitting on the bed waiting while she took care of all of her bathroom business.

"Fine," he said reluctantly, "but if you're not out in fifteen minutes, I'm coming to check on you."

Kate rolled her eyes and shooed him out but couldn't deny the burst of warmth in her belly at the thought of him worrying about her. It had been so long since anyone had fussed over her, she'd forgotten what it felt like.

And the fact that it was Tommy...well, that brought up a whole mess of things she wasn't in any shape to deal with right now. Not to mention, she reminded herself soberly, after yesterday's misadventures, they were no closer to finding Tricia.

She emerged from the bathroom ten minutes later, body scrubbed clean and her hair damp. On the bed was a small pile of clothing. Kate shook it out and found a denim skirt, a blue cotton T-shirt with the word "JUICY" emblazoned across the front, underwear, and a stretchy lace bra.

After an initial burst of jealousy as she wondered where Tommy had come across these women's clothes, she tamped it back and decided to give him the benefit of the doubt. She might have thought him capable of it before, but after last night, Kate was almost certain Tommy wouldn't be so casually cruel as to dress her in clothes that belonged to another lover.

She left his bedroom and followed the sounds of activity and the delicious smells of coffee and toast wafting from the kitchen.

Tommy was standing at the stove, shuffling a pan. He looked over his shoulder, grinning appreciatively when he saw her. "Looks like everything fits. I wasn't sure since Emilia is so much taller than you."

"These are your sister's?" Kate looked down at herself. She'd only met Tommy's little sister a handful of times. The last time she'd seen her, the little girl had been barely nine years old. It was impossible to imagine her big enough to fit these clothes, much less be taller than Kate herself.

"Yeah, from when she was in about ninth grade. Luckily Mom has a problem throwing anything away. I had her run them over while you were still asleep," he said, turning back to the stove. "I figured you'd want something else to wear besides my giant T-shirts."

Despite her talk to herself about getting her head back on the important matters at hand, she started to get a little misty at his consideration.

He set a plate piled high with scrambled eggs and toast on the breakfast bar and motioned her over. "Come eat."

"I can't eat all that," she said, though her stomach rumbled as she sat down and took up her fork.

"Well, you have to eat some," he said, "or else you can't have this," he said, shaking a small brown prescription bottle.

Despite her various aches and pains, she shook her head. "No pain pills. I don't want to be out of it."

"I figured that," Tommy said, "so I had the doctor write you up a prescription for Diclofenac. It's basically high-octane ibuprofen, so you need to take it with food or it will rip your stomach to shreds."

Kate nodded and picked up a forkful of eggs, but it was hard to swallow past the lump in her throat. God, what was wrong with her, getting so emotional over something as silly as Tommy's anticipating her desire to avoid narcotics and fixing her a plate of eggs?

But when was the last time anyone thought about what you wanted or needed, Kate? What would you have done last night if Tommy hadn't been there? If this had happened back in L.A., who would have come to your rescue?

Come on. She tried to snap herself out of her pity party. *You have plenty of friends who care about you.* But not anybody she could count on to be there, anywhere, anytime, without fail.

She'd done that, she realized, by always keeping a certain distance. While she made herself available without question, without limits, to virtual strangers, after what happened to Michael, she'd never expected or asked anyone to do the same for her.

Until this second she hadn't realized how badly she'd missed that. A low whisper in the dark echoed through her consciousness. *I'll always be here for you.*

At that moment she realized Tommy's whisper hadn't been part of another dream.

"Are you okay? Are you in pain?" Tommy's voice was tight with concern and the sound of a spatula hitting the stove echoed through the kitchen.

Kate looked up, startled, and it was only then that she realized she was crying. Mortified, she grabbed up her napkin and swallowed back a sob. "No, I'm fine, I'm sorry—"

Tommy was already at her side, cradling her face gently as he tilted it back so he could look in her eyes. "Is it your head? Your ribs?" Though his voice was calm, his eyes were anxious in a way she would have never expected from the cool, remote man he'd grown into.

"I'm not hurt, not any worse anyway," she said. "I'm just"—*a completely screwed-up emotional mess*—"a little overwhelmed by everything." *And by "everything," I mean you and all the crazy ideas I'm starting to get just because you're being so nice to me.*

"Tell me about it," he said. His hand lingered on her cheek, his thumb brushing slowly against her cheekbone.

He was so close she could see the golden flecks in his deep brown eyes, the individual whiskers that shadowed his hard jaw. "You wouldn't know it from the last few days, but I'm usually much more in control of my emotions," Kate said with a little sniff.

"Nothing like stress and having the crap scared out of you to bring all of it right up to the surface." The way he said it, she wasn't sure he was talking about her.

In which case…Her heart stuttered as she wondered what emotions, exactly, were coming to his surface. Was she an idiot to hope they even came close to matching hers?

Her eyes drifted down to his mouth, studying the fullness of his bottom lip, its softness almost incongruous with the harshness of his features. Her own lips tingled with the need to feel them on hers.

As though he read her mind, Tommy groaned and closed the distance between them. He caught the back of her head, holding her in place as his mouth took hers in a kiss that stole her breath and sent an ache of desire through her that was so fierce it made her other aches and pains seem like nothing.

Kate wrapped her hand around his neck and sucked his tongue into her mouth, drinking in the taste of him, as starved for him as if it had been years instead of days since she'd tasted him last.

He ended the kiss as quickly as it started, jerking away even as Kate tried to hold him close.

"Christ," he said, breathing hard. He closed his eyes and

rested his forehead against hers as Kate tried to slow the galloping pace of her heart. "This can't happen, not right now."

He backed away from her, looking at her as if she were a mountain lion ready to spring.

"But I feel fine," Kate said as she slid off the bar stool to follow him. She hid a wince as she put her weight on her sore hip. Yesterday's attack had left her bruised and battered, not to mention terrified beyond all reason.

It also made her realize how life could turn on a dime, how quickly they could lose everything.

Though Michael's death and her work made her keenly aware of how brutally short life could be, she'd never faced her own mortality as she had yesterday when that hand was closing around her neck. And to think she could have died, without ever seeing Tommy again, touching him, feeling him inside her...

She was afraid, deathly afraid of making another mistake, of getting hurt and hurting him back. But she wasn't going to let that fear stop her from taking what she wanted. And right now she wanted Tommy.

She reached out, slid her hands up his chest, cupping one around his neck to draw his mouth down to hers. "Please, Tommy, I promise I'm fine."

His lips closed over hers on a groan. "I don't want to hurt you," he repeated. Kate felt his hands slide around her waist. She knew she'd won when he pulled her closer and flicked his tongue across her lips, urging hers to part.

Kate tangled her tongue with his and let him guide her backward to the couch. She sank back against the leather cushions, heat pooling between her thighs as Tommy slid his hand up one bare leg...

The phone rang so loud it made her jump, followed by a cry of protest as Tommy stood up, cursing.

"It's the intercom, someone's here," he said as he marched over to the box by the door and pressed a button. "What?" he snapped.

"It's CJ." The speaker filled the room with his voice. "Open up, it's important."

Tommy placed his thumb over a sensor and muttered something that sounded like "cockblocker."

"Did you find out who broke into Kate's?" Tommy said before he'd even fully opened the door to reveal CJ. Instead of his usual uniform, the sheriff was dressed in a T-shirt, nylon shorts, and running shoes. Sweat darkened his hair and ran down the sides of his face. His chest heaving like a bellows. "That's the only reason I can think for you to be bothering me right now."

"What about something that might help us find Tricia?" CJ bit back, his green eyes flashing in irritation. "No offense, Kate, but she's still my first priority."

Kate saw a look of shame flash across Tommy's face as she hurried off the couch. "None taken. What did you find?"

"This."

Kate looked closer, her breath freezing in her chest when she saw what rested in his large palm. A small jar made of frosted glass, with the name of the product written in loopy pink and gold writing across the front.

Beaute D'or.

Chapter 22

Tommy listened intently as CJ described how he'd stumbled across the jar while running on a nearby trail.

"I needed to get out to clear my head," CJ said after he'd gulped the glass of water Kate had brought him. "I didn't want to run into anyone, so took that trail you showed me, the one that you can pick up over by your parents' place."

Tommy knew it well, ran it several times a week any time he was in Sandpoint. "It doesn't get much traffic," Tommy said to bring Kate up to speed. "It goes from the top of this ridge down to the lake, but the trailhead isn't obvious from the beach, and the other access point is from up here. We need to get Jackson in the loop on this," Tommy said.

Tommy lent CJ a pair of jeans and a clean T-shirt. CJ took a quick shower and then the three of them loaded into Tommy's truck and headed to Jackson's house.

Jackson's expression was wary as he opened the door and saw the three of them. "What is it?"

"We may have found something that will help us find Tricia," Kate said simply.

Jackson quickly ushered them into the living room. "Tell me what's going on."

CJ cast a look over Jackson's shoulder at Brooke, who was curled up at the end of a couch. Next to her was Ben

Kortlang, who seemed to have taken Kate's advice about keeping an eye on Brooke very seriously if the protective vibe he was throwing off was anything to go by.

Jackson tracked his look. "This is a family issue, and she deserves to know exactly what's going on as much as I do. As for the kid, well, he seems like a good enough sort, and I think you'll need a crowbar to get him away from her."

CJ and Tommy exchanged a look. "The information we're about to share cannot leave this room. I don't want any of this getting out to the press."

"We won't say anything," Brooke said tightly. "I just want Tricia to come home."

As Jackson absorbed what CJ had found and what it might imply, Tommy unpacked the laptop that never seemed to leave his possession. He quickly pulled up a website that provided maps of the area surrounding the trail and came up with a strategy to conduct the search.

"Most of the trail runs through open areas," Tommy said as he traced his mouse over the line on the map. Kate felt a presence next to her and looked over to see that Brooke and Ben had come to get a closer look at the maps on Tommy's computer screen. "But this area here—it's about a hundred acres or so—" He circled the cursor around the indicated area. "This is private property."

"Will we need a warrant?" Jackson asked.

Kate shook her head. "Not if we have reason to believe Tricia could be in the vicinity."

"And I'm more than happy to put up with a trespassing charge if it means we find Tricia. CJ, you can stay on the other side of the property lines if you're worried it'll come back to bite you in the ass later," Tommy said.

"We'll jump off that bridge when we get to it."

They agreed to keep the search parties small. Other than

Tommy and Jackson, only police officials would be involved in the search. While they wouldn't be able to cover the area as quickly, the more civilians involved, the higher the risk that the press would somehow get wind of it.

"I can't emphasize how important it is to keep this to yourselves," Kate said, giving both Brooke and Ben meaningful looks. "If this turns out to be the break we hope it is and our suspect finds out, it could be disaster."

They both nodded solemnly. "I want to help," Ben said suddenly. CJ started to shake his head, but Ben continued. "I've been out with search parties every day for the last three, and you need all the eyes you can get if you're not going to call in volunteers."

CJ looked like he was going to protest again.

"He can come with me," Tommy said.

CJ shrugged his shoulders as though to say "Suit yourselves."

"I want to go too," Brooke said, her voice shaky.

"Absolutely not." Jackson's voice cracked sharply across the room.

"Why?" Brooke asked, her eyes shiny with tears. "Do you think I'm going to do something to screw it up again?"

"No, Jesus." The fight seemed to drain from him as he walked over to his older daughter. "That's not it at all," Jackson said, awkwardly reaching out his hand and letting it drop before touching her. "I'm just afraid... we might find..."

Kate's throat tightened, mirroring Brooke's sob as she nodded in sudden comprehension.

"I don't want you to have to see that," Jackson finished.

Brooke nodded in horrified silence, and Kate's heart cracked as Jackson turned back to Tommy without another word.

As CJ called in all the deputies for a debrief back at the

station, Tommy packed up his computer and went out to the truck. He returned shortly with a black equipment bag that he set on the wooden dining table.

"What is that?" Kate asked as he passed what looked like a set of earbuds to both Jackson and Ben.

"Communications," Tommy said shortly. "Your standard tactical communication set."

"Can't you just use the radios?" Kate asked, indicating the handset hooked to CJ's belt.

CJ's boots thudded on the wood floor as he walked over. "Usually, but we can't completely secure the frequency, and we wouldn't want anyone picking this up on the scanner."

"You need extras?" Tommy asked.

CJ shook his head. "Thanks, but after I was able to show the bean counters in the capital that the meth kings could monitor our surveillance operations with a scanner, I got them to kick down for better equipment."

Tommy gave a grunt and a nod of approval, and Kate listened as they discussed exchanging frequencies followed by a lot of technical stuff she didn't understand.

Tommy turned to her and held out a set and reached for her ear. Kate held still, forcing herself not to lean into him as he placed the earpiece in her right ear.

"How's that?" Tommy asked, and Kate shivered at the feel of his warm breath skidding across her cheek.

"Fine," she said, and risked a look up to meet his gaze. Big mistake, as the dark fire in his eyes told her he was just as affected by her nearness as she was. Her tongue flicked out to moisten suddenly dry lips as she tried to keep her knees from turning to water.

His eyes locked on her mouth, and he leaned a millimeter closer before he stepped away. But not before his fingers trailed down her neck, underneath her hair in a secret caress that promised all kinds of wickedness when the time was right. "You should be able to hear everything through that."

"What about my mike?"

"You won't need one since you won't be out there with us."

"No, I want to be out there. I need to help—"

"It could take us hours, and we're covering potentially eighty square miles. No way in hell you're up to that."

As much as she wanted to protest, the ache in her ribs and hip told Kate otherwise. She was maintaining, all right, but she could feel her pain levels creeping up even in the brief time she'd spent on her feet.

"Not only that," Tommy said before Kate could concede, "someone should stay here with her," indicating his chin in the direction of Brooke, who was curled up on the end of the couch with her knees pulled tightly to her chest. "I think she needs someone who can understand what she's going through."

Kate nodded and stood by as Tommy made sure all of the communications equipment was working. Then he pulled out four handheld devices and handed one to all the men, including CJ.

"Now this we don't have back at the station," CJ said appreciatively.

"What is it?" Ben asked, turning his up and over in his hand, pushing buttons at random, jumping when the machine let out a shrill beep.

"It's a thermal imager," Tommy said as he swiped it from Ben's grasp and pressed a button to silence the machine. "They're less useful when it's light out, but since nothing came up in that area in the previous foot searches and fly-overs, I figured it could help us find a structure or something underground that was missed."

They all gathered eagerly around Tommy as he went over the features of the state-of-the-art gadget. Boys and their toys, Kate thought with a little grin.

Kate followed them to the door, her heart in her throat, a knot in her stomach that was equal parts anticipation and dread. After nearly five endless days, they might have a real chance of finding Tricia.

The question was, what condition would she be in?

"I don't like leaving you here alone," Tommy said grimly as he gave his equipment one last check.

"We'll be fine," Kate said, but that didn't stop the ripple of unease from skittering down her spine. "No one knows I'm here except you. Even if someone wanted to hurt me, he couldn't find me."

Tommy curved his hand around her neck and leaned close. "Lock the door and set the alarm. Don't open the door to anyone but me, CJ, or Jackson."

Kate nodded and Tommy started out the door.

Brooke's voice stopped him short before he closed it. "Wait," she said, and rose from the couch. "Can I have one of those ear things too?" Crossing her arms around her waist, she walked slowly to him. "I need to know what's happening. I need to know if—" She bit her bottom lip rather than finish the thought.

"Of course," Tommy said with a sad smile that transformed his harsh features. Kate watched, a pinching sensation in her chest as Tommy patiently helped the girl insert the earpiece. When he was done, he pulled Brooke in for a brotherly hug and told her what she desperately needed to hear. "Don't you worry. We're going to get your sister back."

Whether she believed him or not, Brooke nodded and gave him a wobbly smile. "And you need to understand," he added, "none of this is your fault. You didn't do this to your sister."

Tommy looked up over Brooke's head and met Kate's stare, and the look in his eyes demolished any last barrier she might have tried to keep between them.

—⁓—

They agreed that Tommy, Jackson, Ben, and two of CJ's deputies would start out in the area on the east side of the trail, where CJ had initially found the jar. They fanned out, each covering his own quadrant of the map, giving each other regular updates on their position.

CJ and his team searched through the woods on the other side of the trail.

It was tedious work, as they moved slowly, carefully through the brushy terrain, eyes peeled for any sign that anyone was there or had been there in the last five days. One hour passed, then two, and the men were drenched in sweat from the afternoon heat.

Suddenly, one of the deputies in CJ's party began chattering excitedly. "I think I see something—it looks like clothes."

Tommy froze, listening, willing all the other men to shut the fuck up so he could hear what was going on three miles away.

"Everyone, shut the hell up so Roberts can give us a sit rep." CJ's voice crackled into his earpiece. It went dead quiet, then someone—Deputy Roberts, Tommy assumed—began to speak.

"I've found what appears to be a shirt, dark red."

Tommy heard a sharp gasp and figured it was Jackson. Tommy's own stomach rolled over. Tricia had been wearing a red tank top the night she disappeared.

"Oh, shit," Roberts said.

Tommy felt his blood rush from his head to his feet at the man's grim tone. "What?" he said, bracing himself for what was to come.

"It's got Lightning McQueen on it," Roberts said irritably.

"Lightning Mc-what?" Tommy sputtered.

"It's from the kid's movie," CJ broke in wearily. "I think what Roberts is saying is that unless Tricia has a thing for cartoon cars, the shirt doesn't belong to her."

"And since it's a size..." There was a pause, no doubt Roberts searching for the tag. "Five T, I'd say it's too small to belong to our suspect."

Tommy felt himself deflate after the adrenaline rush. "Let's keep moving, guys." As he continued to move, slowly but surely deeper into the woods, he tried to chase away the growing worry that they could search behind every tree trunk and under every boulder in the forest, and they still weren't going to find Tricia.

—⁓—

Brooke had been pacing the great room, brushing off all of Kate's attempts to engage in conversation until Roberts's voice crackled excitedly in their ears. Then she'd stood stock still, her face a mask of mingled hope and fear as he described finding the red shirt.

Kate moved closer to her, unconsciously reaching out to grab the girl's tense, cold hand. Then, as it was revealed that the shirt most likely belonged to a preschooler, Brooke simply crumpled to the floor like all of her bones had turned to rubber.

She buried her face in her hands and sobbed. "They're never going to find her. They're never going to find her. And it's all my fault."

Kate sank to the floor next to her and wrapped her arm around her shoulders. "It's not true. It's not your fault."

"Yes it is." Brooke's head reared back, her face blotchy with tears, her face a mask of pain and guilt. "You don't get it. My mom, before she died, she told me I had to look after Tricia."

Kate's own eyes stung with tears as she remembered a similar admonishment the night Michael died. "Your brother may think he can take care of himself, but he's still only twelve," her father had said sternly. "We're counting on you to look after him." Not as dramatic as a deathbed request, but still...Shame at how casually she'd dismissed him burned through her like acid.

"I know, I know exactly what you're going through."

"Bullshit," Brooke said. She pulled away and scrambled to her feet. "I sent my sister home alone in the middle of the night and she never made it home just so I could be with a guy. And now my dad totally hates me for it and I can't even blame him. I seriously doubt you know exactly what I'm going through."

"You know my background, right? Why I got involved with St. Anthony's?"

Brooke shrugged. "Something about your brother, right? He was taken and—" She paused, swallowed hard.

"Killed," Kate finished for her. "He was taken from the house we were renting, sexually assaulted, and murdered."

Brooke didn't speak, just stared at Kate in morbid fascination.

"But if you go back and read the news stories, you'll see that I was the only one in the house with him that night. My parents were out of town, my sister was at a friend's house, and I was supposed to look after Michael. But instead of staying in the house and keeping an eye on him, I was too busy making out with Tommy Ibarra to care."

Brooke's eyes flew wide. "As in—"

Kate gave a rueful smile.

Brooke gave her a skeptical look. "You're so nice and he's so...scary."

Kate shook her head. "He wasn't always as"—she searched for the right word—"intimidating as he is now. When we were younger he was..." Again, words eluded her. Nice was too tepid, sweet too, well, sweet. "He was pretty awesome." Then, reflecting on the last couple of days, she added, "He's still pretty awesome." She shook her head and tried to wipe what she was pretty sure was a dopey, dreamy look off her face. "Anyway, the point is, I know what you're going through. I completely understand how you feel."

Brooke nodded and swallowed hard, her big dark eyes bright with tears. This time when Kate pulled her close, she didn't pull away.

Kate held her, Brooke's body heaving with sobs as she buried her head against Kate's shoulder. "I just keep thinking of what I said to her when I told her to leave the party. I told her she was an annoying pain in the ass. I can't stop thinking those were the last words she ever heard from me. That she was scared and hurt and maybe dying, and she died thinking I didn't even care about her."

"She doesn't think that. Sisters fight all the time. She knows you love her."

Brooke shook her head. "No, she doesn't. She's probably dead already. Everyone knows it but no one wants to say it out loud."

Kate's mouth pressed in a grim line. "We can't give up hope—"

Brooke pushed away and started to pace, her agitation building as the minutes passed and there was still no progress from the search team. "What if there is no hope? What if she's dead?" She stopped suddenly, sank to the floor, and buried her face in her hands. "What if she's dead? What will I do?"

Kate wished she could feed her some line about how the pain would ease, how the guilt would fade, and eventually she'd be able to focus on the happy memories she and her sister shared together. But she didn't have it in her to lie. "You'll hurt," she said simply. "A lot. For the rest of your life. But if you're lucky, you and your dad will pull together and help each other get through it."

"My father," Brooke said, shaking her head. She suddenly looked beyond weary, and much older than seventeen years. "He'll never forgive me."

Kate wished she could contradict her with conviction. "He shouldn't have to. It wasn't your fault."

"Did you believe people when they tried to tell you that?"

Kate smiled sadly. "No. But then again, it was hard to hear them when so many other people told me that it was."

Brooke cocked her head and looked about to speak, but whatever she was going to say was lost as Tommy's voice crackled in over the earpieces. "I've found something. A structure of some kind. We're heading in."

Chapter 23

It was Ben Kortlang who spotted the tiny scrap of material clinging to a wild rose bush. After years of hunting with his father and uncles, like Tommy, Ben's eye was trained to look for signs of his prey. A footprint, a broken branch, a tuft of hair.

Or a scrap of red cotton, no more than an inch square. "Over here," he called Tommy. "You see that?"

Tommy squinted, but after a few seconds he saw what Kortlang was talking about. Once you got off the trail the undergrowth was pretty thick, but there was no mistaking the outline of a footprint.

They painstakingly picked their way through the brush and followed a half dozen more footsteps before the trail petered out again. Tommy's neck tightened with frustration as he scanned the area and saw nothing.

He held up his thermal imager and turned it in a slow circle, keeping it low to the ground in case it picked up on anything in the underbrush. He hit on a red blob but knew immediately it was too small to be human. They bush-whacked several more yards, cursing as branches snagged on their skin and clothes.

Tommy lifted the sensor, his eyes flying open as it revealed essentially a wall of red somewhere directly in front of him. It was big, big enough to be a vehicle or even a structure of some sort. And though he couldn't see it to save his life, there was no denying its existence.

He quickly let the rest of the team know what he'd discovered and waited for Jackson and Ben to catch up to him before he went any further.

"I don't suppose there's any convincing you to wait for me to arrive," CJ said.

Tommy looked down at his GPS monitor and noted CJ's position. "Not unless you can cover two kilometers in less than thirty seconds."

CJ merely grunted and reminded Tommy not to screw with anything that could be used as evidence.

They didn't see the trailer until they were almost on top of it. Hidden in a thicket of chokecherry trees, painted shades of green and brown to perfectly blend in with the surroundings, it was no wonder it had gone entirely unnoticed by the helicopters that had flown over the area days before.

Tommy, Ben, and Jackson quickly skirted around the edge, and Tommy mentally cataloged the details. The trailer was about twenty feet long, single wide, set up on blocks. From the way the blocks had settled into the earth, it looked like it had been there for a long, long time.

As they circled, he noticed that every single window was boarded up tight, with nails driven into the aluminum sides of the trailer.

The front door was incongruously insecure, the flimsy thing armed only with a standard knob lock and latch. "Ben, you stay behind us," Tommy said as he drew his weapon and watched Jackson do the same. One blow from his booted foot sent the metal door crumpling inward. Tommy froze a minute, allowing his eyes to adjust to the nearly full darkness as he stepped inside. He waited a couple of breaths but heard nothing.

Gun in one hand, Maglite in the other, he swept the beam across the room, his nose wrinkling at the hot, close air in the trailer. There was a musky, dank smell to the air but not, Tommy noticed with relief, the sick rot scent of death.

The room was mostly unfurnished, nothing but a cheap plastic table and a single chair. Off to the right was a short hallway, with a door leading to the trailer's bedroom. Tommy's stomach flipped when he saw the door was secured with an industrial-grade combination lock.

The kind you used only when you really wanted to keep someone out—or in.

"Don't suppose anyone brought bolt cutters?" he muttered. "Hands over ears, guys," he said as he lifted his M9 Beretta a couple inches from the lock. A loud *crack* and the lock popped open.

Tommy barely had the lock off before Jackson was pushing past him through the door.

"Tricia!" Jackson rushed over to the slender figure splayed across the bed, her wrists secured to the headboard by metal cuffs.

His stomach clenched when he saw that Tricia didn't move when Jackson called her name and shook her lightly.

"Is she..." Ben asked.

Jackson had his fingers against Tricia's neck, but they were shaking too hard to get a pulse. Tommy gently pushed him aside and pressed his fingers along the side of Tricia's throat and bent low to hear her breath. "She's alive." There was a chorus of cheers as CJ and the other members of the search party took in the good news.

"But she's unresponsive. Dehydrated and possibly drugged is my guess," he continued. He pressed a hand to her forehead. "She's running a fever." He heard Jackson suck in a breath, and when he focused the flashlight down he saw why.

In addition to the bruises mottling her skin and circling her throat, she had an ugly gash halfway down her thigh. The flesh was red and swollen around the jagged edges.

"She's got a four-inch laceration on her leg that looks infected. She's also sustained some trauma to her face and head—"

"Christ, he beat the crap out of her. He beat my little girl," Jackson said, horrified.

"We need to get her out of here as quickly as possible."

—⁓—

"Her leg is badly infected," Dr. Schmidt said, his face grim. "But the good news is that it doesn't look like we're dealing with antibiotic-resistant bacteria," he said to the group waiting anxiously in the waiting room for an update. "In addition, it appears she's been sedated with something that's still working through her system. She also has mild heatstroke."

"What about her head injury?" Jackson asked tightly.

"She has a slight skull fracture, but there doesn't appear to be any subdural bleeding. I think once we get her fluids up, her fever comes down, and whatever she was sedated with wears off, we should see a lot of improvement."

Kate, Tommy, and the rest of the group echoed Jackson's sigh, and Kate heard Brooke's muffled sob of relief as she buried her head against Ben's chest. The tension eased from her muscles so abruptly Kate felt like she was going to melt like a puddle onto the floor.

"When will we be able to question her?" CJ asked. His hair was rumpled as though he'd run his hands through it, and his uniform was smudged with dirt and ripped in several places.

"She needs to regain consciousness first," the doctor said, the edge in his voice belying his kind eyes. "Then we can determine what she's up for."

CJ nodded grimly. "I'm glad we got her back safe, but I'll be damned if I let whoever did this to her get away with it," he told Jackson. "I'm going to head back to the trailer and make sure the guys don't miss anything while they're processing the scene."

"Can I see her?" Jackson asked.

The doctor nodded and motioned for Jackson to follow.

Kate's stomach knotted as she saw the way Brooke shifted uncertainly in her chair, half rising as though to follow, then sitting back down, unsure of her welcome.

As though he heard her thoughts, Jackson hesitated before he pushed through the double doors leading to the exam room. "Brooke, honey, aren't you coming?"

Brooke nodded eagerly and hurried to her father's side. Kate felt like her heart was going to burst out of her chest when Jackson caught his daughter in a quick, fierce hug and bent his head to whisper something Kate couldn't hear.

Whatever it was, it made Brooke clutch her father harder before they went back to see Tricia.

"They're going to be okay," Tommy said, and covered her hand with his. Kate looked down at their joined hands, warmth coursing all the way up her arm, down to her belly and lower where it pulsed in anticipation.

And just like that, the mood shifted between them from overwhelming relief in the wake of Tricia's rescue to electric, crackling awareness.

Tommy's fingers tightened around hers. "How are you feeling?"

If she really focused on it, somewhere in the background Kate could pick up the dull pain of her injuries. "I hardly feel a thing." It was true. They were easily ignored in favor of the way Tommy's dark eyes glittered hungrily as they raked over her, creating a sharp ache that easily eclipsed any caused by the blow she'd taken to the head.

"Good," Tommy said, his lips pulling in a smile as he raised their clasped hands and placed a firm kiss on the back of hers. "I just need to say goodbye to Jackson."

He was back in under a minute, and in a moment of déjà vu, they were skirting through the exam rooms and sneaking out the back entrance of the hospital. But this time, instead of trying not to throw up from the pain in her head, Kate was giggling like a teenager as they ducked through the hallway in an effort not to be seen.

A nurse passed them, a quizzical look on her face. Kate struggled to keep her composure, straightening her spine and dropping back a little bit to allow more space between herself and Tommy. Still, she worried that anyone passing them could feel the electricity between them and would know exactly what they planned to do as soon as they were alone.

They turned the corner to the back door. "Wait here while I get the truck," Tommy said. Kate nodded. Tommy reached for the door, but a split second before he opened it he reached for Kate instead.

"What are you—" was all Kate could get out before her back was pressed to the wall, Tommy's mouth covering hers in a kiss that threatened to consume her. A tiny voice in the back of her head warned her that this wasn't a good idea, that someone could walk by and see them at any moment.

The voice dissolved in a burst of light and heat at the hot slide of Tommy's tongue against hers, the heat of his big hands wrapping around the curve of her hip, molding her to him. As always, the second he touched her, the rest of the world faded to the background, until all she knew was him.

He pulled away with a groan and reality came crashing back. "Oh my God, we can't do this here," she said shakily, though her arms were still looped around him. Her view was mostly blocked by his broad chest, but she looked around frantically to see if anyone was coming. "Why did you do that? Anyone could have seen us."

"Because I felt like if I didn't get to kiss you my head was going to explode. And no one is around to see." He stepped back, letting her see the empty corridor for herself.

Kate blew out a sigh of relief and pushed him toward the door. "Go get the truck before I let you make me forget we're in a public place again."

As worried as she was about getting caught, that didn't suppress the thrill sizzling through her. The same thrill she'd gotten the first time she snuck out to be with Tommy so many years ago.

As she waited for him, she felt a pinch of doubt. The last time she let her crazy desire for Tommy drive her to break the rules it had ended in disaster. What if...

She pushed the thought firmly aside. She couldn't allow herself to dwell on past tragedies. What had happened was awful and she'd never get over it, but she couldn't let that stand in the way of a second chance at happiness.

With Tommy.

Which was exactly what she wanted, she admitted to herself, equally thrilled and terrified at the realization. But what if he didn't want the same thing?

Tommy's truck pulled up. He got out of the cab, and all of Kate's what-ifs died as she drank in that long-legged, lean-hipped stride, that brick wall of a chest, and most of all at that wide, knowing smile that transformed his harsh features and made her feel like she was the most amazing woman who had ever set foot on planet earth.

He led her around the other side of the truck and opened the door for her, his eyes narrowing appreciatively on Kate's legs as her borrowed skirt rode up her thighs as she climbed in.

As he pulled out of the parking lot, Kate didn't even bother asking where they were going. As far as she was concerned, Tommy could take her anywhere.

—◆—

Maura Walsh blew out a frustrated breath and shifted on her heels, trying to ease the pressure on the balls of her feet. Damn shoes had cost half a month's salary, and while they did amazing things for her legs, if she tried to stand in them for more than ten minutes, she felt like spikes were being driven into the soles of her feet.

She'd been standing on the concrete steps for hours waiting for an update on Tricia Fuller, and now her feet hurt so much she was afraid she was going to end up with nerve damage.

The sheriff—whose rumpled clothes and disheveled hair didn't detract a bit from his overall hotness—had given a brief statement eons ago, and no one else had come out to speak to the press since.

"Let's take a break. I'm starving," grumbled Marshall, her cameraman.

"Not like you couldn't afford to miss a few meals," she shot back with a glare, her nose wrinkling in disgust at the way the buttons of his plaid shirt strained to contain his belly. "I'm not leaving until we get something good." Like maybe a sound bite from Tricia's sister, Brooke. Or even better, some real evidence to prove her hunch that the relationship between Kate Beckett and Fuller's friend Ibarra wasn't just professional. The prospect made her toes curl in her too-tight shoes. After the fallout from Kate's relationship with Graham Miller, the discovery that she was fooling around on yet another case would create the kind of frenzy that would kick Maura out of a backwater market like northern Idaho and straight into the big leagues.

"Hey, where are you going?" she said, snapping out of her reverie as Marshall set his camera down on the steps next to her.

"Gotta take a piss."

Maura gave a shudder of revulsion as he tromped up the stairs. Maybe he was right. They should break. The rest of the press had left already. She'd sent in her reel to air on the six o'clock broadcast. The likelihood of getting something in for the eleven o'clock broadcast was nil.

She slipped out of her shoes and started to limp back to the van when her phone rang. She froze, anticipation swelling in her chest when she saw the caller ID with the hospital's name. "Maura Walsh," she answered.

"Hi, uh, Ms. Walsh? My name is Nancy, I work here at the hospital. I got your card?"

After Kate Beckett's run-in with her intruder, Maura and Marshall had discreetly passed out her business card to several staff members, promising cash rewards for any information they could pass on. "Do you have something you want to share with me, Nancy?"

Nancy hesitated on the other end, and Maura fought back the urge to tell her to spit it out. "N-no one can find out I talked to you," Nancy stammered. "I'll get fired if anyone finds out."

"I always keep my sources confidential," Maura assured her. "Do you have information about Tricia Fuller?"

"Not exactly..."

—๛—

"Can't we stay a little longer?" Brooke asked, her fingers laced tightly with Tricia's. Though Tricia's fingers were limp, they were warm. Warm and alive. The words echoed like a mantra through her head. Tricia was warm and alive and with them.

And—by some miracle—whoever the sicko was who had taken her hadn't raped her. Despite Brooke's tortured imaginings, somehow her baby sister had been spared that. The knowledge took the edge off her guilt, though Brooke knew it would never go away. It didn't matter what everyone said.

Even her father's assurances and tight hug—the first he'd given her in days—couldn't take the weight of the blame from her shoulders.

"She needs undisturbed rest," the doctor said kindly but firmly. "You can come visit again in the morning."

She bent and gave Tricia a kiss on the cheek, her throat tight as she got a close-up view of the mottled bruise on her sister's cheekbone. "I love you, Tricia. I love you so much and I promise to take care of you from now on," she said softly.

When she turned around, she saw her father's eyes were suspiciously wet. "She's going to be okay," Jackson said, and pulled her into a hug. Brooke closed her eyes and breathed in his familiar, comfortable smell. She'd been so busy pushing him away, pretending she didn't need anyone after Mom died, she'd forgotten how good it felt to have her dad hug her. "I'm sorry, Daddy," she said for what felt like the dozenth time today.

"I told you, honey, I don't blame you—"

"I'm not just talking about Tricia," Brooke said, tilting

her head back so she could meet her father's gaze. "I'm sorry I've been such a bitch lately, after Mom—"

"It's okay. We're both having a hard time, and when we get home we all need to work on pulling ourselves back together. We already lost Mom. We can't lose each other."

Brooke stayed close to his side, his arm around her shoulders as they walked out to the waiting room, where Ben was. He stood up eagerly when he saw her.

Her heart shuddered in her chest as she returned his smile. When she'd first met him, she figured they'd hook up a couple times and that would be that. She'd never imagined that he'd end up being someone who'd stick by her unconditionally during one of the most difficult periods in her life.

"I was hoping Ben could give you a ride home," Jackson said, his mouth quirking wryly as Ben eagerly reached out for her hand.

"No problem." Ben nodded enthusiastically.

"What about you?" Brooke turned to her father.

"I'm going to stay here with Tricia. I don't want her to be alone."

"I'll stay too—" Jackson lifted up a hand to silence her.

"You go have fun, get some rest. Tracy will be over at nine to stay the night with you. I don't want you staying alone."

"Sir, I'm happy to stay with Brooke," Ben broke in. "There's no need to bother Tracy."

"Ben, you're a nice kid, and I like you, but no way in hell are you and Brooke staying unchaperoned under the same roof."

Ben's hand dropped from Brooke's shoulder and he jumped away from her like she was on fire. "I didn't—I wouldn't—" Hot color flooded his cheeks and Brooke felt her own cheeks flame.

"And Tracy will be there later to make sure you don't," he said, leveling what Brooke liked to call his drill sergeant look at them.

"Jeez, Dad, don't worry." She rolled her eyes. She leaned up to give him a quick kiss on the cheek. "Promise you'll call if she wakes up or anything?"

Her dad nodded and she and Ben started for the door. "Hold on, I want to say bye to Kate," Brooke said, looking around the waiting room for the other woman.

"She took off with Tommy about ten minutes ago," Ben said, stepping out of the way to let a dark-haired man in a flannel shirt pass them coming the other way.

Her lips pulled into a knowing smile. "I thought they might be hooking up again."

"What do you mean, again?"

Brooke lowered her voice. "You know how Kate's brother was killed?"

"Yeah." Ben grimaced. "By Emerson Flannery. You know Erin who runs the Mary's? He was her uncle."

"Well, the night it happened, Kate was supposed to be watching her brother, but she'd snuck off to fool around with Tommy Ibarra."

Ben's eyes widened in surprise. "Wow, she totally doesn't seem the type. She seems kind of, I don't know, uptight. They both do."

Brooke shrugged. "They were a lot younger then. Anyway, Kate told me her dad had kept all of that out of the press." It occurred to her that Kate might not want that information to get out now either. "And I don't think she wants anyone else to know, so don't say anything to anyone, okay?"

"Promise."

They'd reached the hospital entrance and Brooke paused

for a minute, bracing herself to run the gantlet of reporters milling outside. "No comment, okay? Sheriff Kovacs doesn't want any of us talking to the press until he gets a chance to question Tricia."

Ben nodded and tucked her protectively against his side before he activated the automatic door.

Chapter 24

By the time Tommy got to his place, he was so keyed up he could barely key in the code to unlock his security gate. On the drive over, he'd tried to distract them both by discussing Tricia's case and Kate's plans for dealing with the press over the next few days. Several outlets were contacting Kate to comment on the case, but she wasn't going to give an official statement until CJ was able to question Tricia.

But even speculating on the identity of a violent criminal who preyed on young women didn't do much to take the edge off Tommy's raging desire. He'd never felt anything like this with any other woman. This intensity that went beyond need, beyond lust.

Only with Kate. *Always* with Kate. He'd done everything in his power to keep it locked down, under control, convinced if he let it loose again it would be as disastrous as it had been the first time around.

But as she reached for his hand and let him help her from the truck, an eager glimmer in her eye, he couldn't do anything but give in, give over to it. Being with Kate was as inevitable as the tides, and now that he'd stopped fighting, he realized nothing in his life ever felt as right as when he was with her.

He closed the front door and backed her up against it,

lifting her up so he could take her mouth in a deep, hungry kiss. She wrapped her arms and legs around him and eagerly parted her lips to take him.

He groaned at the first taste of her, sweet and spicy and better than anything he'd ever tasted in his life. His cock, which had been rock hard from the second he'd shut the door to his truck, strained against the fly of his pants until he thought he was going to bust through the seams.

And he hadn't even undressed her yet.

He took a deep breath, willed himself to slow down, ease off. She was still injured, for fuck's sake. He couldn't go after her like a raging bull.

But God, it was hard to slow down when she sucked his tongue into her mouth and made those little high-pitched, needy sounds in the back of her throat.

"God, Katie, I need you, I need you so much," he moaned against her lips.

"I need you too. I've never wanted anyone like I want you."

He sucked and nipped at her lips, savoring the taste of her, absorbing every detail. Her fingers threaded in his hair, sending bolts of electricity through his scalp and rippling down his spine. Her nipples were hard little points against his chest, and the memory of them, so pink and sensitive against his fingers, made his blood go thick.

Her hand curved around his neck, and he let out a surprised hiss as her thumb brushed over a long scratch he must have gotten bushwhacking while he was searching for Tricia.

The tiny jolt of pain pulled him back from the razor's edge, reminding him that he'd spent hours today out in the heat, that his skin was coated in a layer of dried sweat and grit.

He cupped her ass in his hands and pushed away from

the door, his lips never leaving hers as he carried her down the hall.

—⁓—

Kate barely noticed they were moving until Tommy peeled her legs from around his waist and set her feet on the floor.

"I need to clean up," he said, and gave her one last, hard kiss before he stepped away. She blinked, swaying a little as she realized they were in Tommy's bathroom. He quickly turned on the shower and soon the room was filled with steam.

It was on the tip of her tongue to tell him that in the state she was in, it would take more than a little sweat and dirt to put her off. Then Tommy peeled off his T-shirt and the words died in her throat.

She stared hungrily at every inch of flesh that was revealed. God, he was gorgeous, his skin so tan and smooth, stretched tight over muscles that coiled and clenched as he pulled the shirt over his head. And now that she knew how he felt against her, skin to naked skin...

His pants came next, and Kate's mouth practically watered as she took in long legs, thick with muscle. And in between...God, he was so gorgeous he made her mouth water. Long and thick, so hard she could see his pulse beat in the long vein that ran down the side.

As she watched, his own fist closed around the thick shaft, stroking up and down, making her own fingers itch to do the same. She tore her gaze away and lifted it to his face. He met hers with a look so hot she thought she was going to burst into flame.

"You gonna join me?" he said in a thick, gravelly voice that sent a pulse of need straight to her core.

Kate nodded mutely and scrambled to take off her T-shirt, skirt, panties, and bra and join Tommy under the hot spray.

Like everything else in Tommy's house, the shower stall was anything but ordinary. Over sixteen feet square, it had shower heads mounted at various heights so no matter where you stood hot spray hit your body. There was a wide bench on one end. Just in case showering became so tiring you needed to take a rest.

This morning Kate had marveled at the luxury during her quick shower. Now she realized Tommy's shower alone was nothing compared to Tommy's shower with Tommy.

He pulled her to him and ran huge, soap-slicked hands down her arms, back, and legs.

"Don't let me hurt you," he murmured as he ran a gentle hand down her bruised ribs.

Kate was too distracted by the feel of his palms closing over her breasts to even think about pain.

"God, Katie, you're so beautiful," he said as he bent his head and sucked one pink nipple firmly between his lips.

She squeezed her legs together as every lick, every nip, every lash of his tongue on her nipples intensified the pulsing between her thighs. She'd never thought of her breasts as remarkably sensitive, but right now she felt like she could come any second with nothing more than his tongue on her nipples.

"I love how your tits feel in my hands, against my tongue," he groaned.

Kate gave an answering cry as her sex clenched hard and shuddered almost like a mini-orgasm. "Oh, God, Tommy, if you're not careful you're going to make me come before we even get started."

He gave a low chuckle and backed her up a few steps. "Then I guess I better move things along."

He backed her up, urged her down on the bench seat, and sank to his knees in front of her. The hot spray gently pummeled her sides and legs as he threaded his fingers in her wet hair and took her mouth in a deep, tongue-thrusting kiss.

His other hand went back to her breasts. He cupped and squeezed, rolled her nipples between his fingers in a way that had her rocking her hips up off the warm tile, her body yearning in a way she'd never felt before. Never come close.

She'd never experienced anything like this sharp, needy ache that had her begging for his touch, desperate for release.

Desperate for him.

"Tommy," she gasped against his mouth, unable to keep the pleading tone out of her voice. "Tommy, I need...I need you..."

"And I need you too," he groaned, and pulled his mouth from hers and slid it down her neck, chest, his tongue tracing the shallow valley between her breasts before he kissed his way down her belly.

Kate's breath caught in anticipation as Tommy delivered a firm sucking kiss to the skin beneath her navel before he pulled her ass closer to the edge of the bench. She braced her weight on her hands, her sex throbbing in anticipation as Tommy hooked her knees over his shoulders.

The first touch of his tongue sent her cry echoing through the small chamber.

He parted her with his thumbs and took her in long, slow swipes of his tongue, teasing her clit before sucking it in between his lips in a way that made every cell pull tight in anticipation of pleasure.

She'd tried to tell herself she'd been imagining things the other night, that it couldn't possibly have been as good as her memories suggested.

But, oh, God...Kate had enjoyed oral sex in the past—

what wasn't to like?—but somehow it was like Tommy was connected to her body, like he knew exactly how to touch, lick, suck, knowing exactly what she wanted before even she did.

And it wasn't just his skill, it was the way he touched her. Like he was starving for the taste of her. Like he could never get enough of her. Like he was feeling her pleasure almost as keenly as she felt it herself.

Kate was usually modest during sex, preferring to have the lights off and her eyes closed, but with Tommy she didn't want to miss a single detail. Biting her lip, she looked down and gasped. She'd never seen anything more erotic than the sight of Tommy's dark head between her pale thighs, his tongue buried in her folds as he groaned in pleasure.

Then, as she watched, one tan hand stroked up the inside of her leg and she moaned as she felt firm pressure followed by the thick penetration of his fingers sliding into her wetness.

One hand came up to clutch at the slick skin of his shoulder as she rocked her hips against his mouth and fingers, urging him harder, faster as the pleasure pulled tighter and tighter in her core.

She came with a shuddering cry, her body clenching tightly around his fingers, her hips arching eagerly against his mouth. He groaned, continuing to suck and stroke her until the last of her tremors faded.

Kate blinked against the fog as she came back to earth and found herself sprawled on the bench, her body still tingling with little aftershocks.

Tommy still knelt in front of her and pulled her up so he could kiss her. Kate reached dazedly for a bar of soap next to her and lathered her hands and ran them over Tommy's shoulders and back. He groaned, arching under her touch like a jungle cat. As she explored his mouth with lazy strokes of her tongue, she ran her hands over every patch of skin she could reach, discovering the muscles cording his arms, the thick slabs of his chest marred here and there by ropy scars. She traced the ripples of his abdomen and lower.

He gave a harsh groan as her soapy hand closed around his erection, his hips arching helplessly as she squeezed him firmly. She couldn't take her eyes off the sight of her fist closed around his shaft, stroking it up and down as his breath sawed in his chest and his fists clenched at his sides.

Though the last pulses of her orgasm had barely faded, the sight of him in her hand was enough to make her body quiver with the need to feel him buried deep inside of her.

First she wanted something else. "Stand up," she said as she leaned in to chase a rivulet of water down his throat.

He rose to his knees, his dark eyes shimmering with lust as he read her intentions.

"You don't have to—" His words caught in his throat as she closed her lips over the tip of his cock and swirled her tongue around the head.

"I know I don't have to," she said, and traced her tongue up and down his length. She reveled in the tremors that shuddered through his body, loved the power that surged through her, knowing that this man who was a hundred pounds heavier and a million times stronger was totally powerless against the pleasure she was giving him. "I want to."

—⁓—

Tommy clenched his teeth around a groan as he watched Kate's kiss-swollen pink lips close over the head of his cock. Just the sight of it was almost enough to make him come right then and there. He tried closing his eyes but the image was seared in his brain.

And the feel. Oh, Christ, hot wet suction, the firm stroke of her slim hand squeezing him in a firm, steady rhythm. How many times had he dreamed of this, Kate's sweet, soft mouth closing over him, taking him as deep in her throat as she could?

Jesus. He'd never imagined that thing she was doing with her tongue, swirling it around the head and fluttering it against the sensitive spot right below. Everything about it, everything about her was better than any fantasy he'd ever conjured.

Her hair fell in a wet curtain against her cheek, and he brushed it back with trembling fingers so he could watch his cock slide between her lips, then out, its pulsing length slick and shiny.

He could feel his orgasm bearing down, felt his sac pull tighter against his body, his thigh muscles pull tight. "Kate, I'm going to come," he warned. "You should probably stop—"

A harsh groan ripped from his chest as Kate sucked him harder, deeper into her mouth, her fist pumping him in short, fast strokes. Then his whole body shuddered as he came with a force that drained every last bit of strength from his body.

He collapsed to his knees and pulled Kate down on his lap. He kissed her and felt a primitive thrill at the taste of himself in her mouth. Her knees fell on either side of his hips and her arms looped around his as she kissed him back, slow and lazy, as the water cascaded over them.

It didn't take long for their kisses to grow more urgent, and within minutes Tommy could feel himself hardening against the smooth curve of Kate's ass.

Kate gave a little sigh and shifted against him so she could cradle him between her thighs, and Tommy's eyes practically rolled back in his head as he slid against the slick folds between her legs. He slid his hands to her hips, careful of her bruise as he guided her closer, rocking his hips until the head of his cock nudged against her opening. He gave a low groan as the tip squeezed inside, and it was all he could do not to shove himself all the way in.

"Aren't we forgetting something?" Kate asked, even as her hips rolled against him, taking him the barest millimeter deeper. She held herself still, unable to pull away, knowing that they shouldn't go any further. "God, it would feel so good to have you inside me with nothing between us."

His cock surged, seeming to stretch inside her as she perfectly echoed his thoughts. Jesus, just having the tip inside was about to kill him. The thought of taking her in deep, slow strokes, without even a thin layer of latex separating them... "I don't suppose you're on the pill or something," he said.

She laughed, making them both groan at the way it made her clench around him. "Don't I wish. And it's not even really a safe time of the month or else..." She trailed off with a frustrated sigh.

If he fucked her without protection, she might get pregnant. A vision flashed in his head, a little girl with his dark hair and her solemn, blue-gray eyes.

It wasn't the idea of their baby that made him lift her by the hips and set her firmly away. It was the fact that the idea of getting Kate pregnant didn't send him into a full-scale panic. In fact, in what had to be a moment of sheer insanity, it actually struck him as a pretty good idea.

Jesus. Acknowledging the fact that there was something between them worth exploring was one thing, he thought as he helped her to her feet and pushed open the glass door. Entertaining crazy notions of getting her pregnant to tie them together forever was another.

Then he couldn't think about anything but Kate, her wet, naked body pressed against him, her sweet, soft mouth moving eagerly under his own. She felt so good, her slick skin and slim curves moving against him he almost forgot to grab a handful of condoms on the way out.

Hands on her hips, he backed her out of the bathroom to the bed, dragged the comforter and sheets back with a yank of his hands, and urged her back against the pillows. He tossed the condoms on the bedside table and paused a moment, to look at her.

He'd had a moment last night, holding her in his arms, in his bed, where he'd felt like nothing had ever been more right in his life.

But the sight of her, naked in his bed, her lips swollen and dark pink from loving, her flawless pale skin marked here and there from a too-firm kiss or a brush of his beard... it blew everything before this out of the water.

It swelled in his chest, an undeniable force, the realization that he wanted Kate in his house, in his bed, more than he'd ever wanted anything in his life. And not just tonight. He wanted a lifetime of days that ended like this, with her naked, her open arms and knowing smile beckoning him like a siren's song to pleasure beyond his wildest imaginations.

She reached out and traced her fingers down his side, over his hip, before closing it around his rock-hard erection. "I want you inside me, Tommy," she whispered.

He didn't need any more urging, quickly sheathing himself and settling between her legs. His gaze locked with hers as he pulled her hand back to him and covered her hand with his own as she guided him to her slick folds. "Put me inside you," he said.

—⁓—

Kate bit her lip, felt another rush of heat and wetness bathe the head of his cock as she guided him home. His dark, smoldering gaze never left hers as he slid inch by devastating inch until he was buried to the hilt. "Oh, God," Kate murmured, shifting under him, her body already tightening, rippling around him. After the other night, she should have been more prepared for it, the swiftness, the intensity with which her pleasure crashed over her.

But as he covered her mouth with his and started a slow, steady rhythm, Kate was once again shocked at how fast her body responded, already on the edge as though she hadn't just come less than ten minutes ago.

In that, it was just like the first time.

But in every other way, what was happening between them now was completely different. Somehow in the past two days the barriers they'd both been so determined to maintain came crashing down, and now there was no holding back. No pretending that this was nothing more than two people indulging their curiosity.

She was falling in love with him, she realized. Or maybe she'd been in love with him all along. Her body stiffened in shock at the revelation, putting a little crack in the spell Tommy was weaving with his hands, his mouth, his body.

"What is it? Did I hurt you?" he said, breathless, so in tune with her he immediately felt the subtle shift in her.

"No," she quickly reassured him. *Not yet anyway, and not the way you think.*

"Are you sure?" His voice was tight with the effort to restrain himself, his muscles quivering under her hands as he held himself back. He bent his head and kissed her, his tongue sliding against hers. "I never want to hurt you, Katie," he murmured, and bent his head to her breast and gave her nipple a firm tug of his mouth.

Kate cried out as the sensation went straight to her core, making her clench around him and rock her hips to take him even deeper.

"I never want to hurt you again, Katie," he said again, his hips resuming their slow, steady rhythm as he threaded his hands through her hair and locked his stare with hers. "I only want to make you feel good from now on. Let me make you feel good."

There was something in his touch, in his voice, in the very way he moved against her that told her he wasn't just talking about physically. Her fear slipped away as his words rang in her head. *I never want to hurt you. I only want to make you feel good.*

She gave herself over to him, to pleasure, to the crazy connection that fourteen years apart and deep wells of pain couldn't manage to break. She moaned as he hitched one knee higher and thrust deep, punctuating it with a tight circle of his hips that stirred her pleasure to the breaking point.

Her hands circled his back, slid down to the rock-hard muscles of his ass, urging him faster. But he tormented her with those slow, circling thrusts, shoving himself so deep inside her she felt like she could absorb him into her skin. Then the swirling twist that had him touching bundles of nerves she hadn't ever known existed.

Tommy felt himself grow impossibly harder as Kate's moans grew higher, more frantic. The feel of her fingers with their short nails digging into his ass sent a jolt of sensation straight to his cock. He loved this, loved that he could make her so insane with need that she forgot everything else. He didn't want it to end, wanted to draw out their pleasure. He never wanted to leave this place where her world focused only on him and how good he could make her feel.

Just as his world had become centered on Kate and only

Kate. On the taste of her mouth under his, the feel of her arms and legs locking him to her like she never wanted to let him go. And, oh Christ, the sweet, tight perfection of her body rippling and squeezing around his cock with every long, deep thrust.

He pushed so deep his balls nestled against the soft curve of her ass, and still he felt like he couldn't get deep enough, close enough. Like he wanted to get as close to her as he possibly could and never come up for air. He shifted, circled his hips, feeling a burst of satisfaction when she let out another sharp cry as he ground against the needy little bud of her clit.

"Tommy, please," she moaned as he circled again, and he could feel her body stiffen, knew she was right on the edge.

He reached between their bodies and found her clit with his thumb, stroking and circling her in rhythm with his deep, circling thrusts. Her mouth opened on a silent scream and he groaned as she shuddered against him, her body clenching and releasing him in long pulls, as though trying to draw him deeper.

A few hard, fast thrusts and Tommy followed her over the edge.

He collapsed to the pillow and pulled her across his chest as he waited for his breath to slow and his heart to resume a pace that didn't feel like it was going to pound out of his chest. The last aftershocks of his orgasm faded, and as he blinked in soft evening light pouring through his bedroom window, he waited for the urge to bolt to set in.

He got the urge every single time he had sex with a woman, without fail. Didn't matter if it was a one-night stand or a woman he'd been seeing regularly for a while. After the last pulses of pleasure drifted away and the chemical surge drained from his brain, he couldn't drown out the little voice that urged him to get up, get out, get away. He needed space, he needed air, because the aftermath of sex was always just a little too real for him to deal with.

He anticipated it tonight, prepared to push through it as he had in the past when he'd cared for his partner enough to not want to hurt her feelings. And God knew the last thing he wanted to do was hurt Kate's feelings. She was already skittish about what was going on between them. Once he'd been certain he hadn't physically hurt her, he'd recognized the fear that had caused her to freeze up.

And who could blame her, considering the way things had ended up the last time? Hell, he was scared shitless himself, but he was determined to work through it if she was. He didn't have to be a rocket scientist to know that jumping out of bed like she was on fire and secreting himself away in his office was no way to boost her confidence about what was happening between them.

Yet as he lay there, stroking his hand up and down her back, feeling the soft puff of her breath against his chest, the urge never came.

Kate must have felt him stiffen, because she propped herself on his chest and looked up. "What?"

Tommy took a strand of her hair between his fingers, his brows furrowing. "I feel like I never want to leave this bed."

One reddish blond brow quirked. "You make it sound like it's a bad thing."

Tommy shook his head. "Not bad, just different, for me."

She gave him a shy smile and inched her way up his chest until she could reach his mouth. She pressed a soft, lingering kiss to his lips. "Good. Because all of this is very different for me too."

"So what happens now that we've found Tricia?"

Kate's lips pressed together and her pale shoulders

shrugged. "I'll stay a few more days to see if there's any way I can help CJ with the investigation and make sure Tricia, Jackson, and Brooke are connected to people who can help them work through all of this."

"Then what?"

Kate's gaze dropped under his intense stare. "I go back to L.A., continue my work at the foundation."

Tommy hooked her chin with his finger and lifted it until her eyes met his. "I don't suppose you'd have much reason to come back to Sandpoint?"

Kate's lips quirked in a half smile. "Depends on how certain I'd be of my welcome."

Tommy pulled her up his body until her chest was pressed against his and her legs were splayed on either side of his hips. "I think you can rest assured it would be very, very warm."

He trailed soft kisses across her cheek and down her neck. "What about San Francisco?"

"Mm, what about it?" she said as she arched her neck to give him better access.

"I'm consulting for Jackson on the company he's starting in the Bay area, so I'll be spending a lot of time there in the next several months. It's only, what, an hour plane ride from southern California? Then there's my place in Seattle that's easy enough for you to get to for a weekend."

"Sounds like I'll be doing an awful lot of flying," Kate teased.

Tommy settled his hands over the soft curve of her ass and gave her a little squeeze. "I can go to L.A. In fact, I have a whole backlog of potential clients in that area that I haven't taken on. You'd give me a good excuse to build up my business in that region."

Kate kissed him again, then pulled back, her gaze solemn. "You've really thought about this."

Tommy shrugged. "I've thought about you. The rest is just figuring out logistics so I can do more than think about you when you leave town."

Her fingers curled into his chest, and he could feel the tension coiling in her body. "We're really going to do this? After everything that happened, all this time, you really think we—"

He stifled the flood of doubts with a kiss, releasing her only when she let out a soft sigh and relaxed against his chest. "I'm not fool enough to believe we can totally put the past behind us and move on like nothing ever happened. What happened to Michael, what happened after—it changed the way everything went. And it changed us. We became different people because of it. So I'm not looking to get back what we had or get another chance with the girl I fell for once upon a time. I want to be with the Kate you are now, with all baggage, all the scars." He lifted her left wrist to his mouth and placed a hard kiss along the faint white line.

When his eyes met hers again, he saw they were moist with tears. "I want that too," she said.

Chapter 25

They were quiet for a while, and Kate snuggled against Tommy's chest, marveling at the new feeling of closeness between them. Though she'd sensed him thawing in the past couple days, she'd never expected him to flat-out tell her he wanted to be with her. As he'd pointed out, they were different people than they'd been fourteen years ago, and she never would have expected the stoic, stony man Tommy seemed to have become to be so open about what he wanted from her. From them.

Maybe he wasn't as different as he wanted to believe. A tiny prickle of doubt penetrated her dreamy haze. Was it really possible for them to move past what had happened? Could she ever really get past the fear that her total loss of control around him would lead to disaster? Could he really get over the pain and trouble she'd caused, even if it was unintentional?

Speaking of... "Are you ever going to tell me what you said in that letter?"

Tommy grimaced and shook his head. "No point. It was written by a guy who doesn't exist anymore."

"Come on," she urged. "I still see you, lurking underneath that hard-ass front you put on for everybody."

His face settled in grim lines and Kate got a queasy feeling that she'd really upset him. "There's no front, Kate. What you see is what you get." He pulled her hand up to the front of his right shoulder, pressed her fingers against a spot of skin that was ridged with scar tissue. "That scar is real. So's this one." He pulled her hand to a half-inch slit of scar tissue that zigzagged across a couple of ribs. "I spent a lot of time in a lot of places where there wasn't a lot of room for rainbows and unicorns and sweetness and light."

Kate felt her mouth twist in a knowing smile. She was willing to bet she'd seen enough darkness to give him a run for his money. "Who needs rainbows when we can compare scars?" To emphasize her point, she set herself to running her lips and tongue over each one she found.

By the time she found the last one, a starburst of white on his upper left thigh, she barely brushed her lips over it before Tommy was hauling her up by the shoulders and rolling her underneath him. "I stand corrected," she gasped at the first heavy thrust. "There's absolutely nothing soft about you."

—⁓—

Late the next morning, Tommy smiled up at Kate as she padded barefoot into the kitchen dressed in another one of his T-shirts that hung almost to her knees. Kate, seeing he was on the phone, gave him a silent wave and made a beeline for the coffeepot.

"So she can't even give you any basic details," Tommy said, refocusing his attention on his conversation with Jackson, who had called with the news that while Tricia had woken up and was lucid enough for CJ to question her briefly, she couldn't remember anything in enough detail to give a good description of her kidnapper.

"All she can give us is that he's on the tall side, strong build."

Tommy bit back a curse. "That could be anyone. Including the guy who jumped Kate. Hopefully more will come back to her. In the meantime, I'll start digging into the company that bought that property. If we dig deep enough, we're bound to uncover the real owner. That will at least give us a place to start."

"How long do you think that will take you?"

Tommy grimaced. "A couple hours? A couple days? It all depends on how committed this guy is to covering his tracks."

Jackson handed the phone to CJ, who cautioned Tommy about getting too far on the side of illegal in his searches. "We can't use anything like that as evidence."

To Tommy, it was a familiar refrain, but one that never failed to annoy him. "If it points you in the right direction and you do your job right, you'll come up with plenty of your own evidence."

CJ gave a noncommittal grunt. "Let me know if you find anything, but keep the methods to yourself," he said, and rang off.

Tommy snagged Kate around the waist as she walked by and pulled her down into his lap and gave her a proper good morning kiss.

"Was that CJ?" she asked when he came up for air.

"And Jackson."

She raised her eyebrows. "And?"

"Got kind of a good-news, bad-news situation here," he said, and relayed what Jackson had shared.

She let out a relieved sigh. "Thank God she's recovering. That's the most important thing."

"Agreed, but it would be nice to find the fuck who terrorized her and nail him to the wall."

"Ooh, I love it when you get all fierce and protective," Kate teased, and squirmed playfully on his lap.

Already half hard when she'd strolled into the kitchen, Tommy sprang immediately to full, screaming readiness at the feel of that firm little ass nestled against his groin. He gave her another hungry kiss but pulled away before things could go any farther. "As much as I'd like to spend the day in bed with you, I promised Jackson I'd get to work finding out who bought the land where Tricia was found."

Kate made a little sound of regret but didn't protest. "You're right, finding the kidnapper has to be our priority. We can't let ourselves get carried away." She started to walk out of the kitchen and paused. "Speaking of which, we need to keep what's happening between us under the radar for a while."

Tommy's hackles instinctively raised. He didn't know why, but it was like suddenly his nineteen-year-old self came roaring to life, the wounds of losing her still fresh and raw. "What? Afraid of the scandal it will cause when the press finds out the senator's daughter is fucking a lowly rancher's son?"

He regretted the words the second they left his mouth, and the way Kate flinched at his crudeness didn't help.

Before he could apologize, Kate stormed over and got in his face, looking as tough as it was possible for a petitely built woman dressed only in a T-shirt. "Of course I'm not embarrassed or ashamed to be with you. It's just that after everything that's happened, I can't afford for my sex life to be front and center again. This isn't just about my reputation, it's my entire career. Even more important, the focus needs to be on Tricia and finding her kidnapper, not on me and who I'm sleeping with."

"I'm sorry," Tommy said, feeling about two inches big. "I don't even know where that came from." He reached out and pulled her stiff body into his arms, relieved when, after a few breaths, she melted into him once again. "We'll keep it on the down low as long as you want."

Kate smiled up at him. "Fourteen years later and here we are sneaking around again." Then her smile faded, shadows of painful memories darkening her blue eyes.

"Something tells me it's going to work out better this time around."

Fifteen minutes later Tommy dropped her off at her townhouse, refusing to leave until he'd done a thorough search, set the alarm, and heard the dead bolt *thunk* into place behind him. He was heading back to his truck when a female voice called his name.

He didn't need to turn around to know it was the reporter who seemed to have it in for Kate. Tommy didn't even bother to turn around when she called his name again.

"Please, Mr. Ibarra, I know you've been helping on Tricia Fuller's kidnapping, that you were part of the search party who found her."

Tommy paused, his truck door halfway open as he looked at the woman. She was accompanied by a scruffy-looking guy with a camera on his shoulder. "I can't comment, but I'm sure Sheriff Kovac will be happy to answer your questions at the next press conference."

"What about your relationship with Kate Beckett? Can you comment on that?"

Shit. Tommy schooled his face into an expressionless mask. "Kate and I have collaborated with the local authorities to find Tricia."

He started to get in his truck.

"Please, you can't think your sexual relationship with her has remained a secret."

Tommy's fingers tightened around the door frame and he cursed himself for engaging with this bitch in the first place. "Whether or not I'm having sex with Kate Beckett has no bearing on Tricia's disappearance and rescue. Kate has been an invaluable resource and a comfort to the family. You should be focusing on that."

"But you can't deny that she seems to make a habit of getting involved with men she's working with on these high-profile cases."

"I'd hardly call two a habit," he muttered before he could stop himself. His stomach sank as a hard light came into Walsh's eyes. It was a look he knew all too well. The look of a predator going in for the kill.

After Tommy left, Kate showered, dressed, and headed over to the hospital to check on Tricia. Though she was cleared to drive, she opted to walk to the hospital. The weather was beautiful, in the low eighties, the sky the kind of crazy azure blue shade you could only see in the mountains. Not to mention the walk would help her work some of the kinks out of her sore hip as well as all the newly rediscovered muscles that had gotten such a vigorous workout the night before.

Kate felt her mouth stretch into a grin at the thought. She knew she'd better wipe the goofy look off her face before she got to the hospital or she'd have no hope of hiding the fact that she'd spent most of last night rolling around in Tommy's massive bed.

It wasn't just the sex that had her smiling like a fool at nothing in particular. It was the fact that despite all the time and all the battle scars between them, despite the desperate circumstances that had brought them back together, the connection between them was as deep and undeniable as it had ever been. And now, if what Tommy said was true, it looked like they were both ready to stop fighting it and see if, finally, they could find the happiness their bond had once promised.

The sight of the reporters crowded around the entrance to the hospital sobered her up. No matter how amazing it felt to have Tommy back in her life, she knew if the press got wind of it, they'd turn it into something ugly and dirty.

Eventually, if she wanted to be with Tommy—and she did—she knew she'd have to deal with some fallout, but hopefully by the time they went public, there would be enough distance from Tricia's case to soften the impact.

She gave a polite "no comment" to the reporters who peppered her with questions. She noticed with relief that Maura Walsh wasn't anywhere to be seen.

The door to Tricia's room was ajar, and when Kate pushed it open, she found Brooke curled up next to Tricia on the bed, a magazine spread out between them while Jackson dozed in a chair next to the bed. Though her eyes were heavy with fatigue and there were bruises visible on her cheeks, Tricia otherwise seemed well on her way to recovery, laughing as Brooke whispered something Kate couldn't hear.

There was a pinching sensation in her chest as Kate watched the sisters. She and Lauren used to sit like that, heads bent close, having quiet conversations about things they'd never share with anyone else.

They would never have that kind of bond again. While at times like this she felt the ache of missing her sister like a brick to her chest, today it was softened by the fact that this time, with this case, things had ended much differently. And if this start was anything to go by, instead of tearing them apart, this near tragedy was going to pull the Fullers closer together.

She cleared her throat to get their attention. Brooke

looked up, her mouth stretching into a wide smile as she recognized Kate. "Dad, wake up." She gave Jackson a little nudge with her bare foot. "Kate's here."

Jackson stirred and opened his eyes as Kate came forward to introduce herself to Tricia. "It's nice to officially meet you."

Tricia started to smile but it was interrupted by a yawn. "Sorry," she said. "I don't know why I'm still so tired. I think I slept for at least two days straight."

"It's because that asshole drugged you," Brooke said, an unmistakable edge to her voice.

"Brooke," Jackson admonished, "watch your language."

Brooke cocked her eyebrow at her father. "Dad, the guy kidnapped Tricia and hurt her. I can think of a lot worse things to call him."

"But you don't have to say them in front of visitors," he said, inclining his head in Kate's direction.

"Trust me, I've heard a lot worse," she said, flashing a grin at Brooke. Her smile softened as it landed once again on Tricia. "CJ says you never got a good look at the man who took you?"

Tricia shook her head, her mouth tight with frustration. "He always wore a hoodie, even though it was hotter than a sauna in there. He always had it pulled up around his face, and he made sure I never saw his face in the light. I keep thinking maybe it's back there and I'm just blocking it or something."

"It's okay. You've been through a serious trauma. Sometimes it takes awhile for all the circuits to start firing again."

Tricia nodded glumly. "I just want the police to catch him. It's scary, knowing he's still out there. What if he comes after me again?"

"I'll put a bullet in his head," Jackson said, in a voice so hard it sent a shiver down Kate's spine. "But you don't need to worry about it." He reached out and squeezed Tricia's hand. "I won't let anyone near you."

"Me neither," Brooke said. "Never again."

"The best you can do is share anything you can remember, even if you think it's silly. Every detail helps. Other than that, you focus on getting better."

To that end, Kate had pulled together a list of therapists both local to Sandpoint and close to the Fullers' new home in California.

Jackson bristled, a reaction Kate had long since become accustomed to. She was quietly, firmly explaining why having the three of them go, both separately and together, was necessary for them to deal with the aftermath of this latest trauma when they were interrupted by one of the nurses.

"Sorry to bother you," she said, seemingly oblivious to the tension between Kate and Jackson. "But somehow this got separated from the rest of your things"—she held out her hand to Tricia, revealing a gold chain dangling from it—"and I wanted to make sure it got back to you."

Tricia's eyes widened in unmistakable horror, and she tried to scramble away from the nurse's outstretched hand.

"What's wrong?" Brooke asked at the same moment the nurse, confused, said, "Don't you want your necklace back?"

"Get it away from me! It's not mine! *He* put it on me. Get it away from me!"

Jackson was on the phone immediately to CJ. Kate wrapped her own hand in a tissue—no doubt a futile gesture at this point, but at least there would be one less set of prints for the lab to sift through, and held her hand out to the nurse. "I'll give it to Sheriff Kovac when he gets here."

The nurse nodded, her distress evident on her face. "I'm so sorry—I had no idea it would upset her so much. On the news they said she was wearing a necklace when she disappeared. I just assumed that was it."

"It was a locket." Tricia sobbed. "A locket my mom gave me. And he took it and put that, that stupid flower thing on me instead."

Instinctively Kate looked down at the necklace nestled in her palm. Her breath froze in her throat, her body going hot then icy cold as her gaze locked on the gold charm attached to the fine gold chain. It was a flower, leaves of gold fanned out to mimic the shape of a lily. In the center a one-carat diamond threw off the sunlight streaming through the window.

She heard someone talking to her but it was muffled, like she was underwater. A hand waved in her face and she looked up at Brooke, her brows knitted in concern. "Kate? Are you okay? You look kind of pale."

For a few seconds Kate's mouth moved, no sound coming out as she struggled to process what was happening, struggled to come up with an explanation less horrible than the truth staring her in the face. "This necklace," she finally managed. "I recognize it. It was my grandmother's. I haven't seen it since the night my brother was kidnapped."

––––⟋∿⟍––––

When Tommy arrived at the sheriff's station late that afternoon, he found Kate in CJ's office, huddled in one of the guest chairs. She looked shell shocked, so pale and off kilter it sent his protective instincts into overdrive until it was all he could do not to gather her in his arms.

But with her need to keep their relationship under wraps,

he knew that would only add to her stress. As for telling her that the cat might already be out of the bag, based on his encounter with that barracuda of a reporter?

Out of the question. The discovery of the necklace had already knocked Kate for enough of a loop. Right now they needed to figure out what the hell was going on and whether Tricia's kidnapper was in any way involved with what had happened to Kate's brother.

"This—this doesn't make any sense," CJ said, shaking his head as he studied the open file spread out in front of him. "It was an open-and-shut case. Emerson Flannery's truck was seen fleeing the scene, and for God's sake, the man left a suicide note apologizing for what he'd done. I don't see how the two can be related."

"Maybe we were wrong, and Emerson didn't do it. How else can we explain how my necklace—which went missing the night Michael was killed—ended up on Tricia?" Kate said, her voice higher than usual, her body tight with stress.

CJ shook his head. "You don't know that for sure. Think about how hectic the days were after Michael died. Isn't it possible that you lost it then? It could have easily transferred hands several times between then and now. Maybe Tricia's kidnapper picked it up in a pawn shop somewhere."

"Come on, CJ, you know how far-fetched that is," Tommy said.

"No more far-fetched than thinking someone else killed Michael and pinned it on Emerson before killing him too," CJ shot back.

Kate shook her head, staring blankly at the wall. Her lips moved but no sound came out. "Arthur Dorsey," she said softly. "His mother thinks that's what happened. Maybe Emerson..." She cut herself off, threw her hands in the air. "I don't know. All I know is that the Bludgeoner used the same cream that was sitting in my dresser drawer, and he put *my* necklace around Tricia Fuller's neck."

And maybe others, Tommy thought, grimacing as he remembered the ligature marks on the other girls' necks. Kate looked so small, so shocked, he wanted to take her in his arms.

"Emerson would have provided an easy scapegoat," Tommy said.

CJ shook his head again. "You two have been watching too much *CSI*. Nine times out of ten, the simplest answer is the right one."

"And sometimes it's not," Tommy shot back. "Are you telling me that you won't acknowledge the possibility that this could be more than a coincidence?" He shook his head. "Then again, you FBI types aren't exactly known for thinking out of the box."

CJ shot him a glare, then leafed through the folder one more time. His brows knitted and he uttered a soft curse under his breath.

"What?" Tommy asked.

"I missed this the first time through. It said Erin Flannery came in a few days after her uncle was found with Michael. Sheriff Lyons wasn't around to take a statement, so they told her to come back later."

"What did she say?" Kate asked.

"That's just it," CJ said. "There's no record of her statement." He looked up at Kate, then Tommy. "I was planning to talk to her anyway, since one of the few details Tricia remembers is her kidnapper bringing her a sandwich from Erin's restaurant. I can ask her about this too."

"*We* can ask her," Kate said, pushing to her feet.

"I can't have you interfere with official police business—" CJ started.

Tommy silenced him with a raised hand. "You know we'll question her on our own if we have to. Might as well get the same information at the same time."

CJ made an exasperated sound but didn't protest further. "Fine. But when we get there, I'll ask the questions."

Chapter 26

Though Kate had eaten Erin's food several times this week thanks to the woman's generosity toward the volunteers, this was the first time she'd gone inside the restaurant Erin had taken over from Mary Monroe three years ago.

Kate's mind was racing too fast to notice more than the barest details. But she did register that Erin had changed the place substantially from a homey mom-and-pop diner. Erin had replaced the old-fashioned counter with a long mahogany bar. Behind it was a flat-screen TV mounted to the wall, tuned to a local station.

At this time of day, between the lunch rush and the dinner crowd, there were only a few tables with customers. Erin herself seemed to be the only one working the floor.

"I'll be with you in just a moment," she said as she caught them out of the corner of her eye. She finished taking an order and turned to them, her bright smile fading to wariness when she recognized them.

"What's up?"

"We were hoping to ask you some questions," CJ said.

Erin's gray eyes narrowed. "About what?"

"About Tricia Fuller's kidnapping."

"Why would I know anything about that other than what I've seen on the news? And since my brothers are both already in jail, there's no way they had anything to do with it—"

"Jesus, Erin, we're not here to accuse you or anyone in your family of anything," CJ snapped, then closed his eyes and took a deep breath. When he spoke again, his tone was gentler. "Please, it won't take long, and it's possible you have information that could help."

Erin cocked an eyebrow. "Wow, the sheriff asking a Flannery for help? Isn't this a day of firsts. Let me put this order in and get someone to cover the floor."

She returned a few minutes later and directed them to her office in the back. "Sorry it's a little cramped in here," she said as she closed the door. Kate didn't miss the way she skirted around CJ, giving him as wide a berth as possible given the confines of the small room.

Kate and Tommy perched on the couch tucked against one wall. Though she didn't dare give in to the urge to scoot closer and take his hand, she took comfort in his big, solid presence beside her. The sight of the necklace, passed down to Kate after her grandmother's death, had sent her reeling. But even the sound of Tommy's voice on the phone when she'd called him with the news, the fact that he'd dropped everything to be with her then, went a long way in soothing her.

He had better things to do, she acknowledged with a pang of guilt. Like trying to trace the name behind the shell corporation that owned the land. But even her guilt couldn't overcome the amazing feeling of security she got from knowing he was there for her in any way she needed, no matter how big or small. It had been so long since she'd been able to fully trust, fully depend on someone. She'd forgotten how good it could feel.

CJ leaned against one end of the desk while Erin stood

at the other end, arms folded as she leaned back against the wall.

"Before we start," CJ said as he pulled out a digital recorder from his pocket, "you need to know that everything we talk about here has to remain confidential. I don't want any information getting out that could jeopardize the investigation."

"No problem," Erin said.

CJ gave her a hard look. "I mean it. This case is getting a lot of media attention. I can't have you and your family trying to run off and sell a story somewhere."

Erin gave him a long stare, full of meaning Kate couldn't begin to decipher. "Someday you're going to stop lumping me in with the rest of my family," she said finally. "I promise. Whatever we talk about won't leave these four walls."

CJ nodded, apparently satisfied. "Unfortunately, Tricia didn't see her captor closely enough to give us a description, but she did mention he brought her several things he thought she'd enjoy. One of those things was a sandwich off your menu."

Erin's head tilted in inquiry.

"It was the..." CJ paused a few moments, flipping through his notebook. "Ah, it's the grilled chicken with roasted red peppers, arugula, and provolone. Any chance you remember who bought one on Monday?"

Erin gave him a helpless look. "That's one of the most popular items on my lunch menu. This time of year with the Labor Day crowd, I might sell a hundred of them or more a day. Wait." She pushed away from the wall and went over to her computer. "I can run a report for you that links order details with credit card numbers." The sound of keys tapping filled the office.

"Your system can do that?" CJ asked.

"How do you think I manage my food buys if I don't know what's selling?" she replied peevishly.

CJ lifted his hands as though in surrender. "Just a question," he said as the printer on Erin's desk hummed to life. "What about security cameras, surveillance video?"

"Mary had one installed years ago, but I never replaced it when I did the renovation. I figure, it's Sandpoint. Nothing really bad ever happens." Her gaze shifted to Kate, her eyes opening wide in horror as she realized what she said. "Oh my God, Kate, I'm sorry. I didn't mean—"

"It's okay," Kate said. "But speaking of bad things, and that thing in particular, we were also hoping to ask you a few things about the night my brother was kidnapped."

Erin's expression went wary again.

CJ told her about the note they'd found in the case file about her going to the sheriff's station to make a statement. "You never went back."

"I called three more times, but I never was able to talk to Sheriff Lyons," Erin said sharply. She shrugged. "I finally gave up. It wasn't like they'd believe me anyway. No one around here puts much weight on what a Flannery has to say."

Kate's interest piqued as something seemed to ripple between the other woman and the sheriff. "Well, I'm not from around here, and I'd like to hear what you have to say," Kate said.

"I don't think Uncle Emerson was capable of kidnapping and killing your brother," she said in a rush.

"The evidence—" CJ said, shaking his head.

"I know all about the evidence," Erin broke in, "and I can see how it was pretty damning. Look, I'm not even claiming that Emerson wasn't capable of murder. God knows what he did those years in Viet Nam and afterward. But based on what I saw earlier that day, I don't think he was physically capable of pulling it off."

"How do you mean?" CJ asked.

"Well, first off, he was drunk as a skunk by two in the afternoon that day."

Tommy made a scoffing sound. "No offense, Erin, but from what I knew of your uncle, that was pretty much what he did every day."

"No kidding, but he'd hurt his back a week before, so in addition to the usual handle of bourbon, that afternoon he was also popping OxyContin like they were Tic Tacs. He passed out around six and was still totally out of it when I drove him home later that night."

"What time was that?" CJ asked.

Erin looked at the ceiling, searching her memories. "Nine? Ten o'clock?"

Kate exchanged a look with Tommy. Michael had been taken shortly after midnight.

"On top of that he had two ruptured disks in his back," Erin continued.

"And enough Oxy in his system to make sure he was feeling no pain," CJ said.

Erin shrugged. "Even if he'd regained consciousness, does it really seem possible that he could have driven down that road, all the way to the Becketts' house on the lake without crashing into something? Then drag an able-bodied boy from the house, get him back to his place, and then drag him another hundred yards to the hunting shack where he was killed?"

A knot settled in the pit of Kate's stomach. While inconclusive, everything Erin said made sense. "Someone else could have stolen the truck," she murmured, almost to herself.

"I left it in the driveway with the keys in the ignition. It certainly wouldn't have been difficult," Erin said. She swallowed hard. "And I know this isn't a popular opinion to express, especially in this town, and Kate, I hope you'll forgive me, but for all of his faults and bad behavior, Uncle Emerson—the way he hurt your brother..."

Kate nodded. She knew exactly what Erin was talking about.

"Emerson wasn't wired that way, at least, I don't believe he was. He was a bastard to most people, but he was always sweet to me and my brothers, no matter how drunk or stoned he got."

Kate saw the sadness in Erin's eyes. As much as Emerson might have been a drunk and a derelict, it was clear Erin had had affection for the man. All these years Kate had never once considered that Michael wasn't the only innocent victim in what had happened.

CJ scrubbed his hand over his chin. "If everything you're saying is true—"

"I wouldn't lie—" Erin snapped, immediately on the defensive.

CJ held up a hand. "Scratch that. *Assuming* what you say is true and the former sheriff fell down on this investigation, this still doesn't give us anything that points us in the direction of another suspect, or if he's connected to Tricia's kidnapper."

They let out a collective, frustrated sigh, then Erin grabbed the customer activity report off the printer and handed it to CJ. "Hopefully you'll find something in here that will help. I'll let you know if I think of anything else that I didn't tell you."

Kate and Tommy stood and followed Erin back to the main room. The place was still mostly empty, but a few customers had taken seats at the bar. As they started toward the door, she heard Erin say, "Hey look, Tommy, you're on TV!"

Kate automatically turned to the bar, surprised when instead of footage of him storming away from reporters from earlier in the week, there was a picture of Tommy in his football uniform from Idaho State.

The feed switched back to the anchor, and Kate felt her stomach flip over when she recognized Walsh. Then it started to churn as the screen flashed a picture of a teenage Kate. "Can you turn it up?" she asked Erin.

"...to sources Kate Beckett and Tomas Ibarra had struck up a summer romance the summer Beckett's brother, Michael, was kidnapped and murdered. Those familiar with the case will remember that Beckett was left in charge of her brother that night, but it was not widely reported that Beckett was with Ibarra at the time her brother disappeared."

"Crap." Kate swallowed, feeling like the floor was shifting under her. It was okay, she tried to tell herself. No, it wasn't going to be fun to have to live through all of this again, but this was old news.

As long as they didn't find out about—"Now, in what is a shocking development, particularly given Beckett's recent history, it looks as though she and Ibarra have rekindled their romance."

Kate heard Tommy swear viciously next to her, but she couldn't tear her eyes from the huge TV screen. It showed a couple locked in a passionate embrace. Though the video was grainy and the couples' faces were partially obscured, Kate knew without a doubt she was looking at security camera footage from the hospital.

The shot cut to Tommy, in front of her townhouse earlier that morning.

She didn't even get the words out before his voice came blaring out of the TV speakers: "I'm having a sexual relationship with Kate Beckett."

Kate stared, dumbstruck, as the feed went back to the reporter. The blood in her head roared so hard she could only make out snippets of the reporter's commentary, though the pictures flashing up, first of Graham Hewitt, then Madeline Drexler, helped to fill in the blanks. The feed went back to the reporter, and she and the male anchor exchanged banter.

"In this case I guess we should all be thankful Beckett's sex life didn't result in greater tragedy, but I have to wonder how St. Anthony's will feel about her continuing as their primary spokesperson."

Her conversation with Ron Weaver, chairman of the board of St. Anthony's, echoed through her brain. *If you make even one misstep, Kate, it will be disaster for us and for you.* It was like she'd looked into the face of Medusa and been turned to stone as she stood stock still in the middle of Erin's restaurant and felt her world fall apart around her.

It was over. Within the next hour, the story would be all over the country.

"Kate." She heard Tommy's voice in her ear, felt the brush of his hand against her wrist. Her first instinct was to turn to him, grab his hand, and never let go.

Then brutal reality came slamming home and she jerked her arm away as though burned. "Don't."

"Goddammit, Kate, you know they edited that to make it look worse than it was."

"Really? Because that sure looked like me making out with you in the hospital while Tricia Fuller was unconscious down the hall," Kate yelled, heedless of Erin and CJ watching them, wide eyed, while the other restaurant patrons stared transfixed.

"Let's go somewhere and talk about this like reasonable people," Tommy said quietly.

But Kate was beyond reason. All of the sudden she was

a sixteen-year-old girl, staring at the boy who made her so crazy with lust and need and, God help her, love that he made her lose all semblance of control. Until she was hurling herself headlong at him, damn the consequences.

Never mind that she'd already learned the brutal lesson that the way Tommy Ibarra made her feel led to nothing but disaster and destruction.

"Just leave me alone."

Tommy caught her by the shoulders and pinned her with a hard stare. She flinched at the pain that flared in his dark eyes along with a helplessness that matched her own. "We can get through this. It doesn't matter what anyone say—"

"No," Kate said, jerking out of his hold. "This is just like what happened with Graham and Madeline—"

She tried to get away but Tommy held her fast. "What are you talking about? We found Tricia! Nobody died!"

"And I'm grateful for that," she cried, wrenching from his hold. "But you have no idea what this will do to me, my reputation."

"Of course you care more about that than you do about me," he bit out. "How could I ever expect any of that to change?"

It was so much more complicated than that, but right now she didn't have the energy to fight him. "I need you to stay away. Just stay away from me. Every time I let you get too close, I end up losing everything."

He recoiled as though from a blow.

Though her body felt like it had gone numb, somehow she made it to the door, ignoring the stares of the other customers. She stepped out on the sidewalk, squinting in the early evening sunlight. As she fumbled in her bag for her sunglasses, she felt someone touch her arm.

She instinctively jerked away. "Leave me—"

"Kate, it's me."

Kate's hackles lowered when she looked up into CJ's concerned blue eyes. "I'm sorry about the scene, sorry about the mess this is going to cause," she began.

CJ shook his head. "You don't need to apologize to me. Come on, let me give you a lift back to your place before the vultures get wind of your location."

Kate followed him blindly to his cruiser. As she slid into the passenger seat, all of the lingering aches from the last few days came back into searing focus, leaving her feeling as bruised and battered as if she'd gone twelve rounds in the ring.

How could she have been so stupid, letting her defenses down for even a second? Once again he had made her completely lose her head, abandon every shred of common sense. Even knowing what would happen if the press got wind of them, Kate hadn't been able to help herself. She'd thrown herself headlong into their affair, unable to think of anything but him and the wild, crazy desire he stirred in her soul.

Because of her recklessness, she was about to lose everything. Her reputation, the career she'd worked so hard to build. Not to mention the fragile peace she'd made with what had happened to Michael. Once again it was going to be front and center, twenty-four/seven, but with a special new twist as the real truth of what happened that night came to light.

You're nothing but a spoiled brat who let her brother get kidnapped and murdered. Her father's words scorched through her brain, peeling back scar tissue until the wounds were as fresh and raw as the day it had happened.

And for what? Tommy, for all his big talk about wanting to see her, hadn't exactly made any promises. Wanting to "see where this might go" was hardly something any woman with more than two brain cells to rub together would risk the very foundation of her life for.

CJ answered a call on the radio and turned onto First Avenue. "Tommy's a stand-up guy," he said when he got off the call. "You know you can't blame him for what happened."

"I don't," Kate snapped. "I don't blame anyone but myself, for being stupid enough to get carried away. I knew what would happen if it came out that we were sleeping together. I knew it would be a disaster."

CJ gave her a skeptical look. "Don't you think you're being a little melodramatic? It might be headline news for a little while, but eventually something else will catch their interest—"

Kate shook her head wearily. "It's not just the media frenzy, though trust me, you can't really comment unless you've had every aspect of your life dissected. It's the collateral damage—" As though on cue, her phone gave a shrill ring.

Kate's stomach flipped as she recognized the number on the screen. "Hello, Ron."

"Kate." Ron Weaver, chairman of the board of directors for St. Anthony's, managed to instill enough gravity into that one syllable that Kate would have known he was about to deliver bad news even if she hadn't been fully expecting it.

"I assume you've seen the news," Kate said.

"Yes. And in light of what happened last year with Graham Hewitt and the Madeline Drexler case, it's no longer in our best interests to have you working with us on a day-to-day basis, particularly as our key community outreach representative."

"Of course," Kate said, oddly calm now that the blow had been delivered. She listened and gave the appropriate responses as he discussed the details of her termination. "If that's all—" she said.

"Well, there is another matter we need to discuss." Gravity

gave way to uneasiness in Weaver's tone. "While we feel that it's no longer appropriate for you to work with us in such a public fashion, your family has been incredibly generous with the foundation over the years…"

Kate's mouth pulled into a humorless smile. "No need to worry. My family will continue its support. And of course we'll make up for any shortfall should you lose donors over this." She would do whatever she could to mitigate the damage caused by her recklessness. Even if her father decided to pull his support in light of the scandal, Kate's personal trust fund could more than cover the annual donation.

By the time CJ reached her townhouse, the press had already amassed outside. Getting to the front door was like walking a gantlet, and she was grateful for CJ's size as he tucked her behind him and helped her push her way through the hive of microphones and shouted questions.

"What happens now?" CJ asked as he ushered her into her entry, closed the door, and locked it for good measure.

His question brought a sudden piercing memory to the forefront, of herself, lying in Tommy's arms just last night, asking the exact same question. She shoved it away and focused on CJ. "Now that I'm no longer officially employed by the foundation, there's no rush for me to get back to Los Angeles." Coward that she was, part of her wanted to get as far away from Sandpoint and Tommy Ibarra as quickly as possible.

And this time she'd stay gone for good.

But there were questions to answer, matters far more important than her public humiliation. "I'm not leaving until I find out once and for all what happened to my brother."

CJ nodded. "I'm not going to officially reopen the investigation—" He held his hand up to silence her when Kate would have protested. "The key word here is 'officially,'" he said. "With everything going on, there's going to be enough rehashing of Michael's murder as it is. If it gets out that we're taking another look at his case based on evidence from Tricia, it will be like gasoline on a fire. I don't want to risk tipping anyone off."

"Makes sense. So what can I do to help?"

CJ shifted uncomfortably. "No offense, but with all the media frenzy around you, it might be best if you did leave town—"

"Out of the question."

"In that case, the best way to help is to lay low and keep your mouth shut about what we've found out, sit tight, and wait to hear from us."

"But I can give you information about who was around that summer, brainstorm a list of potential leads—"

"I was around that summer too, and so was Tommy. And anything I need from you I can get over the phone when I need it," CJ said calmly.

Kate's shoulders slumped in defeat. CJ pulled her in for a quick hug and Kate weakly returned it. He felt nice, big, strong, solid, smelling pleasantly of laundry starch and soap.

But there was no rush of heat, no sensation of uncontrollable need pulling her to him like a magnet. No need to pull him down the hall to her bedroom, wrap her arms and legs around him and not let him go until he promised to love her forever and never leave her side.

No, that kind of reaction happened only with Tommy. And she couldn't afford to ever feel it again. As exhilarating as it could be, the idea of losing control like that again and the consequences that followed made her throat tight with fear. This time it had cost her her career—relatively mild when compared to what had happened before. But who knew how many ways she could screw up in the future?

She stepped away, blinking back the tears. Tonight, alone in her bed, she could cry, but right now she didn't want to fall apart in front of CJ.

He started for the front door and paused. "I know you've got it in your head that you plus Tommy equals disaster, but if you really care about each other like I think you do, it seems like a shame to let it go because of a little bit of bad luck," he said, and shut the door behind him.

Chapter 27

Tommy barely remembered the drive back to his house, he was reeling so hard from the impact of Kate's words. *Every time I let you get too close, I end up losing everything.*

He felt ripped wide open, instantly regressing back to that foolish nineteen-year-old, blindsided and laid out by her rejection.

What a fucking idiot, he cursed himself as he stormed into his office and flipped open his laptop. He never should have opened himself up, and especially not to her. He should have learned that lesson the first time, learned to think with his head instead of his dick.

Face it, dude, with Kate, your heart has always been as much involved as your dick. You wanted more from her than a quick fuck. You always have.

Yeah, and he should have accepted it a long time ago that he was never going to get it, rather than stepping into the ring for another go-round guaranteed to end up as bad as the last time.

Well, he conceded as he opened up the file on Tavers International and started running a trace on the bank that handled the initial real estate transaction, it didn't end up quite as tragically as last time. This time no one was killed, and Tommy was immune to the wrath of Kate's father. Kate might be devastated by the prospect of another scandal, but deep down, Tommy knew that wasn't the real reason she was pushing him away.

Michael had been killed, and that, Tommy knew, was the true source of Kate's reaction.

Tommy also knew that without the other tragedy between them, they could have worked through the ugliness together. But it was there, lying between them like a stone wall. No matter what Kate said about new starts and second chances while she was lying in his arms, when the shit came down, it was clear she would never forgive Tommy for the role he'd played that night.

Not that she blamed him, at least not nearly as much as Tommy knew he deserved. No, she was too busy blaming herself. Blaming herself for giving in to her feelings for Tommy. For allowing herself to get swept up in the crazy joyride that took over whenever they got close to one another.

It would always be there, always between them. Always guaranteeing that when the shit hit the fan, her first instinct would be to push him away rather than draw him closer.

Even an idiot knew you didn't put your hopes on a woman who runs scared at the first sign of trouble. But acknowledging that truth didn't make the ache in Tommy's chest any less severe. Didn't stop him from wishing there was some way he could convince her to push all the noise of this latest media storm aside and embrace what he knew to be true.

That he loved her, and she loved him. That was all that should matter.

Logically, he knew it could never be that simple. But that didn't stop him from picking up his phone and dialing her number before he could stop himself. Didn't stop the hope from flickering in his gut that she'd pick up, give him an opening.

With each ring that went unanswered that flicker faded, until his call went to voicemail and snuffed it out completely.

He didn't bother to leave a message.

Idiot. Tommy turned back to the screen. But it was impossible for him to concentrate as his brain crowded with memories of working with Kate sitting across the office. Staring at her over his breakfast table just that morning, the taste of her still fresh on his lips.

He told himself not to go there but it was too late. He was buffeted by visions of her in his bed, naked against him, clutching him to her as her body pulsed around him, moaning his name as she came. Then later, the whispers in the dark. Promises to each other about a future smashed to smithereens by one nosy reporter and his careless slip of the tongue.

He paced around his office, edgy and restless like his skin had somehow shrunk a size. For the first time since he moved in, his house didn't feel like a sanctuary. In the brief time she'd spent here, Kate had managed to mark it with her presence. To the point where every time Tommy turned around, he felt a stab of disappointment that she wasn't there.

He was being an idiot, he knew. *You need to stop acting like a sappy loser and get the fuck back to work*, he scolded himself.

An hour later when he hadn't made any more progress, he knew it was a lost cause. Deciding a change of venue was in order, he drove back to the sheriff's headquarters. Stone-faced, he pushed through the handful of reporters out front who perked up when they recognized the male half of Kate's latest sex scandal and joined CJ in his office without waiting for an invite.

"I'm working through the bank records for Tavers International," Tommy said when CJ greeted his entry with a questioning look. "Figure this way I can tell you right away if I hit on anything," he added lamely. But he sure as shit wasn't going to tell CJ that he couldn't stand to be in his own house after what had happened.

But CJ probably figured it out a couple hours later when he announced he was closing up shop to head home.

"It's only seven thirty," Tommy protested.

"And Travis's babysitter has to leave by seven forty-five, which gives me just enough time," CJ said, settling his hat on his head as he rose. "You'll call me as soon as you come across anything?"

"Of course," Tommy said, closing his laptop, pausing a moment as he went through the options of where to go next.

Normally he'd grab a table in the corner at his favorite dive and nurse a beer while he conducted his cyberhunt. But since he'd become headline news, anyplace public was out.

He didn't even consider his parents' place. His mom had already left half a dozen voicemails since the news broke, and he wasn't up to spending the next several hours fending off questions about Kate.

Jackson's house came to mind, but he immediately dismissed it. While Jackson would welcome him with open arms and be eager to learn all the details of the searches Tommy was conducting, he wouldn't feel right imposing. Tricia had just been released from the hospital earlier that afternoon, and they needed time to be together.

As though reading his mind, CJ said, "Why don't you join us for dinner?"

Tommy shook his head. "I couldn't—"

"I'll throw a couple steaks on the grill and we can compare notes."

Feeling equal parts pathetic and grateful, Tommy aimed his truck at the bumper of CJ's cruiser and followed the sheriff to his home a few miles up the lakeshore to a house that was a few streets down from Jackson's rental.

And less than a mile from the house Kate's family had rented every summer, but he wasn't going to dwell on that tonight.

Tommy had been to CJ's house several times in high school and the beginning of college, when he'd run in the same crowd as CJ's older sister, Kelly. But though he and CJ were friendly, he hadn't been to the house since CJ moved back to town.

It looked much the same, though CJ had added a couple touches like a flat-screen that took up most of one wall in the living room.

While CJ cooked up the promised steaks, Tommy sipped a beer and made small talk with Travis, CJ's nephew. Travis pointed interestedly at the tattoo peeking out from the sleeve of Tommy's black T-shirt. "Were you in the Marines too?" At eleven, the kid was all dark hair and skinny limbs. Tommy imagined that when he grew up, he'd look an awful lot like his uncle.

"Marines?" Tommy scoffed, loud enough for CJ to hear. "Marines are for pu—" He caught himself just in time. "Weaklings. I was an Army Ranger."

CJ flipped a steak and said, "Which means he came in and took the credit after we got the enemy to retreat."

With Travis and CJ's mom around, there wasn't much opportunity to discuss the case. Not that they would have been able to get a word in edgewise as Travis peppered him with questions about his time in the Army, comparing it to CJ's time in the Marines.

"He was in for a lot longer than you," Travis said to CJ. "I think that makes him tougher than you." There was no missing the taunting grin on the kid's face.

"Or a lot dumber than me," Tommy said, reaching out and rubbing his hair.

For a split second another kid, another shit-eating grin came to mind. Michael, the night he was kidnapped, torturing Kate with his presence when he knew very well she wanted to be alone with Tommy.

Tommy cleared the table while CJ negotiated TV privileges with Travis. He wandered out on the deck and braced his hands on the railing as he stared out over the water and tried not to think about what Kate was doing at that moment.

He turned at the sound of heavy footsteps and took the beer CJ offered. "You've got a lot on your plate here."

CJ gave a heavy sigh. "Travis is a good kid, so he makes it easier on me..." He shook his head. "One minute I'm single, kicking ass at the Bureau, so close to my next promotion I can smell it, and the next..." He took a sip of his beer. "Amazing how fast everything can change."

Didn't Tommy know it. "You find anything more this afternoon?" While Tommy had been drilling his way into confidential banking information, CJ had been on the phone trying to gather more information about the Bludgeoner's previous victims.

CJ shook his head. "It's going to take awhile to pull the rest of the files and talk to everyone who worked the case. Hopefully someone will remember something that didn't end up in the file."

"What about the necklace, the connection to Michael Beckett's murder? Maybe there's something from that crime scene that was overlooked."

CJ nodded. "I've already got calls in to the lead crime scene analyst and the medical examiner who did the autopsies." He let out a frustrated sigh. "But since everyone worked the scene like it was a suicide, it's likely anything useful would have been lost in the shuffle. I just hope for Kate and her family's sake—" CJ was interrupted by the buzzing of his phone. "Speak of the devil. Hey, Kate," he said, flashing Tommy a look.

Tommy forced himself to the other end of the deck when every cell in his body urged him to lean in so he could catch the mere sound of her voice.

"No, nothing substantial," he heard CJ say.

His fingers curled into a fist as he fought the urge to grab the phone out of CJ's hand. *To say what?* he sneered inwardly. To beg her to listen to him? To give them another chance?

"You want to talk to him yourself? He's right here."

The muscles of his chest and back pulled tight as a bow as he waited for the answer. Even knowing what it would be couldn't stop the wave of disappointment from crashing over him when he heard CJ say, "Fine. I'll keep you posted as soon as we hear anything." He said goodbye and hung up.

"She okay?" Tommy couldn't keep himself from asking.

CJ shrugged. "I'd say she's doing all right, considering she's discovered a potential new twist to her brother's case, found herself starring in a media circus, and lost her job all in the space of one day."

"She got fired from the foundation?" Tommy asked, guilt pinching at his chest. Maybe she was right. Maybe he *was* the cosmic force of doom in her life.

"Yeah—I forgot to tell you. The chairman of the board called her when I was giving her a ride home. Told her the board didn't think it was appropriate for her to have such a public role." CJ shook his head, his lips stretched into a mirthless smile. "Asshole had the nerve to ask her to make sure her family kept up their donations."

Tommy winced. Once again Kate was left alone to weather the storm herself. The desire to go to her was like a physical ache. He should be there for her.

The only thing stopping him was the bitter knowledge that no matter how badly he wanted to help her, he was the last person on earth she wanted to see.

A soft voice wheedled its way through his own pain at her rejection. *Remember what she said about pushing people away? The whole time all she wanted was for someone to ignore all that and just be there for her.*

He knew Kate wouldn't exactly greet him with open arms. But the slim chance that he could push past her defenses and convince her that they could weather this storm better together than apart had him poised to heed that soft voice.

CJ's next words stopped him cold.

"She'll be all right, though. John is coming to get her and take her back to his place so she can get away from the reporters."

Chump. Tommy's grip around his beer bottle tightened until his knuckles shone white but he schooled his face into an expressionless mask. "Nice of him." Kate had said John was one of the few who had had her back when Michael died. Now he could sweep in and be her knight in shining armor all over again.

CJ gave a little chuckle. "I don't know that nice has much to do with it. I guarantee he'll be trying to get in her pants as soon as he gets her in the door."

Tommy took a deep breath through clenched teeth.

"Not that I can blame him," CJ continued. "She was something to look at back when we knew her, with those long legs and that mouth of hers. But now I swear she's only gotten more beautiful—"

"Are you trying to get punched?" Tommy grabbed CJ by the front of his shirt. And immediately regretted it when he saw CJ's smug, knowing grin. He released CJ's shirt and gave him a shove against his chest for good measure.

"I'm just trying to get you to admit that it bothers you that she's turning to someone else when you know she should be with you."

"What the hell am I supposed to do?" Tommy exploded. "You heard what she said."

"She'd just been blindsided by the reporters. She wasn't thinking clearly—"

Tommy held up his hand for silence. "Moments like that are when the truth comes out. Deep down Kate will never get over the fact that she was with me the night Michael was killed. Better to find that out now than before I get in too deep."

"I think you've been in too deep the second Kate walked into Jackson Fuller's place," CJ said, his expression grave.

Tommy repressed a flinch as the truth of CJ's words hit home. Not that there was anything he could do about it. "You know what I think? I think it's time for us to get the fuck back to work."

Chapter 28

"Are you sure I'm not imposing?" Kate asked as she followed John up the stairs from the stretch of beach that abutted his property.

"Of course not. You know I have plenty of room, and now the reporters can't get to you."

Kate felt no small amount of relief at the thought. The past few hours at her townhouse had been torture. Unable to go anywhere because of the dozen or so reporters crowded outside of her door, Kate had been bouncing off the walls while she waited for CJ to call with news.

Of course, it didn't help to be alone with thoughts of Tommy swirling around in her head. The taste of him on her lips, the feel of him deep inside her. The way he talked about a future together like it was a real possibility.

And then the devastation in his eyes when she lashed out.

Part of her hated herself for the way she'd acted, for her knee-jerk reaction to shove Tommy away as the press took something real and beautiful and turned it into a lurid sideshow for the world to criticize and judge.

CJ's words rang in her ears, telling her she was being a fool for allowing her worries about the media's portrayal of her relationship with Tommy to keep her from grabbing this second chance with him and doing everything she could to make it work. And to hell with how that bitch Maura Walsh decided to twist it.

When Tommy called, her heart had leapt to her throat when she recognized the number. Heart pounding, she stared at the phone cradled in her hand, every cell in her body urging her to pick up. To apologize for what she said and take it all back.

But as she went to press the "answer" button, there was a sharp tap on the window next to her kitchen, and she looked up to see the shadow of a man silhouetted in the window, a video camera pointed right at her.

She dropped the phone like it was on fire, darted across the room to yank the curtains shut, then went through the rest of the house to make sure every blind was drawn.

She cursed herself for a coward, but she couldn't make herself pick up the phone and call Tommy back.

Instead she curled on her couch, tuned the TV to a movie channel that guaranteed she wouldn't be assaulted with images of herself, and wondered how long she could stay holed up in the townhouse before she went completely insane.

Fortunately, she didn't have to wait and see. She didn't pick up the phone the first time he called, cringing at the thought of him seeing the news stories. She braced herself as she listened to his message, but instead of sounding scandalized or judgmental, John's voice tone was purely sympathetic.

Hey, I saw the news and wanted you to know that I'm here for you a hundred percent. If you need anything, don't hesitate to call.

Touched, Kate called him back, figuring he deserved a thank-you if nothing else. When he offered for her to come stay with him, initially she'd refused. "There's a swarm of reporters at my front door," she said. "And no offense, but the last thing I need right now is for them to put out a story of me spending the night at yet another man's house."

John chuckled. "I see your point. But what if I could sneak you out without them seeing?"

So they'd hatched a plan for Kate to sneak through the sliding glass door that was one level down from the main entrance on the side of the house that faced the lake. From there it was a short walk down to a spot on the beach where John could pick her up in his boat.

Kate didn't realize how trapped she'd felt in the townhouse until John started motoring to his dock. With the cool evening air on her cheeks and pulling her hair from its ponytail, she felt like she was able to take her first deep breath since she'd left Erin's restaurant that afternoon.

After she'd deposited her overnight bag in one of the many bedrooms, Kate joined John on the deck, where he waited with a glass of wine and a platter of sandwich fixings. "I wasn't sure if you'd had dinner yet," John said, gesturing to the platter. "Magda's off for the evening, and I'm afraid sandwiches are about the extent of my culinary capabilities."

Kate couldn't remember the last time she'd eaten, but the thought of food made her stomach twist with revulsion. "I'm not hungry, but thanks." She took the proffered glass of wine and nearly vomited up the first sip of Pinot Grigio the second it hit her stomach.

She settled in one of the teak armchairs and set the glass on the table beside her.

"You should drink that," John said, settling into the chair next to her. "You deserve a little something after what happened today."

She thought she detected an edge to his voice but couldn't be sure. "I don't think my stomach is up to much of any-

thing right now. It's been crazy—first Tricia and then—"
She stopped herself, realizing she was about to slip the news
of the necklace. "And then this thing in the press…" She
trailed off weakly.

"Is it true?" This time there was no mistaking the edge in his
voice. "Have you and Tommy rekindled your little romance?"

Kate's shoulders stiffened at his snide tone. "Maybe
it wasn't a good idea for me to come here," she said, and
started to push to her feet.

John stayed her with a hand on her arm. "I'm sorry," he
said. "That was rude of me. But just because I accepted that
whatever torch I've been carrying for you will never go anywhere, that doesn't mean I don't get a little jealous, thinking
of you with him."

Kate tried not to notice the way his hand lingered on the
bare skin of her forearm or the way his thumb was tracing
slow circles on the skin of her wrist.

To her relief, he dropped his hand. "Let's talk about
something else," he said, and took a sip of wine. "Is there any
progress in the case? Do I need to get my checkbook out?"

She gave him a wan smile. "Good news is, Tricia is out of
the woods, health wise."

"Has she given them a description of the guy who
took her?"

Kate hesitated before answering. While she trusted John,
she knew too well how harmful a seemingly small confidence could be. "Right now they're focused on getting her
strength up before they start hammering her with questions."

"Hopefully she'll give the police something soon. I imagine whoever did this is busy covering his tracks."

Kate's stomach churned at the thought of whoever did
this to Tricia—and possibly killed those other girls and
maybe even Michael too—slipping through their fingers.

The stress of the day bore down on her, the weight of her crumbling world threatening to crush her. "I really appreciate you giving me a break from the craziness outside my front door. But I'm afraid I'm really terrible company tonight. I really think I should just call it a night."

She was grateful when John didn't protest or act offended even though it wasn't yet nine o'clock. "Get some rest. I suspect you'll need all your reserves to get through the next few days."

Kate bid him good night and retreated to her room. The day had taken its toll both physically and emotionally, but every time she closed her eyes, her mind started racing with questions that had no answers.

Eventually the questions stopped, but still she could find no rest. Because even worse than the endless questions was what replaced them: Tommy.

Memories of him, both past and recent, played in her head on an endless loop. Tommy at age sixteen, howling like Tarzan as he swung out into the lake on a rope swing, taunting Kate mercilessly until she did the same.

Their first kiss, the explosive discovery of how much pleasure she could feel at the slightest brush of his lips.

A pleasure that was nothing compared to what she'd found in his bed the night before. Mind blowing, world altering, all the more powerful because it went so far beyond physical connection. The memory of Tommy looking into her eyes, his features pulled tight with pleasure as he drove her over the edge, brought a pain to her chest so fierce she felt tears leak from the corners of her eyes.

Once started, they wouldn't stop, an endless stream fueled by the memories of his reluctant smiles. The conviction in his voice when he held her in his arms and told her he wanted the Kate she'd become and so carefully traced the faint scar on her wrist.

Kate finally drifted into a fitful sleep. She awoke, gritty eyed and foggy headed, unable to escape the nagging sense that she was going to regret pushing Tommy away for the rest of her life.

She dressed quickly and went down to the kitchen to bolster herself with some caffeine. Magda was at the sink, and Kate brushed off her offer to get coffee for her.

"Mr. Burkhart told me to tell you he's sorry he cannot stay for breakfast, but he has many meetings this morning."

"That's okay," Kate said truthfully. She wasn't up to morning chitchat. She finished her cup of coffee and politely refused Magda's offer to make her breakfast. Her stomach was too twisted up to make room for food.

"You need anything from grocery store? I go soon."

Kate said no and thanked her. After she left, Kate headed out to the lake, hoping the fresh air would help clear her head. As she walked aimlessly along the shore, thoughts of Tommy consumed her.

Now, after the initial shock of seeing Maura Walsh's report had passed, several things became very, very clear. The press could say whatever they wanted about her and Tommy, drag them through the mud until they'd covered every salacious angle.

But that didn't change the fact that she loved him. A deep, passionate love that had survived a terrible tragedy and over a decade of separation but was still there, right underneath the surface. Just waiting to be set free.

More than that, she needed him. Needed him to stand by her side and have her back and hold her at night and tell her everything would be okay. Needed the peace she found in his arms and the excitement she found in his bed to make her feel whole in a way she never had.

And she knew with gut-deep certainty that she would

need his help in the coming weeks, months, however long it took her to find out the truth of what happened to Michael. Not just his skill as an investigator. She needed *him*. Needed his strong, steady presence, his voice rumbling in her ear as he assured her that he was there for her, that he'd never turn his back on her.

She brushed away the tears that streamed down her cheeks, ashamed of how she'd turned on him so quickly, instinctively pushing him away instead of grabbing on and holding tight. Instead of realizing the truth, that whether she ended their relationship or not, the press was going to play the story out for as long as it had legs. In fact, her outburst had no doubt added more fuel to the fire.

But there was an even more basic truth. One that had nothing to do with her reputation.

The truth was that Tommy stirred something up inside of her that she'd never come close to feeling for another human being. Something that made her well up with happiness at the sight of him, something that made her feel like she was lit up from the inside every time he touched her.

And even more mind blowing was that he felt the same way about her.

And even though the things he made her feel were so powerful they were scary, the way they made her throw caution to the wind and act in ways she didn't realize she was capable of, she also knew he had the potential to make her happier than she'd ever dreamed. With Tommy, she had the chance to be happier than most people on the planet had ever dreamed.

She knew that, down to her very core. And if a tragedy like what had happened to Michael couldn't destroy that conviction, she would be an idiot to let a publicity-hungry bitch like Walsh destroy it.

She turned back toward the house, full of renewed purpose, her chest swelling with hope that Tommy would accept her apology and they could get back on track. Doubts nipped at the back of her mind. He'd already been burned by her choosing the need to avoid scandal over him. The man Tommy had become didn't seem big on multiple chances.

—⁂—

She continued down the beach, heart in her throat, mentally scripting exactly how she was going to beg for Tommy's forgiveness. She reached the steps leading to John's deck and was distracted by the figure of a man sitting hunched over a few feet past the wooden staircase, hidden in the shadows.

Panic leapt in her throat a split second before she recognized Magda's son, Christian. His gaze was focused on his cupped hands, and Kate heard the telltale electronic bleeps and blips of some kind of game device. He was so engrossed in his play he didn't even register her approach until Kate called out a greeting.

He jumped up, startled. Instead of saying hello, he darted out from under the deck saying "I'll put it back. Please don't tell" over and over, casting furtive looks at her over his shoulder.

"Don't tell who?" Kate asked.

At that moment Christian caught his foot on a log partially hidden in the sand. He went sprawling and the game device arced up in the air to land a few feet from Kate.

She picked it up, ignoring his panicked protests. "I'm sure it will still work," Kate said as she brushed the sand off. The device was an older one, she realized, with a black-and-white screen and actual buttons to push instead of a touch screen.

Her heart twisted as she recognized that it was very similar to the one Michael had played with so often that summer that they'd joked it was going to graft onto his palm. Then she turned it and felt all the blood rush from her head as she saw the tiny block letters written in permanent marker along the base.

Though time and wear had rubbed some of the ink away, at that moment Kate would have bet her life that it read "PROPERTY OF MICHAEL BECKETT."

In that instant he snatched it from her hand and sprinted down the beach.

"Come back here," Kate shouted as she ran after him. "Tell me what you're doing with that!"

Christian pounded down the boat dock. Kate followed suit, her heart thudding in her ears. He ducked into the boat house at the end of the dock.

It took Kate's eyes a few minutes to adjust to the dark interior, but she saw him in the far corner in front of a chest that held boating and safety equipment. Carefully making her way around the three-foot-wide platform that surrounded John's 25 foot cruiser, Kate came up behind Christian just as he was closing the lid to a small wooden case tucked inside the chest.

"Please," he said, his eyes open so wide with fear Kate could see the whites even in the dim light. "Please don't tell him I found his treasurés."

Treasures? Kate shoved him aside, and though he was taller than her by several inches and outweighed her by at least fifty pounds, he skittered away as quickly as he could.

The roaring in her ears was so loud Kate barely heard his continued pleas for her not to tell on him.

Kate went to flip the lid open, cursing when she met resistance. She looked closer and saw that there was a combination lock holding the latch closed.

"Please, put it away. Put it away so he doesn't find out," he pleaded, from the opposite corner.

Ignoring him, Kate pulled the box out of the chest and carried it to the patch of sunlight that shone through one of the dusty windows. She studied the contents, her breath catching in her throat as she saw several pieces of women's jewelry, a hair clip. And no, she wasn't imagining it. The Game Boy Michael had taken upstairs with him the night he was kidnapped. Kate's breath froze in her chest when she heard heavy footsteps approaching on the dock.

Before she could react, Christian jumped into the water next to the boat and disappeared under the boathouse. Kate stumbled across the platform, scrambling to pull the lid of the chest back into place.

Just as she turned the door was flung open behind her.

Kate turned, her blood turning to ice when she saw John.

"Kate, what are you doing in here?" he asked as he skirted around the back of the boat and walked over to her side.

Her brain scrambled for an excuse, but she couldn't think past the voice screaming at her to get out of there, away from him. "I didn't think you'd be back until later," she said weakly.

"And you thought you'd do a little canoeing?" he replied. His gaze flicked knowingly down to the chest.

Her gaze instinctively followed, and she felt all the breath whoosh from her lungs as she saw that the lid was slightly askew.

An odd, almost satisfied smile stretched across John's face. "I see you've discovered my secret."

Chapter 29

Tommy rubbed at his gritty eyes and took another look at the information displayed across his laptop screen. After he'd left CJ's, he'd headed back to his place and spent the entire night, chasing bank account numbers, connecting transactions to a dozen different shell companies, following the money through wormhole after wormhole. Now he'd parked himself in CJ's office at the sheriff's headquarters and was trying to make sense of it all.

Again he squinted at his screen, wondering if his powers of reason had fully deserted him. It was entirely possible that sleeplessness combined with the emotional stress of what had gone down with Kate was causing him to hallucinate.

Bullshit. You've gone without sleep for days and dealt with the emotional trauma of having your buddy's leg blown off less than two feet away, and you didn't hallucinate then.

"Son of a bitch," he muttered, adrenaline spiking in his blood as the implications hit home.

"You find something?" CJ looked up from the paperwork spread across his desk.

Tommy didn't say a word, just turned his laptop around so CJ could see the website displayed on the screen. "Mountainside Real Estate Development Company," Tommy said grimly. "I traced Tavers International back to it."

CJ's skin paled. "That's the company that bought Burkhart's company."

Tommy nodded and rose to his feet as he closed the laptop. "And kept good old Johnny on as vice president of sales."

"Jesus, you don't really think..." CJ said, trailing off as it became clear that yeah, he really did think too.

"CJ, right now I can't think about much of anything beyond the fact that right now, Kate is alone in a house with a man who likely raped and murdered several women."

—⚬—

"Why," she started, but seemed to choke on the words, her mouth as dry as the Sahara. When she spoke again, her voice came out reedy and thin. "Why do you have Michael's Game Boy?"

John gave her a look that was a mixture of condescension and pity. "I think you know the answer to that."

She struggled to take it all in, her brain unwilling to accept that this man who'd known her for her entire life, who'd been one of the few people to reach out to her in the wake of her brother's death, was the one who'd murdered him.

And murdered at least four other girls after that.

Pure instinct had her hurtling for the door. He caught her arm in a vice grip as she passed. She jerked and kicked, freezing when she felt the cold press of metal and heard the unmistakable *click* of a revolver being cocked.

"Don't," he whispered. That menacing whisper sent a chill down her back, and in that second she knew he was the one who attacked her in her townhouse. "I don't want to shoot you yet. Not when I've waited this long to finally get my hands on you."

The last piece of the puzzle snapped into place. "It was me," she breathed, sick, twisting vertigo making her vision swim and her legs wobble. "You didn't come for Michael. You came for me."

John's hand slid up her chest, his fingers curled around her throat. "Imagine my surprise when I unwrapped that blanket and found Michael instead of you."

"You didn't have to kill him," she choked on a sob.

"Of course I did. The sedative wore off too soon and he saw me. Think about it, Kate, if only you'd kept your legs shut, Michael would still be alive. Now get on the boat."

Frantic sobs ripped from her chest as thoughts of Michael's last moments bombarded her. Waking up confused, drugged, to see a person he recognized and trusted. And to have that person…"Why did you…hurt him?" She couldn't even get the words out.

John shrugged. "I thought it would make it look more convincing."

It should have been me. It should have been me. Fresh guilt crashed over her in a wave, threatening to consume her. *She'd* done this. She'd unwittingly lured the monster to their door. And her brother died because of it.

"Now get on the boat."

Kate shook her head and tried to tear herself from his grip, not stopping even as his hand tightened around her throat while the other pressed the gun barrel against her head with enough force to split the skin.

She couldn't let him take her. If he did she was as good as dead. She felt the sickening pressure of his erection against her spine and knew he wouldn't just kill her outright. She threw her elbow back against his ribs, but the blow was weak as she struggled for air. Her vision tunneled, dimming as she felt herself being dragged onto the boat.

He was going to take her. And this time Tommy wasn't going to show up in time to stop him.

Chapter 30

Tommy hit the parking lot at a dead run, ignoring CJ's shouts for him to wait and let him assess the situation.

Wait? Assess? While Kate was in the same house with a brutal murderer? Fat fucking chance.

As he started to pull out in his truck, he heard the wailing of sirens as CJ and another deputy fired up their cruisers. Realizing that if he went tearing through town he was likely to take down a pedestrian or two, Tommy set himself right on CJ's bumper and drafted off of him all the way to Burkhart's.

If that sick fuck harmed a single hair on Kate's head... Tommy shoved the thought away, trying to convince himself that it wasn't likely Burkhart even knew they were on to him. Even if he'd pumped Kate for information, as far as she knew, Tricia wasn't even close to making an ID. And even in the unlikely event Kate let the new information they had about Michael's case slip, there was no reason for John to think he was under suspicion.

But the fact that Kate hadn't picked up her phone the half dozen times he'd dialed her wasn't reassuring.

As he followed CJ's speeding cruiser through the streets of Burkhart's neighborhood, he couldn't get visions of the man's other victims out of his mind. Their bruised and battered faces and bodies, some with injuries so severe their own parents had trouble identifying them.

The thought of Kate, her delicate nose and chin crushed under the impact of those fists...

As CJ got closer to the house, the sirens ceased. It made sense. If Burkhart heard them coming in hot and got spooked, it could get real ugly, real fast.

He took it as his own cue to settle the hell down. He wouldn't do Kate any good if he lost his head.

He pulled in behind CJ and heard the other cruiser pull in behind him.

Tommy got out of his truck and started to rush the door and shot CJ an annoyed look when the other man grabbed him by the arm to stay him.

"We have no reason to assume there's trouble, so let's not cause any," he cautioned.

Tommy grudgingly obeyed and clenched and unclenched his fists as CJ pressed the doorbell.

"Technically you shouldn't even be here," CJ said as they waited for the door to open.

Tommy shot him and Deputy Roberts a stony glare. "Try and move me."

Deputy Roberts took a half step back. CJ shook his head in exasperation.

After a full minute, two more rings at the doorbell, and no answer, CJ tried the knob.

When he found it locked, he and Tommy exchanged a look. Two size twelve booted feet hit the door in perfect unison, sending the heavy wood swinging in with an ear-splitting *crack*.

"Are you sure this is okay?" Roberts said nervously. "It's not going to look good if we don't have a warrant—"

"You want to wait outside for Burkhart to let you in"—

Tommy wheeled around on him—"you go ahead. I'm not leaving till I know Kate is safe."

Tommy felt the hairs stand up on his arms as the three did a quick sweep of the downstairs. It was empty and eerily silent, though the dishes on the table suggested recent activity, and the sliding glass door that opened onto the deck was open, letting fresh air in through the screen.

Tommy started up the stairs, pausing when he heard what sounded like crying coming from outside.

His stomach lurching, he called for CJ as he ran over to the screen door and slid it open, his boots pounding on the deck as he followed the sound down to the beach.

It took him a moment to realize the sound was coming from under the deck. Tommy ducked underneath and saw that the sobbing was coming from a large male figure. As his eyes adjusted to the shadows he recognized Burkhart's housekeeper's kid huddled in a ball, sobbing incoherently.

Tommy's stomach clenched with dread. He'd seen the kid around town, knew there was something not quite right about him, but had no idea whether the kid might be violent.

"Where's Kate?" Tommy shouted.

At the sound of his shout, the boy's head shot up, his expression full of fear. "I was only looking at the treasures, I didn't mean to get her in trouble."

"Get who in trouble? Kate?" CJ asked as he ducked under the deck.

"The lady, from the TV. I didn't want her to see the treasures. And he, he got so mad."

Tommy's stomach churned with fear. "What did he do? What did he do to the lady from the TV?"

"T-took her. Like he t-took the others," Christian choked out.

"Where?" Tommy fought the urge to grab the kid by the shoulders and shake it out of him.

"What's going on? What you are doing?" A thickly accented female voice rang through the air. Magda ran over and shoved Tommy out of the way to kneel next to her son. She cupped his face in her hands and crooned to him in an Eastern European language he couldn't quite decipher.

"Ask him what happened to Kate," Tommy said through clenched teeth, feeling like his chest was about to explode.

"He took her on a boat," Magda said. "He had a gun and he took her on the boat."

"Do you know where?" Tommy asked, fear turning his blood to ice.

"No," Magda said softly. "Christian doesn't know where he took her. He never takes them to the same place twice."

The realization that Magda must have known about John's activities before now sent a ripple of shock through him.

"You're the one who gave Kate the newspaper clipping," CJ said. Tommy surged to his feet and walked out from under the deck.

"I thought I could help," Magda said softly as she walked out after him, clinging to Christian's arm. "I give a clue, point in the right direction—"

"It would have helped if you'd gone to the police years ago and stopped him!" Tommy wheeled around on her.

Magda began to cry softly. "He would send me back to Hungary without Christian, told me he would hurt him."

"We're not going to let anything happen to you or Christian," CJ said quietly, "as long as you tell us everything you know."

Tommy wanted to punch a wall, he was so infuriated. Magda might have finally had a crisis of conscience and given them a crucial clue, but there was nothing she could do to help them find Kate.

He listened impatiently as CJ scrambled a helicopter and several search and rescue boats. Within ten minutes, a boat from Bonner County Marine Patrol pulled up to the dock to pick up Tommy, CJ, and Deputy Roberts. In the meantime, another deputy had arrived to take a statement from Magda and Christian.

"I have no idea what his end game is or how he thinks he's going to get away from us," CJ said as the boat rumbled out into the water

Tommy's jaw clenched. "There's over a hundred miles of coastline and lots of places to hide for someone who knows the lake well."

"Every boater and Jet Skier on the lake will be looking for him. We'll find her, Tommy."

Chapter 31

Kate didn't think she was out for long, but it was long enough for John to bind her hands and feet tightly with zip ties and shove her to the deck of the boat. He hadn't gagged her, but the rumble of the boat's engine was loud enough to drown her out if she tried to scream.

CJ knows you were with John. Tommy does too. As long as you're still alive, you can be found.

But how long would it take before they even thought to look for her? The only person who knew she was in trouble was Christian, and he'd bolted in a panic when John arrived. Would he think to tell anyone what he saw?

She'd stayed quiet, keeping a wary eye on John as he sped over the water, his head darting anxiously around, keeping his distance as much as possible from the other boats. After a while he slowed the boat down and finally parked it along the shore in a U-shaped cove that backed into a densely wooded area that looked completely deserted.

"I'd hoped to have more time to prepare for our trip," John said tightly as he jumped down onto the beach to drive the anchor into the sand. "But your little discovery pushed up my schedule a bit." He hopped back on the boat and stood over her, shaking his head like she was a disobedient child. "There you go again, Kate, ruining my plans. I was already going to punish you for Tricia. Now I'm afraid it's going to be much, much worse."

He moved so quickly she didn't even have a chance to brace herself before his foot connected with her stomach. She gasped in pain, barely able to breathe as he drove all the breath from her lungs.

She curled into a ball, bracing herself for a blow that didn't come. Instead he was digging through the storage bins under the padded benches that lined the sides, clearly agitated when he didn't find what he was looking for.

Kate tracked him as he paced, tapping his foot, checking his watch and the sky.

She didn't know what he was waiting for, but if she had to guess, she'd say he was waiting until dark to start moving again.

Eventually he sat down in the captain's chair, and though Kate tried to ignore it, she could feel his stare burning a hole through the top of her bent head.

"It could have been so different, you know," he finally said. "If you had only understood how much I loved you."

Her head snapped up. "You *loved* me? Is that why you planned to kidnap, rape, and kill me like you did to those other girls?"

"I never wanted to hurt you. I thought if I could get you alone for a while you would understand how much I cared for you—"

Her mind reeling, Kate said, "Is that why you kidnapped and beat Tricia? Because you cared for her? You think Ellie Cantrell and Stephanie Adler felt cared for when you were beating them to death? You're a monster. I don't know how I never saw it."

"I'm not a monster!" John roared.

Fear pulsed through her as he surged to his feet and loomed over her, his face a furious mask, a thick vein throbbing in his forehead.

"I loved them! I loved them all! All I wanted was to love them and to care for them, but they were all a bunch of ungrateful bitches who weren't capable of understanding how I honored them."

His hands reached for her and Kate scrambled away until her back hit one of the bench seats.

Then with a shake of his head he seemed to catch himself, the fury dimming. "I never wanted to hurt any of them," John said, sounding almost grief stricken. "But they would be so mean to me, so disrespectful, and I would get so angry..." His voice trailed off. "It always started out as a punishment."

Kate swallowed back a surge of nausea, remembering his promise to punish her.

"It all worked out for the best, though," he said, his voice matter-of-fact, stripped of any trace of grief. "If they couldn't accept my love, I could hardly let them go."

"So you had to kill them," Kate said.

"I can't let betrayal go unpunished," he replied. For a brief second, a softer, wistful expression came over his face. It quickly disappeared, his expression once again stone cold. "But then she tried to leave me too. For eight years I gave her everything she could have ever wanted, and she showed me her gratitude by trying to sneak off in the middle of the night."

"Jennifer didn't commit suicide then," Kate said.

"No one ever gets to leave me," John said coldly.

Kate felt a surge of pity for the woman.

Something of it must have shown on her face, because he

sneered, "Don't feel sorry for her. She was living in a trailer park with her meth-head mother who made her do disgusting things in front of a web camera to pay for her drugs when I rescued her. And when you think about it, you can blame her for what happened to Tricia."

"How so?" Kate could barely choke the words out, disgust made her throat so tight.

"If she hadn't tried to leave, I wouldn't have needed to find someone new to love," he said as though the answer were obvious.

"And now you're back to me, full circle. You think you're somehow going to convince me to love you?"

His mouth pulled into a smile that sent a chill straight to the bottom of her soul. "You think I want to be loved by Tommy Ibarra's whore?" He squatted down until he was on her eye level. "You lost your chance a long time ago. But I realized the other day, when I had my hand around your neck, your body against mine, you could serve another purpose."

Kate swallowed back a surge of bile as he reached out with one hand and ran his hand over her shoulder, down her chest until it covered her breast. His fingers closed over the curve, squeezing until tears gathered, but she wouldn't give him the satisfaction of crying out in pain.

"While I want my lovers to give themselves to me freely, I find that being around them inspires certain urges—" He gave her breast a meaningful squeeze to make his point. "After everything you've put me through, I think it's a fitting punishment for you to be the one to satisfy them."

As he bent closer, her gaze zeroed in on the gun held loosely in his other hand. If she could just get her hands on it...

She flung her head forward as hard as she could, satisfaction surging through her as she heard the crunch of bone as her head made contact with his nose. He staggered back, and she hurled herself at his gun hand, her bound feet making her clumsy.

She scrambled with her bound wrists and managed to knock the gun out of his hand. She threw herself on the deck, grunting as his knee landed in her back. He flipped her over and she struggled to secure her hold on the handle as her thumb fumbled with the hammer. A metallic *click*, her index finger closed over the trigger—

In that split second John grabbed her wrists and twisted. There was a sharp *pop*, and pain exploded in Kate's chest.

The gun clattered to the deck as Kate fell back against the bench. She was vaguely aware of him picking up the gun and shoving it in his waistband, screaming something about her not getting off this easy.

She wanted to tell him the pain wracking her was anything but easy, but she couldn't get the words past her lips.

She chalked up the dimming of his voice and the retreating of his footsteps to her battle to stay conscious, and it took her a couple moments to realize he'd left the boat. Was he coming back? Had he left her there to die?

Either way she had to do something or she *was* going to die, either tonight from the gunshot or later when he was finished with her. Adrenaline rushed through her as her body gave a last gasp to save itself. She pushed to her elbows and knees, forcing past the pain as she inchwormed herself over to the captain's chair.

—ᴍᴍ—

It took several minutes, but she managed to struggle to her feet. Though she knew it was a long shot, disappointment wracked her when she saw the empty ignition.

She was about to sink back to the floor when her gaze

snagged on a panel built into the dashboard. Her heart kicked into a flutter as she read the dark, glossy lettering of the built-in GPS system. Tommy had used the GPS on her phone to track her that day in the woods.

Kate hoped this worked the same way, because her strength was fleeing as adrenaline faded.

She fumbled her bound hands toward the on button, keeping a wary eye out for Burkhart all the while.

She pressed the button, uttering a prayer of thanks as the display lit up. *It's working.*

Tommy spent the next few hours in an agony of helpless frustration as he fruitlessly scanned the lake for any sign of Burkhart's boat from the deck of the sheriff's rescue cruiser. Dozens of volunteers were searching the lake and the beaches by water and air and had thus far come up cold.

With a little digging into the purchase history of Burkhart's boat, Tommy was able to get a line into the onboard GPS system.

Which would give them the ability to pinpoint Burkhart's exact location. That is, if it had been turned on.

Psychotic or not, Burkhart was clever enough not to risk it, just as he hadn't risked taking his or Kate's cell phone with him on the boat.

Which left Tommy's electronic tracking skills essentially worthless. If they wanted to find Kate, they would have to rely on good old-fashioned eyes in the sky and feet on the street. Or on the lake, as it were. Unfortunately, Burkhart's boat, similar to so many others, had been spotted going in every direction imaginable, which narrowed the search area to roughly one hundred fifty square miles of water.

And that was assuming he hadn't ditched the boat already and found another mode of transportation.

While Tommy fruitlessly scanned the lake, he thought about what he'd learned from Burkhart's banking records.

Judging from the sizable transfers Burkhart made overseas within the past thirty-six hours, he'd been preparing to run. Tommy felt his stomach clench at the amounts in question. With that amount of wealth and the relative ease with which he could access it, if Burkhart managed to get over the border, he'd have unlimited resources for a life on the run.

You can run, but you can't hide, motherfucker. I will not lose her again, not to you, not to anybody.

As though the universe heard him, there was a shrill beep and vibration from the phone in his pocket. He jumped, startled, as he dug it out. His eyebrows shot up to his hairline at what he saw on the display.

"What?" CJ asked.

"I think we might have found her," Tommy said, unable to keep the excitement out of his voice.

Though he didn't want to get his hopes up—it was possible Burkhart had ditched the boat at the location displayed on the GPS tracking app Tommy had set up and someone else had turned the system on—he couldn't stop the rush of anticipation.

After a hoot of excitement, CJ took down the coordinates. "He's up toward Oden Bay. I'll get everyone out in that direction ASAP."

Tommy frowned. "If we go that way, he'll see you coming three hundred yards out. You spook him, he could hurt Kate." Assuming he hadn't…he didn't even want to go there.

"There's no other way to access the shore there," CJ said impatiently.

"That's not true. If you go up Sunnyside there's a trail that goes down to the beach. It's only about two miles through the forest."

"I've never heard of any trails up there."

"It's not on a map—it's just an old game trail we used for hunting."

"So where exactly is it, and how is that better than approaching from the water?" CJ asked, still sounding skeptical.

Tommy tried to explain. "You got about four miles up Sunnyside from where it splits off Railroad. Trust me, it's the best way."

CJ studied him for a moment, then: "Deputy, take us back to Burkhart's. We'll take Tommy's truck up to the trailhead."

Even though Tommy was sure this was their best chance at getting the drop on Burkhart, his gut was twisted with doubt. If he was wrong, if he fucked up, if Kate got hurt…

"I hope I'm not making a huge fucking mistake trusting you," CJ muttered as they motored up to the dock in front of Burkhart's house.

"That makes two of us," Tommy said grimly.

Hang on, Kate. Hang on and I'll be there as soon as I can.

Chapter 32

Tommy broke several traffic laws as he sped his truck to the trailhead, CJ and Deputy Roberts following in the cruiser. Even though the app would sound an alarm if Burkhart's boat moved from the current location, Tommy checked the screen compulsively. He pulled to a stop just past the split tree and loaded his Beretta while CJ pulled the cruiser up behind him. He pulled his M1A hunting rifle from behind his front seat, along with a pair of binoculars that could switch to night vision mode once the sun went down, and strapped his KA-BAR Tanto to his calf for good measure.

"You're certainly prepared," CJ remarked as he loaded up his own M1A. "How accurate are you with that thing?" he asked, eyebrow cocked as he looked pointedly at the rifle slung over Tommy's shoulder.

"A thousand yards, iron sights. I was first in my class in sniper training, and I've made sure to keep up my skills. You?" He nodded at CJ's gun.

"Last fall I caught a bull elk in the eye at six hundred yards. Foggy day too."

Tommy gave a grunt of approval, checked the magazine on his Beretta, and tucked it into his waistband. "Hopefully we won't have to find out who's the better shot." He slipped on an earpiece and a mike and headed into the trees.

—ɯ—

I should just leave the bitch to die, John thought viciously as he paced up and down the beach. He'd had to get away from her, afraid he would pull out the gun and finish the job, once and for all.

No. That would be too easy. After the way she treated him, turned her nose up at him, ruined everything for him, she deserved far worse than to die of a simple gunshot wound.

But as he climbed back on the boat and saw Kate slumped on the deck, he was afraid matters were out of his hands. Cursing viciously, he bent and slid his hand to her throat. Her pulse fluttered weakly against his fingers, but if she didn't get medical attention soon...

His plan was to wait until dark to slip into a marina, boost a car, and from there head to the Canadian border. As he looked at Kate, her naturally pale complexion gone nearly gray, her lips bleached of all color and her chest moving in short, shallow breaths, he knew she wouldn't make it that long.

He flung himself in the captain's chair. The sun was heading behind the mountains, but full dark wouldn't come for another hour and a half. Dammit. He would just have to go now and take the chance of someone seeing him.

So what if someone does? he reassured himself. *There's no reason for anyone to think Kate is in trouble or that you're even involved. By the time anyone figures it out, you'll both be long gone.*

He grasped onto that, pushing the doubts aside. He'd had close calls before, and still no one ever had a clue. This wouldn't be any different.

As he went to insert his key into the ignition, something out of the corner of his eye caught his attention. His stomach pitched to the floor when he registered what it was.

The green light, indicating that the GPS navigation system had been turned on.

Locating them would be child's play for a technical expert like Tommy.

Panic and fury roared through him, drowning out the voice of reason trying to reassure him that so what if Tommy *could* find them, it didn't matter because there was no reason for him to be looking.

Yet he couldn't escape the sensation that the walls were closing in on him, the end was rushing up, and he couldn't do anything to stop it.

He surged from the chair, pulled the gun from his waistband as he loomed over Kate. "How long has that been on?" he shouted. "How long!" he repeated, kicking her in the leg when she didn't respond.

Kate gave a feeble whimper and tried to open her eyes. "Don't," she whispered when she saw the gun pointing at her head.

Oh god, this is it, Kate thought through the haze of pain. *He's going to finish it.*

Her eyes drifted shut, but she could hear him cursing, call her a host of filthy names. She blocked it out. *I'm sorry, Tommy,* she thought, as though somehow he'd pick up her thoughts in the ether. *I'm sorry I pushed you away.*

She could hear the scuff of John's feet on the deck, assumed he was getting in better position to aim.

Maybe I'll get to see Michael again.

Chapter 33

He and CJ were halfway down the trail when they heard a gunshot, followed immediately by a shrill alarm from Tommy's phone indicating that the GPS signal was lost.

Panic surged in his chest. *Holy shit, he killed Kate. I'm too late, and he killed her.* The thought echoed through his head as he took off at a flat-out sprint, CJ following close behind. "Call in the boats, get them to block him off," Tommy said, unnecessarily, it turned out. Before he even finished the sentence, he heard CJ shouting the orders into his mike. Burkhart had parked the boat in a narrow, U-shaped cove no more than fifty yards wide. They'd completely lost the element of surprise, but it would be easy to block off the escape route. Within a minute a voice came through his earpiece assuring them the boats were in position.

As they got closer to the lake, the brush thickened, and Tommy felt branches tearing at his arms as he crashed through the foliage. When they were close enough to hear the rumble of the boat engine, they slowed their pace to keep the noise level down.

Burkhart had only gotten about twenty yards off the shore before the boats pinned him in.

Over the noise of the boat's engine, one of the deputies

called through a megaphone, "Put down your weapon and release the girl."

Tommy's stomach flipped as he raised the binoculars to his eyes to confirm what he already dreaded. Burkhart was standing at the helm, and though he didn't have a clear view of Kate, it was obvious by the man's stance he was holding a gun to her head.

There was a moment of relief. Despite the gunshot they'd heard, if he was using Kate as a hostage, it meant she was alive.

The relief fled immediately as he focused in on her and got a better look. She was unconscious, he realized, her head slumped forward. And—Jesus Christ, his heart froze in his chest—the front of her shirt was covered in blood.

She looked like she was dead.

He shoved the thought away, forcing himself into mission mode. If she was dead...He couldn't go there. He had to keep it together. Because if she was alive and he lost his shit right now and didn't get her to the hospital in time, her death would be as much on his head as Burkhart's.

Tommy and CJ locked eyes. CJ pointed at him, then at the north end of the U. Making his way carefully through the brush so Burkhart wouldn't see him, Tommy moved until he was parallel with Burkhart's boat while CJ took up the same position on the opposite side of the cove.

"I've known you for a long time. I know this isn't who you really are," the deputy called over the speaker. "John," the deputy said in a softer tone.

"You don't have a fucking clue who I am and what I'm capable of," Burkhart screamed.

"It's clear she's wounded. I know you don't want her to die. Let her go."

Burkhart's response was to pull Kate tighter against him and dig the barrel deeper into her temple.

Tommy pulled his rifle off his shoulder and put his eye to the scope, which allowed him to take in the scene in excruciating detail. "You in position?" he said to CJ.

"Affirmative," CJ's answer came clearly through Tommy's earpiece.

So CJ too could see Kate's pale, unresponsive face and the fact that not only did Burkhart have a gun to her head, he had his hand wrapped firmly around her throat.

"If you don't move in five seconds, she's dead. Five, four…" Kate's head lolled to one side. Just the opening he needed.

"I have a shot." Tommy took a deep breath and settled the M1A more firmly against his shoulder.

"So do I," CJ said into his ear. "Let's do this."

"Three, two…"

A loud *crack*, another following a millisecond later. Time seemed to stop for a moment as Tommy watched Burkhart's head explode into a bloody pulp, his body falling lifeless to the ground.

Tommy was sprinting down the hill before Kate hit the deck.

—⁓—

"Excuse me? Sir?"

It took a few seconds to realize the doctor was speaking to him. "Yes?" Tommy looked up to see a lanky guy in his mid-forties dressed in scrubs. Tommy recognized him from around town but couldn't place the name.

"You came in with Kate Beckett, correct? I'm Dr. Shreeve, her surgeon."

Tommy nodded eagerly and shot to his feet. "How is she?"

The doctor's mouth pulled into a grim line that sent Tommy stomach hurtling for his feet. "Because it took a couple hours for her to get treatment, she lost a lot of blood. And with bullet wounds there's the risk of extensive tearing."

Tommy's vision swam, his throat so tight he couldn't breathe as the doctor's words sank in. *She's dead. Oh, God, she's dead. She's dead and I never told her I love her.*

He felt his knees go watery beneath him as the doctor continued to speak, his voice sounding like it was coming from the bottom of a well.

"...but with physical therapy should recover fully."

Tommy snapped to alertness as the doctor's words sank in. "Wait, she's not dead?"

Shreeve's bushy eyebrows knitted together over the bridge of his nose. "No. As I said, though the injury is serious, I expect her to make a full recovery."

Again his knees threatened to buckle, this time with relief. "Here's a tip, Doc: How about next time you lead with that."

Despite the doctor's reassurances, the sight of Kate, so pale and still in the recovery room, hit Tommy like a blow to the chest. With her eyes closed, oxygen mask over her face, and the sheets and blanket pulled over her, it was hard to believe she was breathing.

Logically, he knew she had to be, otherwise the half dozen or so machines she was hooked up to would be setting off all kinds of alarms. Still, he couldn't draw a breath until he got close enough to see the shallow rise and fall of her bandaged chest, until he took her hand in his and felt her fingers curl slightly in response.

"Hey, sweetheart," he said, his voice thick. The doctor had warned him that it could take awhile for her to regain consciousness, and even then she would be out of it from the morphine drip.

So he was surprised when her eyelids fluttered at the sound of his voice, and she murmured something that sounded like his name behind the oxygen mask.

His fingers curled more tightly around hers and he felt his mouth stretch into a grin even as his eyes burned with tears. "Katie girl, you've got to stop scaring me like this."

Her eyes crinkled a little bit above her mask. And he couldn't be sure, because it was muffled by the mask, but it sounded like she said "Keep you on your toes."

Her little comeback sent a surge of tangled emotions through him—relief, joy, gratitude. And on top of it all, a love that felt so big it was going to swallow him up.

He bent his head close to where hers rested on the pillow. Through the smells of antiseptic, he got a whiff of pure Kate. He took a deep breath, filling himself with the scent of grass, flowers, and the sweet musk that was uniquely her. "I was so damn scared I was going to lose you," he said. "When I saw you there…" The words choked off at the image of her on the boat, so pale and small, blood staining her entire torso crimson. "I don't know what I would have done if I'd lost you."

Her fingers squeezed feebly at his hand. It took him a few moments to realize she was trying to say something else. He lifted his head, moved his ear right next to the oxygen mask.

"Sorry," he heard her whisper. "Sorry I pushed you away…told you that you ruin everything." The single tear rolling from the corner of her eye hit Tommy like a punch in the gut.

"Don't, it's okay." Tommy's throat felt like it was being closed in a vice.

Her eyelids slid closed and when several moments passed he thought she'd fallen asleep. But then she whispered, "You don't ruin anything. Only you make everything right."

Tommy's eyes burned as he brought her hand to his mouth and pressed his lips to her knuckles. "*We* make everything right," he whispered fervently. "And I should have told you this a lot sooner, but I love you, Katie."

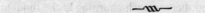

The only reason Kate knew she was really awake this time was because of the pain. The grinding pressure started in the upper right part of her chest and radiated all the way down to her hand. Though the pain made her gasp, she resisted the urge to give herself an extra dose from her morphine drip.

She wasn't sure exactly how long she'd drifted in and out of her drugged half sleep, plagued with strange dreams and visions so vivid it was hard to know what was real and what wasn't.

She opened her eyes, and even through the pain she felt her heart surge with happiness at the sight of the man asleep in the chair next to her, his body bent in half so his arms and torso rested on the bed next to her. She had no idea when he'd come in—there was only a vague impression of a deep voice rumbling in her ear.

I love you. Her heart clenched at what she hoped was an actual memory, not just a fantasy cooked up by her overmedicated brain.

Her arm felt like it weighed a thousand pounds but she willed it to move so her hand could come to rest on Tommy's head, her fingers coiling in the short thick strands of hair.

He raised his head and greeted her with a smile so full of warmth she felt like the sun had risen right there in her hospital room.

"You're here," she whispered with an answering smile.

He took her hand in his, pulled it to his mouth, and pressed a kiss in the center of her palm. "I never left."

Kate felt the burst of joy ebb as she dug back through her foggy memory bank and remembered the events leading up to her surgery.

"John?" she asked, her stomach churning at the thought of the man.

"Dead," Tommy said. There was no missing the satisfaction in his voice. "Got him with a clean shot to the head."

She must have been unconscious at that point, she thought with a shudder. While part of her was glad not to have the memory of John's death, after all of the evil he'd inflicted on Kate, her family, and so many others, part of her wished she'd been able to see him take Tommy's bullet to the head.

"You mean *I* got him with a clean shot to the head." Kate turned her head and saw CJ standing in the doorway.

Tommy rolled his eyes and shook his head, a rueful smile tugging at his lips. "Whatever, Marine. You keep that fantasy alive as long as you want, but we both know the truth."

"Acing sniper school and hitting a moving target are two totally different things, Ranger boy," CJ retorted. Then, his expression serious, he continued, "I don't want to intrude, but I just wanted to check in, see for myself you're on the mend."

Kate shifted in the bed, wincing at the shaft of pain driving through her chest. "It hurts like a bitch, but the doctors seem to think I'll be fine."

"I can't tell you how happy I am to hear that. I also wanted to let you know that I spoke to Agent Torrance at the FBI. They're going to formally reopen the Bludgeoner case with Burkhart as the key suspect. I'm going to reopen Michael's case as well."

At the mention of her brother's name, Kate felt another wave of pain pour through her that had nothing to do with the wound in her chest. All at once, the soul-crushing truth she had discovered came crashing down over her. "Oh, God," she whispered, tears flooding her eyes as she clutched her free hand against her chest.

Tommy immediately sprang to attention. "What is it? Are you in pain? I'll call the doctor—"

"No," Kate whispered. "It's not that." The pain from her wound was nothing in comparison. "It was supposed to be me."

"What do you mean?" Tommy asked. Her throat closed up over the words, as though somehow by not saying them, she could pretend they weren't true.

"He didn't come for Michael that night. He was coming for me."

— ᨁ —

Though it made a weird sort of sense that Kate was the intended target—all of Burkhart's other targets had been female—that didn't stop Tommy's mind from reeling as Kate repeated what Burkhart had told her.

"As soon as he realized he'd grabbed Michael and not me, he decided to kill him." The pain reverberating in Kate's voice felt like it was leaching from her skin under his own.

"So he grabbed Emerson Flannery and made it look like a murder-suicide," CJ said through gritted teeth. "That sick fuck."

Kate was sobbing softly now, the sound cutting at Tommy like shards of glass. He bent his head until it rested against hers on the pillow. "Kate." He didn't have the words to comfort her.

"It should have been me," she sobbed. "If I'd only been there, in my own bed like I should have been, Michael would still be alive."

"And you would be dead!" Tommy said, too harshly, but

even the thought of it was almost too much for him to deal with. "You think that would have been better?"

She turned so her face was buried in the curve of his neck. He could feel her tears soaking his skin, burning him like acid. "My family would say so."

Tommy blinked back his own tears and threaded his fingers through Kate's hair. "And I say they're full of shit. I say the only person to blame for any of that is that sick fuck who took advantage of your family's trust and then tore it apart."

CJ excused himself. Tommy didn't even spare him a glance.

"If he hadn't been after me—"

"He would have been after someone else. He was a sick killer, and if it hadn't been Michael, or you, it would have been someone else. You can't beat yourself up for the rest of your life for what he did. You're as much a victim as Michael or any of those other girls."

"How can you say that when I'm alive and they're not?"

"Barely," Tommy snapped, "or did you forget the part where he put a bullet in your chest?"

She started to turn her face from him. He caught her chin, gently but firmly keeping her eyes locked on his.

He knew she was at a breaking point, that if he didn't pull her back from the edge he was going to lose her again. For good this time.

"Don't. Don't push me away again. I know it feels impossible now, but you can get past this. I'll be with you, every step. I'm not going to let you go through this alone."

She started to open her mouth but before she could speak, he continued. "You wanted to know what I said in the letter? I said a lot of things, but the most important thing I said was that I love you."

She stiffened against him and her throat spasmed on a hard swallow. "You did?"

"I did. And I do. Love you, I mean. And I know at the very least you need me right now, even more than you needed me then. And I'm not going to turn my back on you again, no matter how hard you try to push me away."

Kate lay next to Tommy, her fingers clutching his hand like a lifeline. She didn't know it was possible to feel such intense grief and intense joy at the same time.

But Tommy's confession sent a burst of happiness through her, immediately followed by a rush of shame. What right did she have to be happy after everything that had happened?

"Do you love me, Kate?" It tugged at her heart, the way he sounded almost tentative.

"Yes, but—"

"Then don't let him take this away from us too. He already tore your life apart. Don't let him take our future."

Kate moved her hand to rest against his cheek. She soaked in the different sensations, the scratchy feel of stubble against her palm, the softness of his lips as she brushed her thumb against them.

She looked into his eyes, so close she could see the flecks of gold in their dark depths. It was as though the years had fallen away and he was looking at her with all the love and intense devotion he'd once felt in his young heart, no trace of the hardened warrior he'd become.

Every fiber of her being wanted to drink it all in and give it right back to him, but the guilt was still there, a yawning cavern in her soul, threatening to consume her. Telling her she didn't deserve any of it.

She told Tommy as much.

"What do you think Michael would want?" Tommy shot back, the frustration evident in his voice. "Do you really think he'd want you to spend the rest of your life miserable, doing penance? If the tables were turned, would you want him to do the same?"

"Of course not," she said, choking on a sob. "But you don't know what it's like—"

"You think I don't know what it's like to have someone's death on my conscience? I was there the night Michael died too. I've gone back and replayed that night thousands of times, wishing I hadn't pressured you to sneak out."

"I was the one who went. I was the one—"

Tommy pressed two fingers gently against her lips. "We both should have made different decisions. But the truth of the matter is that the only guilty party in all of this was John. He almost took you from me today. When I thought you were dead, I felt like my life was over. I never got over losing you the first time."

He covered her mouth with his, sending a rush of warmth tingling through her body, sweet and pure, cutting through all the ugliness John had left in his wake.

"Don't let him kill our future. I love you, so much," he murmured against her lips. "And I know we can get through this together."

Though she would live with the pain of what happened to Michael for the rest of her life, she knew in her heart Tommy was right. John had already taken so much from her already. She wasn't going to let him steal her one chance at happiness too.

"I love you too," she said, feeling the words down to her very core. "I love you and I want to be happy. With you."

Tommy gave her one of those blinding smiles and kissed again. The taste of him, the feel of his mouth moving against hers made her blood run thick and chased the last shreds of darkness away, leaving only bright hope for the future. And love, deep and true. Strong enough to survive tragedy and years of separation. Strong enough to get them through whatever life threw at them.

With Tommy at her side, she could make it through anything.

Epilogue

"Come on, just a few more bites," Tommy insisted.

Kate dutifully took one more swallow of the chicken soup Erin had dropped off a little while ago, then firmly pushed the spoon he brandished out of her face. Well, as firmly as she could considering two days after being shot in the chest she was still weak as a kitten.

"You're not going to get your strength up if you keep eating like a damn bird," Tommy groused as he put the lid back on the soup carton and set it aside.

"I'll have a little bit more later," she promised, hiding her half smile. Of all the insane happenings of the last several days, the fact that Tommy Ibarra was here, glued to her side as he had been for the last two days straight, watching over her, catering to her every need, struck her as the craziest.

Craziest and, besides Tricia's rescue, the only wonderful thing that had come of all of it. Kate clutched at it, the wonder, the happiness as she tried to keep the horrors of the last few days at bay. Eventually she would have to deal with it, she knew. Face the press. Hell, face a therapist to help her unwind the twisted mess that John had left behind.

"It's going to be okay," Tommy said, as though he could read the unpleasant thoughts trying to wheedle their way into her brain. She loved the way he said it, not as a hollow reassurance, but forcefully, as a statement of truth. A statement she had no choice but to believe.

Even more, she loved the way he followed it up with a sweep of his broad palm across her cheek, followed by a soft press of his lips. Warm, reassuring, telling her with his touch what he'd told her in words so many times the past two days. *I will always be here for you, Kate. I'm never letting you go again.*

Kate turned her head to catch his mouth with hers and tried to shift closer. The movement sent a shock of pain through her right side. She tried to stifle her gasp, but Tommy, attuned to every wince and frown, immediately pulled away.

"Dammit, you should have kept the morphine drip for another couple of days."

She didn't take offense at the sharpness of his tone, accompanied as it was by the helplessness in his dark eyes. He hated seeing her in pain, a point he'd made abundantly clear. However, Kate was already over the weird drunk and disconnected feeling she experienced from the morphine, and Tommy's aversion to seeing her hurt wasn't a good enough reason for her to keep taking it.

"Let me call the nurse—"

Kate stopped him with a firm squeeze of his hand and shook her head. She breathed softly, pushing through it until the stabbing pain receded to a dull ache. "I promise I'll let them give me something if it gets worse," she said as she settled back against the pillows he'd tucked behind her.

He shook his head in mock exaggeration, flipped open his laptop and clicked over to a video streaming site. "What will it be? Another movie? Or should we start another season of *Mad Men*?"

This was how they had spent most of Kate's waking

hours between brief visits from Jackson, Brooke, CJ, and Tommy's parents.

Not once had they turned on the TV or looked at the news to see what was being said about the case. She could imagine the media storm occurring outside the four walls of this room, and knew that soon enough she and Tommy would be at the very center of it. But not yet.

They'd just finished the opening credits of another episode when there was a sharp rap on the door.

"Come in," Tommy called as he paused the movie and slid his chair away from the bed to make room for the nurse who was no doubt outside the door.

But instead of the nurse, it was Deputy Roberts, who was taking a shift guarding the door to Kate's room to make sure no reporters or other unwanted visitors snuck in, who opened the door.

"Kate, Senator Beckett—I mean, your father's out here to see you."

A shock went through Kate, making her stomach seize up.

"He didn't seem happy when I told him I needed to check with you first," Roberts continued.

That would account for the uneasy look on the deputy's face. The senator wasn't used to being asked to wait, and no doubt made sure the deputy knew that.

Tommy was up immediately. "I'll tell him to hit the bricks," he said and started for the door, the lines of his back and shoulders tense, ready for confrontation.

"No," Kate said softly. She'd known in the back of her mind that when the truth about Michael's death came out, she would have to face her father. Face the cold accusation in his eyes once again. Though the identity of Michael's killer no doubt shocked her father to his core, it still didn't erase the mistakes Kate had made that night. And Kate didn't hold any hope that it would change her father's attitude toward her.

"Are you sure?" Tommy asked, his face carved into harsh lines as he returned to her side and took her hand in a firm grip. "You've been through too much already and I don't want you upset."

"It will be fine," Kate said with a confidence she didn't feel. But she'd known this confrontation would come. Now that her father was here, forcing the issue, she just wanted to get it over with.

Tommy nodded an OK at Deputy Roberts. "I swear to God, one word out of line and I will throw his ass out of here," he murmured under his breath.

As the senator stepped through the door, Tommy positioned himself in front of Kate, a human brick wall.

"Hello, Kate," her father said. To her shock, his voice held none of the cold, emotionless quality she'd come to expect. Instead it was deep and thick with emotion. And when she met his eyes, there was none of the angry accusation she'd seen so many times. Instead they were dark, stormy with grief and regret.

"Hello..." she trailed off, not sure how to address him.

Her father grimaced uncomfortably and ran his hand through his still thick silver hair. "I realize we should have called first, but I couldn't, I didn't—"

Kate squeezed Tommy's hand, unsure what to make of her father, seemingly unsure of himself when he'd always dominated every situation.

"We weren't sure you'd talk to us," a wry female voice cut him off. At that moment Kate realized her father wasn't alone. Lauren and her mother were behind him, her view of them blocked by Tommy's broad back.

Her mother, small and birdlike, hovered at her father's arm, her face thin and pinched as she remembered, her normally flawless complexion blotchy, her eyes puffy and red.

Lauren didn't hesitate as she hurled herself at the bed, ignoring the way Tommy stiffened as she grabbed for Kate's free hand.

"God Kate, we're so glad you're okay," Lauren barely got the words out before she burst into tears. "And I'm sorry, I'm sorry I've been so distant after what happened, after Michael…"

Kate felt her own eyes fill as she wrapped her fingers around her sister's.

"We're all sorry, Kate," her father said, hovering at the foot of her bed. "Me especially. The things I said to you, blaming you. I was so wrong, about everything…I…"

Kate felt like her entire world was spinning off of its axis as her father uttered words she'd never expected to come out of her mouth.

"I spent so much time blaming you for what happened, and I had no idea I'd brought that monster into our lives. If I hadn't been so close to Phillip —"

"Don't," Kate said quietly. She knew exactly what her father was going through, the way the what ifs and the second guesses could drag you down a rabbit's warren of guilt. "You couldn't have known. None of us did."

Her father reached out a hand, awkwardly, uncertain whether or not to approach her. Kate dropped Lauren's hand, more from shock than anything else, and reached out to her father. His hand closed around hers, the fingers still strong, though the skin felt papery, more weathered. Long forgotten memories bubbled up at the contact, of her slipping her hand in to his as they crossed a crowded street.

Her mother covered their joined hands with her own, the

familiar scent of her perfume settling over Kate like a soft blanket.

"When we heard the news, about John, what he'd done to you, to Michael—" her father choked on a sob.

"We had to make sure you were really all right," Lauren said, her voice thick with tears.

"And tell you that we love you, Katie," her mother said in a voice tight with grief and regret. As Kate met her mother's gaze, she saw that she'd lost that dazed, cloudy look she'd had the last time Kate had seen her. Bright, alert, as though someone had jolted her awake after years of sleepwalking.

Kate could relate.

"We love you, Kate," her father and Lauren echoed.

Kate sat in stunned silence, struggling to take it all in.

"I'll leave you alone, let you catch up."

Kate looked up at Tommy's voice, saw him standing in the corner. His arms were folded across his chest, taking in the scene, his expression carefully guarded.

But she could see it there, the tightness in his mouth and shoulders as he watched her, surrounded by her family. *She's got them, she won't need me anymore.* He didn't have to say it out loud.

"No!" she said, a jolt of panic hitting her at the thought of him leaving. She gently tugged her hand from her father's and reached out to Tommy. "Please don't go. I need you." Because in a strange way, as amazing as her family's desire to reach out to her was, it was in its own way as traumatic as anything else that had happened in the past few days. There was no way she was going to get through it without him.

A fact that was driven home as his big hand swallowed hers up and she immediately felt a rush of warmth, of peace. That feeling that with Tommy at her side, everything really *would* be okay. "I need *you*, Tommy."

He brought her hand to his lips, his eyes crinkling at the corners in a smile she couldn't help but return.

Her father cleared his throat uncomfortably. "Tommy, there are of course, things I need to say to you as well. I'm not entirely sure where to start—"

"How about thank you for saving Kate's life," Lauren broke in. She reached over and grabbed Tommy in a quick hug. He stiffened at first, but gave her a gentle pat on the back.

"Of course," the senator said gruffly. "We're of course incredibly grateful. But I also owe you an apology, for what I did after Michael's death," he glanced guiltily at Kate before turning his attention back to Tommy.

Kate could feel Tommy's fingers stiffen against hers. "What's done is done. All I care about now is seeing Kate through all of this so we can get on with our life."

She didn't miss a single detail, not the way he said *our life*, their future already intertwined. And not the way his entire body seemed to loom larger in challenge, making it clear to her father, to her family, they could apologize all they wanted, but Kate was his now.

As he was hers.

Her father nodded and turned his attention back to Kate. "I don't expect you to forgive me right away," he said gruffly, "or ever. I just want the chance to be in your life again. We all would."

Tears stung Kate's eyes as she stared at their faces, apprehensive, afraid she would turn them away as they'd once turned from her.

While she would always bear the scars of Michael's death and the aftermath, she knew if she turned them away now, it would be out of pure spite. It wouldn't be what she wanted.

More importantly, it wouldn't be what Michael wanted. "I'd like that," she said, her throat tight with tears.

They left a few minutes later, with promises to visit again the next day.

"I really wanted to punch him in the face," Tommy said when the door closed behind them.

Kate smiled. "After what he did to you, no one would blame you."

Tommy stretched out onto the bed next to her, careful not to jostle her. He pressed a kiss to her cheek and murmured, "It would have been for you. I don't care what he did to me."

Warmth pooled in her chest and she snuggled closer. Sensing she wasn't quite ready to talk, Tommy started the movie up again while she tried to make sense of her jumbled emotions. She was happy her family wanted to reach out, pull her back into the fold, but wary too.

She felt like a puzzle whose pieces had warped and worn over the years; complete, but not quite fitting together seamlessly like everything should.

She didn't even realize she was crying until Tommy brushed his thumb across her cheek. She wrapped her good arm around his waist, drinking in the feel of him, the scent of him, the sound of his heartbeat thudding steadily against her cheek.

"It's so strange," she said, as much to herself as him. "How everything works. I lost everyone I loved the night Michael died. And finding out the truth has brought them all back to me."

"You're never going to lose me again," Tommy whispered. "You know that, right?"

Kate nodded against his chest. "I love you."

He pressed a kiss to the top of her head. "I love you too, Kate," he replied, his voice suspiciously thick. "More than you even know."

As she lay there, folded in his arms, something welled

up in her, pushing through the cracks of her puzzle pieces, washing past the tangle of conflicted emotions raging inside her.

Happiness.

After everything that had happened, it had seemed impossible, and she still wasn't sure she deserved it.

But it was here. It was hers. She was going to hold it tight and never let it go.

All Talia Vega wants is a quiet, normal life.

But a brutal killer from her past has come back to haunt her—and Jack Brooks, the man she swore she'd never let herself depend on again, is the only man she can trust...

Please turn this page for an excerpt from

Run from Fear

Chapter 3

"Y ou can go ahead and file a report," the officer, who was not nearly as nice as Officer Roberts, said in a voice that managed to convey the emptiness of that gesture. "But your landlord admitted the lock is old and the house had been previously burglarized. There's no proof those scratches are from the other night—"

"They look fresh," Jack interrupted. "Had they been from the previous burglary, they would have been smoothed out—"

"So being a high-priced rent-a-cop makes you an expert in forensics?" the cop said, adjusting his belt under his hefty gut as he puffed his chest out.

Ben rolled his eyes and went back into the house. Talia was pretty sure that crunching sound was Jack biting on his tongue. "What else do you suggest I do, Officer?"

"Keep your doors locked and your alarm on," he said with a smirk, and left.

Jack muttered something under his breath.

"Tal, do you want me to stay with you for a little while?" Rosario asked, her hand on Talia's arm the only warm spot on her body.

Talia shook her head. "I'll be fine." Rosario loved living on campus, and Talia would never take that away from her. And maybe she was being paranoid, but if someone was specifically targeting her, she wanted Rosie well away, safe in her dorm, protected by the university's own rigorous security protocols. "Just do me a favor—no missing any curfew calls this week. Deal?" When Talia had agreed to let Rosario live on campus, they'd agreed Rosario would call her every single night, no matter what, at eleven p.m. to let her know where she was. In the eight months since school started, Rosario had gotten a little lax. And try as she did not to overreact, nothing sent Talia into a tailspin faster than not being able to get ahold of Rosie. There had even been one humiliating—according to Rosario—incident involving her dorm RAs and the campus police.

"Deal," Rosario replied with a smile. "Eleven o'clock, on the dot, unless I go to bed early, and if I can't call, I promise to text." She gave Jack a quick hug good-bye and ran inside to get her stuff together.

"Talia—" Jack got cut off as his phone beeped. He let out a low curse. "I'm sorry, but we have to go." He nodded at Ben, who emerged from her house with his bag of gear. "We need to move it if we're going to make it on time," he called over Talia's head, then focused back on her. "I'm on a personal security detail over in Atherton—our client has been receiving death threats, so they're temporarily relocating from London. It's going to be twenty-four-seven, so the next few weeks—"

Talia held up her hand. "Jack, you don't have to explain to me that you have a job to do. I know you didn't come down from Seattle to see me. You don't have to babysit me. I'll be fine."

He cocked an eyebrow and looked meaningfully in the direction of her garage door.

Talia shrugged and said, "Like Officer Friendly said, that probably happened ages ago."

"You don't buy that bullshit any more than I do."

"Let's move," Ben said. "And I'm driving. You drive like a grandma."

Jack didn't budge. "The system is wired now to call Gemini headquarters and my cell phone if the alarm trips. I'll get here as fast as I can, but if I can't someone else will. And if anything else happens, you call me immediately. I'll have my phone on and with me at all times."

Talia rolled her eyes. "It was probably just some dumb kid looking to steal beer—"

"Immediately," Jack bit out. "And if I don't answer, you call Danny, Derek, or Ethan directly."

"Or me!" Ben interjected.

"Not Ben," Jack said with a smile so slight she wondered if she was imagining it. "He's an asshole."

Did the iceman just make a joke? "I promise," she conceded. "But don't expect to hear from me. And I won't expect to hear from you," she said. But she couldn't ignore the hollow feeling that washed over her as she watched Jack and Ben climb into the car and drive away.

It was stupid, she told herself as she walked back into the house, the way seeing him left her with that strange, hollow ache. A faint yearning for him to stick around, for her to unglue her tongue and figure out what to say instead of her halfhearted efforts to push him away. A wish that maybe they could have . . . something.

Right, like that was possible, she thought, and gave herself a mental kick. What she and Jack had, so oddly intimate yet so excruciatingly uncomfortable, could never be untangled enough to go anywhere good.

She drove Rosario back to campus and contemplated what to do for the rest of the afternoon. Maybe she should see if Susie was up for a movie, she thought, then quickly dismissed the idea. Talia was in a weird, melancholy mood and had no business inflicting herself on anyone.

Besides, she had only a few hours to kill before she had to work. Maybe she'd do some laundry. The house phone rang, cutting off her mental meanderings. She started to ignore it—anyone she knew would have called her cell. She picked up the handset to turn the ringer off, hesitating when she saw the number on the caller ID display.

Wireless caller. Her brow furrowed as she recognized the Washington State area code and Seattle exchange.

Without thought, her thumb pressed the TALK button. "Hello?"

"Talia Vega?" an unfamiliar male voice asked.

"Who's calling?"

"Is this Talia Vega?" he repeated.

Her grip on the phone tightened. "Who wants to know?"

The phone went dead.

Cold sweat filmed her forehead. *They'd found her.* Just like that, she was back down in that black hole of panic and fear, leaving the safe house only when necessary. Breath held, constantly looking over her shoulder, dreading the moment when he or one of his lackeys would snatch her from her bed or, worse, take Rosario and use her as bait to flush Talia out.

No, stop. She took a deep breath, reminded herself that David was dead, his organization blown to smithereens. There was no more "they." No one had bothered to come after her in nearly two years. Why would they now?

But whoever called knew her name, knew her phone number.

It wasn't like she was in hiding, the rational, calming part of her brain argued. She'd kept her information unlisted, but she knew there were ways to find out that sort of thing if someone was motivated enough.

That last thought wasn't at all comforting. She picked up the phone and brought the number up on the caller ID. She knew it was overkill, but she could call someone back at Gemini's office and have them trace it. She didn't want to bother Jack—

The phone rang in her hand. It was him again.

"What do you want?" she asked sharply.

"Talia Vega?"

She didn't answer.

"Sorry about before. I went through a canyon and my cell dropped the call. I'm trying to get in touch with Talia Vega. Can you at least tell me if I have the right number?"

"And I'll ask you again," she said, irritation doing its part to chase away some of the fear, "who wants to know?"

"My name is Greg Fitzhugh," he said. "I'm working on a book for *Seattle Magazine* about the fallout from the Grayson-Maxwell scandal—"

"I have nothing to say on the matter."

"Please," he said, "if it hadn't been for you, no one would have ever connected him to Karev's operation," he said.

Talia wasn't sure if he was genuinely impressed or just kissing her ass.

"If it weren't for you helping Deputy PA Slater, the corruption would have gone unchecked, and none of those people would have been arrested."

Her fingers started to go numb at the tips. The last thing she wanted to do was remind all of those people of her existence and, worse, make it seem like she was bragging about her part in bringing them down. Hell, at one time she'd been as knee-deep in the shit as the rest of them. She had nothing to brag about.

"I know you took a bit of a beating in the press before," he said at her continued silence, "but you don't have to worry about how you'll be portrayed."

What, like they could somehow turn the mistress of a notorious criminal—who, among other things, had twisted her testimony to help send an innocent man to death row and stood numbly by while half a dozen women were butchered—into a heroine for justice? "I'm sorry, I'm afraid I can't help you."

She hung up and immediately unplugged the phone in case Greg Fitzhugh decided to call back, then realized she'd forgotten to ask him where he'd gotten the number.

You should have changed your name. Not for the first time, Talia questioned her decision not to change her identity. Jack assured her that as long as they held up their cover stories, he could create a cover for them that was all but bulletproof.

Everything in her had rebelled at the idea. David Maxwell had nearly taken everything from them. She wasn't going to let him take their identities. Most importantly, it wasn't fair to force Rosie to live this lie with her.

And deep in her heart, Talia didn't feel like she deserved to disappear into anonymity. Her own bad choices had gotten her into trouble, and part of her penance was living with that truth. For better or worse.

This, she supposed, was the worse part.

Nothing to do but move past it. What was done was done, and unless she wanted to turn her and Rosie's lives upside down all over again, she had to accept reality: If a person was motivated to find Talia Vega, there wasn't much to keep them from tracking her down.

THE DISH

Where Authors Give You the Inside Scoop

From the desk of Debra Webb

Dear Reader,

I can't believe we've already dug into case five of the Faces of Evil—REVENGE.

Things are heating up here in the South just as they are in REVENGE. The South is known for its story-telling. I can remember sitting on the front porch in an old rocking chair and listening to my grandmother tell stories. She was an amazing storyteller. Most of her tales were ones that had been handed down by friends and family for generations. Many were true, though they had changed through the years as each person who told them added his or her own twist. Others were, I genuinely hope, absolute fiction. It would be scary if some of those old tales were true.

Certain elements were a constant in my grandmother's tales. Secrets and loyalty. You know the adage, "blood is thicker than water." Keeping family secrets can some-times turn deadly and in her stories it often did. Then there were those dark secrets kept between friends. Those rarely ended well for anyone.

Jess Harris and Dan Burnett know a little something about secrets and I dare say in the next two cases, REVENGE and the one to follow, *Ruthless*, they will understand that not only is blood thicker than water but the blood is where the darkness lurks. In the coming cases Jess will need Dan more than ever. You're also going to meet a new and very interesting character, Buddy Corlew, who's a part of Jess's past.

Enjoy the summer! Long days of gardening or romping on the beach. But spend your nights with Jess and Dan as they explore yet another case in the Faces of Evil. I promise you'll be glad you did.

I hope you'll stop by www.thefacesofevil.com and visit with me. There's a weekly briefing each Friday where I talk about what's going on in my world and with the characters as I write the next story. You can sign up as a person of interest and you might just end up a suspect! We love giving away prizes, too, so do stop by.

Enjoy the story and be sure to look for *Ruthless* next month!

Cheers!

Debra Webb

From the desk of Katie Lane

Dear Reader,

One of the highlights of my childhood was the New Mexico State Fair. Every year, my daddy would give me a whole ten dollars to spend there. Since I learned early on what would happen if you gorged on turkey legs and candy apples before you hopped on the Tilt-a-Whirl, I always went to the midway first. After a couple hours of tummy-tingling thrills, my friends and I would grab some food and head over to the coliseum to watch the cowboys practice for that night's rodeo.

Sitting in the box seats high above the arena, I would imagine that I was a princess and the cowboys were princes performing great feats of agility and strength in order to win my hand in marriage. Of course, I was never interested in the most talented cowboys. My favorites were the ones who got bucked off the broncos or bulls before the buzzer and still jumped to their feet with a smile on their face and a hat-wave to the crowd.

It was in this arena of horse manure and testosterone that a seed was planted. A good forty years later, I'm happy to announce that my rodeo Prince Charming has come to fruition in my newest contemporary romance, FLIRTING WITH TEXAS.

Beauregard Cates is a cowboy with the type of smile and good looks that make most gals hear wedding bells. But after suffering through a life-threatening illness, he has no desire to be tied down and spends most of his time traveling around the world…until he ends up on a runaway Central Park carriage ride with a sassy blonde from Texas.

Jenna Jay Scroggs is a waitress who will go to any length to right the injustices of the world. Yet no matter how busy her life is in New York City, Jenna can't ignore the sweet-talkin', silver-haired cowboy who reminds her of everything she left behind. And when her hometown of Bramble gets involved, Beau and Jenna will soon be forced on a tummy-tingling ride of their own that will lead them right back to Texas and a once-upon-a-time kind of love.

I hope y'all will join me for the ride. (With or without a big ol' turkey leg.)

Much Love,

Katie Lane

♥ ♥ ♥ ♥ ♥ ♥ ♥ ♥ ♥ ♥ ♥ ♥ ♥ ♥ ♥ ♥

From the desk of Erin Kern

Dear Reader,

A few months ago, my editor put me on assignment to interview Avery Price. Little did I know that Avery would end up being the heroine of my latest book, LOOKING FOR TROUBLE. I got such a kick out of following her journey that led her to Trouble, Wyoming, and into the arms of Noah McDermott, that I jumped at the opportunity to revisit with her. What better way to spend my afternoon than having a heart-to-heart with the woman who started it all?

We settle on the patio of her home in the breathtaking Wyoming foothills. After getting seated, Avery pours me a glass of homemade lemonade.

ME: Thank you so much for taking the time to meet with me. I know how much you value your privacy.

AVERY: (*Takes a sip of lemonade, then sets her drink*

down.) Privacy is overrated. And I should be thanking you for making the drive out here.

ME: It's nice to get out of the city every once in a while. Plus it's beautiful out here. I can see why you chose this place.

AVERY: I'd say it chose me. *(Her lips tilt up in a wry little smile.)* I actually didn't plan on staying here at first. But anonymity is something anyone can find here.

ME: Is that why you left Denver?

AVERY: *(Pauses a moment.)* If I wore a pair of heels that were too high, it got commented on in the society pages. No one cares about that kind of thing here. It's refreshing to be able to be my own person.

ME: That's definitely a tempting way of life. Your family must miss you terribly, though. Are you planning on being an active part in your father's campaign?

AVERY: I'll always support my father no matter what he does, which he's almost always successful at. No matter what happens with the race, he'll always have the support of his children. But I've had my fill of the public eye. That life suits my parents and brother just fine. I think I'll leave the campaigning to them.

ME: That's right. Your brother, Landon Price, is one of the biggest real estate developers in Denver. Are you two close?

AVERY: We grew up pretty sheltered so the two of us were really all the other had. I'd say we're closer than your average brother and sister.

ME: Do you think your brother will be moving up here with you any time soon?

AVERY: *(She chuckles before answering.)* Even though we're very close, my brother and I are very different people. He lives and breathes city life. Plus my parents aren't nearly as concerned with his activities as they are mine.

ME: Meaning?

AVERY: *(Pauses before answering.)* Maybe because he has a different set of genitals? *(Laughs.)* Who knows? For some reason they focus all their energy on me.

ME: Is that the reason you're not active in your father's business? Is this a rebellion?

AVERY: I wouldn't really say it's a rebellion. I made a decision that I thought best suited me. The corporate life isn't for me, anyway. I doubt I'd have anything valuable to offer. My father has enough VPs and advisers.

ME: *(I smile as I take my first sip of lemonade.)* I've got to say, you are a lot more down to earth than I expected. And there are a lot of girls in this country who wished they were in your shoes.

AVERY: *(She lifts a thin shoulder beneath her linen top.)* Everybody always thinks the grass is greener on the other side. Growing up in the public eye isn't for everyone. I've developed thick skin over the years. But I wouldn't change my life for anything.

ME: Well, I certainly appreciate you granting me this interview. Good luck with your father's campaign.

<u>AVERY:</u> Thank you. I'm going to grab a copy of the magazine when the article is printed.

Erin Kern

From the desk of Jami Alden

Dear Reader,

As I look back on the books I've written over the course of my career, I'm struck by two things:

1) I have a very twisted, sinister imagination, if my villains are anything to go by!
2) I love reunion romances.

Now in real life, if you ran into someone who was still hung up on her high school boyfriend and who held on to that person (consciously or not) as the one true love of her life, you might think she had a screw loose. Unless you've ended up with your high school or college sweetheart, most of us grow up and look back at those we dated in our youth—hopefully with fondness but sometimes with less affection. But rarely do we find ourselves pining for that boy we went to senior prom with.

So I wondered, why do I love this premise so much in romance? Well, I think I may have figured it out. In real life, for most of us, those early relationships run their natural course and fizzle out with little more than a whimper and a gasp.

But in romance novels, those relationships that start out with unbridled intensity end with drama and more drama and leave a wagonload of unfinished business for our hero and heroine. It's that lingering intensity, combined with the weight of unfinished business, that draw our hero and heroine together after so many years. So when they finally find themselves back in the same room together, the attraction is as undeniable as gravity.

When I was coming up with the story for GUILTY AS SIN, I found myself fascinated by the history between my hero, Tommy Ibarra, and my heroine, Kate Beckett. Caught up in the giddy turmoil of first love, they were torn apart amid the most excruciating and tragic circumstances I, as a parent, could ever imagine.

And yet, that intensity and unfinished business lingered. So when they're brought back together, there's no force on Earth that can keep them apart. Still, to say their road to true love is a rocky one is a huge understatement. But I hope in the end that you feel as I do. That after everything Tommy and Kate went through, they've more than earned their happily ever after.

Happy Reading!

Jami Alden